A Book Of

COMPUTER GRAPHICS

Semester IV : Paper - VI

For Third Year B.Sc. Computer Science
As Per Revised Syllabus
Effective from June 2015

Ms. Manisha Bharambe
M.Sc. (Computer Science), M.Phil. (IT)
Associate Professor
Department of Computer Science
MES Abasaheb Garware College
PUNE

Mrs. Veena Gandhi
M.C.S., M.Phil. (Computer Science), UGC-NET
Lecturer in Computer Science Department
Abeda Inamdar Senior College
PUNE

Ms. Renuka Zope
M.Sc. (Computer Science), UGC-NET
Lecturer in Computer Science Department
MIT Group of Institutions
MAEER's Arts, Commerce and Science College
PUNE

NIRALI PRAKASHAN
ADVANCEMENT OF KNOWLEDGE

N0898

COMPUTER GRAPHICS **ISBN 978-93-5164-913-7**

Second Edition : January 2017

Published By : **Polyplate**

NIRALI PRAKASHAN
Abhyudaya Pragati, 1312, Shivaji Nagar,
Off J.M. Road, Pune – 411005
Tel - (020) 25512336/37/39, Fax - (020) 25511379
Email : niralipune@pragationline.com

➢ DISTRIBUTION CENTRES

PUNE

Nirali Prakashan : 119, Budhwar Peth, Jogeshwari Mandir Lane, Pune 411002, Maharashtra
Tel : (020) 2445 2044, 66022708, Fax : (020) 2445 1538
Email : bookorder@pragationline.com, niralilocal@pragationline.com

Nirali Prakashan : S. No. 28/27, Dhyari, Near Pari Company, Pune 411041
Tel : (020) 24690204 Fax : (020) 24690316
Email : dhyari@pragationline.com, bookorder@pragationline.com

MUMBAI

Nirali Prakashan : 385, S.V.P. Road, Rasdhara Co-op. Hsg. Society Ltd.,
Girgaum, Mumbai 400004, Maharashtra
Tel : (022) 2385 6339 / 2386 9976, Fax : (022) 2386 9976
Email : niralimumbai@pragationline.com

➢ DISTRIBUTION BRANCHES

JALGAON

Nirali Prakashan : 34, V. V. Golani Market, Navi Peth, Jalgaon 425001,
Maharashtra, Tel : (0257) 222 0395, Mob : 94234 91860

KOLHAPUR

Nirali Prakashan : New Mahadvar Road, Kedar Plaza, 1st Floor Opp. IDBI Bank
Kolhapur 416 012, Maharashtra. Mob : 9850046155

NAGPUR

Pratibha Book Distributors : Above Maratha Mandir, Shop No. 3, First Floor,
Rani Jhanshi Square, Sitabuldi, Nagpur 440012, Maharashtra
Tel : (0712) 254 7129

DELHI

Nirali Prakashan : 4593/21, Basement, Aggarwal Lane 15, Ansari Road, Daryaganj
Near Times of India Building, New Delhi 110002 Mob : 08505972553

BENGALURU

Pragati Book House : House No. 1, Sanjeevappa Lane, Avenue Road Cross,
Opp. Rice Church, Bengaluru – 560002.
Tel : (080) 64513344, 64513355,Mob : 9880582331, 9845021552
Email:bharatsavla@yahoo.com

CHENNAI

Pragati Books : 9/1, Montieth Road, Behind Taas Mahal, Egmore,
Chennai 600008 Tamil Nadu, Tel : (044) 6518 3535,
Mob : 94440 01782 / 98450 21552 / 98805 82331,
Email : bharatsavla@yahoo.com

Preface ...

We take an opportunity to present this book entitled as **"Computer Graphics"** to the students of T.Y.B.Sc. Computer Science as per the revised syllabus, June 2015.

The book covers theory of Introduction to Computer Graphics, Input Devices and Interaction Tasks, Presentation and Output Devices, Raster Scan Graphics, Transformations, Clipping, 3D Transformation and Viewing and Hidden Surfaces Elimination.

A special word of thanks to Shri. Dineshbhai Furia, Mr. Jignesh Furia for showing full faith in us to write this book. We also thank to Mr. Amar Salunkhe, Mr. Akbar Shaikh, Ms. Chaitali Takle of M/s Nirali Prakashan for their excellent co-operation.

Although every care has been taken to check mistakes and misprints, any errors, omission and suggestions from teachers and students for the improvement of this text book shall be most welcome.

Our efforts shall be more than rewarded if this book proves beneficial to the students.

Authors

Syllabus ...

1. Introduction to Computer Graphics **[4 L]**

1.1 Introduction to Computer Graphics and Graphics Systems.

1.2 Components of Computer Graphics Representation, Presentation, Interaction and Transformations.

1.3 Applications of Computer Graphics.

1.4 Pixel/Point, Raster v/s Vector, RGB Color Model, Intensity.

1.5 Programming essentials – Event Driven Programming, OpenGL Library.

2. Input Devices and Interaction Tasks **[4 L]**

2.1 Logical Interaction – Locator, Valuator, Pick and Choice.

2.2 Physical devices used for Interaction – Keyboard, Mouse, Trackball, Spaceball, Tablets, Light pen, Joystick, Touch panel, Data glove.

2.4 Keyboard, Mouse Interaction in OpenGL.

2.5 Graphical User Interfaces - Cursors, Radio buttons, Scroll bars, Menus, Icons.

2.6 Implementing GUI in OpenGL.

3. Presentation and Output Devices **[4 L]**

3.1 Presentation Graphics - Frame Buffer, Display file, Lookup table.

3.2 Display Devices, Random and Raster Scan Display Devices; CRT.

3.3 Hardcopy Devices - Plotters and Printers.

4. Raster Scan Graphics **[10 L]**

4.1 Line drawing algorithms; DDA Algorithm, Bresenham's Line Drawing Algorithm, Circle Generation Algorithm.

4.2 Scan Conversions - Generation of the Display, Image Compression.

4.3 Displaying Lines and Characters.

4.3 Polygon Filling - Scan Converting Polygons, Fill Algorithms, Boundary Fill Algorithm, Flood Fill Algorithm.

5. Transformations **[7 L]**

5.1 Basic Transformations: Translation, Rotation, Scaling; Matrix Representations and Homogeneous Coordinates, Reflection, Shear.

5.2 Transformation of Points, Lines, Parallel Lines, Intersecting Lines. Viewing Pipeline.

5.3 Window to Viewport Co-ordinate Transformation. Setting Window and Viewport in OpenGL.

6. Clipping **[7 L]**

6.1 Clipping Operations, Point Clipping.

6.2 Line Clipping; Cohen Sutherland Algorithm, Midpoint Subdivision Algorithm, Cyrus Beck Algorithm.

6.3 Polygon Clipping, Sutherland Hodgman Algorithm, Weiler-Atherton Algorithm.

7. 3D Transformation and Viewing **[6 L]**

7.1 3D transformations: Translation, Rotation, Scaling and Other transformations.

7.2 Three Dimensional Viewing, Parallel and Perspective Projections.

7.3 View Volumes and General Projection Transformations.

7.4 3 D Clipping.

8. Hidden surfaces Elimination **[4 L]**

8.1 Depth Comparison, A-buffer Algorithm, Back face detection; Depth - Buffer.

8.2 Scan-line Method - BSP tree method, the Painter's Algorithm, Area-subdivision Algorithm.

Contents ...

CHAPTER 1

Introduction to Computer Graphics

Contents ...

Objectives...

- To Understand Basic Concepts of Computer Graphics
- To Study Computer Graphics System
- To Learn Basic Components of Computer Graphics
- To Study Applications of Computer Graphics
- To Understand OpenGL

1.1 INTRODUCTION TO COMPUTER GRAPHICS AND GRAPHICS SYSTEM

- The computer is an information processing machine. It is a tool for storing, manipulating and retrieving data. There are many ways to communicate the processed information to the user.
- The computer graphics is one of the most effective and common way to communicate the processes information to the users.
- Computer Graphics (CG) displays the information in the form of graphics objects. Such as pictures, diagrams, and graphs instead of simple text. That means with the help of computer graphics, we can express the data in pictorial form.
- In CG, pictures and graphics objects are presented as a collection of picture elements called pixel. The pixel is the smallest addressable screen element.
- Computer graphics is the field of science, which studies the manipulation of visual and geometric information using computational techniques.
- In this chapter we study basic concepts of computer graphics.

1.1.1 Introduction to Computer Graphics

- Graphics (from Greek graphikos) are visual images or designs on some surface, such as a wall, canvas, screen, paper, and so on.
- Graphics are used to inform, illustrate or entertain. It may includes pictorial representation of data, as in computer-aided design and manufacture, in typesetting and the graphic arts, digital images, geometric designs and maps.
- Graphics may be in black-and-white, grayscale or color and may contain text.
- Images that are generated by a computer are called computer graphics which displays information in the form of graphics objects as windows, graphs, diagrams etc. Thus, computer graphics express data in pictorial form.
- In other word, we can say that computer graphics is an art of drawing pictures on computer screens with the help of programming. It involves computations, creation, and manipulation of data.

- Computer graphics is a rendering tool for the generation and manipulation of images.
- Today, computer graphics used routinely in such diverse areas like Science, Engineering, Medicine, Business, Industry, Government, Art, Entertainment, Advertising, Education, and Training.

Graphics Standards:

- A good computer graphics system includes good software, as well as, a compatible hardware.
- Both computer graphics vendors as well as users identified some needs to have some graphics standards. The needs are as follows:
  1. Software portability.
  2. Image data portability.
  3. Text data portability.
  4. Model database portability.
- The search for standards began in 1974, to fulfill these needs both at the USA and International levels. As a result of worldwide efforts, various standards at different levels of the graphics systems were developed.
- The standards are as follows:
  1. **GKS (Graphics Kernel System):** It is an ANSI (American National Standards Institute) and ISO (International Standards Organization) standard. It interfaces the application program with graphics support package.
  2. **CORE (Core of a Graphics Systems):** Developed by the graphics standard planning committee of the Association for Computing Machinery (ACM). CORE is also termed SIGGRAPH (Special Interest Group on Graphics) of ACM.
  3. **IGES (Initial Graphics Exchange Specification):** It is an ANSI standard. It enables art exchange of model database among computer graphics software.
  4. **PHICS (Programmer's Hierarchical Interactive Graphics System):** It supports workstations and their related computer graphics applications. It supports three-dimensional modelling of geometry, segmentation and dynamic display.
  5. **CGM (Computer Graphics Metafile):** It defines functions needed to describe an image. Such description can be stored or transported from one graphics device to another.
  6. **CGI (Computer Graphics Interface):** It is designed to interface plotters to GKS or PHIGS. It is the lowest device independent interface in a graphics system.
- Commonly used graphical packages include Autocad, Paint, Photoshop, Coreldraw, etc. for Windows, and Xfig, Xpaint etc., for Unix or Linux.

Operations of Computer Graphics:

- Computer graphics deals with creation, manipulation, representation and production of graphical objects on output devices either in animated or in non-animated forms.

- The basic operations of computer graphics thus can be listed as follows:
  1. Creation of elementary objects.
  2. Creating basic shapes.
  3. Creating solid objects.
  4. Sizing and positioning.
  5. Projection on 2D.
  6. Shading and colouring.
  7. Viewing and clipping.
  8. Hidden surface elimination.
  9. Producing animated views.

Overview of a Graphics Systems:

- The operation of a typical graphics system can be split into a three-part sequence as shown in Fig. 1.1.

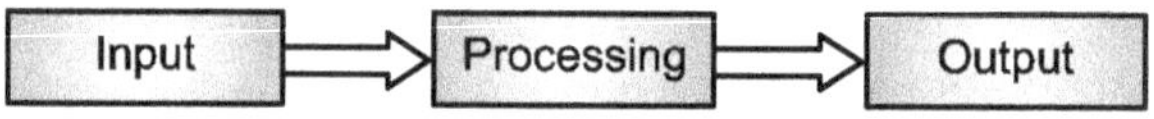

Fig. 1.1: Operation of a typical graphics system

- The simplest example of this is when you click on a thumbnail image in, say, Facebook and a video clip pops up and begins to play. The click is the input. Your computer then reacts to this input by processing, which involves downloading the movie file and running it through the Adobe Flash Player, which in turn outputs video frames to your monitor.

1.1.1.1 Definition

- Computer Graphics (CG) is "the discipline of producing pictures or images using a computer including modeling - creation, manipulation and storage of geometric objects and rendering, converting a scene to an image, or the process of transformation, rasterization, shading, illumination and animation of the image".

OR

- Many definitions of computer graphics have been given but the following is the most understandable definition:

  Computer Graphics = Data structures + Graphics algorithm + Languages

  where, Data Structure means those data structures that are suitable for computer graphics. Graphic algorithms for picture generation and transformation. Languages i.e., higher-level languages for generation of grapics objects or pictures.

OR

- Computer Graphics (CG) involves "the generation, representation, manipulation, processing or evaluation of graphics objects by a computer as well as the association of graphic objects with related non-graphic information residing in computer files".

- Basically there are two types of computer graphics as explained below:

1. **Interactive (Active) Computer Graphics:**

- In active computer graphics, the user has control over contents, structure and appearance of objects on display devices.
- For example, in video games a user has a lever in his hand to control level of the game.

2. **Non-interactive (Passive) Computer Graphics:**

- In passive computer graphics, the user has no control over picture. The user can only see the contents of the picture.
- For example, in TV monitor user has no control over picture he/she cannot move picture, translate, rotate picture and so on.

1.1.1.2 Common Terms in Computer Graphics

- Some most common terms in computer graphics are explained below:

1. **Pixel or Pel:**

- Pixel or Pel is defined as "the smallest addressable screen element". Pixel is one spot in a rectilinear grid of thousands of such spots that are individually painted to form an image.
- Each pixel has its own intensity, name or address by which we can control.
- Pixel is a measure of screen position.
- Fig. 1.2 shows pixel position.

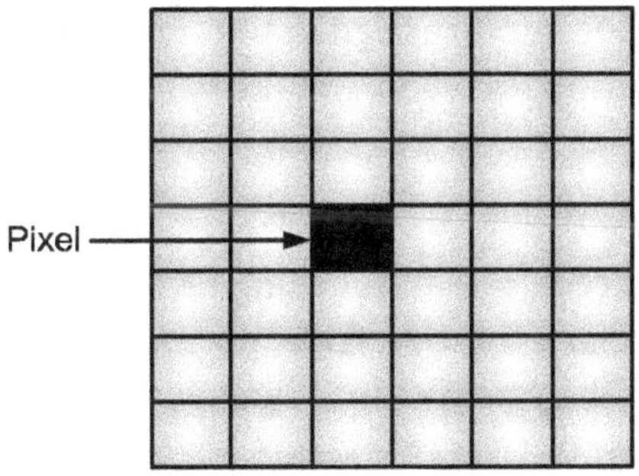

Fig. 1.2: A Pixel or Pel

2. **Frame or Refresh Buffer:**

- Frame buffer is a large, contiguous piece of memory into which the intensity values for all pixels are placed.
- Frame buffer is an array and graphical display devices can access this array. It contains an internal representation of the image called as a frame buffer.

3. **Aliasing:**

- Usually, common display devices have two pixel states i.e., ON or OFF. For these displays, lines may have jagged (or staircase) appearance because the sampling process digitizes the coordinate points on an object to discrete integer pixel positions. This process of distortion of information due to low frequency sampling or undersampling is called as aliasing.

4. **Resolution:**

- It is the ratio of width and height of output of the display device. Usually, we talk of two types of resolutions:
  (i) **Image Resolution** is defined as "the distance from one pixel to the next pixel i.e., pixel spacing".
  (ii) **Screen Resolution** is defined as "the number of pixels in the horizontal and vertical directions on the screen".

5. **Antialiasing:**

- It is the process which compensates the consequences of undersampling process.

6. **Bit Map and Pixel Map and Apixmap:**

- An image of two colors is called as a bitmap.
- On a black and white system with one bit per pixel, the frame buffer is commonly called as a bitmap.
- An image of more than two colors is called as a pixel map.
- For systems with multiple bits per pixel, the frame buffer is called as a apixmap.

7. **Bit Depth or Color Depth:**

- It is defined as "the number of bits assigned to each pixel in the image".
- Bit depth specifies the number of colors that a monitor can display. For example, One byte (8 bits) per pixel represents $2^8 = 256$ colors for each pixels.

8. **Pixel Phasing:**

- Pixel phasing is a hardware based antialiasing technique in which the graphics system shifts individual pixels from their normal positions in the pixel grid by a fraction (typically 0.25 and 0.5) of the unit distance between the pixels.
- By moving pixels closer to the time line, this technique is very effective in smoothing out the stair steps without reducing the sharpness of the edges.

9. **Interlacing:**

- It is used when the perpetual threshold is greater than the frequency of standard line voltage. The refresh rate and persistence of phosphor must be matched because of following reason:
  (i) If refresh rate > phosphor's persistence then their moving objects become blurred.
  (ii) If refresh rate < phosphor's persistence then it creates flickering.
- Interlacing is used to break the raster-line into two sweep patterns consisting of half the number of raster lines in the original patterns.

10. Dot Pitch:

- It is the measurement of the diagonal distance between two liked-colored (RGR) pixels on a display screen.
- Dot pitch is measured in millimeter (mm).

11. Display Area:

- The difference between the screen size or boundary and the displayed image is known as a display area.
- This gap is important so that the picture is not lost from the first or last column or row.

12. Refresh Rate:

- It is the number of times per second the pixels are recharged so that the image does not flicker.
- For a monitor, it is measured in hertz (Hz). Here, it is also called as a frame rate, horizontal scan rate, refresh rate, vertical frequency or vertical scan rate.
- Normally, the refresh rate varies from 60 to 75 Hz. A refresh rate of 75 Hz means that the image is redrawn 75 times a second.

1.1.1.3 Characteristics of Computer Graphics

- The characteristics of computer graphics are as follows:
  1. It is interactive in nature.
  2. It provides a tool called as motion dynamics which allows users to move objects.
  3. It has the ability to show moving pictures i.e., animations.
  4. It is very user-friendly.
  5. It provides an update dynamics facility which allows users to change the shape, color and other properties of objects being viewed.

1.1.1.4 Advantages of Computer Graphics

- Some of the major advantages of computer graphics, can be enlisted as follows:
  1. Information becomes more communicative when it is represented graphically.
  2. Mathematical models of hyperspace objects can be easily realized using computers.
  3. Visual form of data may be more relevant to realize their characteristics.
  4. Using motion dynamics simulation experiments of moving objects can be performed.
  5. A huge table of numbers may be replaced by a simple graph or chart diagram.
  6. Creation of engineering designs and architectural blue-prints can be fully automated.

1.1.2 Graphics System/Components of Computer Graphics

- The Fig. 1.3 shows the high level conceptual framework for interactive graphics and it consists of input and output devices, graphics system, application program and application model.

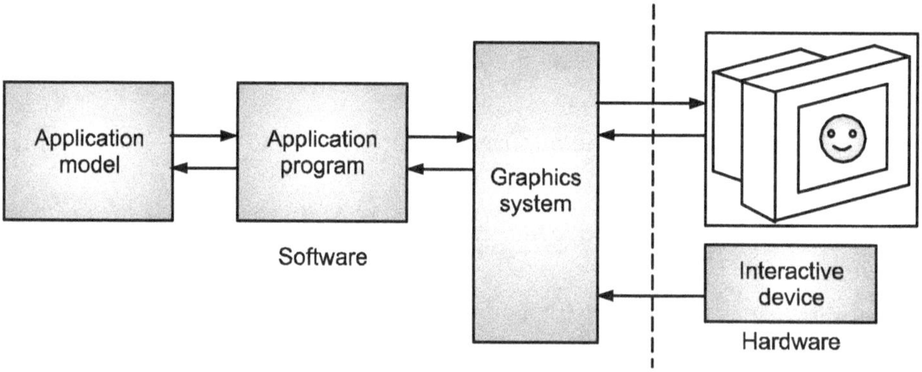

Fig. 1.3: The high level conceptual framework

- A computer receives input from input devices, and output images to a display device.
- The input and output devices are called the hardware components of the conceptual framework.
- At hardware level, the computer receives input from interactive devices and show images on display devices.
- At software level, there are three components i.e., application program, application model and graphics system.

1. **Application Program:**

- Application program creates, stores, retrieves picture from the second component, application model.
- The application program creates the application model and communicates with it to receive and store the data and information of object's attributes.
- It also handles user input and it produces views by sending a series of graphics output commands to the graphics system.
- The application program is also responsible for interaction handling and it does this by event handling loops.

2. **Application Model:**

- Application model represents the data or object to be pictured on the screen.
- It captures all the data and objects to be pictured on the screen and it also captures the relationship among the data and objects these relationship are stored in the database called application database, and referred by the application programs.

3. Graphics System:

- Graphics system is a series of graphics commands that contain both — what is to be viewed and how it is to be viewed?
- Graphics system is an intermediately between the application program and the display hardware. It accepts the series of graphics output commands from application program.
- It is responsible for actually producing the picture from the detailed descriptions and for passing the user's input to the application program for processing.

1.2 COMPONENTS OF COMPUTER GRAPHICS REPRESENTATION [Oct. 16]

- The screen is represented by a 2D array of locations called pixels, (See Fig. 1.4).

Fig. 1.4: Zooming in on an image made up of pixels

- The convention in these notes will follow that of OpenGL, placing the origin in the lower left corner, with that pixel being at location (0, 0). Be aware that placing the origin in the upper left is another common convention.
- One of 2^N intensities or colors are associated with each pixel, where N is the number of bits per pixel. Greyscale typically has one byte per pixel, for $2^8 = 256$ intensities. Color often requires one byte per channel, with three color channels per pixel: red, green, and blue. Color data is stored in a frame buffer. This is sometimes called an image map or bitmap.

Primitive operations:

1. `setpixel(x, y, color)`: Sets the pixel at position (x, y) to the given color.
2. `getpixel(x, y)`: Gets the color at the pixel at position (x, y).

- Scan conversion is the process of converting basic, low level objects into their corresponding pixel map representations. This is often an approximation to the object, since the frame buffer is a discrete grid.

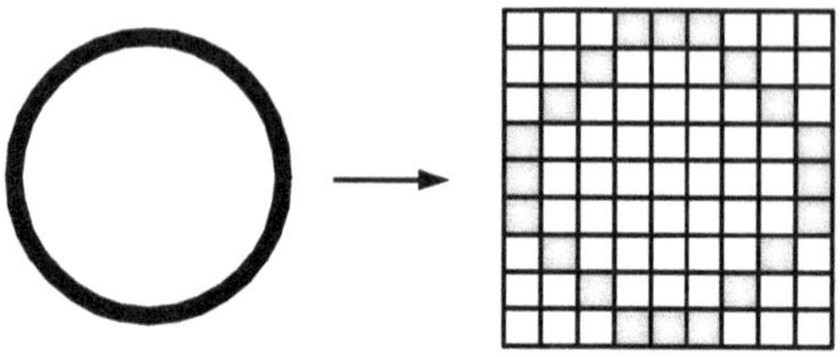

Scan conversion of a circle

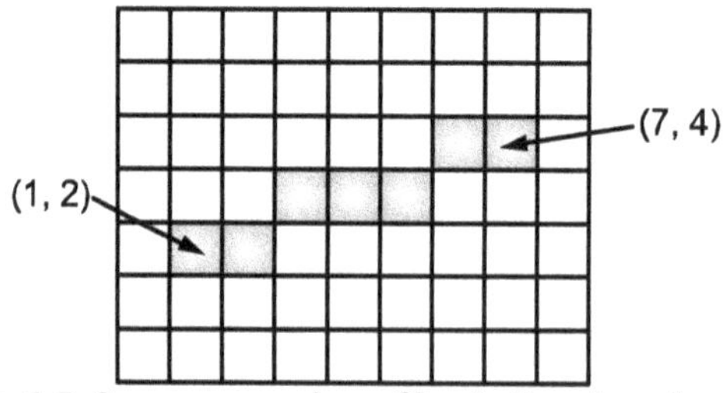

Fig. 1.5: Scan conversion of basic line drawing

Basic Line Drawing:

- It is a basic element in graphics. A line can be presented by two points.
- A line connects two points. To draw a line, you need two points between which you can draw a line.
- Characteristics of a good line drawing algorithm:
  1. Lines should appear straight.
  2. Lines should have constant density.
  3. Lines should be drawn rapidly.
  4. Lines should start and terminate accurately.

  Syntax : line(x_1, y_1, x_2, y_2);

  Where, (x_1,y_1) are coordinates of starting point of line and (x_2,y_2) are co-ordinates of end point of line.

  Example : line(10,10,100,100);

  It will draw a line from point (10,10) to point (100,100).

  Output : It draws only a line not a box on screen.

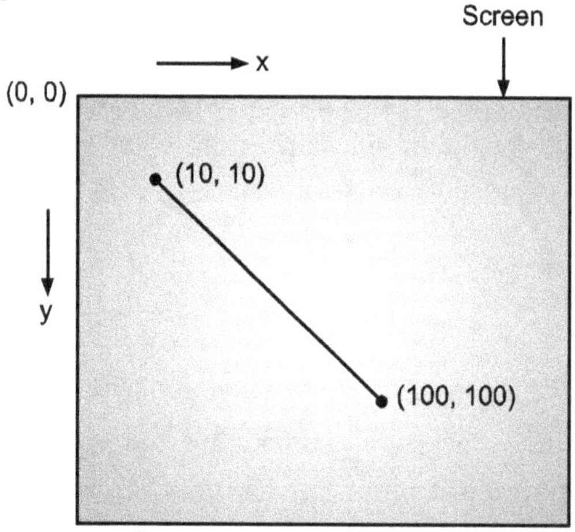

Fig. 1.6: Basic line drawing

1.2.1 Presentation

1.2.1.1 Curves

- A curve is an infinitely large set of points. Each point has two neighbors except endpoints.
- Curves and surfaces can have explicit, implicit, and parametric representations. Parametric representations are the most common in computer graphics.

1. **Implicit Curves:**

- Implicit curve representations define the set of points on a curve by employing a procedure that can test to see if a point in on the curve.
- Usually, an implicit curve is defined by an implicit function of the form:

  $f(x, y) = 0$

- It can represent multivalued curves (multiple y values for an x value). A common example is the circle, whose implicit representation is:

  $x^2 + y^2 - R^2 = 0$

2. **Explicit Curves:**

- A mathematical function $y = f(x)$ can be plotted as a curve. Such a function is the explicit representation of the curve.
- The explicit representation is not general, since it cannot represent vertical lines and is also single-valued.
- For each value of x, only a single value of y is normally computed by the function.

3. **Parametric Curves:**

- Curves having parametric form are called parametric curves.
- The explicit and implicit curve representations can be used only when the function is known. In practice the parametric curves are used.
- A two-dimensional parametric curve has the following form:

  $P(t) = f(t), g(t)$ or $P(t) = x(t), y(t)$

- The functions f and g become the (x, y) coordinates of any point on the curve, and the points are obtained when the parameter t is varied over a certain interval [a, b], normally [0, 1].

1.2.1.2 Ellipse

- An ellipse is defined as the set of points such that the sum of the distances from two fixed positions (foci) is the same for all points.

  Syntax: ellipse (x,y,start,end,xrad,yrad);

where,

x, y - are coordinates of centre point.

start, end - starting and ending angle of ellipse.

xrad, yrad – x-axis and y-axis radius respectively.

- For full ellipse, the start and end should be 0 and 360 else it will draw an arc on screen.

Example: ellipse (100, 100, 0, 360, 20, 10);

Output:

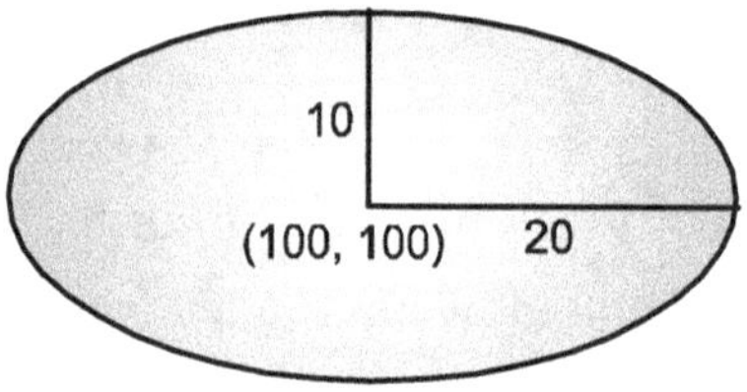

Fig. 1.7

Example: Ellipse(100, 100, 0, 360, 10, 20);

Output:

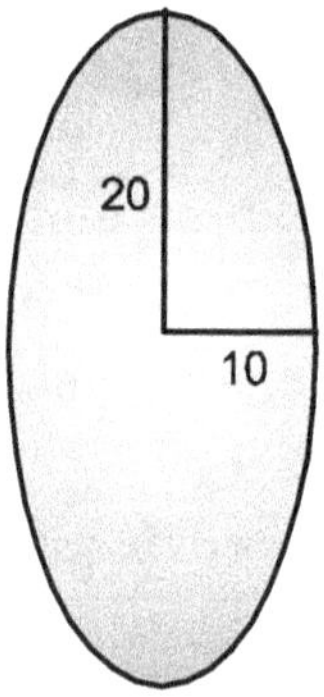

Fig. 1.8

Implicit:

- $\frac{x^2}{a^2} + \frac{y^2}{b^2} = 1$. This is only for the special case where the ellipse is centered at the origin with the major and minor axes aligned with y = 0 and x = 0.

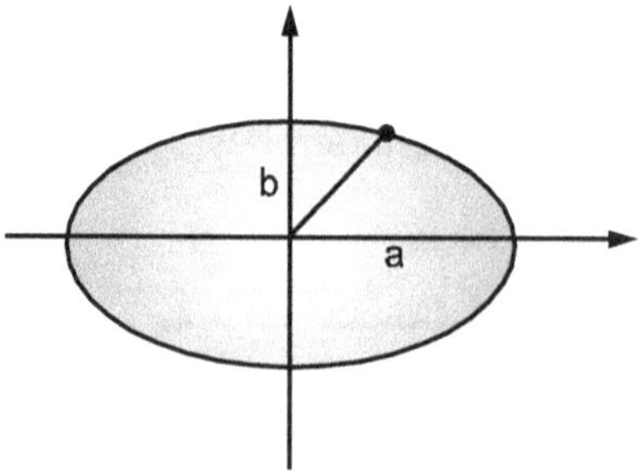

Fig. 1.9

Parametric:

$x(\lambda) = a\cos(2\pi\lambda)$, $y(\lambda) = b\sin(2\pi\lambda)$ or in vector form

$$\bar{p}(\lambda) = \begin{bmatrix} a\cos(2\pi\lambda) \\ b\sin(2\pi\lambda) \end{bmatrix}$$

- The implicit form of ellipses and circles is common because there is no explicit functional form. This is because y is a multifunction of x.

1.2.1.3 Polygon

- An object with more than two vertices is called as a polygon.
- A polygon is an ordered list of vertices.
- A polygon is a continuous, piecewise linear, closed planar curve.
- A simple polygon is non self-intersecting.
- A regular polygon is simple, equilateral, and equiangular.
- An n-gon is a regular polygon with n sides.
- A polygon is convex if, for any two points selected inside the polygon, the line segment between them is completely contained within the polygon.

  Example: To find the vertices of an n-gon, find n equally spaced points on a circle.

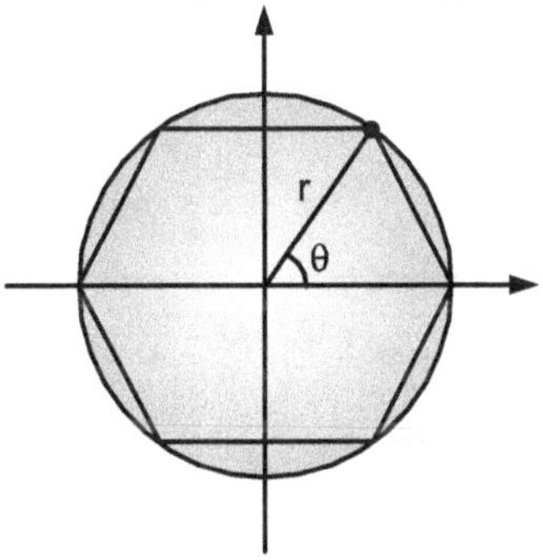

Fig. 1.10: A polygon

- In polar coordinates, each vertex $(x_i, y_i) = (r\cos(\theta_i), r\sin(\theta_i))$, where $\theta_i = i\frac{2\pi}{n}$ for $i = 0 \ldots n = 1$.
  - To translate: Add (x_c, y_c) to each point.
  - To scale: Change r.
  - To rotate: Add $\Delta\theta$ to each θ_i.

1.2.1.4 Rectangle

- It is a four sided flat shape with straight sides where all interior angles are right angles (90°), (See Fig. 1.11).

- Also opposite sides are parallel and of equal length.

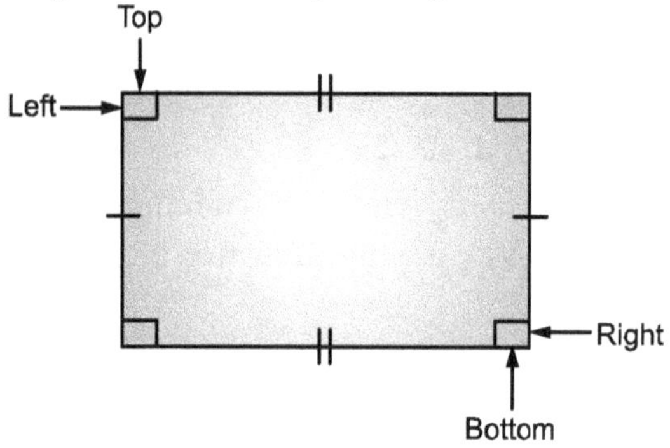

Fig. 1.11: A rectangle

Example: A square is a special type of rectangle.

Syntax : Rectangle(x_1, y_1, x_2, y_2);

Where, (x_1, y_1) are co-ordinates of top left corner point of rectangle and (x_2,y_2) are co-ordinates of bottom right corner point of rectangle.

Example : rectangle(10, 10, 100, 100);

It will draw a rectangle as shown in following output.

Output :

Fig. 1.12

1.2.1.5 Circle

- A circle is a simple shape in Euclidean geometry.
- It is the set of all points in a plane that are at a given distance from a given point, the centre; equivalently it is the curve traced out by a point that moves so that its distance from a given point is constant. The distance between any of the points and the centre is called the radius.
- A circle with circumference (C), diameter (D), radius (R) and centre (O), (See Fig. 1.13).

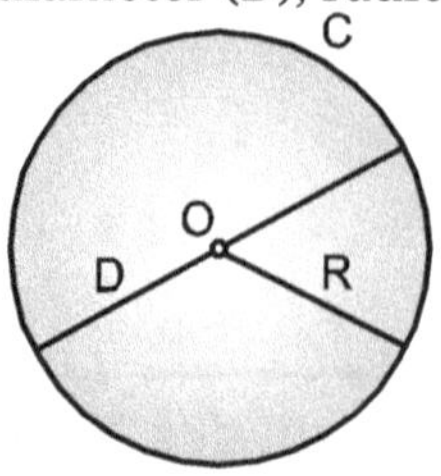

Fig. 1.13: A circle

Syntax : circle(x, y, r);

Where, (x, y) are co-ordinates of centre of circle and r is radius of circle.

Example : circle (50,50,10)

It draws a circle with centre 50,50 and radius 10.

Output :

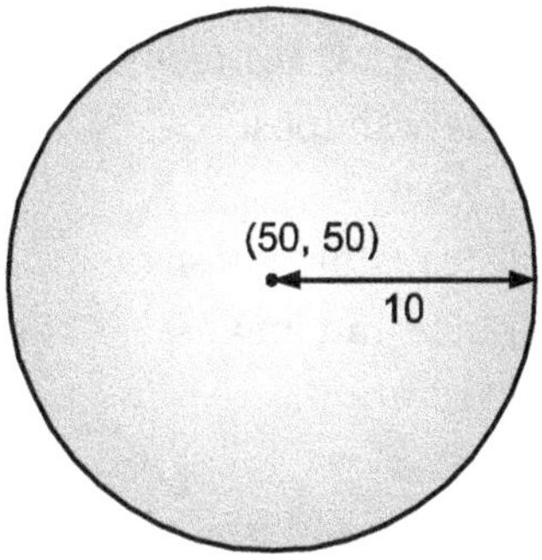

Fig. 1.14

1.2.2 Interaction

- Interaction is the one of the most advances in computer technology – to interact with computer displays, e.g. interactive computer graphics, i.e. the user sees an image on the display/screen.
- He/she reacts to this image by means of an interactive device, such as a mouse. The image changes in response to her input. He/she reacts to this change, and so on.
- The interaction can be logical interaction and physical interaction.
- The devices working over logical interaction are locator, valuator, pick and choice. The basic idea behind logical interaction is to make graphics packages independent of computer hardware.
- Where physical interaction itself include hardware components such as keyboard, mouse, trackball, spaceball, tablets, light pen, joy stick, touch panel, data glove. The devices will be discussed in Chapter 2.

1.2.3 Transformations

- Transformations play an important role in computer graphics to reposition the graphics on the screen and change their size or orientation.
- Transformation means changing some graphics into something else by applying rules. We can have various types of transformations such as translation, scaling up or down, rotation, shearing and so on.

1. **2D Transformations:**

- When a transformation takes place on a 2D plane, it is called 2D transformation.
- Given a point cloud, polygon, or sampled parametric curve, we can use transformations for several purposes:
  (i) Change coordinate frames (world, window, viewport, device, etc).
  (ii) Compose objects of simple parts with local scale/position/orientation of one part defined with regard to other parts. For example, for articulated objects.
  (iii) Use deformation to create new shapes.
  (iv) Useful for animation.
- There are three basic classes of transformations:
  (i) Rigid body: Preserves distance and angles.
  Examples: Translation and rotation.
  (ii) Conformal: Preserves angles.
  Examples: Translation, rotation, and uniform scaling.
  (iii) Affine: Preserves parallelism. Lines remain lines.
  Examples: Translation, rotation, scaling, shear, and reflection.

Transformation of Points:

- The result of the multiplication of a matrix (x, y) containing the coordinate of a point P and a general 2×2 transformation matrix:

$$[X]\,[T] = [x\ \ y]\begin{bmatrix} a & b \\ c & d \end{bmatrix} = [(ax + cy)\ (bx + dy)]$$
$$= [x^*\ \ y^*]$$

- The mathematical notation means that the initial coordinates x and y are transformed to x^* and y^*.

Special Cases:

Case 1:

$a = d = 1$ and $c = b = 0$

$$[X]\,[T] = [x\ \ y]\begin{bmatrix} 1 & 0 \\ 0 & 1 \end{bmatrix} = [x\ \ y] = [x^*\ \ y^*]$$

As we have multiplex X with the identity matrix, there is no change in the coordinates of point P. The reason is that in matrix algebra, multiplying by the identity matrix is equivalent to the original matrix.

Case 2:

$d = 1$ and $b = c = 0$

$$[X]\,[T] = [x\ \ y]\begin{bmatrix} a & 0 \\ 0 & 1 \end{bmatrix} = [ax\ \ y] = [x^*\ \ y^*]$$

$x^* = ax$ produces a scale change in the x-coordinates of the position vector.

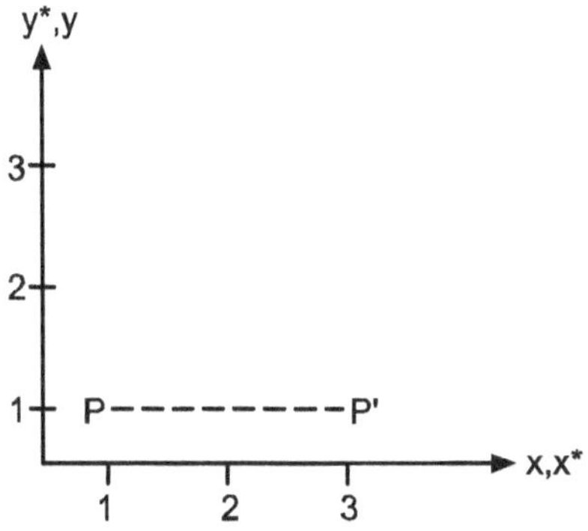

Fig. 1.15

Case 3:

b = c = 0

$$[X]\,[T] = [x\ \ y]\begin{bmatrix} a & 0 \\ 0 & d \end{bmatrix} = [ax\ \ dy] = [x^*\ \ y^*]$$

This yields scaling of both x and y coordinates of the original position vector.

- If $a \neq d$ then scaling is not equal.
- If $a = d > 1$ then pure enlargement or scaling of coordinates of P occurs.
- If $0 < a = d < 1$, then compression of the coordinates P.

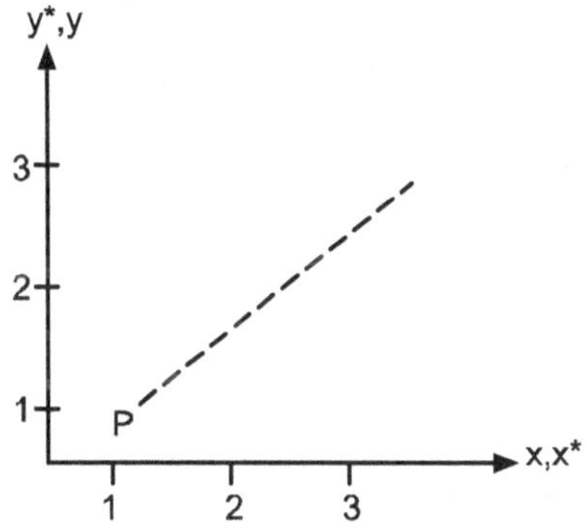

Fig. 1.16

Case 4:

b = c = 0, d = 1 and a = – 1

$$[X]\,[T] = [x\ \ y]\begin{bmatrix} -1 & 0 \\ 0 & 1 \end{bmatrix} = [-x\ \ y]$$

$$= [x^*\ \ y^*]$$

The reflection through an axis or plane occurs in the above case through y-axis as shown below.

If b = c = 0, a = 1 and d = – 1, then reflection through x-axis occurs. If b = c = 0, a = d < 0, then reflection through the origin occurs.

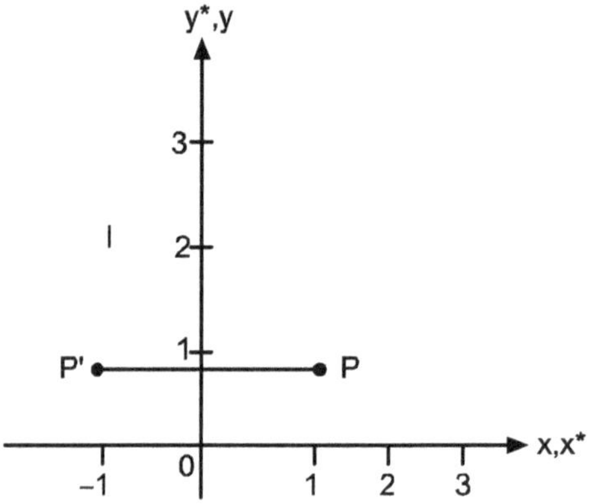

Fig. 1.17

Examples of Transformations:

- **Translation by vector** $\vec{t}$: $\bar{p}_1 = \bar{p}_0 + \vec{t}$.

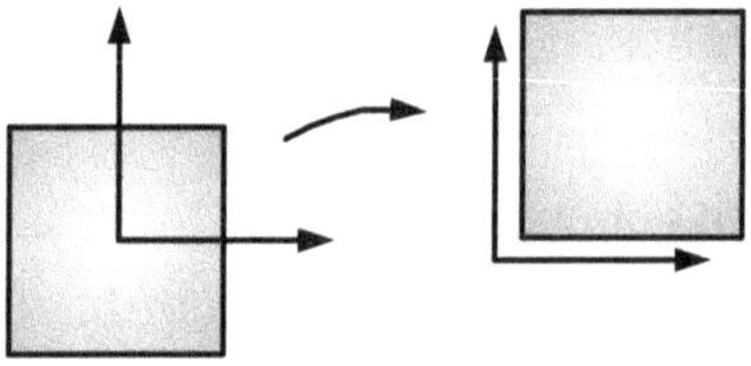

Fig. 1.18: Translation by vector

- **Rotation:** Counterclockwise by θ : $\bar{p}_1 = \begin{bmatrix} \cos(\theta) & -\sin(\theta) \\ \sin(\theta) & \cos(\theta) \end{bmatrix} \bar{p}_0$.

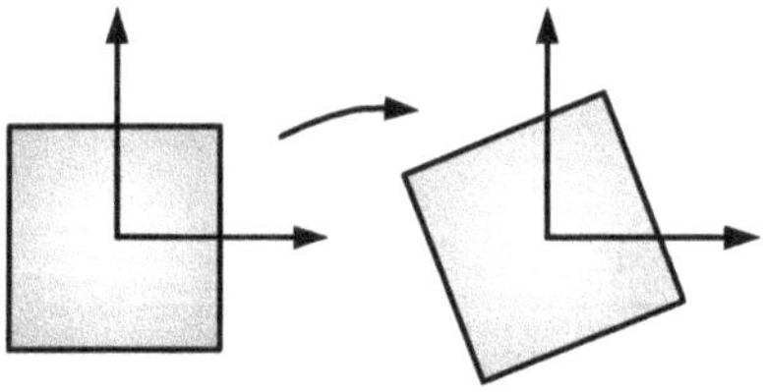

Fig. 1.19: Rotation

- **Uniform scaling** by scalar a : $\bar{p}_1 = \begin{bmatrix} a & 0 \\ 0 & a \end{bmatrix} \bar{p}_0$.

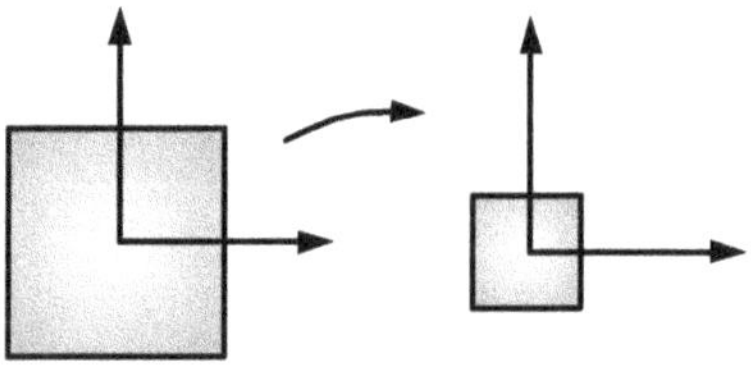

Fig. 1.20: Uniform scaling

- **Non-uniform scaling** by scalar by a and b : $\bar{p}_1 = \begin{bmatrix} a & 0 \\ 0 & b \end{bmatrix} \bar{p}_0$.

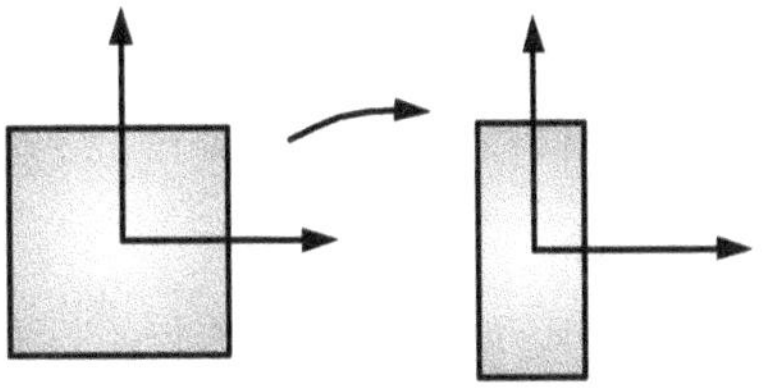

Fig. 1.21: Non-uniform scaling

- **Shear by** scalar h : $\bar{p}_1 = \begin{bmatrix} 1 & h \\ 0 & 1 \end{bmatrix} \bar{p}_0$.

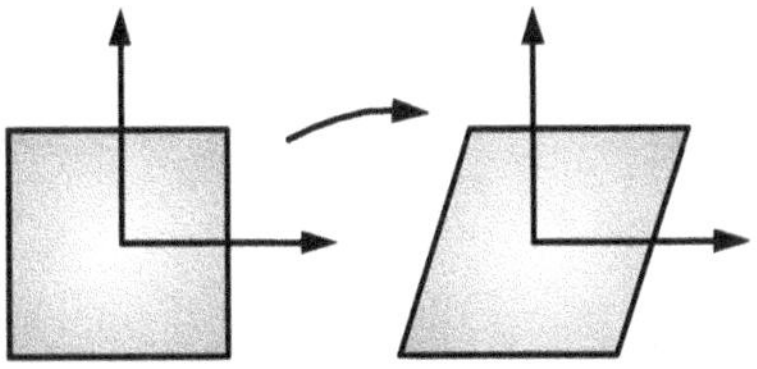

Fig. 1.22: Shear by scalar h

- **Reflection** about y-axis: $\bar{p}_1 = \begin{bmatrix} -1 & 0 \\ 0 & 1 \end{bmatrix} \bar{p}_0$.

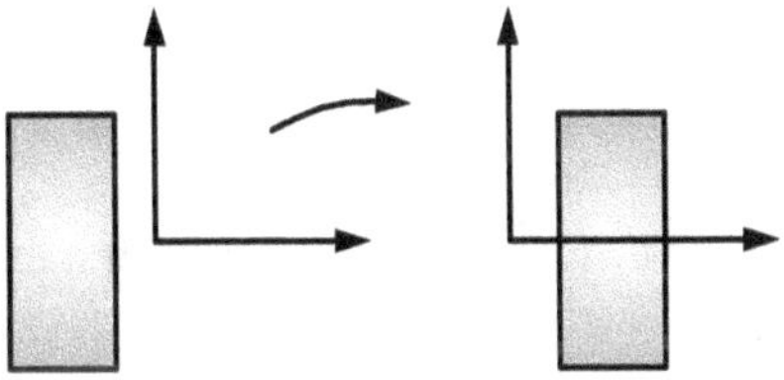

Fig. 1.23: Reflection

2. **Affine Transformations:**

- An affine transformation takes a point $\bar{p}$ to $\bar{q}$ according to $\bar{q} = F(\bar{p}) = A\bar{p} + \vec{t}$, a linear transformation followed by a translation. You should understand the following proofs.

(i) The inverse of an affine transformation is also affine, assuming it exists.

Proof: Let $\bar{q} = A\bar{p} + \vec{t}$ and assume A^{-1} exists, i.e. $\det(A) \neq 0$.

Then $A\bar{p} = \bar{q} - \vec{t}$, so $\bar{p} = A^{-1}\bar{q} - A^{-1}\vec{t}$. This can be rewritten as $\bar{p} = B\bar{q} + \vec{d}$, where $B = A^{-1}$ and $\vec{d} = -A^{-1}\vec{t}$.

Note: The inverse of a 2D linear transformation is,

$$A^{-1} = \begin{bmatrix} a & b \\ c & d \end{bmatrix}^{-1} = \frac{1}{ad - bc}\begin{bmatrix} d & -b \\ -c & a \end{bmatrix}$$

(ii) Lines and parallelism are preserved under affine transformations.

Proof:

To prove lines are preserved, we must show that $\bar{q}(\lambda) = F(\bar{l}(\lambda))$ is a line, where $F(\bar{p}) = A\bar{p} + \vec{t}$ and $\bar{l}(\lambda) = \bar{p}_0 + \lambda\vec{d}$.

$$\begin{aligned}\bar{q}(\lambda) &= A\bar{l}(\lambda) + \vec{t} \\ &= A(\bar{p}_0 + \lambda\vec{d}) + \vec{t} \\ &= A(\bar{p}_0 + \vec{t}) + \lambda A\vec{d}\end{aligned}$$

This is a parametric form of a line through $A\bar{p}_0 + \vec{t}$ with direction $A\bar{d}$.

Given a closed region, the area under a affine transformation $A\bar{p} + \vec{t}$ is scaled by det(A).

Note:

- Rotations and translation have det(A) = 1.
- Scaling $A = \begin{bmatrix} a & 0 \\ 0 & b \end{bmatrix}$ has det(A) = ab.
- Singularities have det(A) = 0.

Example: The matrix $A = \begin{bmatrix} 1 & 0 \\ 0 & 0 \end{bmatrix}$ maps all points to the x-axis, so the area of any closed region will become zero. We have det(A) = 0, which verifies that any closed regions area will be scaled by zero.

(iii) A composition of affine transformations is still affine.

Proof:

Let $F_1(\bar{p}) = A_1\bar{p} + \vec{t}_1$ and $F_2(\bar{p}) = A_2\bar{p} + \vec{t}_2$.

Then,
$$\begin{aligned}F(\bar{p}) &= F_2(F_1(\bar{p})) \\ &= A_2(A_1\bar{p} + \vec{t}_1) + \vec{t}_2 \\ &= A_2A_1\bar{p} + (A_2\vec{t}_1) + \vec{t}_2)\end{aligned}$$

Letting $A = A_2A_1$ and $\vec{t} = A_2\vec{t}_1 + \vec{t}_2$, we have $F(\bar{p}) = A\bar{p} + \vec{t}$, and this is an affine transformation.

3. **Homogeneous Coordinates:**

- Homogeneous coordinates are another way to represent points to simplify the way in which we express affine transformations.

- Normally, book-keeping would become tedious when affine transformations of the form $A\bar{p} + \vec{t}$ are composed. With homogeneous coordinates, affine transformations become matrices, and composition of transformations is as simple as matrix multiplication.
- With homogeneous coordinates, a point $\bar{p}$ is augmented with a 1, to form $\hat{p} = \begin{bmatrix} \bar{p} \\ 1 \end{bmatrix}$.

  All points $(\alpha\bar{p}, \alpha)$ represent the same point $\bar{p}$ for real $\alpha \neq 0$.

4. **Hierarchical Transformations:**

- It is often convenient to model objects as hierarchically connected parts. For example, a robot arm might be made up of an upper arm, forearm, palm, and fingers.
- Rotating at the shoulder on the upper arm would affect all of the rest of the arm, but rotating the forearm at the elbow would affect the palm and fingers, but not the upper arm.
- A reasonable hierarchy, then, would have the upper arm at the root, with the forearm as its only child, which in turn connects only to the palm, and the palm would be the parent to all of the fingers.
- Each part in the hierarchy can be modeled in its own local coordinates, independent of the other parts. For a robot, a simple square might be used to model each of the upper arm, forearm, and so on.
- Rigid body transformations are then applied to each part relative to its parent to achieve the proper alignment and pose of the object.
- For example, the fingers are positioned to be in the appropriate places in the palm coordinates, the fingers and palm together are positioned in forearm coordinates, and the process continues up the hierarchy. Then a transformation applied to upper arm coordinates is also applied to all parts down the hierarchy.

5. **Transformations in OpenGL:**

- OpenGL manages two 4 × 4 transformation matrices i.e., the modelview matrix, and the projection matrix.
- Whenever, you specify geometry (using glVertex), the vertices are transformed by the current model view matrix and then the current projection matrix. Hence, you don't have to perform these transformations yourself.
- You can modify the entries of these matrices at any time. OpenGL provides several utilities for modifying these matrices.
- The model view matrix is normally used to represent geometric transformations of objects; the projection matrix is normally used to store the camera transformation.

1.3 APPLICATIONS OF COMPUTER GRAPHICS [April 16]

- Now-a-days computer graphics is used in variety of fields ranging from daily routine activities to very high end specialized areas.
- Some of major applications of computer graphics are shown in Fig. 1.24.

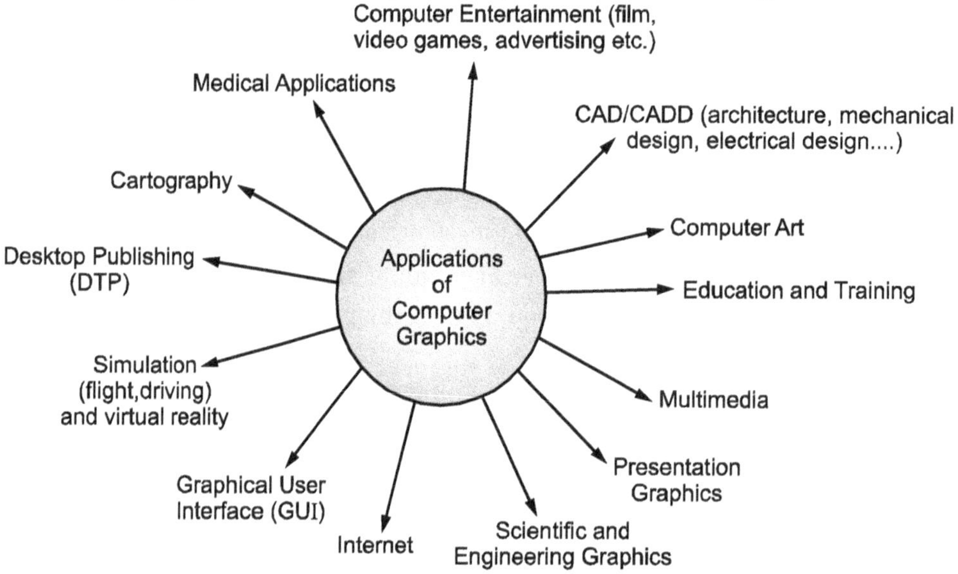

Fig. 1.24: Applications of computer graphics

1. **DTP (DeskTop Publishing):**

- DTP is used in office automation and electronic publishing. The use of graphics for the creation and dissemination of information has increased enormously since, the advent of desktop publishing on personal computers.
- Number of organizations whose publications used to be printed by outside specialists can now produce printed materials inhouse.
- Office automation and electronic publishing can produce both traditional printed (hard copy) documents and electronic (soft copy) documents that contain text, tables, graphs, and other forms of drawn or scanned-in graphics.
- DTP is related to the production of journals, printing newsletters, book publishing in small organisation.

2. **Graphical User Interface (GUI):**

- One cannot use any software package of recent times without observing the many graphic items present and available on the screen to guide the user.
- Number of software developed today must have a GUI for user-friendly and interactive operation.

3. **Medical Applications:**

- Computer graphics has now become a powerful tool of diagnosis and treatment in the hands of doctors, particularly surgeons, MRIs, CAT scans, etc.

4. **Computer Art:**

- Computer graphics methods are widely used in both fine art and commercial art applications.
- Artists use a variety of computer methods, including special-purpose hardware, artist's paintbrush (such as Lumens), other paint packages (such as Pixel-paint and Super-paint), specially developed software, symbolic mathematics packages (such as Mathematics), CAD packages, desktop publishing software, and animation packages that provide facilities for designing object shapes and specifying object motions.

5. **Presentation and Business Graphics:**

- Presentation graphics deals with graphical representation of information.
- The presentation of data/information in a condensed, visual, convenient form has always been an aid to understanding and promoting any idea. The visual (pictorial) medium is more powerful than the written (text) medium or the audio (sound) medium.
- Computer graphics has raised such presentations like brochures, posters, transparencies, etc., for publicity and training purposes—to an art form, by making the visuals attractive and colourful, without the special artistic skills, time and effort involved in their production by human agency.

6. **Computer Aided Design/Drafting (CAD/CADD):**

- A major use of computer graphics is in design processes, particularly for engineering and architectural systems, but almost all products are now computer designed.
- Generally, referred to as CAD, (Computer-Aided Design) methods are now routinely used in the design of buildings, automobiles, aircraft, watercraft, spacecraft, computers, textiles, and many, many other products.

7. **Computer Games and Entertainment:**

- Computer games, with colourful and animated screen displays were among the first applications of computer graphics.
- Computer graphics methods are now commonly used in making motion pictures, music videos, and television shows. Sometimes, the graphics scenes are displayed by themselves, and sometimes graphics objects are combined with the actors and live scenes.

8. **Computer-Aided Learning (CAL):**

- The computer is being used more and more in the teaching/learning process in almost every, field in the developed countries, especially to perform repetitive tasks in complex training areas.

- For repeated study of various components of an object, concept or process, pictures can be more effectively used than words.
- Computer graphics tools such as Microsoft PowerPoint are very heavily used in teaching, seminar and conference presentations, on almost every subject at every level.
- The interactive nature of the computer graphics is a vital component of the teaching-learning process.

9. **Animations:**

- Moving pictures are must and this facility is provided by computer graphics using animation.

10. **Cartography:**

- Computer graphics is used to produce accurate and schematic representation of geographical and other natural phenomena front measurement data.
- For example, geographic maps, relief maps, exploration maps for drilling and mining, oceanographic charts, weather maps, contour maps and population density maps.

11. **Simulation and Virtual Reality:**

- Simulation is another recent development that permits expensive anti complex phenomena and processes to be modeled in the computer and pictorially presented to the user.
- Using simulation techniques, astronauts, aircraft and ship pilots, and even automobile drivers, can be trained to perfection in a complex and expensive piece of equipment, without risking life or property.
- Simulation has now been taken to such lengths that wearing such special devices on the eyes, ears and fingers, a user can interact with a computer to get into virtual reality inside a virtual universe in which the user call activate a number of scenarios in a variety of environments.

12. **Education:**

- Computer-generated models of physical, financial and economic systems are often used as educational aids.

1.4 PIXEL/POINT [April 16]

1. **Pixel:**

- A pixel (short for picture element, using the common abbreviation "pix" for "picture") is one of the many tiny dots that make up the representation of a picture in a computer's memory.
- In a computer, the smallest dot that can be displayed on the screen is a pixel, usually rectangular in shape.
- Pixel has finite dimensions, however small. Hence, a computer line is made up of a finite number of dots.

2. **Point:**

- A point is a position on a plane or in space.
- In short, a position in a plane/space is known as a point.
- Graphics involves first, the location of points; next, the definition of lines as connecting or passing through points in a specified fashion, then the definition of surfaces as bounded by lines and finally the representation of solids as bounded by surfaces.

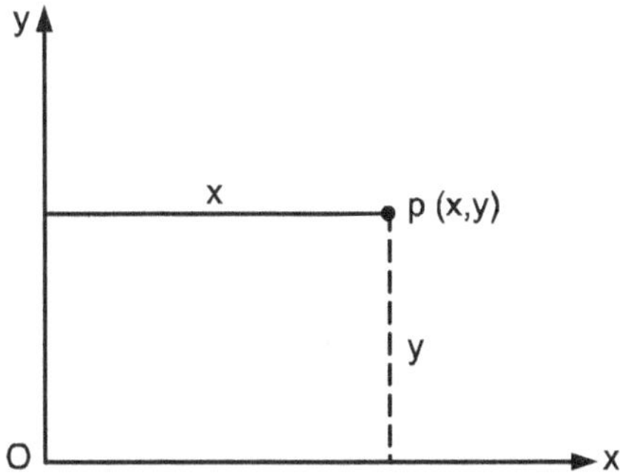

Fig. 1.25: Point

- The point itself is just the location and it has no size. A line is a set of points. It is theoretically made up of an infinite number of points because it is a finite length divided by zero - the theoretical length of the point.

1.5 RASTER VS VECTOR [April 16]

1. **Raster:**

- Raster is a rectangular array of points or dots. Each row of pixels is called a raster line or scan line.
- A raster image is a collection of dots called pixels as shown in Fig. 1.26.

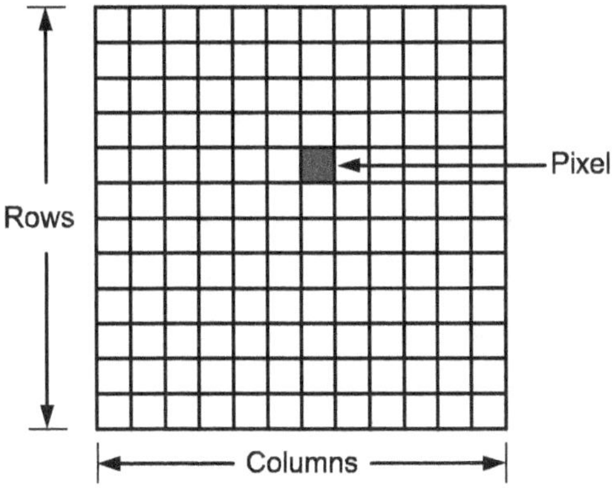

Fig. 1.26: A raster image

- A raster graphics image is a dot matrix data structure representing a generally rectangular grid of pixels, or points of color, viewable via a monitor, paper, or other display medium. Raster images are stored in image files with varying formats.
- A raster file is usually larger than a vector graphics image file. A raster file is usually difficult to modify without loss of information, although there are software tools that can convert a raster file into a vector file for refinement and changes.
- Examples of raster image file types are BMP, TIFF, GIF, and JPEG files.

2. **Vector:**

- Vector graphics is the use of geometrical primitives such as points, lines, curves, and shapes or polygons - all of which are based on mathematical expressions—to represent images in computer graphics.
- Vector graphics are based on vectors (also called paths), which lead through locations called control points or nodes.
- A vector is a directed line segment that has magnitude and direction. A vector is defined as the difference between two point positions as shown in Fig. 1.27.

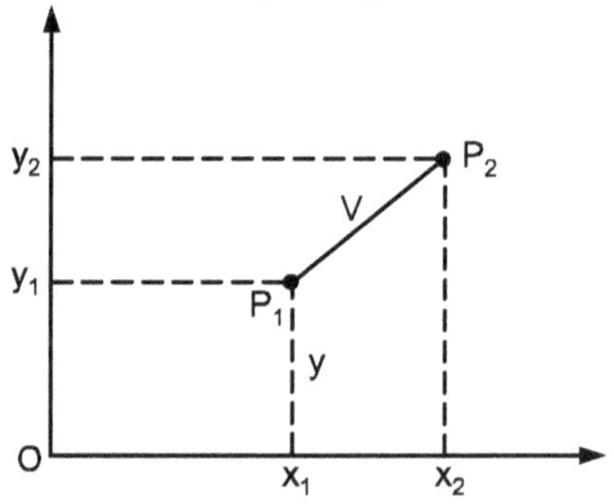

Fig. 1.27: A vector

So for a 2D vector, we have

$$V = P_2 - P_1$$
$$= (x_2 - x_1, y_2 - y_1)$$
$$= V_x, V_y$$

where, the Cartesian components V_x and V_y are projections of V onto the x and y-axis. Also, we can say that,

V_x - Movement along x-direction

V_y - Movement along y-direction

The magnitude of vector, V is given by

$$|V| = \sqrt{V_x^2 + V_y^2}$$

and its direction in terms of angular displacement from x-axis is given by,

$$\alpha = \tan^{-1}\left(\frac{V_y}{V_x}\right)$$

Some Special Vectors:

1. **Unit Vector:** A vector of unit magnitude is called as a unit vector.
   For example: A vector a, is said to be a unit vector if,
   $$|a| = 1$$
2. **Zero Vector/Null Vector:** A vector of zero magnitude with no direction associated with it is called as a zero or null vector.
   For example: A vector a, is said to be a Null/Zero vector if $|a| = 0$.
3. **Equal vectors:** Two vectors R and S having the same magnitude and same or parallel directions are said to be equal. We write it as follows:
   $$R = S$$
4. **Negative Vector:** A vector $\overrightarrow{AB}$ represents the negative of $\overrightarrow{BA}$.

Raster Vs Vector:

Sr. No	Raster	Vector
1.	Raster graphics are composed of pixels.	Vector graphics are composed of paths.
2.	Raster graphics are resolution dependent.	Vector graphics are resolution independent.
3.	More expensive	Less expensive.
4.	Raster graphics, become "blocky," since each pixel increases in size as the image is made larger.	Because vector graphics are not made of pixels, the images can be scaled to be very large without losing quality.
5.	A raster graphic, such as a gif or jpeg, is an array of pixels of various colors, which together form an image.	A vector graphic, such as an .eps file or Adobe Illustrator file, is composed of paths, or lines, that are either straight or curved.
6.	Raster images are pixel-based, they suffer a malady called image degradation.	Vector-based graphics are more malleable than raster images
7.	Less versatile, flexible and difficult to use.	More versatile, flexible and easy to use.
8.	Large dimensions and detailed images equal large file size.	A large dimension vector graphic can maintain a small file size.
9.	A raster is usually difficult to modify (editing) without loss of information,	Easy to modify without loss of information.
10.	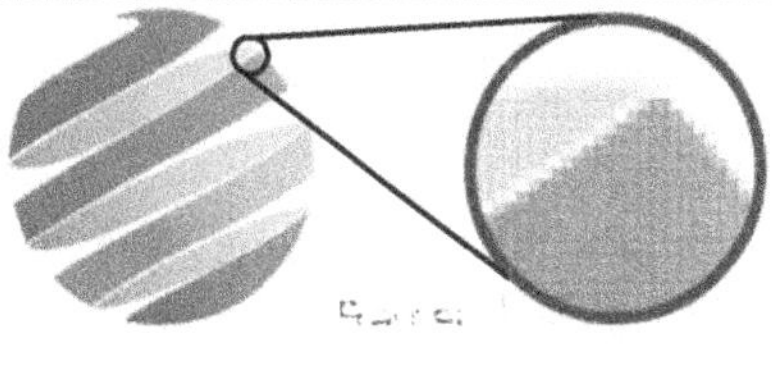	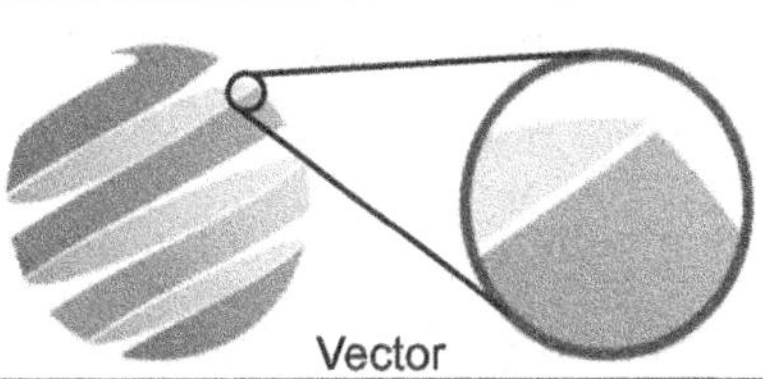

1.6 RGB COLOR MODEL

- Color is the aspect of things that is caused by differing qualities of light being reflected or emitted by them.
- There are several ways to specify colors. A color model is a unique representation of a color.
- The most common of these is the RGB color model.
- The RGB color model specifies the Red, Green and Blue components of color.
- The main purpose of the RGB color model is for the sensing, representation, and display of images in electronic systems, such as televisions and computers, though it has also been used in conventional photography.
- RGB color model is the standard model used in a color monitor for TV or computer.
- The RGB model defines a color by giving the intensity level of Red, Green and Blue light that mix together to create a pixel on the display.

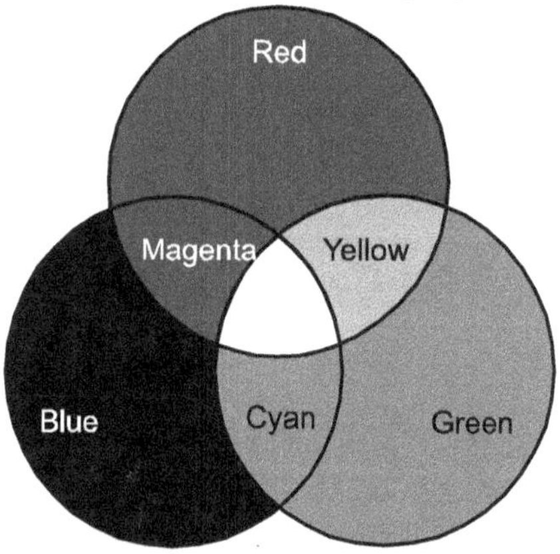

Fig. 1.28: The RGB model

- Fig. 1.29 shows the RGB color model, defining colors with an additive process within the unit cube.
- The cube represents all of the colors that can be represented in the RGB system. When the value of blue is zero, the bottom face of the cube has varying shades of black, green, red and yellow.
- Likewise, when the value of red is one, the front right face has varying shades of red, magenta, yellow and white.

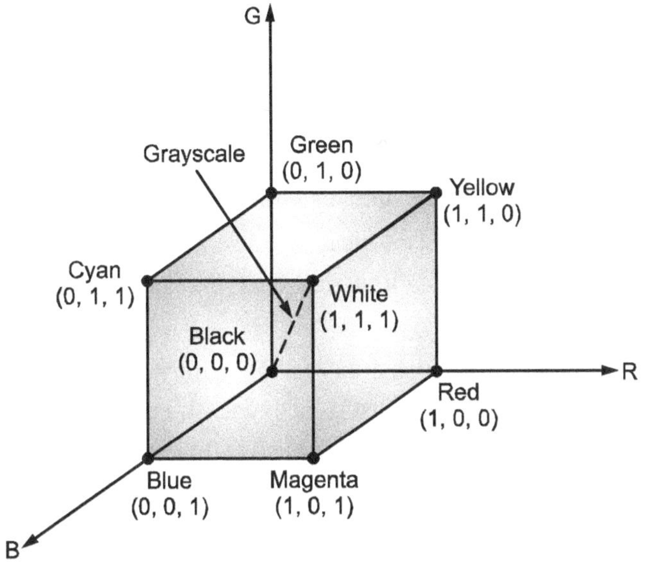

Fig. 1.29: The RGB color model

- What RGB model states, that each color image is actually formed of three different images. Red image, Blue image and Black image. A normal grayscale image can be defined by only one matrix, but a color image is actually composed of three different matrices.
- One color image matrix = Red matrix + Blue matrix + Green matrix.
- This can be best seen in following example and shown in Fig. 1.30.

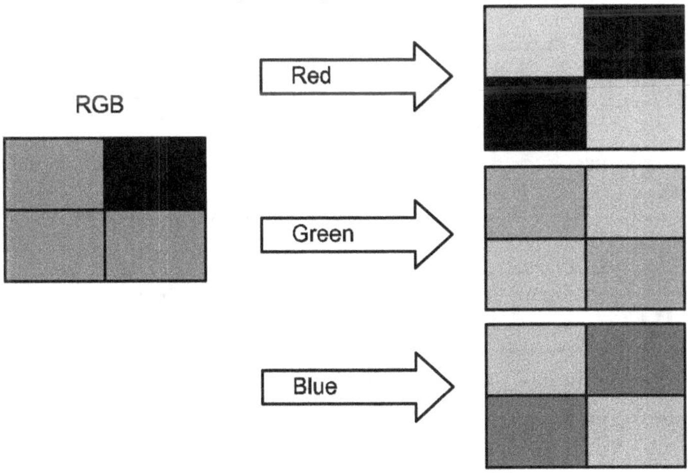

Fig. 1.30: Gray Scale Image

- **Gray Scale Image:** The image which results an intensity of light at each pixel in a single band of electromagnetic spectrum (like infrared, visible light, ultraviolet etc.)

Applications of RGB:

1. Liquid Crystal Display (LCD).
2. Cathode Ray Tube (CRT).
3. A compute monitor or a large scale screen.
4. Plasma Display or LED display such as a television.

- The RGB model is so important to graphic design because it is used in computer monitors. The screen you are reading this very article on is using additive colors to display images and text.
- Therefore, when designing websites (and other on-screen projects such as presentations), the RGB model is used because the final product is viewed on a computer display.
- With most of today's displays, the intensity of each color can vary from 0 to 255, which gives 16,777,216 different colors. (Older displays with less memory might only allow 256 colors, and really ancient displays might have only 16).
- Here are some example colors and their red, green and blue intensity values:

Color	Red	Green	Blue
Red	255	0	0
Green	0	255	0
Blue	0	0	255
Yellow	255	255	0
Cyan	0	255	255
Magenta	255	0	255
White	255	255	255
Black	0	0	0

1.7 INTENSITY

- The RGB color model is used for specifying colors. This model specifies the intensity of red, green, and blue on a scale of 0 to 255, with 0 (zero) indicating the minimum intensity.
- The settings of the three colors are converted to a single integer value by using this formula:

  RGB Value = Red + (Green*256) + (Blue*256*256)

- The following table shows examples.

Red	Green	Blue	RGB value	Color
255	0	0	255	Red
0	255	0	65280	Green
0	0	255	16711680	Blue
0	255	255	16776960	Cyan
255	0	255	16711935	Magenta
255	255	0	65535	Yellow
255	255	255	16777215	White
128	128	128	8421504	Gray
0	0	0	0	Black

1.8 PROGRAMMING ESSENTIALS

- The process of developing and implementing various sets of instructions to enable a computer to do a certain task is called as programming.
- Computer programming (often shortened to programming) is a process that leads from an original formulation of a computing problem to executable computer programs.
- A program is a specific set of ordered operations for a computer to perform. Programming involves activities such as analysis, developing understanding, generating algorithms, verification of requirements of algorithms including their correctness and resources consumption, and implementation (commonly referred to as coding) of algorithms in a target programming language.
- The purpose of programming is to find a sequence of instructions that will automate performing a specific task or solving a given problem.

1.8.1 Event Driven Programming

- Event-driven programming is a programming paradigm in which the flow of program execution is determined by events - for example a user action such as a mouse click, key press, pen light, joystick motion or a message from the operating system or another program.
- An event-driven application is designed to detect events as they occur, and then deal with them using an appropriate event-handling procedure.

- Event-driven programs can be written in any programming language, although some languages (Visual Basic for example) are specifically designed to facilitate event-driven programming, and provide an Integrated Development Environment (IDE) that partially automates the production of code, and provides a comprehensive selection of built-in objects and controls, each of which can respond to a range of events.
- Virtually all object-oriented and visual languages support event-driven programming. Visual Basic, Visual C++ and Java are examples of such languages.
- The central element of an event-driven application is a scheduler that receives a stream of events and passes each event to the relevant event-handler. The scheduler will continue to remain active until it encounters an event (e.g. "End_Program") that causes it to terminate the application.
- Under certain circumstances, the scheduler may encounter an event for which it cannot assign an appropriate event handler. Depending on the nature of the event, the scheduler can either ignore it or raise an exception (this is sometimes referred to as "throwing" an exception).
- Within an event-driven programming environment, standard events are usually identified using the ID of the object affected by the event (e.g. the name of a command button on a form), and the event ID (e.g. "left-click").
- The information passed to the event-handler may include additional information, such as the x and y coordinates of the mouse pointer at the time the event occurred, or the state of the Shift key (if the event in question is a key-press).
- Events are often actions performed by the user during the execution of a program, but can also be messages generated by the operating system or another application, or an interrupt generated by a peripheral device or system hardware. If the user clicks on a button with the mouse or hits the Enter key, it generates an event. If a file download completes, it generates an event.
- And if there is a hardware or software error, it generates an event. The events are dealt with by a central event-handler (usually called a dispatcher or scheduler) that runs continuously in the background and waits for an even to occur.
- When an event does occur, the scheduler must determine the type of event and call the appropriate event-handler to deal with it.
- The information passed to the event handler by the scheduler will vary, but will include sufficient information to allow the event-handler to take any action necessary.
- Fig. 1.31 illustrates the relationship between events, the scheduler, and the application's event-handlers.

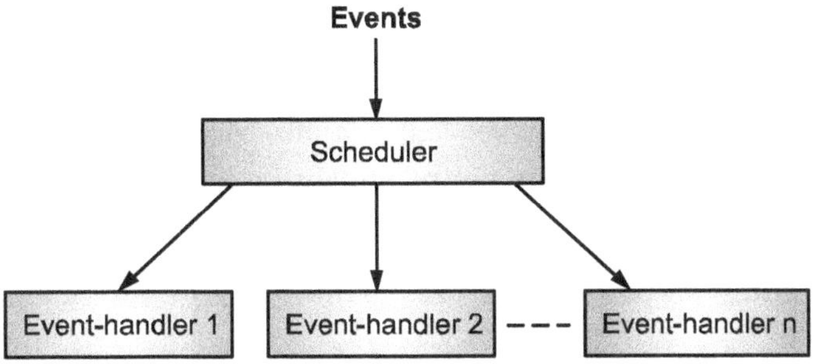

Fig. 1.31: A simple event-driven programming paradigm

1.8.2 Overview of OpenGL

- OpenGL is mainly considered an API (Application Programming Interface) that provides us with a large set of functions that we can use to manipulate graphics.
- Different computers operating systems, and graphics processors all have a different set of commands to control the output on a computer screen.
- For this a series of different standards has been developed through the years, with OpenGL being one of the more recent standards.
- OpenGL is a set of graphics libraries that is available for UNIX, Linux, the X Window System, Microsoft Windows, and Macintosh. These libraries handle different sets of tasks, with the most basic tasks being handled by the core OpenGL library.
- There is also an OpenGL Utility Library (GLU) that includes more advanced object modeling tasks. There are libraries to handle windowing tasks for most computer systems including the X Window System (GLX), Microsoft Windows (WGL), IBM OS/2 (PGL) and Apple Macintosh (AGL). Kilgard has written a windowing system independent library called the OpenGL Utility Toolkit (GLUT) that sits on top of these and hides some of the complexities of the different windowing systems.
- OpenGL routines can be called from Ada, Cp C++, FORTRAN, Python, Perl, and Java. C and C++ are the main languages used in computer graphics.
- OpenGL is a state-based system. A number of state variables within OpenGL determine how the objects appear when rendered. For example, the current color is a state variable. When a particular color is set in OpenGL, all objects are drawn using that color until a new color is specified.

1.8.3 OpenGL Library [April 16, Oct. 16]

- OpenGL is a software interface to graphics hardware. This interface consists of about 150 distinct commands that you use to specify the objects and operations needed to produce interactive three-dimensional applications.

- OpenGL is designed as a streamlined, hardware-independent interface to be implemented on many different hardware platforms.
- OpenGL doesn't provide high-level commands for describing models of three-dimensional objects. Such commands might allow you to specify relatively complicated shapes such as automobiles, parts of the body, airplanes, or molecules. With OpenGL, you must build up your desired model from a small set of geometric primitives - points, lines, and polygons.
- OpenGL (Open Graphics Library) is a cross-language, multi-platform Application Programming Interface (API) for rendering 2D and 3D vector graphics. The API is typically used to interact with a Graphics Processing Unit (GPU), to achieve hardware-accelerated rendering.

Associated Libraries:

- The earliest versions of OpenGL were released with a companion library called GLU, the OpenGL Utility Library. It provided simple, useful features which were unlikely to be supported in contemporary hardware, such as mipmap generation, tessellation, and generation of primitive shapes.
- The GLU specification was last updated in 1998, and the latest version depends on features which were deprecated with the release of OpenGL 3.1 in 2009.

Context and Window Toolkits:

- These toolkits are designed specifically around creating and managing OpenGL windows. They also manage input, but little beyond that.
  1. **GLFW:** A cross platform windowing and keyboard/mouse/joystick handler. Is more aimed for creating games.
  2. **freeglut:** A cross platform windowing and keyboard/mouse handler. Its API is a superset of the GLUT API, and it is more stable and up to date than GLUT.
  3. **GLUT:** An old windowing handler, no longer maintained.
- Several "multimedia libraries" can create OpenGL windows, in addition to input, sound and other tasks useful for game-like applications.
  1. **Allegro 5:** A cross-platform multimedia library with a C API focused on game development.
  2. **SDL:** A cross-platform multimedia library with a C API.
  3. **SFML:** A cross-platform multimedia library with a C++ API.
- **Widget Toolkits:**
  1. **FLTK:** A small cross-platform C++ widget library.
  2. **Qt:** A cross-platform C++ widget toolkit. It provides a number of OpenGL helper objects, which even abstract away the difference between desktop GL and OpenGL ES.
  3. **wxWidgets:** A cross-platform C++ widget toolkit.

Extension Loading Libraries:

- Given the high workload involved in identifying and loading OpenGL extensions, a few libraries have been designed which load all available extensions and functions automatically. Examples include GLEE, GLEW and glbinding. Extensions are also loaded automatically by most language bindings, such as JOGL and PyOpenGL.
- Table 1.1 shows the beginning letters for each of the OpenGL libraries.

Table 1.1: OpenGL routine prefixes

core OpenGL library	gl
OpenGL Utility library	glu
OpenGL Utility Toolkit	glut
X Window System Library	glX
Microsoft Windows Library	wgl
IMB OS/2 Library	pgl
Apple Macintosh Library	agl

- The OpenGL system could be represented as shown in Fig. 1.32.

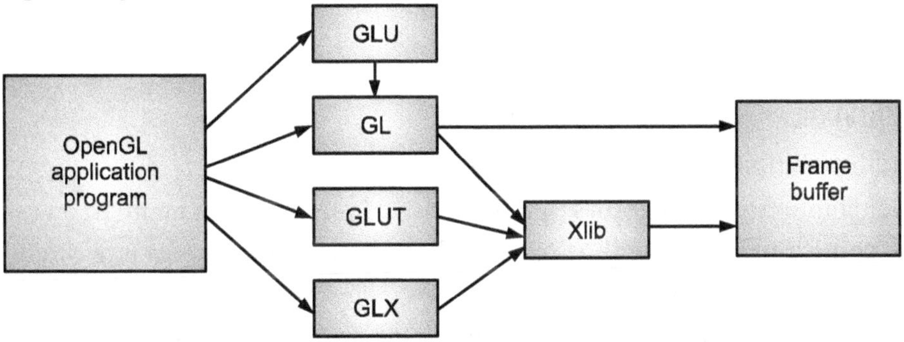

Fig. 1.32: The OpenGL system

- To access the system, application programmers used a library called GL. GL is our basic graphics library and consists of all the primitive functions, GLU is the graphics utility library and uses GL, GLUT is the graphics utility library toolkit and interfaces with the windowing system.
- The library is constantly expanding. The final component, GLX for X Windows, or on Microsoft Windows wgl communicates with the X windowing system, or the Windows window subsystem.

Getting Ready to Render:

- Before starting to draw things in OpenGL, GLUT must be initialized. Then GLUT is given details about how things will be specified, and how it should function.

- After this initialization, the drawing window can be opened. These tasks are done with calls to the routines glutInit, glutInitDisplayMode and glutCreateWindow, respectively.
- A size and position for the window can be recommended with the functions glutInitWindowsSize and glutInitWindowPosition but the actual size and position will be determined by the windowing system itself.
- The following code segment shows the use of above functions:

```
int main(int argc, char **argv)
{
    glutInit(&argc, argv);
    glutInitDisplayMode(GLUT_SINGLE | GLUT_RGB);
    glutInitWindowSize(400, 400);
    glutInitWindowPosition(80, 80);
    glutCreateWindow("example in OpenGL");
    .
    .
    .
}
```

Functions:

1. `void glutInit (int *argc, char **argv);`

   The call to glutInit takes two parameters:

   argc: A pointer to the program's unmodified argc variable from main. Upon return, the value pointed to by argc will be updated, because glutInit extracts any command line options intended for the GLUT library.

   argv: The program's unmodified argv variable from main. Like argcp, the data for argv will be updated because glutInit extracts any command line options understood by the GLUT library.

2. `void glutInitDisplayMode(unsigned int mode);`

   glutInitDisplayMode sets the initial display mode. The initial display mode is used when creating top-level windows, subwindows, and overlays to determine the OpenGL display mode for the to-be-created window or overlay.

3. `void glutInitWindowSize(int width, int height);` and

   `void glutInitWindowPosition(int x, int y);`

   glutInitWindowPosition and glutInitWindowSize set the initial window position and size respectively.

The initial value of the initial window position GLUT state is -1 and -1. If either the X or Y component to the initial window position is negative, the actual window position is left to the window system to determine. The initial value of the initial window size GLUT state is 300 by 300. The initial window size components must be greater than zero.

A GLUT program should use the window's reshape callback to determine the true size of the window.

4. **int glutCreateWindow(char *name);**

glutCreateWindow creates a top-level window. The name will be provided to the window system as the window's name (ASCII character string). The intent is that the window system will label the window with the name.

Event Loops and Callback Functions:

- Once, the window or windows are set up and the objects are drawn inside those windows, there is still a lot more that can happen. The user/programmer can click a mouse button, or can minimize, resize, or close the window. Any of these actions is considered an event and that event needs to be recognized and then processed.
- The GLUT of OpenGL has the capability to recognize these events and can do some simple work with them, but there are some things that only the program can do.
- For example, when the user clicks a mouse button, the program needs to decide what that means and how to handle it. If the user resizes the window, the program needs to determine how to handle the ability to draw in this new window. So, how is the interaction between the GLUT and the program handled? It is done through functions that we write, but that the GLUT calls.
- Your next question might be, "how does the GLUT know which of my functions to call?" There are a set of routines in the GLUT that register which of the functions are to be used for which tasks. The program functions are called "callback" functions because the GLUT calls back to them when their work is needed.
- An example of a complete main program that uses a couple of these callback registration functions follows:

```
int main(int argc, char **argv)
gluInit(&argc, argv);
glutInitDisplayMode(GLUT_SINGLE | GLUT_RGB);
glutInitWindowSize(400, 400);
glutInitWindowPosition(80, 80);
glutCreateWindow("example in OpenGL");
initialize();
```

```
glutDisplayfunc(drawImage);
glutReshapeFunc(reshapeWindow);
glutMouseFunc(handleMouse);
glutKeyboardFunc(handleKeyboard);
glutMainLoop();
return 0;
```

Functions:

1. **`void Initialize( )`**: This is a programmer written function that does any initialization that is only needed at the start of the program. This function can, for example, set the background color to use when the window is cleared; define the type of shading OpenGL should do when drawing images; and set parameters about lighting.
2. **`void glutDisplayFunc(void (*func)(void))`**: glutDisplayFunc sets the display callback for the current window. When GLUT determines that the normal plane for the window needs to be redisplayed, the display callback for the window is called. Before the callback, the current window is set to the window needing to be redisplayed and (if no overlay display callback is registered) the layer in use is set to the normal plane. The display callback is called with no parameters. The entire normal plane region should be redisplayed in response to the callback (this includes ancillary buffers if your program depends on their state).

   GLUT determines when the display callback should be triggered based on the window's redisplay state. The redisplay state for a window can be either set explicitly by calling glutPostRedisplay or implicitly as the result of window damage reported by the window system. Multiple posted redisplays for a window are coalesced by GLUT to minimize the number of display callbacks called.
3. `void glutReshapeFunc(void (*func)(int width, int height))`: glutReshapeFunc sets the reshape callback for the current window. The reshape callback is triggered when a window is reshaped. A reshape callback is also triggered immediately before a window's first display callback after a window is created or whenever an overlay for the window is established. The width and height parameters of the callback specify the new window size in pixels. Before the callback, the current window is set to the window that has been reshaped.
4. **`void glutMouseFunc(void(*func) (int button, int state, int x, int y))`**: There are a wide variety of things that must be known about a button event on a mouse for it to be processed. The first thing to know is the button that was used with the options being GLUT_LEFT_BUTTON, GLUT_MIDDLE_BUTTON and

GLUT_RIGHT_BUTTON. If a mouse has just two buttons, the middle option is not available, and if a mouse has a just one button, it will generate only the left option. The second thing to know is the button state, with the options being GLUT_DOWN and GLUT_UP, where down occurs when the button is pressed and up occurs when the button is released. The last thing to know is where the mouse was positioned within the window when the event occurred. In the example code, the mouse function is called handleMouse, which must be declared somewhere in the program files as:

```
void handleMouse(int button, int state, int x, int y)
void glutKeyboardFunc(void(*func)(unsigned char key, int x, int y)
```

Above routine resistors a function to handle when keys are pressed on the keyboard. In the example code, the keyboard function is called handleKeyboard which must be declared somewhere in the program files as void handleKeyboard (unsigned char key, int x, int y), where the key is an ASCII value of the key pressed and x and y gives the location of the mouse when the key was pressed. The location of the mouse can be necessary if the program needs to write the letters pressed into window where the mouse is located.

5. `void glutMainLoop(void)`: glutMainLoop enters the GLUT event processing loop. This routine should be called at most once in a GLUT program. Once called, this routine will never return. It will call as necessary any callbacks that have been registered.

Simple Program to Create Window in OpenGL:

```
#include <GL/gl.h>
#include <GL/glu.h>
#include <GL/glut.h>
void myinit(void)
{
glClearColor(1.0,1.0,1.0,0.0);
glColor3f(0.0, 0.0f, 0.0f);
glPointSize(4.0);
glMatrixMode(GL_PROJECTION);
glLoadIdentity();
gluOrtho2D(0.0, 600.0, 0.0, 400.0);
}
```

```
void myDisplay(void)
{
int i;
glClear(GL_COLOR_BUFFER_BIT);
glBegin(GL_POINTS);
glVertex2i(40,40);
glEnd();
glFlush();
}
int main(int argc, char **argv)
{
glutInit(&argc, argv);
glutInitDisplayMode(GLUT_SINGLE|GLUT_RGB);
glutInitWindowSize(600,400);
glutInitWindowPosition(300,300);
glutCreateWindow("My First Program");
glutDisplayFunc(myDisplay);
myinit();
glutMainLoop();
}
```

- The compilation and execution procedure is as follows:

```
$cc myfirst.c -lGLU -lglut -lGL -o myfirst
$./myfirst
```

- For every program, initialization function and main function remain almost the same but the display function will vary.

SUMMARY

- Computer graphics is an art of drawing pictures on computer screens with the help of programming.
- In simple words, computer graphics is a rendering tool for the generation and manipulation of images.
- Basically there are two types of computer graphics namely, interactive Computer Graphics involves a two way communication between computer and user. In non interactive computer graphics otherwise known as passive computer graphics. it is the computer graphics in which user does not have any kind of control over the image.
- A point has no dimensions; it represents a location in space.
- A vector, on the other hand, has no well-defined location and its only attributes are direction and magnitude.
- A pixel short for picture element is one of the many tiny dots that make up the representation of a picture in a computer's memory.
- When a diagonal line or a curved arc drawn on the screen looks as if it was made out of bricks, when it looks like stair steps instead of a slide, the effect is technically called aliasing.
- Antialiasing is a technique employed in computer graphics to smooth the jagged appearance of text and lines by applying varying shades of colour.
- Resolution refers to the sharpness, or detail of the usual image. It's a primary function of the monitor and it's determined by the beam size & dot pitch. The screen is made up of a number of pixels.
- When choosing a monitor, one of the factors that the customer usually considers is the refresh rate.
- The dot pitch of a color monitor measures the size of the tiny individual dots of phosphorescent material that coat the back side of the picture tube's face. The dot pitch helps determine how sharp the image looks, independent of the resolution (which is measured in pixels).
- Computer graphics can be used in many disciplines. Charting, Presentations, Drawing, Painting and Design, Image Processing, Animation, Simulation and Scientific Visualization are some among them.
- Transformation means changing some graphics into something else by applying rules. Transformations play an important role in computer graphics to reposition the graphics on the screen and change their size or orientation.
- Transformations is a process of changing the position of the object or may be combination of these. We know that an image of picture is drawn using the picture

coordinates. This image of picture when displayed on display devices, we need to convert these picture coordinates to the display devices coordinates. This task is done by transformation.

- When a transformation takes place on a 2D plane, it is called 2D transformation.
- Color is the aspect of things that is caused by differing qualities of light being reflected or emitted by them.
- A color model is a unique representation of a color. The most common of these is the RGB color model. RGB stands for Red, Green and Blue.
- The RGB color model is used for specifying colors. This model specifies the intensity of red, green, and blue on a scale of 0 to 255, with 0 (zero) indicating the minimum intensity.
- The process of developing and implementing various sets of instructions to enable a computer to do a certain task is called as programming.
- Event-driven programming is a programming paradigm in which the flow of program execution is determined by events - for example a user action such as a mouse click, key press, or a message from the operating system or another program.
- OpenGL (Open Graphics Library) is a cross-language, multi-platform Application Programming Interface (API) for rendering 2D and 3D vector graphics.

PRACTICE QUESTIONS

1. What is mean by pixel?
2. List out any four application of computer graphics.
3. Define Computer graphics.
4. What is Intensity?
5. What is GLUT?
6. Differ pixel and point.
7. Discuss various components of Computer Graphics Representation.
8. Give difference between Raster vs Vector.
9. Write short note on OpenGL library functions.
10. What do you mean by event driven programming?
11. Explain the concept of Transformation in computer graphics.

■■■

CHAPTER 2

Input Devices and Interaction Tasks

Contents ...

Objectives...

- To Understand Input Devices and Interactive Tasks
- To Learn GUIs Concpets
- To Study Implemnting GUI in OpenGL

2.1 INTRODUCTION

- Interactivity is an important component of many computer graphics applications.
- OpenGL, however, does not support interaction directly. This is because system architects who designed OpenGL wanted to increase its portability by allowing the system to work in a variety of environments.
- Consequently, windowing and input functions were left out of the API. However, any program must have at lease minimal interaction with the rest of the computer system.
- An interaction technique is the fusion of input and output, consisting of all software and hardware elements, that provides a way for the user to accomplish a task.
- Fig. 2.1 shows interaction between I/O devices and CPU in computer system.
- A computer accepts (input) information and manipulates (processes) it to get desired result (output) on a sequence of instructions.
- In computer terminology devices can be referred as "a unit of hardware, which is capable of providing input, to the computer or receiving output or both".
- An input device captures information and translates into the form that is understandable by computer and output devices translate information into the form that is understandable by human beings.
- Through input devices users talk to the computer, through output devices, the computer and communicates with the users.
- In simple words, Input/Output devices are the means of communication between a computer system and the external world.

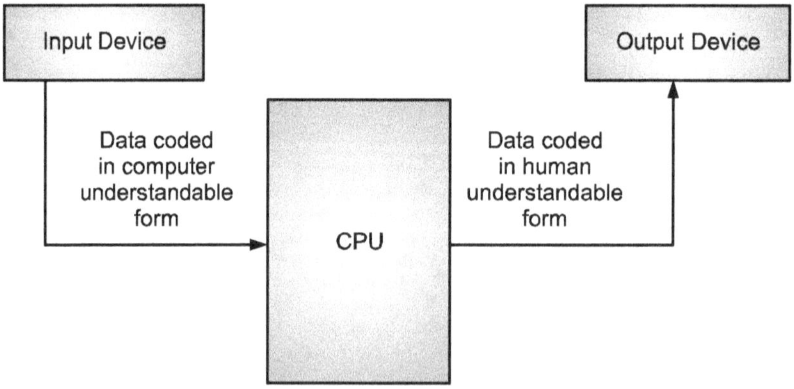

Fig. 2.1: Interaction between I/O devices and CPU in computer system

- The common input devices are keyboards and mouse. The common output devices are monitors and printers.
- There are two basic types of graphical interaction i.e., pointing at items already on the screen and positioning new items.

- The need to interact in these ways requires the development of a number of different types of graphical input devices, classified into positioning devices and pointing devices.
- Pointing and positioning are two basic types of graphical interactions.

1. **Pointing Devices:**

- Pointing refers to location of items already on the screen. Pointing is also known as selection.
- These are the devices used to select the items already on the screen. Some of the commonly used pointing devices are mouse, trackball, joystick, light pen and so on.

2. **Positioning Devices:**

- Positioning refers to location of new items. Positioning is sometimes known as locating.
- Positioning devices are used to add new items on the screen.
- Positioning devices give position information. These devices provide the coordinate of a point.
- Positioning devices are also known as locators.
- Keyboard is an common example of positioning device.

2.2 LOGICAL INTERACTION [Oct. 16]

- Graphics programs are several kinds of input data. Picture specifications need values for coordinate positions, values for the character-string parameters, scalar values for the transformation parameters, values specifying menu options, and values for identification of picture parts.
- To make graphics packages independent of the particular hardware devices used, input functions can be structured according to the data description to be handled by each function. This approach provides a logical input-device classification in terms of the kind of data to be input by the device.
- Input devices are used to communicate information from the external/outside world to the computer system.

Logical Classification of Input Devices:

- The following six logical device classifications used by PHIGS and GKS:
  1. **Locator:** A device for specifying a coordinate position (x, y).
  2. **String:** A device for specifying text input.
  3. **Choice:** A device for selecting menu options.

4. **Pick:** A device for selecting picture components.
5. **Stroke:** A device for specifying a series of coordinate positions.
6. **Valuator:** A device for specifying scalar values.

2.2.1 Locator Devices

- Locator devices provide position information to the computer i.e., using a locator we can indicate the position of an object on the screen. Example includes mouse, jockstick, trackball etc.
- A standard and common method for interactive selection of a coordinate point is by positioning the screen cursor.
- We can do this with a mouse, joystick, trackball, spaceball, thumbwheels, dials, a digitizer stylus or hand cursor or some other cursor-positioning device.
- When the screen cursor is at the desired location, a button is activated to store the coordinates of that screen point.
- Keyboards can also be used for locator input. The keyboard has four cursor control keys that move the screen cursor up, down, left and right and with an additional four keys, it is possible to move the cursor diagonally as well.
- Alternatively, a joystick, trackball, or thumbwheels can be mounted on the keyboard for relative cursor movement.
- Light pens have also been used to input coordinate positions, but some special implementation considerations are necessary.
- The locator supports following different types of echoes for different interactions:
    1. Implementation standard.
    2. Digits display a numeric representation of the current locator position.
    3. Rubber band line is the line drawn between current locator position and initial locator position.
    4. Rubber-band rectangle is a rectangle is drawn using the current locator position for one corner and initial locator position at another corner.
    5. Cross hair.
    6. Tracking cross.

2.2.2 Valuator Devices

- This logical class of devices is employed in graphics systems to input scalar values.
- A valuator returns a single numeric value within a given range, such as might be entered by a dial.
- The valuator can be simulated by using a graphical input device to point to a position on a scale, or even by using a keyboard to type digits.

- Valuators are used for setting various graphics parameters like rotation angle and scale factors, and for setting physical parameters associated with a particular application (temperature settings, voltage levels, stress factors, etc.).
- The valuator device defines following three kinds of echo :
  1. **Dial:** Some sort of dial is displayed, and the user identifies a value on it.
  2. **Digits:** A string of digits is displayed in the echo area.
  3. **Implementation standard:** In the IBM/PGS implementation, a digital representation of the value is displayed in the echo area.
- Any keyboard with a set of numeric keys can be used as a valuator device. A user simply types the numbers directly in floating-point format, although this is a slower method than using dials.
- Joysticks, trackballs, tablets, and other interactive device, can be adapted for valuator input by Interpreting pressure or movement of the device relative to a scalar range.
- Another technique for providing valuator input is to display sliders, buttons, rotating scales, and menus on the video monitor. Locator input from a mouse, joystick, spaceball, or other devices is used to select a coordinate position on the display, and the screen coordinate position is then converted to a numeric input value.

2.2.3 Pick Devices

- Graphical object selection is the function of this logical class of devices. Pick devices are used to select parts of a scene that are to be transformed or edited in some way.
- Typical devices used for object selection are the same as those for menu selection, the cursor-positioning devices. With a mouse or joystick, we can position the cursor over the primitives in a displayed structure and press the selection button.
- A pick device returns a pick identifier and segment number to identify a graphical object the user has chosen by pointing.
- The pick identifier is an output primitive attribute that is set before creating an output primitive.
- The rules for determining which object is identified by a pick are not very precise. If the cursor is accurately positioned over an isolated geometric object, it is picked.
- The following conditions may result in some errornous or unpredictable results:
  1. A fill area with hollow interior style.
  2. Overlapping of two objects.
  3. If the cursor is not near any detachable object. But "definition of "near" is not precise.
  4. Intersection of two objects.

- The pick device offers following three different methods of echoing the picked object i.e., of making it visible in some way.
  1. **Pick identifier group** is the group of primitive in the same segment and with the same pick identifier as the picked primitive is highlighted.
  2. The entire **segment** containing the picked primitive is highlighted.
  3. **Implementation standard.**

2.2.4 Choice Devices

- Graphic packages use menus to select programming options, parameter values, and object shapes to be used in constructing a picture.
- A choice device is defined as one that enters a selection from a list (menu) of alternatives. Commonly used choice devices are a set of buttons, a cursor positioning device such as a mouse, trackball, or keyboard cursor keys and a touch panel.
- The computer user selects one of a fixed number of alternatives; the index of the selected alternative is returned. Its principal use is for entering commands from a small, fixed set.
- Different echo types for choice device offer various ways to present the user with the choices.
  1. **Lamps:** Some workstations have a box of illuminated buttons, which can be used to enter a choice.
  2. **String Command:** A set of string is displayed in the echo area.
  3. **Implementation standard:** The implementation may use any technique for echoing the user's choice.
  4. **Symbol menu:** A specific segment is displayed in the echo area in order to show a menu and the user picks one the menu entries.
  5. **String menu:** A set of strings is displayed in the echo area and the user selects one of them. The user types one of the choices on the keyboard.

2.3 PHYSICAL INPUT DEVICES FOR INTERACTIONS

- Each device has properties that make it more suitable for certain tasks than for others.
- Two primary types of physical devices are:
  1. **Pointing devices:** Allow the user to indicate a position on the screen, and
  2. **Keyboard devices:** A physical keyboard, but can be generalised to include any device that returns character codes to a program – ASCII.

2.3.1 Keyboard

- An alphanumeric keyboard on a graphics system is used primarily as a device for entering text strings.
- The keyboard is an efficient device for inputting such nongraphic data as picture labels associated with a graphics display.
- Keyboards can also be provided with features to facilitate entry of screen coordinates, menu selections, or graphics functions.
- The layout of the keyboard is like that of traditional typewriter, although there are some additional keys provided for performing additional functions.
- Using a keyboard data is entered into a computer by simply pressing various keys.
- The layout of a keyboard comes in various styles such as QWERTY, DVORAK, AZERTY but the most common layout is the QWERTY. It is name so because the first six keys on the top row of letters are Q, W, E, R, T and Y.
- The number of keys on a typical keyboard varies from 82 keys to 108 keys.
- Portable computers like laptops quite often have custom keyboards that have slightly different key arrangements than a standard keyboard.
- A keyboard is the easiest input device, as it does not require any special skill, it is supplied with a computer so no additional cost is incurred.
- The maintenance and operation cost of keyboard is also less. However, using a keyboard for data entry may be a slow process.

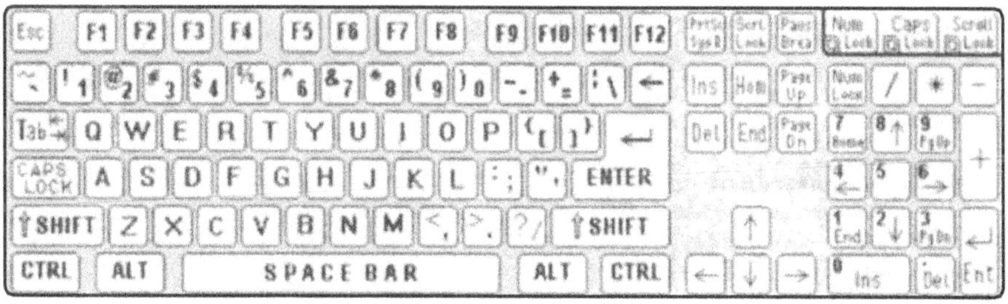

Fig. 2.2: Keyboard

- The keys on the keyboard are as follows:
  1. **Typing Keys:** These keys include the letter keys (A-Z) and digit keys (0-9) which generally give same layout as that of typewriters.
  2. **Numeric Keypad:** It is used to enter numeric data or cursor movement. Generally, it consists of a set of 17 keys that are laid out in the same configuration used by most adding machines and calculators.
  3. **Function Keys:** The twelve function keys are present on the keyboard which are arranged in a row at the top of the keyboard. Each function key has unique meaning and is used for some specific purpose.

4. **Control keys:** These keys provide cursor and screen control. It includes four directional arrow keys. Control keys also include Home, End, Insert, Delete, Page Up, Page Down, Control(Ctrl), Alternate(Alt), Escape(Esc).
5. **Special Purpose Keys:** Keyboard also contains some special purpose keys such as Enter, Shift, Caps Lock, Num Lock, Space bar, Tab, and Print Screen.

2.3.2 Mouse

- Mouse is most popular pointing device.
- Mouse was invented by Douglas Englebart of Standard Institute of 1963.
- A mouse is small hand-held box pointing device used to position the screen cursor with a rubber ball or wheel embedded at it slower side and buttons on the top.
- Wheels or rollers on the bottom of the mouse can be used to record the amount and direction of movement.
- Usually a mouse contains two or three buttons, which can be used to input commands or information.
- The mouse may he classified as a mechanical mouse or an optical mouse, based on technology it uses as shown in Fig. 2.3.
  1. **Mechanical Mouse:** It uses a rubber ball at the bottom surface, which rotates as the mouse is moved along a flat surface, to move the cursor.
  2. **Optical Mouse:** It uses a light beam instead of a rotating. ball to detect movement across a specially patterned mouse pad. As the user rolls the mouse on a flat surface, the cursor on the screen also moves in the direction of the mouse's movement.

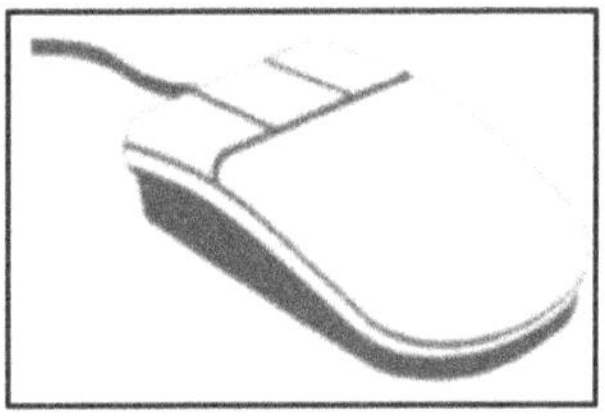

(a) Mechanical mouse

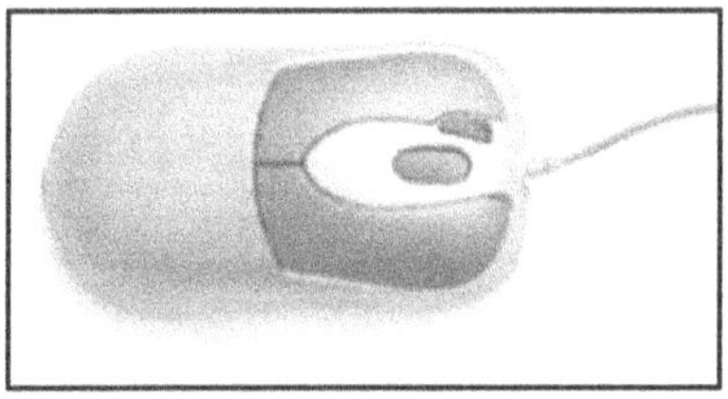

(b) Optical mouse

Fig. 2.3

2.3.3 Trackball and Spaceball

1. **Trackball:**

- Trackball is an input device that is mostly used in notebook or laptop computers.
- Trackball is a ball which is half inserted and by moving fingers on ball, pointer can be moved as shown in Fig. 2.4. (a).

- A trackball can be rotated with the fingers or palm of the hand, to produce screen-cursor movement.
- Trackballs are often mounted on keyboards and it is a two-dimensional positioning device.

2. **Spaceball:**

- Fig. 2.4 (b) shows a spaceball.
- A spaceball provides six degrees of freedom. Unlike the trackball, a spaceball does not actually move.
- The spaceball itself consists of a pressure-sensitive ball which can distinguish different kinds of forces, including forward/backward, lateral and twist, responding by moving and orienting the selected object.
- Spaceballs are used for three-dimensional positioning and selection operations in virtual-reality systems, modeling, animation, CAD, and other applications.

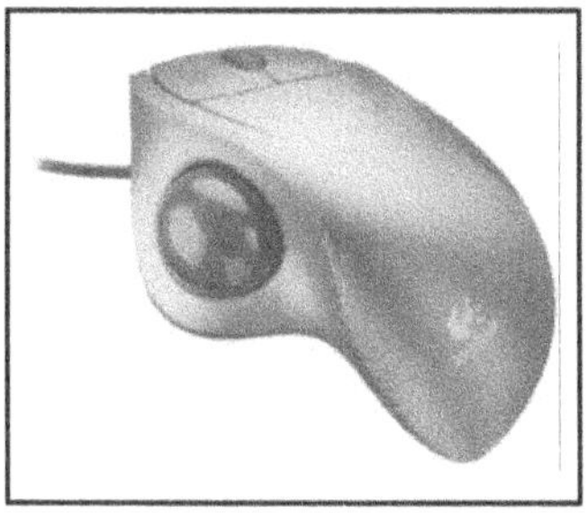

(a) Trackball

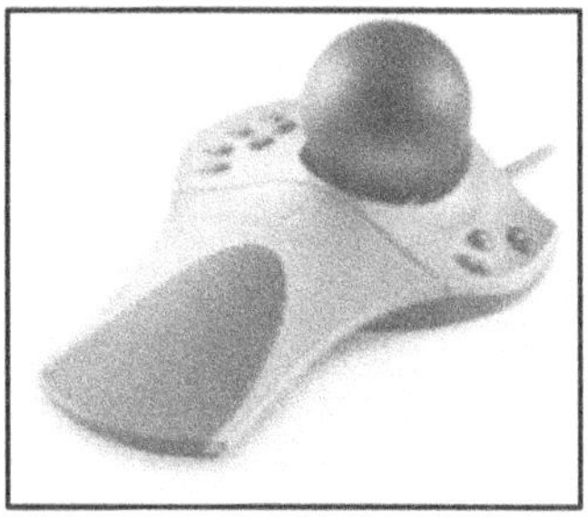

(b) Spaceball

Fig. 2.4

2.3.4 Tablets

- A common and popular device for drawing, painting or interactively selecting coordinate positions on the object is a Digitizer.
- These devices can be used to input coordinate values in either a two-dimensional or a three-dimensional space.
- In simple words, a graphics tablet (data tablet) or digitizer is a computer input device that enables a user to hand-draw images, animations and graphics, similar to the way a person draws images with a pencil and paper.
- Fig. 2.5 shows a digitizer.

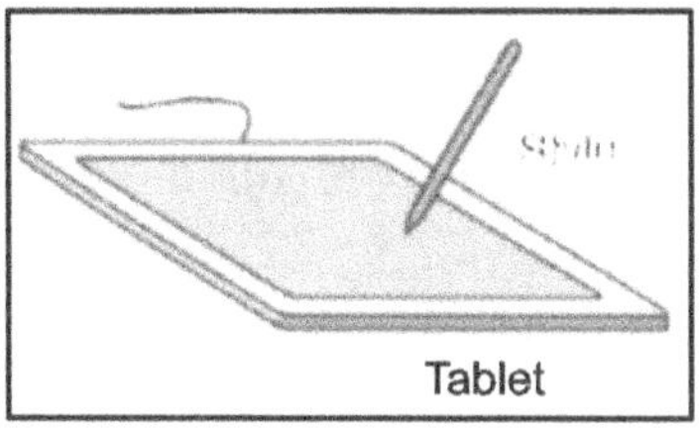

Fig. 2.5: Tablet

- The device consists of a flat surface upon which the user may "draw" or trace an image using an attached stylus, a pen-like drawing apparatus.

2.3.5 Light Pen

- Light pen is a pointing device.
- Light pen is a pen-shaped device used to select screen positions by detecting the light coming from points on the CRT screen, (See. Fig. 2.6).

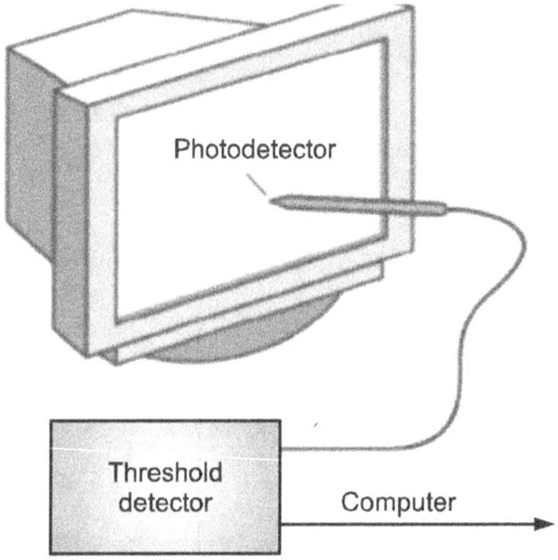

Fig. 2.6: Light pen

- The pen will send a pulse whenever phosphor below it is illuminated. While the image on a refresh display may appear to be stable, it is fact blinking ON and OFF faster than the eye can detect.
- This blinking is not too fast, for the light pen. The light pen is easily determines the time at which the phosphor is illuminated.
- Since, there is only one electron beam on the refresh display, only one line segment can be drawn at a time and no two segments are drawn simultaneously.

2.3.6 Joystick

- Joystick is also a pointing device which is used to move cursor position on a monitor screen.
- A joystick consists of a small, vertical lever called the stick and mounted on a base that is used to steer the screen cursor around.
- Most joysticks select screen positions with actual stick movement; others respond to pressure on the stick.
- The distance that the stick is moved in any direction from its center position corresponds to screen-cursor movement in that direction.

- Fig. 2.7 shows a typical joystick.

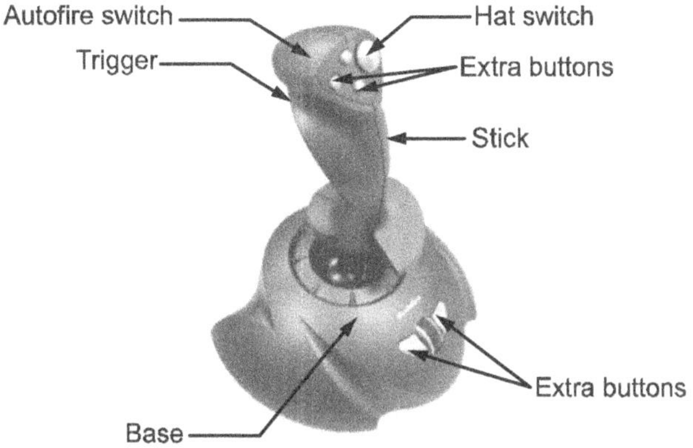

Fig. 2.7: A typical joystick

- The function of joystick is similar to that of a mouse. It is mainly used in Computer Aided Designing (CAD) and playing computer games.

2.3.7 Touch Panels [April 16]

- A touch panel is a piece of equipment that lets users interact with a computer by touching the screen directly.
- Incorporating features into the monitor like sensors that detect touch actions makes it possible to issue instructions to a computer by having it sense the position of a finger or stylus.
- A typical application of touch panels is for the selection of processing options that are represented with graphical icons.
- Some systems like plasma panels are designed with touch screens.
- Fig. 2.8 shows a typical touch panels.

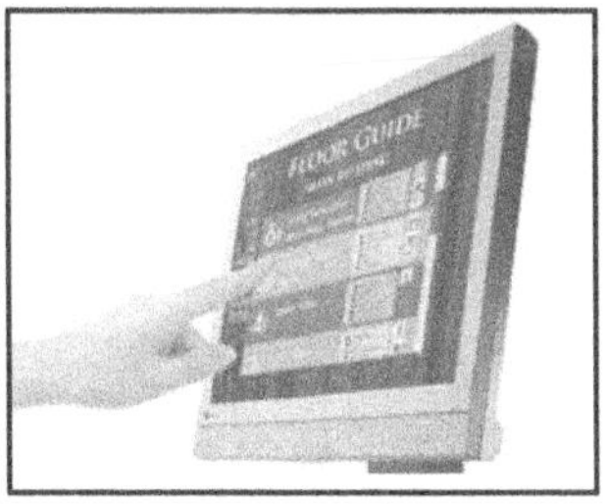

Fig. 2.8: A typical touch panels

2.3.8 Data Glove

- A data glove that can be used to graph a "virtual" object.
- Data glove device is used particularly in virtual reality environments which are programmed to react to the position of the gloves, the direction in which fingers are pointing, as well as to hand motion and gestures.

- A glove equipped with sensors that sense the movements of the hand and interfaces those movements with a computer.
- A data glove is an interactive device, resembling a glove worn on the hand, which facilitates tactile sensing and fine-motion control in virtual reality.
- The glove is constructed with a series of sensors that detect and finger motions.
- Electromagnetic coupling between transmitting antenna and receiving antennas is used to provide information about the position and orientation of the hand.
- A two-dimensional projection of the scene can be viewed on a video monitor, or a three-dimensional projection can be viewed with a headset.
- Data gloves are commonly used in virtual reality environments where the user sees an image of the data glove and can manipulate the movements of the virtual environment using the glove.
- Fig. 2.9 shows a data glove.

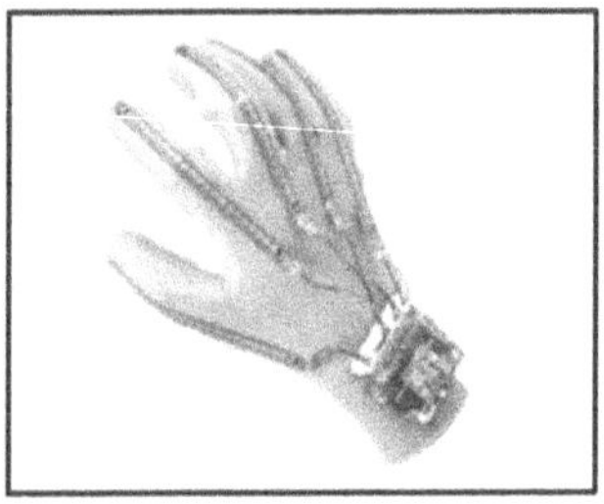

Fig. 2.9: Data glove

2.4 KEYBOARD AND MOUSE INTERACTION IN OPENGL

[April 16]

- Two ways for the user to give input to a program are through the mouse and keyboard. In an elaborate graphics program, a user can click locations to indicate object vertices; drag across the screen to select objects; type text to be placed into the scene; or type commands to change the image.
- OpenGL can be defined as "a software interface to graphics hardware".
- Following are the some functions used for input and interaction. The user submits a pointer to a function that should be called when the corresponding event occurs.
- GLUT provides an easy-to-use interface,

```
glutMouseFunc(function); // click mouse
glutMotionFunc(function); // move mouse
glutPassiveMotionFunc(function); // no button
glutReshapeFunc(function); // window resize
glutKeyboardFunc(function); // keyboard
```

```
glutSpecialFunc(function); // arrows, pgup
glutJoystickFunc(function); // joystick
glutIdleFunc(function); // animation
glutDisplayFunc(function); // draw primitives
```

Note: Refer Section 2.6 to know the structure of OpenGL program.

Keyboard Interaction:

```
int main(int argc, char **argv)
{
    initGLUT(argc, argv);
    initGL(); //Set the display callback
    glutDisplayFunc(draw); //Set the keyboard callback
    glutKeyboardFunc(keyboard); //Start the GLUT main event loop.
    glutMainLoop();
    return 0;
}
//keyboard callback
 void keyboard(unsigned char key, int x, int y)
 {
    switch(key)
    {
    case 'r':
        r=1.0;
        g=0.0;
        b=0.0;
        break;
    case 'g':
        r=0.0;
        g=1.0;
        b=0.0;
        break;
    }
    glutPostRedisplay();
 }
```

```
// Display Function
void draw()
{
    //draw a polygon
   glColor3f( r, g, b );
   glBegin( GL_POLYGON );
   glVertex2f( 0.25, 0.25 );
   glVertex2f( 0.75, 0.5 );
   glVertex2fv( point2 );
   glEnd();
}
```

- After r-key press the red color vertex is displayed. After g-key press green color vertex is displayed on window.

Mouse Interaction:

```
int main(int argc, char **argv)
{ ...
    //Set the keyboard callback
   glutKeyboardFunc(keyboard);
   glutMouseFunc(mouse);
    glutPassiveMotionFunc(passiveMotion);
   glutMotionFunc(motion);
... }
// mouse callback
void mouse(int button, int state, int x, int y)
{
    if( button == GLUT_LEFT_BUTTON && state == GLUT_DOWN )
   {
        printf("Left mouse button pressed");
    }
}
// mouse motion callback
void motion(int x, int y)
{
    pos_x=x/WINDOW_SIZE_X;
   pos_y=1-(y/WINDOW_SIZE_Y);
   glutPostRedisplay();
}
```

- After pressing left mouse button, the message displayed is Left mouse button pressed.

2.5 GRAPHICAL USER INTERFACES

- A Graphical User Interface (GUI) is an interface through which a user interacts with electronic devices such as computers, hand-held devices and other appliances.
- This interface uses icons, menus and other visual indicator (graphics) representations to display information and related user controls, unlike text-based interfaces, where data and commands are in text.
- Graphical user interface elements are those elements used by GUIs to offer a consistent visual language to represent information stored in computers. These make it easier for people with few computer skills to work with and use computer software.
- Today's major operating systems provide a graphical user interface. Applications typically use the elements of the GUI that come with the operating system and add their own graphical user interface elements and ideas.

Interaction elements:

- Some common idioms for interaction have evolved in the visual language used in GUIs.
- Interaction elements are interface objects that represent the state of an ongoing operation or transformation, either as visual remainders of the user intent (such as the pointer), or as affordances showing places where the user may interact.
- Elements of a GUI include such things as windows, pull-down menus, buttons, scroll bars, iconic images, wizards, the mouse, and many other things.
- With the increasing use of multimedia as part of the GUI, sound, voice, motion video, and virtual reality interfaces seem likely to become part of the GUI for many applications.

2.5.1 Cursor

- Cursor or pointer is a symbol that appears on the display screen and that you move to select objects and commands.
- Usually, the pointer appears as a small angled arrow. Text-processing applications, however, use an I-beam, pointer that is shaped like a capital I.
- A cursor is an indicator used to show the position on a computer monitor or other display device that will respond to input from a text input or pointing device.
- The idea of a cursor being used as a marker or insertion point for new data or transformations, such as rotation, can be extended to a 3D modeling environment.
- In most command-line interfaces or text editors, the text cursor or caret navigation, is an underscore, a solid rectangle, or a vertical line, which may be flashing or steady, indicating where text will be placed when entered (the insertion point).

- In text mode displays, it was not possible to show a vertical bar between characters to show where the new text would be inserted, so an underscore or block cursor was used instead.
- The blinking of the text cursor is usually temporarily suspended when it is being moved; otherwise, the cursor may change position when it is not visible, making its location difficult to follow.

2.5.2 Icons

- Icons as parts of the graphical user interface of the computer system, in conjunction with windows, menus and a pointing device (mouse), belong to the much larger topic of the history of the graphical user interface that has largely supplanted the text-based interface for casual use.
- Icons are small pictures that represent commands, files, or windows. By moving the pointer to the icon and pressing a mouse button, you can execute a command or convert the icon into a window.
- Icons are a quick way to execute commands, open documents, and run programs.
- Icons are also very useful when searching for an object in a browser list, because in many operating systems all documents using the same extension will have the same icon.
- As it can serve as an electronic hyperlink or file shortcut to access the program or data. The user can activate an icon using a mouse, pointer, finger, or recently voice commands. Their placement on the screen, also in relation to other icons, may provide further information to the user about their usage.
- In activating an icon, the user can move directly into and out of the identified function without knowing anything further about the location or requirements of the file or code.

2.5.3 Menus

- Menus allow the user to execute commands by selecting from a list of choices. Options are selected with a mouse or other pointing device within a GUI. A keyboard may also be used.
- Menus are convenient because they show what commands are available within the software. This limits the amount of documentation the user reads to understand the software.
- Some common menu components/elements are:
    1. A **menu bar** is displayed horizontally across the top of the screen and/or along the tops of some or all windows. A pull-down menu is commonly associated with this menu type. When a user clicks on a menu option the pull-down menu will appear.

2. A **menu** has a visible title within the menu bar. Its contents are only revealed when the user selects it with a pointer. The user is then able to select the items within the pull-down menu. When the user clicks elsewhere the content of the menu will disappear.
3. A **context menu** is invisible until the user performs a specific mouse action, like pressing the right mouse button. When the software-specific mouse action occurs the menu will appear under the cursor.
4. **Menu extras** are individual items within or at the side of a menu.
5. **Sub-menus:** Menus are sometimes hierarchically organized, allowing navigation through different levels of the menu structure. Selecting a menu entry with an arrow will expand it, showing a second menu (the sub-menu) with options related to the selected entry.

- A common use of menus is to provide convenient access to various operations such as saving or opening a file, quitting a program, or manipulating data. Most widget toolkits provide some form of pull-down or pop-up menu.
- Pull-down menus are the type commonly used in menu bars (usually near the top of a window or screen), which are most often used for performing actions, whereas pop-up (or "fly-out") menus are more likely to be used for setting a value, and might appear anywhere in a window.

2.5.4 Radio Button

- A radio button or option button is a graphical control element that allows the user to choose only one of a predefined set of options, an exclusive or.
- Radio buttons are arranged in groups of two or more and displayed on screen as, for example, a list of circular holes (O) that can contain white space (for unselected) or a dot (for selected ⊙).
- Each radio button is normally accompanied by a label describing the choice that the radio button represents.
- The choices are mutually exclusive; when the user selects a radio button, any previously selected radio button in the same group becomes deselected (making it so only one can be selected). Selecting a radio button is done by clicking the mouse on the button, or the caption, or by using a keyboard shortcut.

2.5.5 Scrollbar

- A scrollbar is a graphical control element with which continuous text, pictures or anything else can be scrolled including time in video applications, i.e., viewed even if it does not fit into the space in a computer display, window, or viewport. It was also known as a handle in the very first GUIs.

- Scrollbars are present in a wide range of electronic devices including computers, graphing calculators, mobile phones, and portable media players. They usually appear on one or two sides of the viewing area as long rectangular areas containing a bar (or thumb) that can be dragged along a trough (or track) to move the body of the document as well as two arrows on either end for precise adjustments.
- Example of horizontal and vertical scrollbars around a text box as shown in Fig. 2.10.

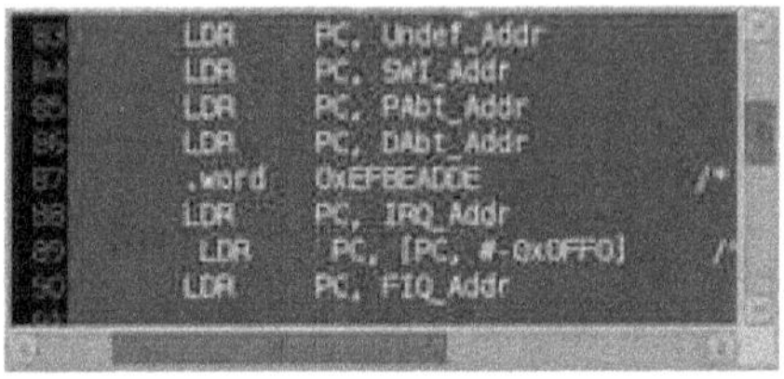

Fig. 2.10: Horizontal and vertical scrollbars around a text box

2.6 IMPLEMENTING GUI IN OPENGL

Writing Graphics Programs Using OpenGL:

- Every graphics program contains three main parts:
  1. An initialization function which performs all the initialization.
  2. A display function that contains the code required to display picture according to the requirements of the application.
  3. The main function that contains the necessary code for creating and displaying window, registering the display function as a callback function and also a call to the initialization function.

```
// include the OpenGL libraries
void myinit(void)
{
// do all the necessary initializations here
}
void myDisplay(void)
{
// The application specific code will be written here.
}
void main(int argc , char ** argv)
{
// will contain the standard code using GLUT library functions
}
```

- A simple graphics program for creating and presenting a picture will include the first three libraries. The following include statements are essential.

```
#include <GL/gl.h>
#include <GL/glu.h>
#include <GL/glut.h>
```

Basic GL Functions:

- Basic Graphics Library functions start with gl. Most gl functions have several versions depending on the number and type of arguments:

  glColor3f(..) indicates no of arguments as 3 and data type as float.

  glVertex2iv(..) indicates no of arguments as 2 , data type as integer and that the arguments, in vector form. All commands do not have vector form

- The basic openGL data types and the corresponding C data types are shown in following table.

Character	ubC-Language Type	OpenGL Type
b	signed char	GLbyte
s	Short	GLshort
i	Int	GLint, GLsizei
f	Float	GLfloat, GLclampf
d	Double	GLdouble, GLclampd
ub	unsigned char	GLubyte, GLboolean
us	unsigned short	GLushort
ui	unsigned int	GLuint, GLenum
	Void	GLvoid

Program 1: The display functions for some points on window.

```
#include <GL/gl.h>
#include <GL/glu.h>
#include <GL/glut.h>
//GLint x,y;
void myinit(void)
{
glClearColor(1.0,1.0,1.0,0.0);
glColor3f(0.0, 0.0f, 0.0f);
glPointSize(4.0);
glMatrixMode(GL_PROJECTION);
glLoadIdentity();
gluOrtho2D(0.0, 600.0, 0.0, 400.0);
}
```

```
void myDisplay(void)
{
int i;
GLint x,y;
glClear(GL_COLOR_BUFFER_BIT);
glBegin(GL_POINTS);
for(i=0;i<100;i++)
{
  x=rand()%600;
  y=rand()%400;
  glVertex2i(x,y);
}
glEnd();
glFlush();
}
int main(int argc, char **argv)
{
glutInit(&argc, argv);
glutInitDisplayMode(GLUT_SINGLE|GLUT_RGB);
glutInitWindowSize(600,400);
glutInitWindowPosition(300,300);
glutCreateWindow("My First Program");
glutDisplayFunc(myDisplay);
myinit();
glutMainLoop();
}
```

Output:

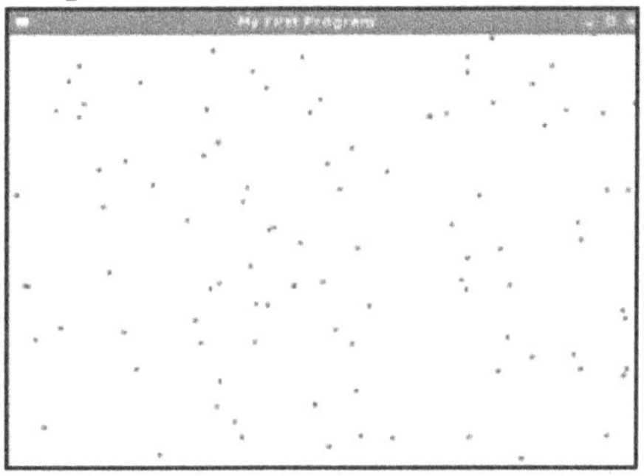

Program 2: Divide the display surface into four quadrants by drawing x and y axis.

```
// Program to divide surface
#include <GL/gl.h>
#include <GL/glu.h>
#include <GL/glut.h>
void myinit(void)
{
glClearColor(1.0,1.0,1.0,0.0);
glColor3f(0.0, 0.0f, 0.0f);
glPointSize(4.0);
glMatrixMode(GL_PROJECTION);
glLoadIdentity();
gluOrtho2D(0.0, 600.0, 0.0, 400.0);
}
void myDisplay(void)
{
int i;
glClear(GL_COLOR_BUFFER_BIT);
glBegin(GL_LINES);
glVertex2i(0,200);
glVertex2i(600,200);
glVertex2i(300,0);
glVertex2i(300,400);
glEnd();
glFlush();
}
int main(int argc, char **argv)
{
glutInit(&argc, argv);
glutInitDisplayMode(GLUT_SINGLE|GLUT_RGB);
glutInitWindowSize(600,400);
glutInitWindowPosition(300,300);
glutCreateWindow("My First Program");
glutDisplayFunc(myDisplay);
myinit();
glutMainLoop();
}
```

Output:

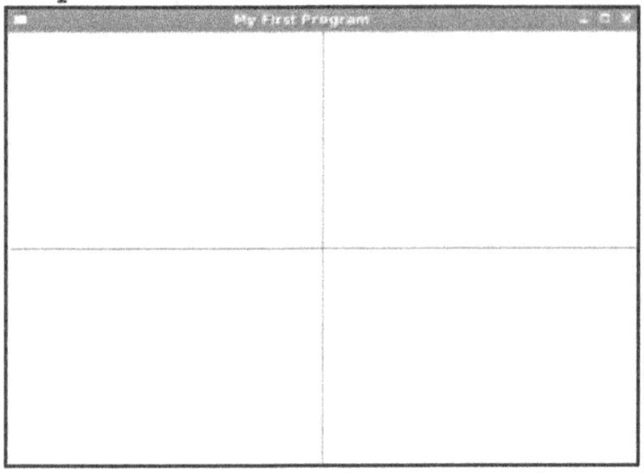

Program 2: Program for Keyboard interaction - Use four arrow Keys to view the effect.

```
#include <stdio.h>
#include <string.h>
#include <stdlib.h>
#include <GL/glut.h>
GLenum doubleBuffer;
/* *INDENT-OFF* */
double plane[4] = {
  1.0, 0.0, -1.0, 0.0
};
float rotX = 5.0, rotY = -5.0, zTranslate = -65.0;
float fogDensity = 0.02;
GLint cubeList = 1;
float scp[18][3] = {
  {1.000000, 0.000000, 0.000000},
  {1.000000, 0.000000, 5.000000},
  {0.707107, 0.707107, 0.000000},
  {0.707107, 0.707107, 5.000000},
  {0.000000, 1.000000, 0.000000},
  {0.000000, 1.000000, 5.000000},
  {-0.707107, 0.707107, 0.000000},
  {-0.707107, 0.707107, 5.000000},
  {-1.000000, 0.000000, 0.000000},
  {-1.000000, 0.000000, 5.000000},
  {-0.707107, -0.707107, 0.000000},
  {-0.707107, -0.707107, 5.000000},
```

```
  {0.000000, -1.000000, 0.000000},
  {0.000000, -1.000000, 5.000000},
  {0.707107, -0.707107, 0.000000},
  {0.707107, -0.707107, 5.000000},
  {1.000000, 0.000000, 0.000000},
  {1.000000, 0.000000, 5.000000},
};
static float ambient[] = {0.1, 0.1, 0.1, 1.0};
static float diffuse[] = {1.0, 1.0, 1.0, 1.0};
static float position[] = {90.0, 90.0, 0.0, 0.0};
static float front_mat_shininess[] = {30.0};
static float front_mat_specular[] = {0.0, 0.0, 0.0, 1.0};
static float front_mat_diffuse[] = {0.0, 1.0, 0.0, 1.0};
static float back_mat_shininess[] = {50.0};
static float back_mat_specular[] = {0.0, 0.0, 1.0, 1.0};
static float back_mat_diffuse[] = {1.0, 0.0, 0.0, 1.0};
static float lmodel_ambient[] = {0.0, 0.0, 0.0, 1.0};
static float fog_color[] = {0.8, 0.8, 0.8, 1.0};
/* *INDENT-ON* */
/* ARGSUSED1 */
static void
Key(unsigned char key, int x, int y)
{
  switch (key) {
  case 'd':
    fogDensity *= 1.10;
    glFogf(GL_FOG_DENSITY, fogDensity);
    glutPostRedisplay();
    break;
  case 'D':
    fogDensity /= 1.10;
    glFogf(GL_FOG_DENSITY, fogDensity);
    glutPostRedisplay();
    break;
  case 27:
    exit(0);
  }
}
```

```
/* ARGSUSED1 */
static void
SpecialKey(int key, int x, int y)
{
  switch (key) {
  case GLUT_KEY_UP:
    rotX -= 5;
    glutPostRedisplay();
    break;
  case GLUT_KEY_DOWN:
    rotX += 5;
    glutPostRedisplay();
    break;
  case GLUT_KEY_LEFT:
    rotY -= 5;
    glutPostRedisplay();
    break;
  case GLUT_KEY_RIGHT:
    rotY += 5;
    glutPostRedisplay();
    break;
  }
}
static void
Draw(void)
{
  glClear(GL_COLOR_BUFFER_BIT | GL_DEPTH_BUFFER_BIT);
  glPushMatrix();
  glTranslatef(0, 0, zTranslate);
  /* XXX hooky dual axis rotation! */
  glRotatef(rotY, 0, 1, 0);
  glRotatef(rotX, 1, 0, 0);
  glScalef(1.0, 1.0, 10.0);
  glCallList(cubeList);
  glPopMatrix();
```

```
    if (doubleBuffer) {
      glutSwapBuffers();
    } else {
      glFlush();
    }
}
static void
Args(int argc, char **argv)
{
    GLint i;
    doubleBuffer = GL_TRUE;
    for (i = 1; i < argc; i++) {
      if (strcmp(argv[i], "-sb") == 0) {
        doubleBuffer = GL_FALSE;
      } else if (strcmp(argv[i], "-db") == 0) {
        doubleBuffer = GL_TRUE;
      }
    }
}
int
main(int argc, char **argv)
{
    GLenum type;
    glutInit(&argc, argv);
    Args(argc, argv);
    type = GLUT_RGB | GLUT_DEPTH;
    type |= (doubleBuffer) ? GLUT_DOUBLE : GLUT_SINGLE;
    glutInitDisplayMode(type);
    glutInitWindowSize(300, 300);
    glutCreateWindow("Fog Test");
    glFrontFace(GL_CW);
    glEnable(GL_DEPTH_TEST);
    glLightfv(GL_LIGHT0, GL_AMBIENT, ambient);
    glLightfv(GL_LIGHT0, GL_DIFFUSE, diffuse);
    glLightfv(GL_LIGHT0, GL_POSITION, position);
    glLightModelfv(GL_LIGHT_MODEL_AMBIENT, lmodel_ambient);
```

```
glLightModeli(GL_LIGHT_MODEL_TWO_SIDE, GL_TRUE);
glEnable(GL_LIGHTING);
glEnable(GL_LIGHT0);
glMaterialfv(GL_FRONT, GL_SHININESS, front_mat_shininess);
glMaterialfv(GL_FRONT, GL_SPECULAR, front_mat_specular);
glMaterialfv(GL_FRONT, GL_DIFFUSE, front_mat_diffuse);
glMaterialfv(GL_BACK, GL_SHININESS, back_mat_shininess);
glMaterialfv(GL_BACK, GL_SPECULAR, back_mat_specular);
glMaterialfv(GL_BACK, GL_DIFFUSE, back_mat_diffuse);
glEnable(GL_FOG);
glFogi(GL_FOG_MODE, GL_EXP);
glFogf(GL_FOG_DENSITY, fogDensity);
glFogfv(GL_FOG_COLOR, fog_color);
glClearColor(0.8, 0.8, 0.8, 1.0);
/* *INDENT-OFF* */
glNewList(cubeList, GL_COMPILE);
  glBegin(GL_TRIANGLE_STRIP);
    glNormal3fv(scp[0]);
    glVertex3fv(scp[0]);
    glNormal3fv(scp[0]);
    glVertex3fv(scp[1]);
    glNormal3fv(scp[2]);
    glVertex3fv(scp[2]);
    glNormal3fv(scp[2]);
    glVertex3fv(scp[3]);
    glNormal3fv(scp[4]);
    glVertex3fv(scp[4]);
    glNormal3fv(scp[4]);
    glVertex3fv(scp[5]);
    glNormal3fv(scp[6]);
    glVertex3fv(scp[6]);
    glNormal3fv(scp[6]);
    glVertex3fv(scp[7]);
```

```
        glNormal3fv(scp[8]);
        glVertex3fv(scp[8]);
        glNormal3fv(scp[8]);
        glVertex3fv(scp[9]);
        glNormal3fv(scp[10]);
        glVertex3fv(scp[10]);
        glNormal3fv(scp[10]);
        glVertex3fv(scp[11]);
        glNormal3fv(scp[12]);
        glVertex3fv(scp[12]);
        glNormal3fv(scp[12]);
        glVertex3fv(scp[13]);
        glNormal3fv(scp[14]);
        glVertex3fv(scp[14]);
        glNormal3fv(scp[14]);
        glVertex3fv(scp[15]);
        glNormal3fv(scp[16]);
        glVertex3fv(scp[16]);
        glNormal3fv(scp[16]);
        glVertex3fv(scp[17]);
      glEnd();
    glEndList();
    /* *INDENT-ON* */
    glMatrixMode(GL_PROJECTION);
    glLoadIdentity();
    gluPerspective(45.0, 1.0, 1.0, 200.0);
    glMatrixMode(GL_MODELVIEW);
    glutKeyboardFunc(Key);
    glutSpecialFunc(SpecialKey);
    glutDisplayFunc(Draw);
    glutMainLoop();
    return 0;             /* ANSI C requires main to return int. */
}
```

Output:

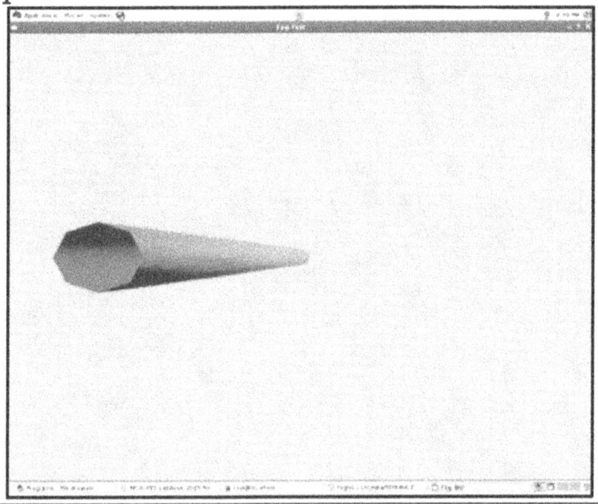

SUMMARY

- Interaction – one of the most advances in computer technology – to interact with computer displays, e.g. interactive computer graphics, i.e. the user sees an image on the display.
- A computer accepts (input) information and manipulates (processes) it to get desired result (output) on a sequence of instructions. In computer terminology.
- Pointing and positioning are two basic types of graphical interactions.
- The common interactions devices are:
  - Locator
  - Stroke
  - String
  - Valuator
  - Choice
  - Pick.
- An alphanumeric keyboard on a graphics system is used primarily as a device for entering text strings.
- Keyboards are of two sizes 84 keys or 101/102 keys, but now keyboards with 104 keys or 108 keys are also available for Windows and Internet.
- A mouse is a pointing device that detects two-dimensional motion relative to a surface. This motion is typically translated into the motion of a pointer on a display, which allows for fine control of a graphical user interface.

- A trackball is a pointing device consisting of a ball held by a socket containing sensors to detect a rotation of the ball about two axes—like an upside-down mouse with an exposed protruding ball. The user rolls the ball with the thumb, fingers, or the palm of the hand to move a pointer.
- A joystick is an input device consisting of a stick that pivots on a base and reports its angle or direction to the device it is controlling.
- A light pen is a computer input device in the form of a light-sensitive wand used in conjunction with a computer's CRT display.
- A digitizer tablet (also known as a digitizer or graphics tablet) is a tool used to convert hand-drawn images into a format suitable for computer processing. Images are usually drawn onto a flat surface with a stylus and then appear on a computer monitor or screen.
- Spaceball is a graphical input device that is based on a fixed spherical ball. It inputs six different values defined by the orientation of the ball and the pressure together with the direction that is applied to it.
- A data glove is an interactive device, resembling a glove worn on the hand, which facilitates tactile sensing and fine-motion control in virtual reality. Data gloves is an input device for virtual reality in the form of a glove which measures the movements of the wearer's fingers and transmits them to the computer.
- Virtual reality is a set of perceived relationships (i.e. vision , sound) from a medium called cyberspace.
- A graphics tablet (or digitizer, digitizing tablet, graphics pad, drawing tablet) is a computer input device that allows one to hand-draw images and graphics, similar to the way one draws images with a pencil and paper.
- A touchscreen or touch panels is an input device normally layered on the top of an electronic visual display of an information processing system.
- A graphical user interface is fondly called "GUI" pronounced "gooey." The word "graphical" means pictures; "user" means the person who uses it; "interface" means what you see on the screen and how you work with it. So a graphical user interface, then, means that you (the user) get to work with little pictures on the screen to boss the computer around, rather than type in lines of codes and commands.
- In computer user interfaces, a cursor is an indicator used to show the current position for user interaction on a computer monitor or other display device that will respond to input from a text input or pointing device.

- Cursor is Latin for 'runner.' A cursor is the name given to the transparent slide engraved with a hairline that is used for marking a point on a slide rule. The term was then transferred to computers through analogy.
- The ScrollBar enables the user to select a value by positioning it at the desired location. It consists of a bar with arrows at each end. Visual basic provides two types of scroll bars-Horizontal scroll bar and vertical scroll bar. A vertical or horizontal bar commonly located on the far right or bottom of a window that allows you to move the window viewing area up, down, left, or right.
- An icon is a small graphical representation of a program or file that, when clicked on, will be run or opened. Icons are used with Graphical User Interface (GUI) operating systems, such as Microsoft Windows and the Apple Mac OS, to help quickly identify a type of file or program associated with the icon.
- As menu is a list of commands or choices offered to the user. Menus are commonly used in GUI operating systems and allow a user to access various options the software program is capable of performing.

PRACTICE QUESTIONS

1. What is meant by Locator?
2. List out different devices use for graphics interaction
3. What is meant by Cursor?
4. List out the use of scroll bar in computer graphics.
5. Highlights the use of radio buttons.
6. What do you meant by valuator?
7. Give the difference between trackball and spaceball.
8. What is data glove?
9. What do you mean by logical interaction also Explain any 2 devices for it.
10. Explain the structure of light pen and joy stick.
11. How does mouse interaction happens in computer graphics
12. Write a code for mouse interaction in computer graphics
13. How does keyboard interaction happens in computer graphics
14. Write a code for keyboard interaction in computer graphics
15. Explain the concept of GUI also explain any two interface components (controls).
16. Explain the general structure of OpenGL code.
17. “Touch panel is the future of computer graphics “ , comment.

■■■

CHAPTER 3

Presentation and Output Devices

Contents ...

Objectives...

- To Understand Output Devices and Presentations
- To Learn various Display Devices like Monitor, CRT, Plasma Display, DVST etc.
- To Study Hard Copy devices such as Plotter and Printer

3.1 PRESENTATION GRAPHICS

- Presentation graphics deals with graphical representation of information.
- Presentation graphics is commonly used to summarize financial, statistical, mathematical, scientific, and economic data for research reports, managerial reports, consumer information bulletins and other types of reports.

3.1.1 Frame Buffer

- In a raster-scan system, the electron beam is swept across the screen, one row at a time from top to bottom. As the electron beam moves across each row, the beam intensity is turned ON and OFF to create a pattern of illuminated spots.
- Picture definition is stored in a memory area called the refresh buffer or frame buffer. This memory area holds the set of intensity values for all the screen points.
- Stored intensity values are then retrieved from the refresh buffer and 'painted' on the screen one row (scan line) at a time. Each screen point is referred to as a pixel or pel (shortened form of picture element).
- The storage area in a raster scan display system is arranged as a two-dimensional table. Every row column entry of this table stores information such as brightness - and/or color value or the corresponding pixel on the screen.
- In a frame buffer each pixel can be represented by 1 to 24 or more bits depending on the quality (resolution) of the display system.
- Commands to plot a point/line are converted into intensity and colour values of the pixel array or bitmap of an image by a process called Scan Conversion.
- The display system cycles through the refresh or frame buffer row by row at speeds of 30 or 60 times per second to produce the image on the display. The intensity values picked up from the frame buffer are routed to the Digital/Analog (A/D) converter which produces the necessary deflection signals to generate the raster scan.
- A flicker-free image is produced by interlacing; all odd-numbered scan lines are displayed first from top to bottom and then all even-numbered scan lines are displayed. The effective refresh rate to produce the picture becomes much greater than 30 Hz.
- Different kinds of memory have been used in frame buffers.
- Basic types of frame buffers are rotating memory frame buffer, shift register frame buffer, modern frame buffers and multiple plane frame buffer etc. as discussed below:
    1. The earliest type of frame buffers used drums and disks with rotational frequency compatible to the rate of refresh. Such frame buffers were called **rotating-memory frame buffers**.
    2. But the relatively lower costs of integrated-circuit shift registers saw the rotating-memory frame buffer being replaced by **shift-register frame buffers**.
    3. Another type of frame buffer is the **multiple-plane frame buffer**, where the frame buffer can be treated as consisting of several frames or planes, each containing information (intensity and/or color) values of a separate image.

- A frame buffer can be constructed with a number of shift registers, each representing one column of pixels on the screen. Each shift register contribute- one bit per horizontal scan line. However changing a given spot on the screen is not very easy with shift registers. So shift registers are not suitable for interactive applications.
- Today's, **modem frame buffers** use random-scan integrated circuits where the pixel intensities are represented by 1, 2, 4, 8, 16 or 24 bits. Encoding text and simple images does not require more than say, 8 bits per pixel. But to produce a good quality colored image more than 8 bits, something like 24 bits, are required.
- An 8-bit per pixel frame buffer can be made to represent a single image with 8-bits of intensity precision or it can represent two images each of 4-bit intensity precision or eight black and white images with 1-bit intensity precision each. A variety of image mixing can be done.

Implementation of Frame Buffer:

- Fig. 3.1 shows the implementation of frame buffer using shift register.
- In Fig. 3.1, one shift register is required per pixel an a scan line and the length of shift register in bits is equal to number of scan lines. Here, them are 8 pixels per scan line and there are in all 5 scan lines.
- Therefore, 8 shift registers, catch of 5 bit length are used to implement frame buffer. The synchronization between the output of the shift register and the video scan rate is maintained data corresponding to particular scan line is displayed correctly.

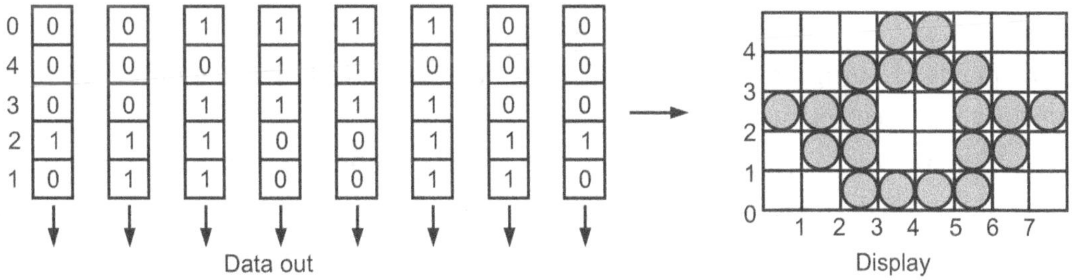

Fig. 3.1: Frame buffer using eight 5-bit shift registers

- Both rotating memory and shift register frame buffer implementations have low levels of interactivity. The interactivity in rotating memory is limited due to disk access time and it is reduced in shift register implementations because changes can only be made as bits are being added to the register.

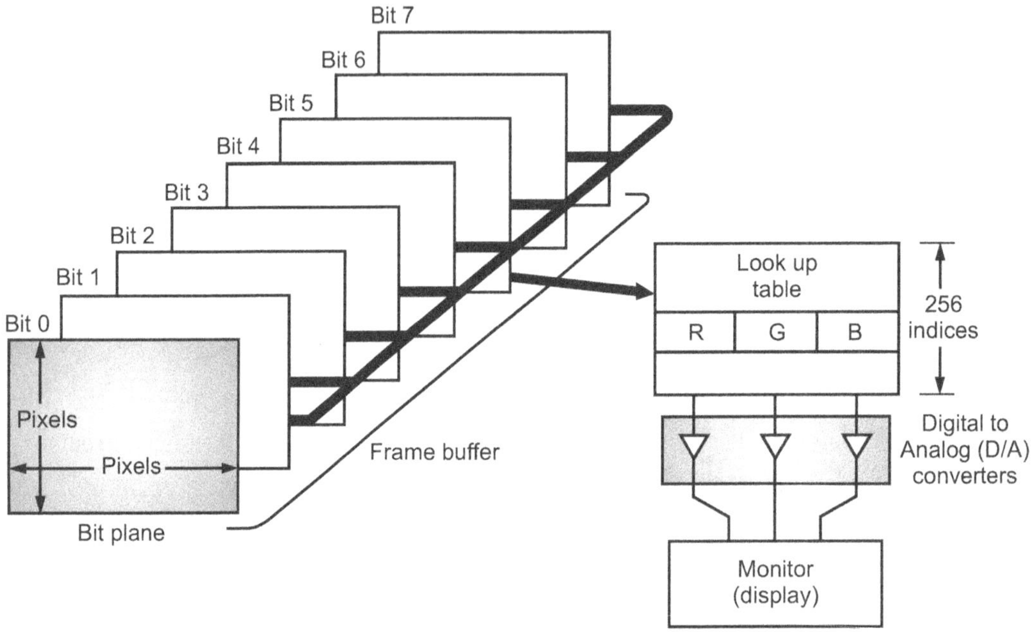

Fig. 3.2: Concept of bit plane

3.1.2 Frame Buffer Graphics System

- Fig. 3.3 shows typical frame buffer graphics system.
- Frame buffer graphics system consists of CPU, frame buffer, display controller and video monitor.

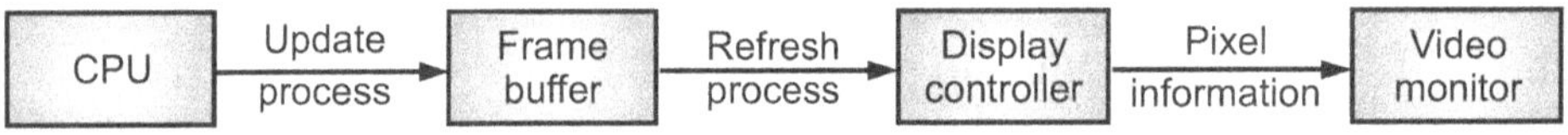

Fig. 3.3

- An application program running in the computer updates the frame buffer as per the picture information.
- The display controller cycles through the frame buffer in scan line order (top to bottom) and passes the corresponding information to the video monitor to refresh the display.
- The frame buffer can be part of computer memory itself or it can be implemented with separate memory as shown in the Fig. 3.4 (a).

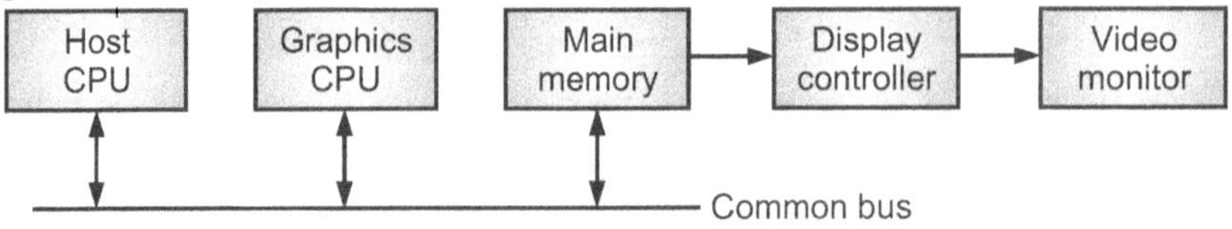

Fig. 3.4: (a) Frame buffer as a part of computer memory

- Generally, separate graphics processor is used to improve the performance of graphics system. The graphics processors manipulates the frame buffer as per commands issued by main processor.
- The performance of the graphics system is also affected by sharing of single memory done by two processors.
- The performance of the graphics system thus can be improved by having separate frame buffer memory as shown in the Fig. 3.4 (b).

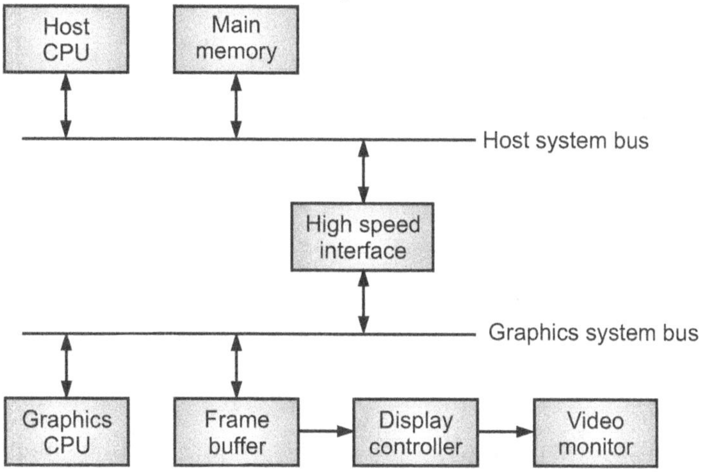

(b) Separate frame buffer

Fig. 3.4: Frame buffer architectures

3.1.3 Display File

- The raster frame buffer stores not only the end points but also all pixels in between as well as all other pixels not on the line. While vector refresh display stores only the commands required for drawing the line segments and input to the vector generator is saved instead of its output.
- The file in which all these are saved is called as a display file.
- Display file provides an interface between the image specification process and the image display process.
- Display files also defines a compact description of image which may be saved for later display. Also note that these concepts may be applied to devices other than refresh displays. These files are called as pseudo-display files or metafiles.

Structure of Display File:

- Each display file command contains two parts as given below:
  1. **An operation code (opcode)** identifies the command like draw line, move cursor etc.

2. **An operand** provides the coordinates of a point to process the command.

For example, Move (10, 10)

↓ ↓

Opcode Opcode

- Let us, consider two commands Move and Line. Initialize opcode 1 for Move command and opcode 2 for Line command.

Opcode	Command
1	Move
2	Line

- As operand is having both x and y parameters we have to separate them. So we will store the x co-ordinate in x operand and y co-ordinate in y operand.

So now our command move (10, 10) will become,

Op code	x-(op)	y-op
1	10	10

- This is what about one command. But in display file there will be many commands. So, we will use arrays to store opcodes and operands.

Opcode (op) array	x-op	y-op

- Now we can access a particular commands from this display file very easily.

For example,

Opcode (op) array	x-op array	y-op array
1	10	10

- Suppose we want to access second command then we will just say,

op[2], x-op [2]; y-op[2].

Now let us take an example:

Suppose we want to draw rectangle ABCD. Then we will perform following steps:

Step 1: Move to point A which may be (x_1, y_1), (See Fig. 3.5).

So our command will be Move (x_1, y_1)

We will represent this command in opcode and operand form by $(1, x_1, y_1)$

Where, 1 means Move command

x_1 indicates x co-ordinate of point A

y_1 indicates y co-ordinate of point A

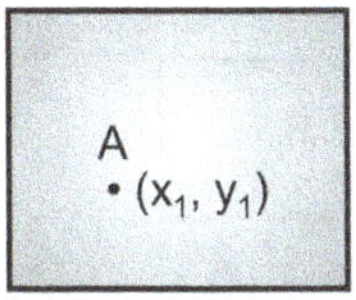

Fig. 3.5

Step 2: Draw line from A to B

So command will be, line (x_2, y_2).

Where, (x_2, y_2) are the co-ordinates of point B

We will represent this command in the form of opcode and operand as $(2, x_2, y_2)$.

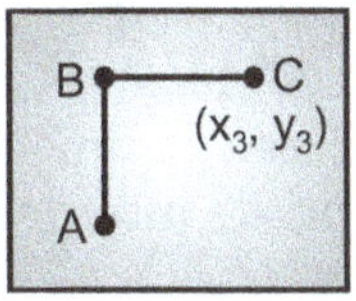

Fig. 3.6

Step 3: Draw line from B to C.

So command will be line,

(x_3, y_3)

where (x_3, y_3) are the coordinates of point C

We will represent this command in the form of opcode and operand as, $(2, x_3, y_3)$.

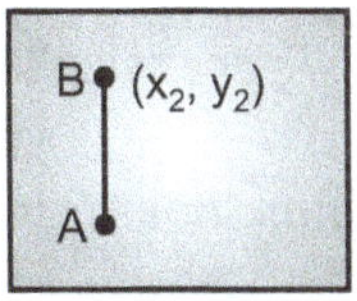

Fig. 3.7

Step 4: Draw line from C to D.

So command will be, line (x_4, y_4)

where (x_4, y_4) are the coordinates of point D

We will represent this command in the form of opcode and operand as, $(2, x_4, y_4)$.

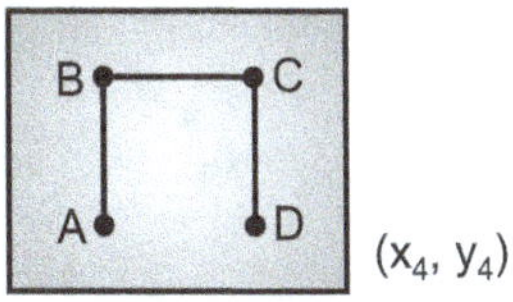

Fig. 3.8

Step 5: Draw line from D to A.

So command will be, line (x_1, y_1)

where (x_1, y_1) are the coordinates of point A

We will represent this command in the form of opcode and operand as, $(2, x_1, y_1)$.

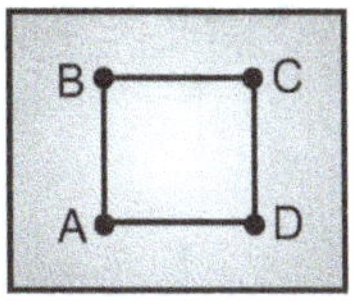

Fig. 3.9

Display File Interpreter:

- The display file contains information necessary to construct picture. This information is in the form of commands.
- The program which converts these commands into actual picture is called display file interpreter.
- Display file interpreter is an interface between graphics representation in the display file and device as shown in Fig. 3.10.

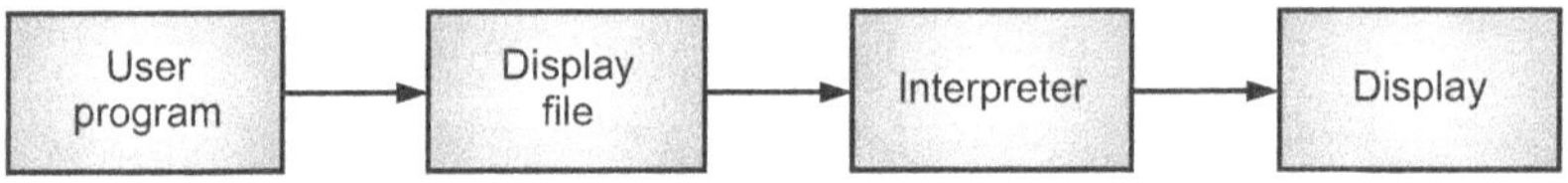

Fig. 3.10: Display process

- Display process is divided into two steps:
  1. The image is stored in the display structure, and
  2. Then it is interpreted by an appropriate interpreter to get the actual image.
- Instead of this if we store actual image for particular display device it may not run of other displays. To achieve the device independence the image is stored in raw format i.e. in the display file format and then it is interpreted by an appropriate interpreter to run on required display.

3.1.4 Look Up Table (LUT)

- The number of bits per pixel i.e., bit depth stored in the frame buffer to achieve pixel color requires large storage space, this problem can be reduced if a storage space is introduced in between the frame buffer and monitor. This storage space is called as a Look Up Table (LUT).
- LUT is also implemented as a separate table and is known as color lookup table or video look-up table. So, a LUT has many entries pixel values.
- For example, say a pixel at coordinates (x, y) has a eight bit value in the frame buffer as shown in Fig. 3.11.

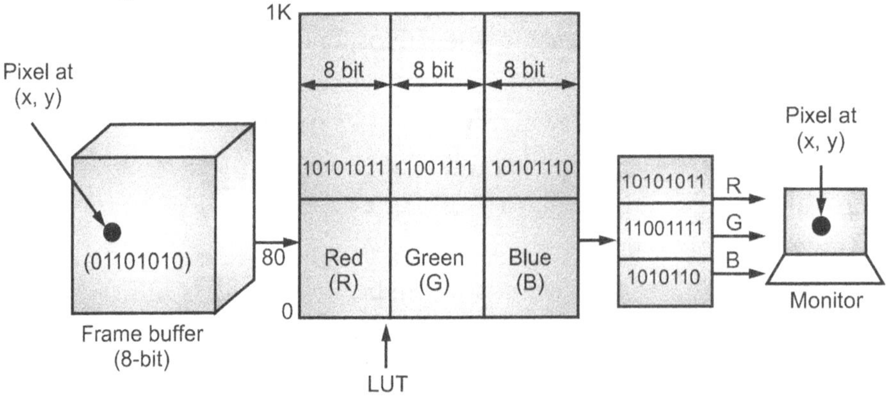

Fig. 3.11: Look Up Table

- Here, there is LUT of size 0 to 1 K. So, each entry of LUT has a $8 \times 3 = 24$ bits RGB color value.

- **Image depth:** It is the number of bytes per pixel.
- An image with a higher image depth has a greater number of possible intensity values which improves the quality of filtering.
- Please remember the following points now:
  1. If we decrease resolution, the width and height of the image will increase.
  2. If we increase resolution, the width and height of the image will decrease.
  3. If we increase the width or height of the image, the resolution will decrease.
  4. If we decrease the width or height of the image, the resolution will increase.
- **Bit-mapped graphics:** Images that are stored as a collection of bits in memory locations corresponding to pixels on the screen represent a bit-mapped graphics.
- **Vector Graphics:** It is a method of generating images that use mathematical descriptions to find the position, length and direction in which lines are to be drawn.

3.2 DISPLAY DEVICES

- The computer processes input data to produce useful information and this information can be displayed on a monitor, printed on a printer, or listened through speakers or a headset, or it can be stored in the secondary memory device for further processing or future reference.
- These different ways of output can be broadly categorized as hard copy output and soft copy output as explained below.

1. **Soft Copy Output:**

- The electronic version of an output, which usually resides in computer memory or on disk, is known as soft copy. Soft copy is not a permanent form of output.
- Soft copy is transient and is usually displayed on the screen. This kind of output is not tangible, that is, it cannot be touched.
- Soft copy output includes textual or graphical information displayed on a computer monitor is a soft copy form of output.

2. **Hard Copy Output:**

- The physical form of output is known as hard copy.
- In general, hard copy refers to the recorded information copied from a computer onto paper or some other durable surface, such as microfilm.
- Hard copy output is permanent and relatively stable form of output.
- Paper is one of the most widely used hard copy output media. The principal examples are printouts, whether text or graphics from printers considered a hard copy output.

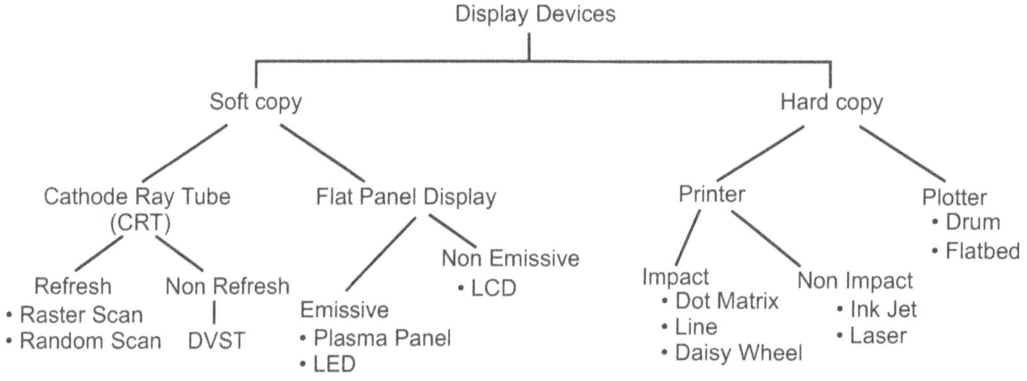

Fig. 3.12: Classification of display devices

3.2.1 Monitor

- The device that displays graphics as well as text characters on a screen, much like a TV, is known as Display Processing Unit or DPU and more commonly a Visual Display Unit or VDU or simply as the Monitor.
- Monitor is the part of computer system used to display information to user.
- The purpose of display device is to convert electrical signals into visible images. i.e. to display picture.
- The primary output device in a graphical system is the video monitor. The main element of a video monitor is the Cathode Ray Tube (CRT).

3.2.1.1 CRT [Oct. 16]

- Fig. 3.13 shows simplified representation of CRT.
- A CRT is an evacuated glass tube. An electron gun at the rear of the tube produces a beam of electrons which is directed towards the front of the tube (screen).
- The inner side of the screen is coated with phosphor substance which gives off light when it is stroked by electrons.
- It is possible to control the point at which the electron beam strikes the screen and therefore the position of the dot upon the screen, by deflecting the electron beam.

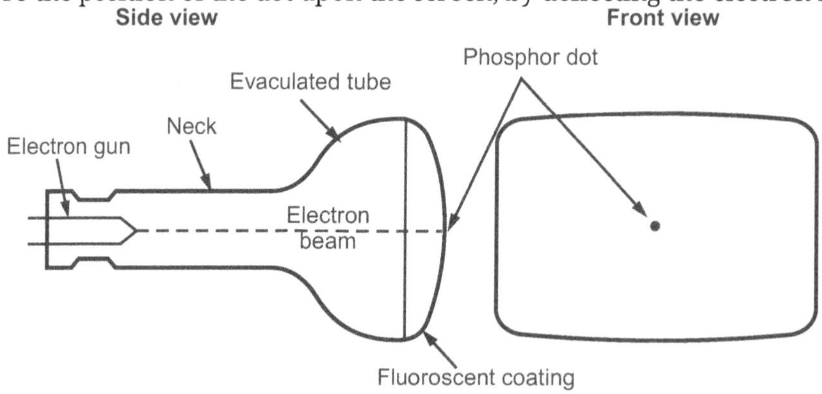

Fig. 3.13: Simplified representation of CRT

Operation of CRT:

- The electron gun emits a beam of electrons (cathode rays).
- The electron beam passes through focusing and deflection systems that direct it towards specified positions on the phosphor-coated screen.
- When the beam hits the screen, the phosphor emits a small spot of light at each position contacted by the electron beam.
- It redraws the picture by directing the electron beam back over the same screen points quickly.

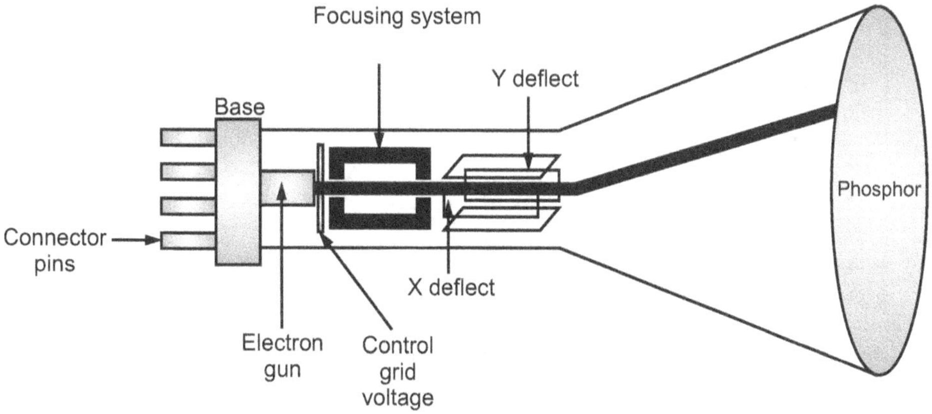

Fig. 3.14: Operation of CRT

- There are two ways (Random scan and Raster scan) by which we can display an object on the screen.

1. Random Scan CRT:

- In this technique CRT draw a picture line by line and one line at a time and hence called as vector display.
- It is also called as stroke writing or calligraphic display.
- Here, picture definition is stored as a set of line drawing commands in refresh display file.
- Fig. 3.15 shows block diagram of random scan display.

Fig. 3.15: Block diagram of random scan display

- Fig. 3.16 shows the random scan display architecture. It consists of display controller, Central Processing Unit (CPU), display buffer memory and a CRT.

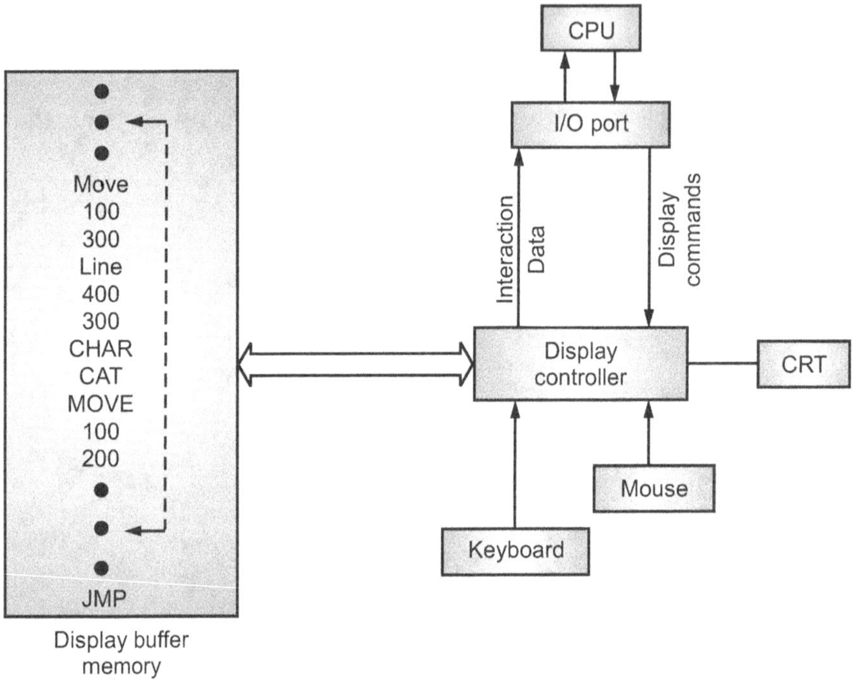

Fig. 3.16: Random scan display architecture

- Picture definition is stored as a set of line-drawing commands in an area of memory referred to as the refresh display file.
- To display a specified picture, the system cycles through the set of commands in the display file, drawing each component line in turn.
- After all the line-drawing commands are processed, the system cycles back to the first line command in the list.
- Random-scan displays are designed to draw all the component lines of a picture 30 to 60 times each second.

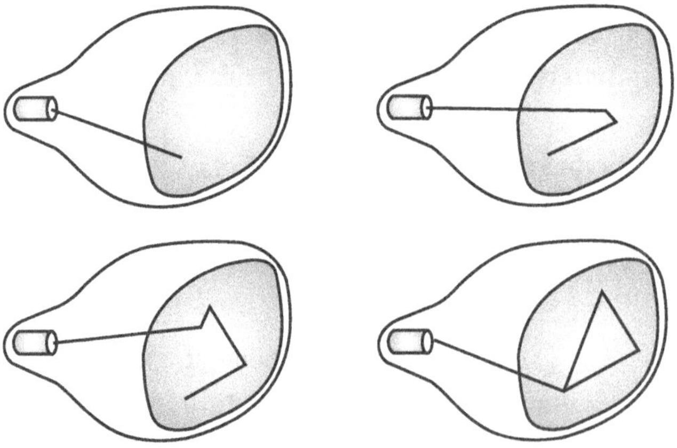

Fig. 3.17: Process of line-drawing

- **Example:** Pen plotter is the best example of random scan, hard copy device. In this, for example, if we want to draw a line pq, electron beam directly moves from point p to q making all points on line visible as shown in Fig. 3.18.

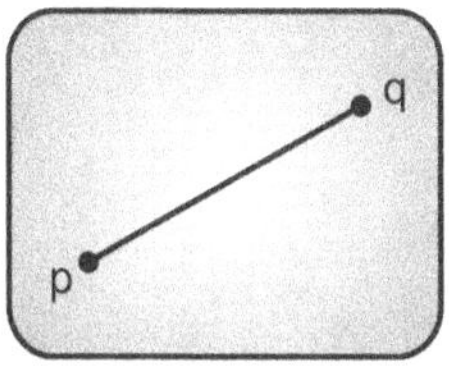

Fig. 3.18: Random Scan CRT

2. **Raster Scan CRT:**

- In a CRT, the raster is a sequence of horizontal lines that are scanned rapidly with an electron beam from left to right and top to bottom, in much the same way as a TV picture tube is scanned.
- In a raster scan system, the electron beam is swept across the screen, one row at a time from top to bottom.
- As the electron beam moves across each row, the beam intensity is turned on and off to create a pattern of illuminated spots.
- Fig. 3.19 shows block diagram of a raster scan display.

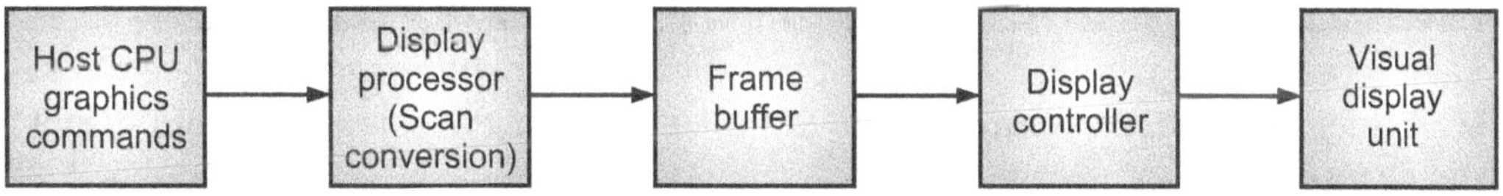

Fig. 3.19: Block diagram of a raster scan display

- As shown in the Fig. 3.20, the display image is stored in the form of 1s and 0s in the refresh buffer. The video controller reads this refresh buffer and produces the actual image on the screen.
- It does this by scanning one scan line at a time, from top to bottom and them back to the top, as shown in the Fig. 3.20.
- Fig. 3.20 shows architecture of a raster display.

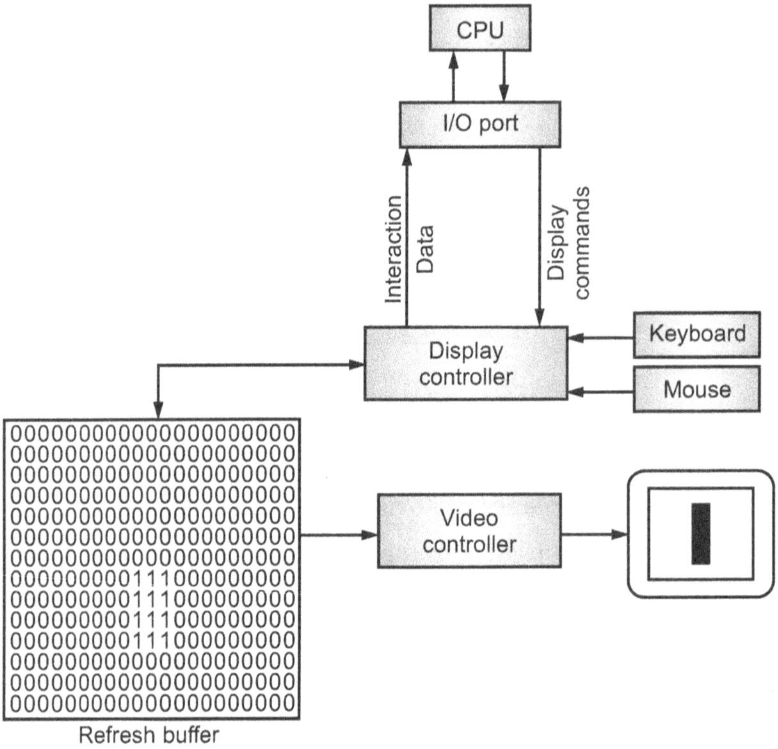

Fig. 3.20: Architecture of a raster display

- Picture definition is stored in memory area called the Refresh Buffer or Frame Buffer. This memory area holds the set of intensity values for all the screen points.
- Stored intensity values are then retrieved from the refresh buffer and "painted" on the screen one row (scan line) at a time as shown in the following illustration.
- Each screen point is referred to as a pixel (picture element) or pel. At the end of each scan line, the electron beam returns to the left side of the screen to begin displaying the next scan line.

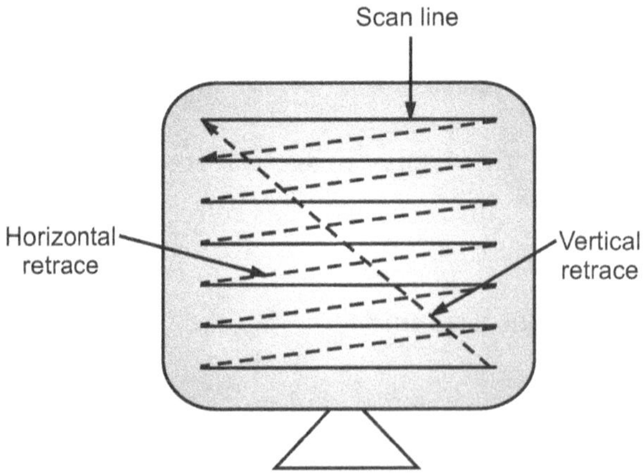

Fig. 3.21

- The return to the left of the screen, after refreshing each scan line, is called the Horizontal Retrace of the electron beam. And at the end of each frame, the electron beam returns (vertical retrace) to the top left corner of the screen to begin the next frame.
- On some raster-scan systems (and in TV sets), each frame is displayed in two passes using an interlaced refresh procedure.

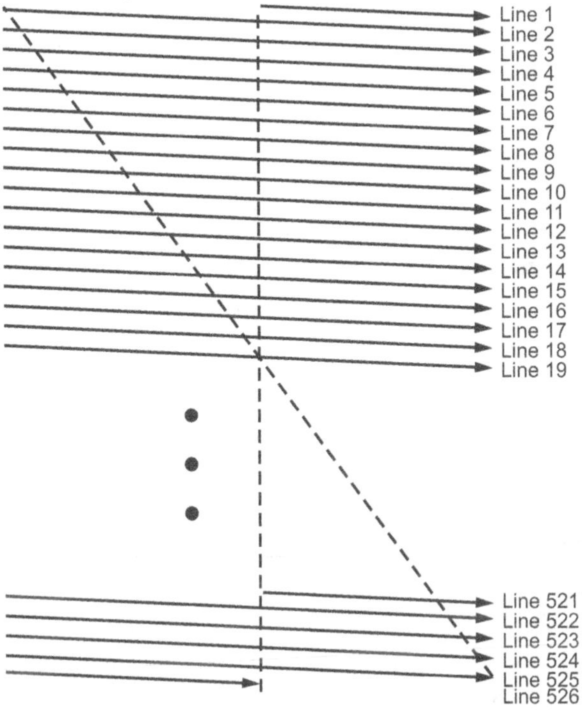

Fig. 3.22: Two passes using an interlaced refresh procedure

- In the first pass, the beam sweeps across each other scan line from top to bottom. Then after the vertical retrace, the beam sweeps out the remaining scan line.
- Interlacing of the scan line in this allows us to see the entire screen displayed in one-half the time it would have taken to sweep across all the lines at once from top to bottom.
- Interlacing is an effective technique for avoiding flicker, providing that adjacent scan lines contain similar display information.

Difference between Vector Scan Display and Raster Scan Display:

Sr. No.	Vector Scan Display	Raster Scan Display
1.	Vector displays draw lines and characters.	Raster display can draw areas filled with colours or patterns.
2.	These displays have higher resolution.	The displays have lower resolutions.
3.	The draw continuous and smooth lines.	They draw by approximating them with pixel on the raster grid.
4.	It does not user interlacing.	It uses interlacing.
5.	Editing is easy.	Editing is difficult.
6.	It uses beam-penetration method.	It uses shadow-mask method.
7.	In vector displays, the beam is moved between the end points of the graphics primitives.	In raster display, the beam is moved all over the screen one scan line at a time from top to bottom and then back to top.
8.	The refresh rate depends directly on picture complexity.	The refresh rate is independent of picture complexity.
9.	Scan conversions are not required.	Scan conversions are done.
10.	More expensive.	Less Expensive.

3.2.1.2 Colour CRT

- A colour CRT monitor can display colour pictures by using combination of phosphor that emit different coloured lights. Different colours are produced by combining emitted colour light from different phosphor.
- The two basic techniques used for producing colour display on CRT are beam penetration and shadow mask.

1. **Beam Penetration Technique :**

- It is used with random scan monitors. In this, normal CRT screen is coated with two phosphor layers. Here, red phosphor layer is deposited behind green phosphor layer.
- A slow electron beam excites only red phosphor layer and thus produces only red trace.
- A very fast beam penetrates through red layer and excites green layer also and thus gives green trace.
- A beam with intermediate speed gives red and green combination.

- The beam accelerating voltage controls the speed of beam and hence produces different screen colours.
- It is a cheap technique for colour display. Drawbacks of this technique are :
  (i) Limited range of colours are produced.
  (ii) Need to change beam accelerating voltage, which is difficult.

2. **Shadow Mask Technique :**

- It can display much wider range of colours than beam penetration technique. In this type of CRT a metal plate having small round holes in triangular pattern called shadow mask is inserted behind phosphor layer.
- Electron gun consist of three electron guns grouped in a triangle, where each gun is responsible for red, green and blue component of light of phosphor. These three beams encounter a hole in mask, pass through and strike the phosphor.
- Since, they originate at three different points they strike the phosphor in three slightly different spots.
- Therefore, in shadow mask CRT phosphor is laid down in groups of three spots as red, green and blue, under each hole in mask in such a way that each spot is struck only by beam from appropriate gun.
- Thus, when three phosphor spots of red, green and blue placed very close to each other are activated, a single phosphor spot is made visible on screen.
- By varying the intensity of three electron beams, we can retain different colours.
- Fig. 3.23 shows shadow mask CRT.

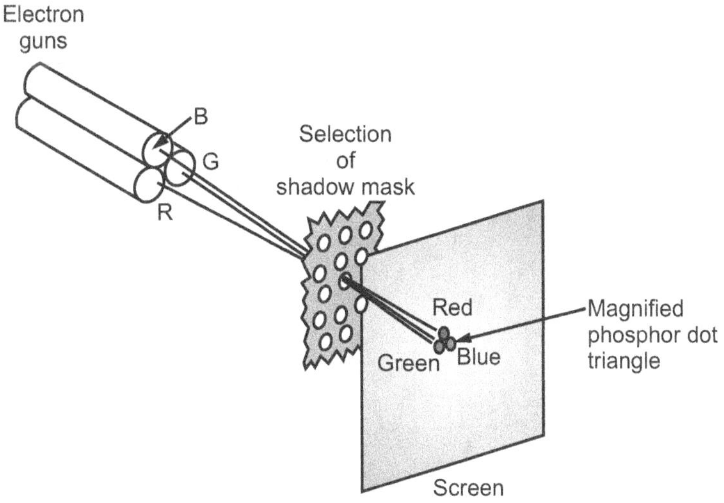

Fig. 3.23: Shadow mask CRT

Advantages of Shadow-mask CRT:

1. The whole of the screen is constantly updated.
2. It allows even the solids to be displayed.
3. It leverages low-cost CRT hardware.
4. It is a bright light-emitting display technology.

Disadvantages of Shadow-mask CRT:

1. It requires a very large memory array equal to that of our screen size.
2. It performs discrete spatial sampling of pixels.
3. Varying angles of e beam, approach the CRT face. Hence, convergence is difficult.
4. It results in spurious X-ray radiations also.
5. It requires proper matching of shadow-mask and dot-pitch frequencies.

3.2.1.3 Direct View Storage Tube (DVST)

- DVST is based on inherent image storage capability. It stores the picture information as a discharge distribution just behind the phosphor coated screen.
- DVST is very similar to CRT but has extremely long persistence phosphor, as image on the screen will remain visible for up to an hour.

Need of DVST:

- In raster display and all refresh display we need to refresh the screen to maintain consistent image on screen else flickering occurs. An alternative solution to this is display devices with inherent image storage capability, which stores image in display device for displaying.
- DVST uses a storage grid which stores picture information as a charge distribution just behind phosphor coated screen.
- The general arrangement of DVST is shown in Fig. 3.24.

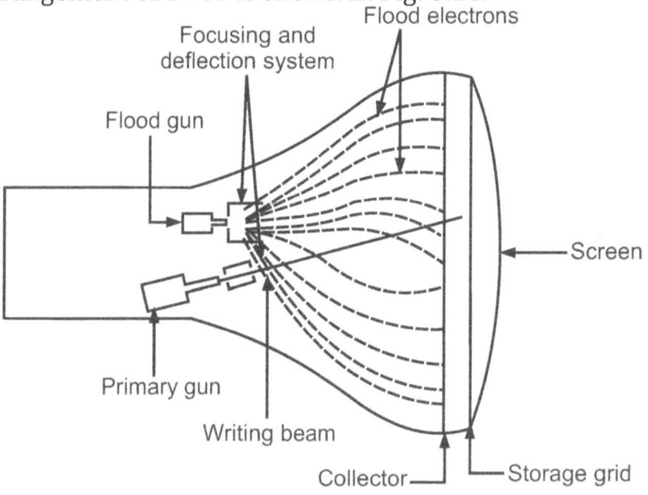

Fig. 3.24: Direct View Storage Tube

- DVST consist of two electron guns as writing gun and flood gun.
- Writing gun stores picture pattern as a positive charge on storage grid. This picture pattern is transferred to phosphor by continuous flood of electron generated from flood gun.
- Flood electrons passes through collector which smoothes out flow of electrons.
- Electrons pass through collector at low speed and are attracted by positively charged picture pattern on storage grid and are repelled by rest.
- The attracted electrons by positive picture pattern pass right through it and strike on phosphor making it visible on screen.

Advantages of DVST:

1. It has a flat screen.
2. Refreshing of CRT is not required.
3. Even complex pictures can be displaced at a very high resolutiojn with flicker as refreshing is required.

Disadvantages of DVST:

1. It produces relatively poor contrast and gradual degradation of picture quality.
2. DVST's performance is some what inferior to the refresh type of CRT.
3. Only a single level of intensity can be displayed.
4. It does not display colors and that selected parts of picture cannot be erased.
5. Erasing is not easy because it requires the removal of charge on the storage grid.

3.2.1.4 Flat Panel Display

- Flat panel display devices are very thinner than CRT. These display devices have low volume, weight and power requirement as compared to CRT.
- The main two types of flat panel display are – emissive display and non–emissive display.
  1. **Emissive Display:** These devices convert electrical energy into light. e.g. devices – plasma panels, light emitting diodes etc.
  2. **Non–Emissive Display:** They use optical effects to convert sunlight or light from some other source into graphics patterns. For example, Liquid crystal device and laser scan display. Let's see one example device of each type.

3.2.1.5 Plasma Panels

- PDPs (Plasma Display Panels) are also called as gas-discharge displays. They are essentially a matrix of very small fluorescent tubes with RGB phosphors.
- Fig. 3.25 shows construction of plasma panel display.

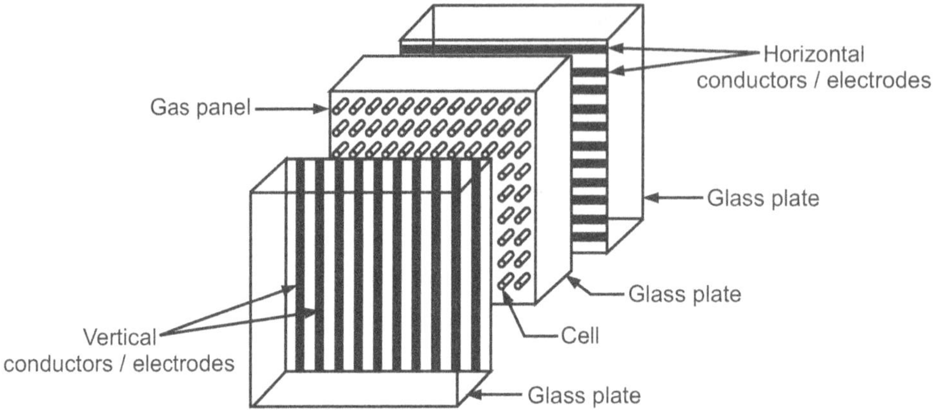

Fig. 3.25: Construction of plasma panel display

- It consist of two sheets of glass with thin and closed spaced gold electrodes attached to inner faces and covered with dielectric material. These are attached as series of vertical conductors on one glass plate and horizontal on other glass plate.
- The space between two glass plate, is filled with neon based gas and is sealed. By applying voltage between electrodes the gas within panel is divided into tiny cells and each cell is independent of its neighbours.
- Firing voltage applied to pair of horizontal and vertical conductors cause the gas at intersection cell to break down into glowing plasma. This glow can be sustained by maintaining high frequency alternating voltages across cell.

Advantages:

1. Light weight, less bulky the CRTs.
2. Produces flicker free image.
3. Refreshing is not required.
4. They have excellent color reproduction property.
5. They have large viewing angle.
6. They are promising for large format displays.

Disadvantages:

1. Costly.
2. They have poor resolutions (about 60 dpi).
3. They have complex addressing and writing requirement.
4. It is an expensive device.

3.2.1.6 Liquid Crystal Display (LCD)

- LCD is a flat panel display, electronic visual display, or video display that uses the light modulating properties of liquid crystals.
- This display use nematic (thread like) liquid crystal compounds that tend to keep the long axes of rod shaped molecules aligned. These nematic compounds have crystalline arrangement of molecules, yet they flow like a liquid and hence termed as liquid crystal display.

- Liquid crystal material is filled in between two glass plates. One glass plate have horizontal transparent conductors are built into same glass plate and other end glass plate have vertical light polarizer and vertical conductors are built into it.
- The intersection of two conductors defines pixel position. Polarized light passing through material is twisted so that it will pass through opposite polarizer.
- The light is then reflected back to the viewer. To turn OFF pixel, we apply voltage to two intersecting conductors to align molecules so that light is not twisted.
- Picture definitions are stored in refresh buffer and screen is refreshed at the rate of 60 frames per second.

Principle of LCD:

- The polarizing characteristics of certain organic compounds are used to modify the characteristics of color LCD. Certain organic compounds which exists in mesophase are stable at temperatures between the liquid and solid phases. Hence, the name LCD.
- LCD shows three types of mesophase i.e., Smectic, nematic (thread like) and cholestric. In mematic phase, the long axis of liquid crystal molecules align parallel to each other. The alignment direction is sensitive to temperature, surface tension, pressure and electric and magnetic fields. The optical characteristics of Liquid crystal are also sensitive to these effects.

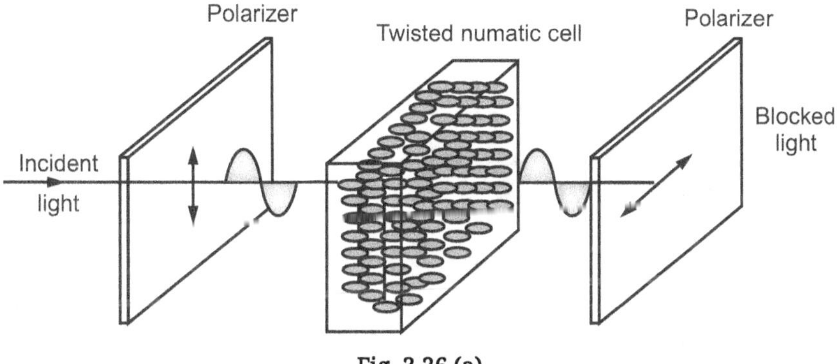

Fig. 3.26 (a)

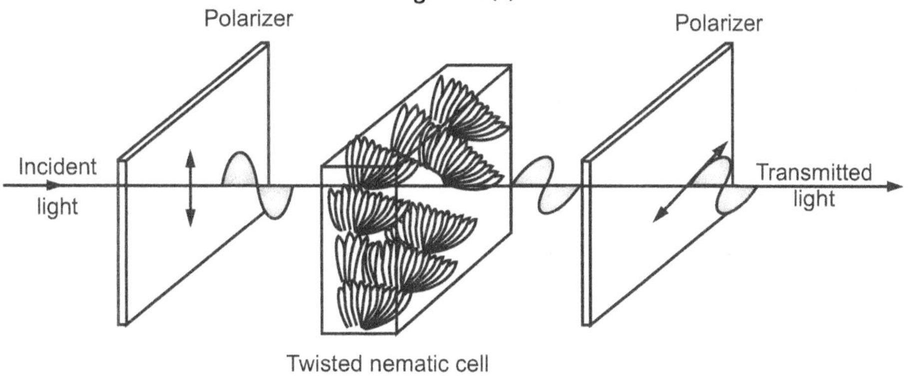

Fig. 3.26 (b): Liquid Crystal Display

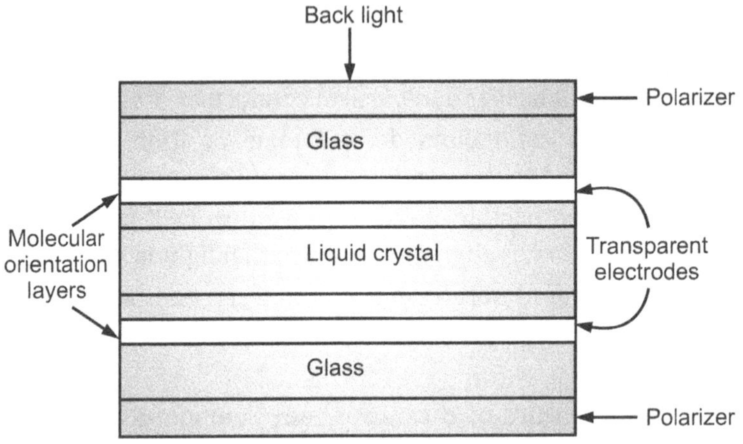

Fig. 3.26 (c)

Advantages of LCDs:

1. Lower power consumption.
2. They have low weight.
3. LCDs are flat.

Disadvantages:

1. LCD are temperature dependent i.e. the operating temperatures must be between 0° to 70° Celsius.
2. High cost.

3.3 HARD COPY DEVICES

- Output which is produced on a paper is known as hard copy output and they are permanent in nature.
- Among the wide variety of the hard copy output devices, printers and plotters are the most commonly used.
- A printer is used to produce printouts of the documents stored on a computer's disk drive while a plotter is a pen-based output device, which is used for producing high quality output by moving ink pens across the paper.

3.3.1 Plotters

- The plotter is a computer printer for printing vector graphics.
- A plotter gives a hard copy of the output. It draws pictures on a paper using a pen.
- Plotters are used to print designs of ships and machines, plans for buildings and so on.
- Plotters are divided into two types namely Drum plotters and Flatbed plotters.

1. **Drum Plotter:**

- A drum plotter is also known as Roller Plotter.
- It consists of a drum or roller on which a paper is placed and the drum rotates back and forth to produce the graph on the paper.
- It also consists of mechanical device known as Robotic Drawing Arm that holds a set of colored ink pens or pencils.
- The Robotic Drawing Arm moves side to side as the paper are rolled back and forth through the roller. In this way, a perfect graph or map is created on the paper. This work is done under the control of computer.
- Drum Plotters are used to produce continuous output, such as plotting earthquake activity.
- Fig. 3.27 shows a drum plotter.

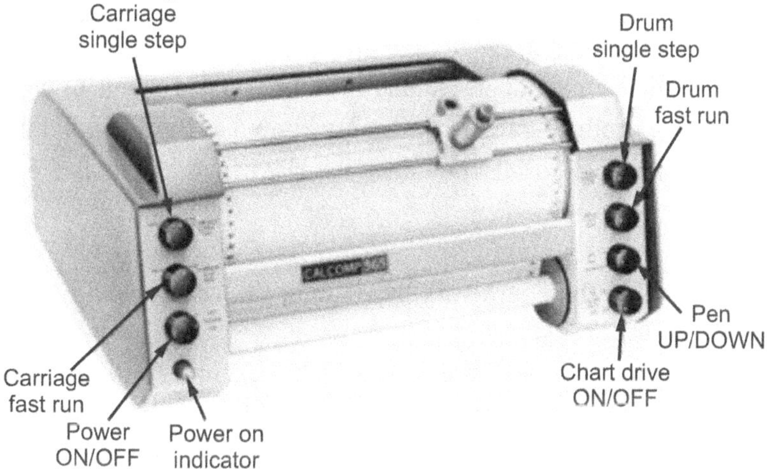

Fig. 3.27: A drum plotter

2. **Flatbed Plotter:**

- A flatbed plotter is also known as Table Plotter.
- It plots on paper that is spread and fixed over a rectangular flatbed table. The flatbed plotter uses two robotic drawing arms, each of which holds a set of colored ink pens or pencils.
- The drawing arms move over the stationary paper and draw the graph on the paper. Typically, the plot size is equal to the area of a bed.
- The plot size may be 20- by-50 feet. It is used in the design of cars, ships, aircrafts, buildings, highways etc.
- Flatbed plotter is very slow in drawing or printing graphs.
- The large and complicated drawing can take several hours to print. The main reason of the slow printing is due to the movement mechanical devices.

- Fig. 3.28 shows a flatbed plotter.

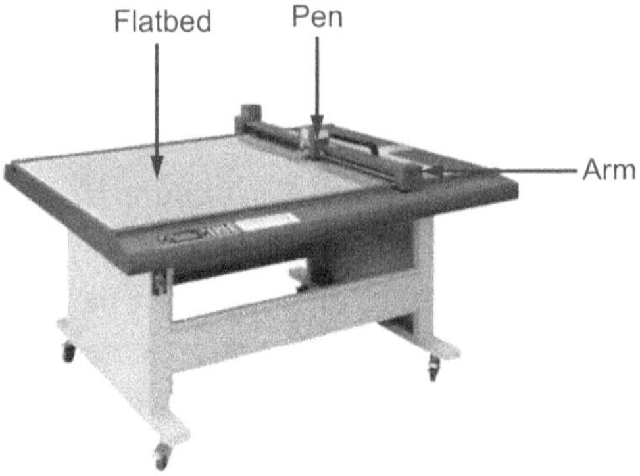

Fig. 3.28: A flatbed plotter

3.3.2 Printers [April 16]

- A printer is a device that accepts text and graphic output from a computer and transfers the information to paper, usually to standard size sheets of paper.
- Printers are used to produce paper (commonly known as hard copy) output.
- Based on the technology used they can be classified as impact and non-impact printers.

1. **Impact Printers:**

- The printer that prints the characters by striking the ribbon and onto the paper, are called impact printers.
- For example, dot-matrix printers, daisy wheels, line printers and drum printers etc.

2. **Non-Impact Printers:**

- Those printers that print a complete page at a time are called as non-impact or page printers. The print head does not make any contact with the paper. No ink ribbon is required.
- For example, ink jet and laser printers.
- Impact printers are of two types i.e., character printers and line printers.

1. **Character Printers:**

- Character printer are the printers which print one character at a time. These are further divided into two types i.e. Dot Matrix Printer (DMP) and Daisy Wheel Printer.

(i) **Dot Matrix Printer:**

- In the market one of the most popular printers is Dot Matrix Printer. These printers are popular because of their ease of printing and economical price.
- Each character printed is in form of pattern of dots and head consists of a Matrix of Pins of size (5*7, 7*9, 9*7 or 9*9) which come out to form a character that is why it is called Dot Matrix Printer.

- A typical dot-matrix printer is shown in the Fig. 3.29. It consists of a print head, sheet guide assembly, platen knob, and covers.

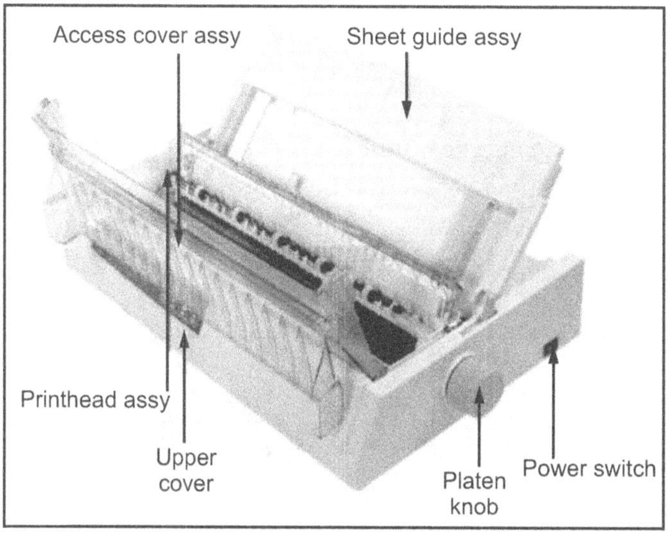

(a) Parts of dot matrix printer

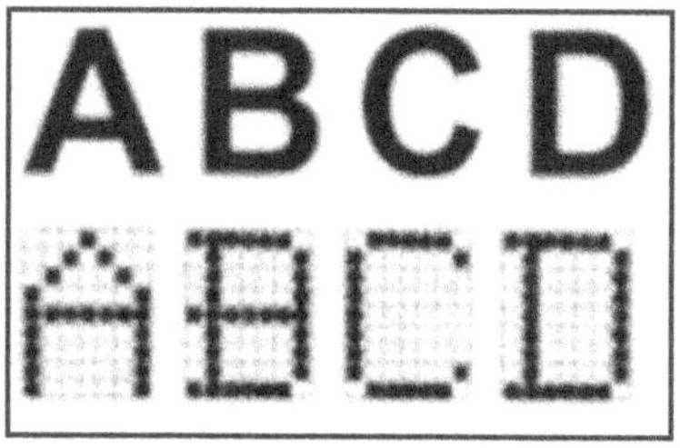

(b) Characters in dot matrix printer

Fig. 3.29

Advantages of Dot-matrix Printers:

1. They can print on multi-part stationary or carbon copies.
2. Lower printing costs compared with inkjet or laser printers.
3. These can withstand unclean or dusty environment whereas inkject or laser jet printers require clean environment.
4. Suitable for traction fed paper or continuous paper feed. Sometimes you may need to print an activity using continuous paper feed. Inkjet and Laser printers use discrete sheets of paper, and normally do not use continuous paper feed.
5. Using these printers require negligible operator training.
6. These printers usually cost less (initial purchase cost may be more, but running cost is negligible).

Disadvantages:

1. Slow speed.
2. Poor quality.
3. Noisy.

(ii) Daisy-Wheel Printers:

- Head is lying on a wheel and pins corresponding to characters are like petals of Daisy (flower name) that is why it is called Daisy Wheel Printer.

- These printers are generally used for word-processing in offices which require a few letters to be sent here and there with very nice quality.
- A Daisy-Wheel Printer works on the same principle as ball-head typewriter. The daisy wheel printer consists of a disk made of plastic or metal on which characters stand out along the outer edge.
- The printer rotates the disk to print a character until the desired letter is facing the paper, after which a hammer called solenoid strikes forcing the character to hit an ink ribbon making a mark of the character on the paper.
- Their speed is rated by cps (number of characters per second).
- Fig. 3.30 shows a daisy-wheel printer.

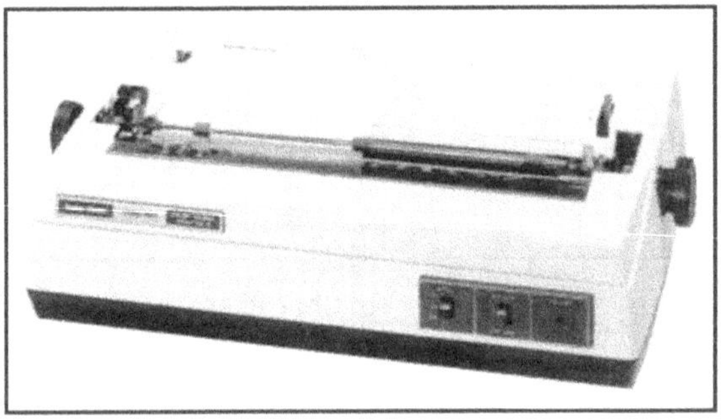

(a) Daisy-wheel printer

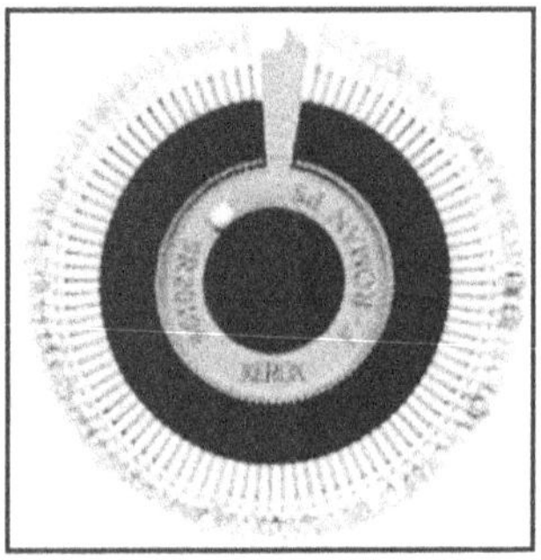

(b) A disk in Daisy-wheel printer

Fig. 3.30

Advantages:

1. More reliable than DMP.
2. Better quality.
3. The fonts of character can be easily changed.

Disadvantages:

1. Noisy when they printing.
2. These kinds of printers cannot print graphics.
3. Printing speed is slow.
4. More expensive than DMP.

2. Line Printers:

- Line printers are the printers which print one line at a time. These are of further two types i.e., Drum Printer and Chain Printer.

(i) Chain printer:

- An early line printer that used type slugs linked together in a chain as its printing mechanism. In this printer, chain of character sets are used so it is called Chain Printer.

- A standard character set may have 48, 64, or 96 characters. The chain spins horizontally around a set of hammers.
- When the desired character is in front of the selected print column, the corresponding hammer hits the paper into the ribbon and onto the character in the chain.
- Chain and train printers gave way to band printers in the early 1980s.

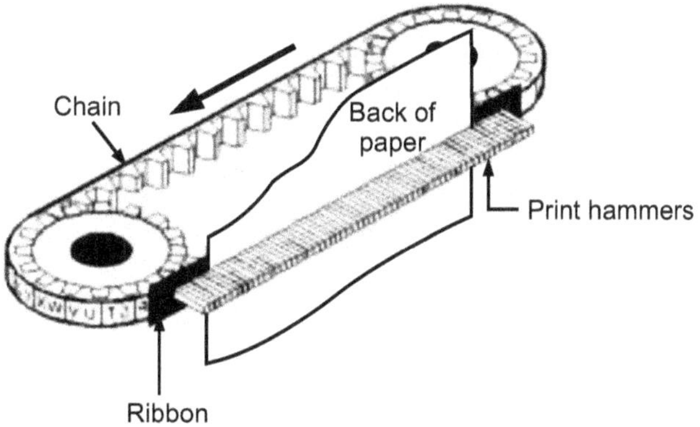

Fig. 3.31: Chain Printer Mechanism

- When the required character in the chain has revolved to the selected print column, the hammer pushes the paper into the ribbon and against the type slug of the letter or digit.

Advantages:

1. Character fonts can easily be changed.
2. Different languages can be used with the same printer.

Disadvantages:

1. Noisy.

(ii) Drum Printers:

- This printer is like a drum in shape so it is called drum printer. Drum printer consists of a cylindrical drum.
- The surface of drum is divided into number of tracks. Total tracks are equal to size of paper i.e. for a paper width of 132 characters, drum will have 132 tracks.
- A character set is embossed on track. The different character sets available in the market are 48 character set, 64 and 96 characters set. One rotation of drum prints one line.
- Drum printers are fast in speed and can print 300 to 2000 lines per minute. One complete set of characters is embossed on all the print positions on a line, as shown in the Fig. 3.32. The character to be printed is adjusted by rotating drum.

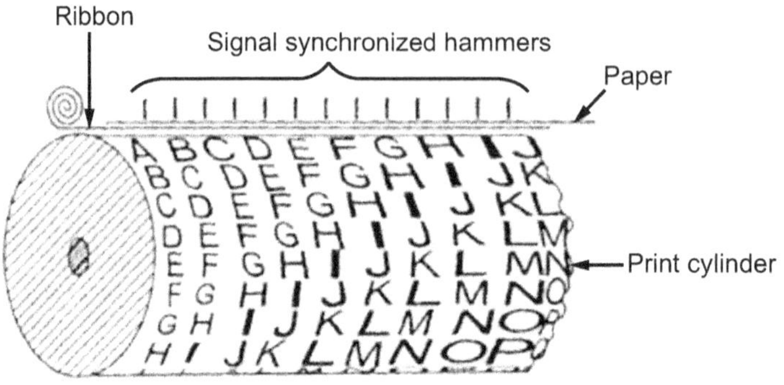

Fig. 3.32: Drum printers

Advantages:

1. Very high speed.

Disadvantages:

1. Very expensive.
2. Characters fonts cannot be changed.

- Non-impact printers are of two types i.e., Laser Printers and Inkjet Printers.

(i) Laser Printer:

- Laser printers are the fastest and most popular printers on the market today. They produce extremely high quality images – some near photo quality.
- The main principle in the working of laser printer is static electricity i.e., they use electro photography, or an electrophotostatic process, to form images on paper. The basis of the principles involved here is the science of atoms – oppositely-charged atoms are attracted to each other, so opposite static electricity fields cling together.
- The basic parts that a laser printer consists of are toner cartridges, photosensitive drum, erase lamp, primary corona, transfer corona, fuser assembly. Each of these parts have a very important role to play in the printing process.
- The laser printer uses electrostatic charges to (1) create an image on the drum, (2) adhere toner to the image, (3) transfer the toned image to the paper, and (4) fuse the toner to the paper.
- The laser creates the image by "painting" a negative of the page to be printed on the charged drum. Where light falls, the charge is dissipated, leaving a positive image to be printed.

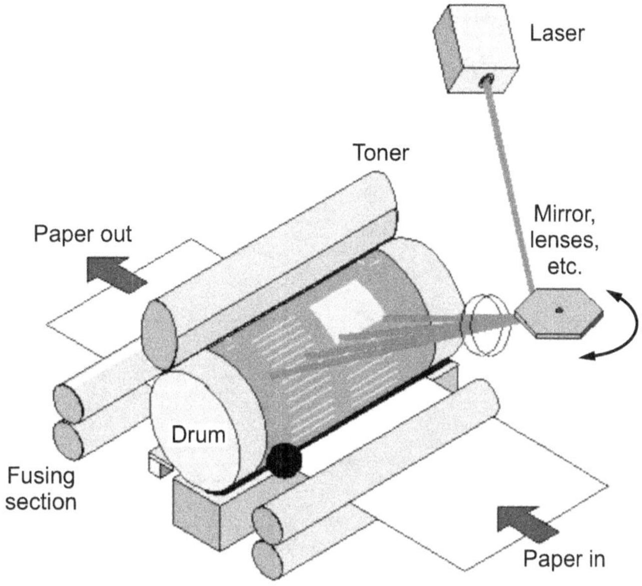

Fig. 3.33: The Laser mechanism

Advantages:

1. Very high speed.
2. Very high quality output.
3. Give good graphics quality.
4. Support many fonts and different character size.

Disadvantages:

1. Expensive.
2. Cannot be used to produce multiple copies of a document in a single printing.

(ii) Inkjet Printers:

- Inkjet printers are non-impact character printers based on a relatively new technology.
- Inkjet printers produce high quality output with presentable features. Inkjet printers are those that place extremely small droplets of ink onto paper to create an image. They use a reservoir of aqueous ink, a pump and an ink nozzle to accomplish this.
- These dots are extremely small and can have different colors combined together to create photo-quality images. They essentially work by shooting ink onto paper.
- Both inkjet and laser printers are non-impact printers in the sense that they do not have mechanisms that physically touch paper in order to create images.

- However, unlike laser printers, inkjet printers use aqueous ink that spontaneously colors the paper (unlike toner from laser printers that has to be fused into the paper with a fuser).
- Parts of a typical ink jet printer are shown in the Fig. 3.34.

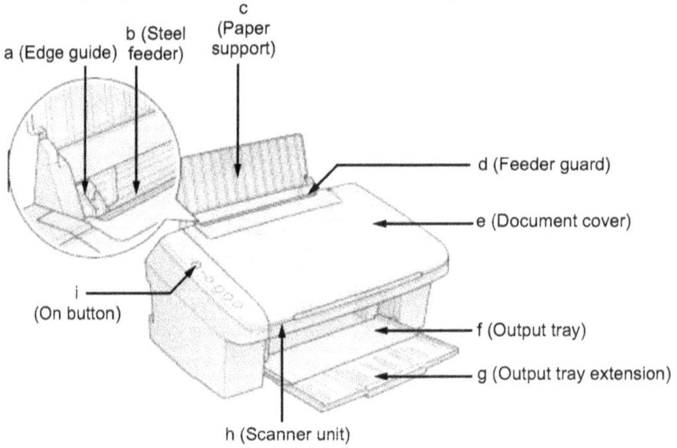

Fig. 3.34: A typical ink jet printer

- Above Fig. 3.32 shows following ports of inkjet printer.
  - (a) **Edge guide:** Helps load the paper straight. Adjust the left edge guide so that it fits snugly to the width of your paper.
  - (b) **Sheet feeder:** Feeds a stack of paper automatically.
  - (c) **Paper support:** Supports the paper loaded in the sheet feeder.
  - (d) **Feeder guard:** Prevents objects placed on the document cover from falling inside the printer when opening the document cover.
  - (e) **Document cover:** Open and close when you place a photo or document.
  - (f) **Output tray:** Receives ejected paper.
  - (g) **Output tray extension:** Supports the ejected paper.
  - (h) **Scanner unit:** Open and close when you replace an ink cartridge.
  - (i) **On button:** Turns the printer on and off.

Advantages:

1. High quality printing.
2. More reliable.

Disadvantages:

1. Expensive as cost per page is high.
2. Slow as compared to laser printer.

SUMMARY

- A frame buffer is a large, contiguous piece of computer memory. At a minimum there is one memory bit for each pixel in the rater; this amount of memory is called a bit plane. The picture is built up in the frame buffer one bit at a time.
- An application program along with graphics package is present in the system memory. The graphic commands is the program and translated by the graphics package and stored in the display file. In other records the file used to store the commands necessary for drawing the line segments is called the Display file. The program which converts these commands into actual picture is called the Display file Interpreter.
- The number of bits per pixel (bit depth) stored in the frame buffer to achieve pixel color requires large storage space. This problem can be reduced if a storage space is introduced in between the frame buffer and monitor. This storage space is called as a Look Up Table (LUT).
- LUT is also implemented as a separate table and is known as color look up table or video look up table. So, a LUT has many entries pixel values.
- A lookup table is an array or matrix of data that contains items that are searched. Lookup tables may be arranged as key-value pairs, where the keys are the data items being searched (looked up) and the values are either the actual data or pointers to where the data are located.
- A display device is an Output device for presentation of Information for Visual reception. The Display Systems are often referred to as Video Monitor or Video Display Unit (VDU).
- A soft copy (sometimes spelled "softcopy") is an electronic copy of some type of data. A hard copy (or "hardcopy") is a printed copy of information from a computer. Sometimes referred to as a printout, a hard copy is so-called because it exists as a physical object.
- A Cathode Ray Tube (CRT) is a specialized vacuum tube in which images are produced when an electron beam strikes a phosphorescent surface. Most desktop computer displays make use of CRTs. The CRT in a computer display is similar to the "picture tube" in a television receiver.
- In random scan system, an electron beam is directed to only those parts of the screen where a picture is to be drawn. The picture is drawn one line at a time, so also called vector displays or stroke writing displays. After drawing the picture the system cycles back to the first line and design all the lines of the picture 30 to 60 time each second.
- In a raster scan system, the electron beam is swept across the screen, one row at a time from top to bottom. When electron beam moves across each row the beam

intensity is turned ON and OFF to create a pattern of illuminated spots. Picture definition is stored in a memory called frame buffer which holds the set of intensity values, which are then retrieved from the frame buffer and pointed on the screen one row at a time.

- The plasma panel is composed of two sheets of glass with a series of ribs (like corrugated cardboard) filled with color phosphors in between. The top glass with embedded electrodes seals and forms a pixel where the junctions of the channels and the plate come together. Inside the sealed pixel, is a mixture of rare gases- typically argon and neon, although xenon has also been used.
- A color CRT monitor displays color picture by using a combination of phosphors that emit different colored light. By combining the emitted light a range of colors can be generated. Two basic methods for producing color displays are Beam Penetration Method and Shadow-Mask Method
- Random scan monitors use the beam penetration method for displaying color picture. In this, the inside of CRT screen is coated two layers of phosphor namely red and green. A beam of slow electrons excites only the outer red layer, while a beam of fast electrons penetrates red layer and excites the inner green layer. At intermediate beam speeds, combination of red and green light are emitted to show two additional colors- orange and yellow.
- Raster scan system are use shadow mask methods to produced a much more range of colors than beam penetration method. In this, CRT has three phosphor color dots. One phosphor dot emits a red light, second emits a green light and third emits a blue light. This type of CRT has three electrons guns and a shadow mask grid.
- LCD (Liquid Crystal Display) A display technology that uses rod-shaped molecules (liquid crystals) that flow like liquid and bend light. Unenergized, the crystals direct light through two polarizing filters, allowing a natural background color to show. When energized, they redirect the light to be absorbed in one of the polarizers, causing the dark appearance of crossed polarizers to show. The more the molecules are twisted, the better the contrast and viewing angle.
- Printers are the most commonly used output devices for producing hard copy output. Generally there are two types of printers those are impact and Non-impact. Impact Printers are those which strikes characters against the Ribbon for Printing like dot matrix printer. Non-impact Printers are those which uses Spray Method for Printing or in those printers no hammering action is performed like injet printer.
- A dot matrix printer or impact matrix printer is a type of computer printer with a print head that runs back and forth, or in an up and down motion, on the page and prints by impact, striking an ink-soaked cloth ribbon against the paper, much like a

typewriter. Unlike a typewriter or daisy wheel printer, letters are drawn out of a dot matrix, and thus, varied fonts and arbitrary graphics can be produced. Because the printing involves mechanical pressure, these printers can create carbon copies and carbonless copies.

- Inkjet printers form characters and images by spraying small drops of ink on to the paper. They are the most common type of computer printer for the general user due to their low cost, high quality of output, capability of printing in different colors, and ease of use.
- Laser Printers are those printers which first heats a Paper , for heating a entire paper a drum is used which Rotates the Paper and heat that Paper and then Toner is applied i.e. Ink is sprayed on that Paper , Then the heated area is Printed.
- A plotter is a printer that interprets commands from a computer to make line drawings on paper with one or more automated pens. Unlike a regular printer, the plotter can draw continuous point-to-point lines directly from vector graphics files or commands.
- There are a number of different types of plotters: a drum plotter draws on paper wrapped around a drum which turns to produce one direction of the plot, while the pens move to provide the other direction; a flatbed plotter draws on paper placed on a flat surface; and an electrostatic plotter draws on negatively charged paper with positively charged toner. Plotters were the first type of printer that could print with color and render graphics and full-size engineering drawings.

PRACTICE QUESTIONS

1. List out different types of frame buffers.
2. What is bit-plane.
3. List out the components of display file.
4. What is Look-Up Table (LUT)
5. What is soft copy and hard copy?
6. What is shadow mask?
7. Give advantages of shadow masking.
8. Advantages of DVST.
9. Disadvantages of shadow masking.
10. What is flat panel display.
11. Advantages of LCD.
12. What is impact printer.
13. Explain the concept of frame buffer with it's type.

14. Write a short note on display file.
15. Highlight look up table with it's uses for image storage.
16. Explain the concept of Monitor.
17. Differentiate Random scan CRT and Raster scan CRT.
18. Explain the concept of DVST.
19. What is mean by flat panel display. Highlight it's merits and demerits.
20. Explain the concept of plotter.
21. List out advantages and disadvantages of dot matrix printer.
22. Write a note on Printer.
23. Highlight the use of non-impact printer over impact printers.
24. Write a note on laser printer.
25. Explain the concept of Inkjet printer with it's advantages over laser printer.

■■■

CHAPTER 4

Raster Scan Graphics

Contents ...

Objectives...

- To Study Raster Scan Graphics
- To Learn various Line Drawing Algorithms
- To Study Scan Conversions
- To Understand Polygon and Polygon Filling Concpets

4.1 INTRODUCTION

- The very beginning of computer graphics, many algorithms have been developed to generate such complex graphic objects like cubes, circles, canes, ellipses etc.
- Independent of the algorithms being used, the computer can produce raster images on raster devices only by turning the appropriate pixels ON or OFF. The process of representing continuous graphics objects as a collection of discrete pixels, is called scan conversion.

- Computer graphics can be created as either raster or vector images.
- Raster graphics are bitmaps. A bitmap is a grid of countless individual dots (called pixels) that collectively compose an image. Each pixel is coded in a specific color, hue or shade.
- Raster graphics are best used for non-line art images such as digitized photographs, scanned artwork or detailed graphics. Non-line art images are best represented in raster form because they typically include subtle chromatic gradations, undefined lines and shapes, and complex composition.
- Common raster formats include TIFF, JPEG, GIF, PCX and BMP files.
- This chapter examines the procedures for drawing complex objects. It will explain various line drawing algorithms like DDA, Bresenham line drawing as well as circle drawing algorithm.

4.2 LINE DRAWING ALGORITHMS

- Line (actually a straight line), together with point, is a basic concept of elementary geometry.
- Point, together with line, a basic concept of elementary geometry.
- The idea of point is an abstraction that distills our understanding of the concept of location.
- The screen of a computer is divided into rows and columns. The intersection area of these rows and columns is known as a pixel, as shown in Fig. 4.1.
- In order to draw a line on the screen, first we have to determine which pixels are to be switched ON (i.e., are to be brightened).
- The process of determining which combination of pixels provide the best approximation to the desired line, is known as Rasterization.
- When rasterization is combined with rendering of the picture in scan-line order, then it is known as scan-conversion.
- The choice of the pixels is determined by the orientation of the line which is to be drawn.

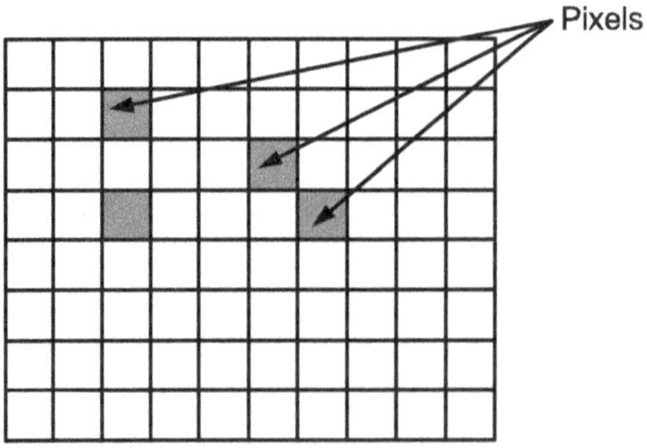

Fig. 4.1: Pixel

- A line connects two points. To draw a line, you need two points between which you can draw a line. In the following three algorithms, we refer the one point of line as X_0, Y_0 and the second point of line as X_1, Y_1.
- Before discussing specific line drawing algorithms, it is useful to consider general requirements for such algorithms. Let us see what are the desirable characteristics needed for these lines.
- The primary design criteria of line are as follows:
  1. Straight lines appear as straight lines.
  2. Straight lines start and end accurately.
  3. Displayed lines should have constant brightness along their length, independent of the line length and orientation.
  4. Lines should be drawn rapidly.
- The goal of any line drawing algorithm is to construct the best possible approximation of an ideal line given the inherent limitations of a raster display.

4.2.1 Digital Differential Analyzer (DDA) Algorithm

- This algorithm generates a line from differential equations of line and hence the name DDA.
- DDA algorithm is an incremental scan conversion method.
- A DDA is hardware or software used for linear interpolation of variables over an interval between start and end point.
- DDAs are used for rasterization of lines, triangles and polygons.
- DDA method is referred by this name because this method is very similar to the numerical differential equations. The DDA is a mechanical device that solves differential equations by numerical methods.
- There are two DDA techniques for straight-line namely, Simple DDA and Symmetrical DDA.
- **Working Principle:** DDA works on a principle that we simultaneously increment x and y by small steps proportional to the first derivative of x and y.

  The slope (m) of a straight line is given as,

$$M = \frac{y_2 - y_1}{x_2 - x_1} \qquad \dots (4.1)$$

- Where (x_1, x_2) and (y_1, y_2) are two end points of a line. This equation (4.1) can be used to obtain a straight line

$$\text{x interval} = \Delta x = x_2 - x_1$$

$$\text{y interval} = \Delta y = y_2 - y_1$$

∴ Equation (4.1) can be written as

$$\frac{\Delta y}{\Delta x} = \frac{y_2 - y_1}{x_2 - x_1} \quad \ldots (4.2)$$

For any given x interval (Δx); we can calculate corresponding y interval (Δy). From equation (4.2) as,

$$\Delta y = \frac{y_2 - y_1}{x_2 - x_1} \Delta x$$

Similarly, for given Δy, we can calculate corresponding Δx as

$$\Delta x = \frac{x_2 - x_1}{y_2 - y_1} \Delta y$$

Once, intervals are known, the values for next x and next y on straight line can be obtained as

$$x_i + 1 = x_i + \Delta x$$

and $$y_i + 1 = y_i + \Delta y$$

1. **Simple DDA:**

- For simple DDA either Δx or Δy whichever is larger is selected as line length estimate (i.e. it is taken as length of line to draw). Therefore, either Δx or Δy will be of unit magnitude. Let us see the algorithm to draw straight line.

Algorithm:

Steps 1: Read the end points of line.

Steps 2: $\Delta x = \text{abs}(x_2 - x_1)$ and

$\Delta y = \text{abs}(y_2 - y_1)$

Step 3: if Δx ≥ Δy then

length = Δx

else

length = Δy

end if

Step 4: $\Delta x = (x_2 - x_1)/\text{length}$

Step 5: $\Delta y = (y_2 - y_1)/\text{length}$

Step 6: $x = x_1 + 0.5 * \text{sign}(\Delta x)$

$y = y_1 + 0.5 * \text{sign}(\Delta y)$

Step 7: i = 1

```
while (i ≤ length)
{
    plot (integer (x), integer (y))
    x = x + Δx
    y = y + Δy
    i = i + 1
}
```

Step 8: End

- **Note:** Here step (4) makes either Δx or Δy equal to 1 because length is either abs (x_2, x_1) or abs (y_2, y_1). Therefore, incremental value for either x or y is one. Sign function of step 6 makes algorithm to work in all quadrants and the factor 0.5 makes it possible to round the values in integer function rather than truncating them.

2. **Symmetrical DDA:**

   In this, 2^{-n} represents the line length estimate such that

   $$2^{n-1} \leq \max (|\Delta x|, |\Delta y|) < 2^n$$

- This algorithm generates accurate lines as next dot on true line is never greater than one half of one pixel and thus neither Δx nor Δy exceeds unit magnitude whereas in simple DDA either Δx or Δy is of unit magnitude. Therefore, it adds unit value either to x if Δx is greater or to y if Δy is greater.

Advantages of DDA Algorithm:

1. It is the simplest algorithm and it does not require special skills for implement-tation.
2. It is a faster method for calculating pixel positions than the direct use of equation y = mx + b. It eliminates the multiplication in the equation by making use of raster characteristics, so that appropriate increments are applied in the x or v direction to find the pixel positions along the line path.

Disadvantages of DDA Algorithm:

1. Floating point arithmetic in DDA algorithm is still time-consuming.
2. The algorithm is orientation dependent. Hence end point accuracy is poor.

Ex. 1: Consider the line from (0,0) to (4,6). Use the simple DDA algorithm to rasterize this line.

Sol. Evaluating steps 1 to 5 in the DDA algorithm we have,

$X_1 = 0 \quad Y_1 = 0$

$X_2 = 4 \quad Y_2 = 6$

Length = $|Y_2 - Y_1| = 6$

$$\Delta X = |X_2 - X_1| / \text{Length}$$
$$= 4$$
$$= 6$$
$$\Delta Y = |Y_2 - Y_1| / \text{Length}$$
$$= 6/6 = 1$$

Initial value for,

$$X = 0 + 0.5 \times (4) = 0.5$$
$$6$$
$$Y = 0 + 0.5 \times (1) = 0.5$$

Tabulating the results of each iteration in the step 6 we get,

i	Plot	x	y
		0.5	0.5
1	(0, 0)		
		1.167	1.5
2	(1, 1)		
		1.833	2.5
3	(1, 2)		
		2.5	3.5
4	(2, 3)		
		3.167	4.5
5	(3, 4)		
		3.833	5.5
6	(3, 5)		
		4.5	6.5

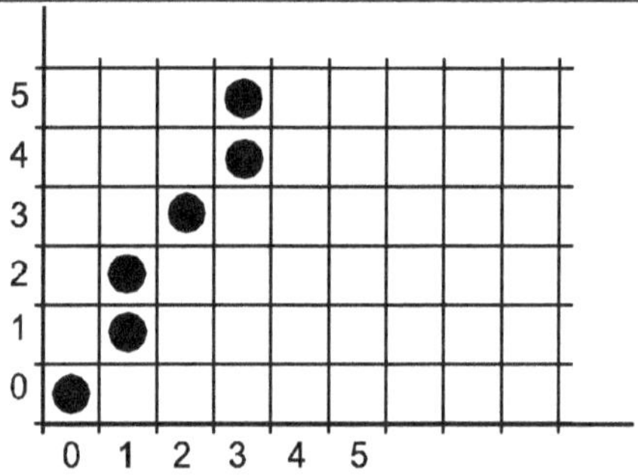

Fig. 4.2

- The results are plotted as shown in the Fig. 4.2. It shows that the rasterized line lies to both sides of the actual line, i.e. the algorithm is orientation dependent.

Ex. 2: Consider the line from (0, 0) to (-6, -6). Use the simple DDA algorithm line.

Sol.: Evaluating steps 1 to 5 in the DDA algorithm we have

$X_1 = 0$ $\quad Y_1 = 0$

$X_2 = -6$ $\quad Y_2 = -6$

$$\text{Length} = |X_2 - X_1| \; |Y_2 - Y_1| = 6$$

$$\Delta X = \Delta Y = -1$$

Initial values for,

$$X = 0 + 0.5 \times (-1) = -0.5$$

$$Y = 0 + 0.5 \times (-1) = -0.5$$

Tabulating the results of each iteration in the step 6 we get,

i	Plot	x	y
		− 0.5	− 0.5
1	(−1, −1)		
		− 1.5	− 1.5
2	(−2, −2)		
		− 2.5	− 2.5
3	(−3, −3)		
		− 3.5	− 3.5
4	(−4, −4)		
		− 4.5	− 4.5
5	(−5, −5)		
		− 5.5	− 5.5
6	(−6, −6)		
		− 6.5	− 6.5

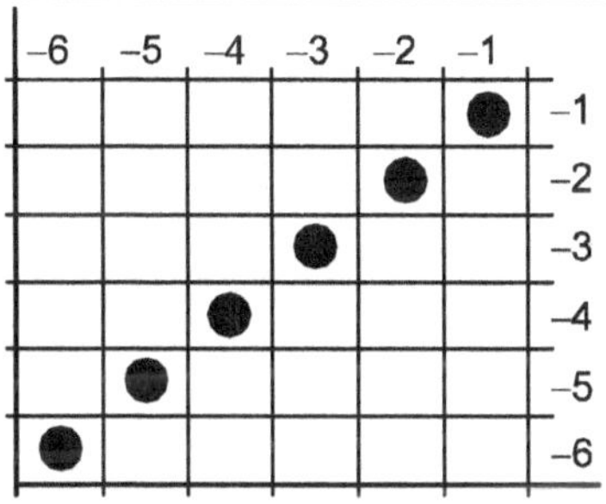

Fig. 4.3

- The results are plotted as shown in the Fig. 4.3. It shows that the rasterized line lies on the actual line and it is 45° line.

4.2.2 Bresenham's Line Drawing Algorithm [April 16]

- The drawbacks of DDA algorithm have been overcome in Bresenham's algorithm. This algorithm was developed by Jack E. Bresenham in 1962 at IBM.
- The Bresenham algorithm is another incremental scan conversion algorithm. The big advantage of this algorithm is that, it uses only integer calculations. Moving across the x axis in unit intervals and at each step choose between two different y coordinates.
- For example, as shown in the following illustration (See Fig. 4.4), from position (2, 3) you need to choose between (3, 3) and (3, 4). You would like the point that is closer to the original line.

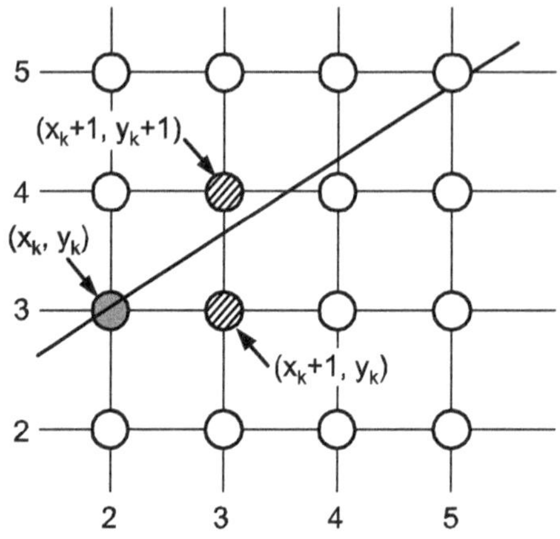

Fig. 4.4

- At sample position $X_k + 1$, the vertical separations from the mathematical line are labelled as d_{upper} and d_{lower}.

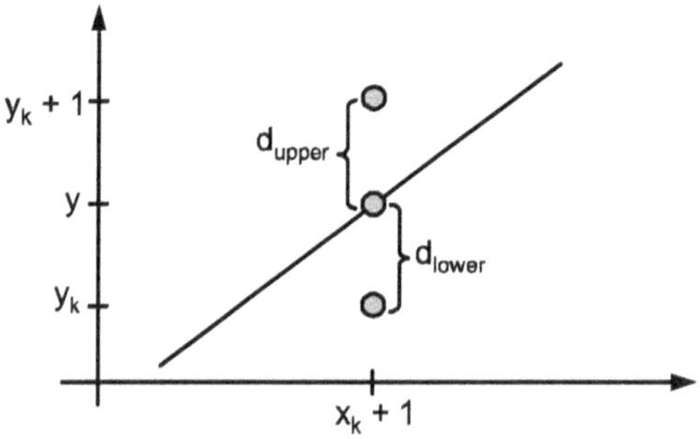

Fig. 4.5

- From the above illustration (Fig. 4.5), the y coordinate on the mathematical line at $x_k + 1$ is:

$$Y = m(X_k + 1) + b$$

So, d_{upper} and d_{lower} are given as follows:

$$d_{lower} = y - y_k$$
$$= m(X_k + 1) + b - Y_k$$

and $$d_{upper} = (y_k + 1) - y$$
$$= Y_k + 1 - m(X_k + 1) - b$$

- You can use these to make a simple decision about which pixel is closer to the mathematical line. This simple decision is based on the difference between the two pixel positions.

$$d_{lower} - d_{upper} = 2m(x_k + 1) - 2y_k + 2b - 1$$

- Let us substitute m with dy/dx where dx and dy are the differences between the end-points.

$$dx(d_{lower} - d_{upper}) = dx(2dydx(x_k + 1) - 2y_k + 2b - 1)$$
$$= 2dy.x_k - 2dx.y_k + 2dy + 2dx(2b - 1)$$
$$= 2dy.x_k - 2dx.y_k + C$$

So, a decision parameter P_k for the kth step along a line is given by:

$$p_k = dx(d_{lower} - d_{upper})$$
$$= 2dy.x_k - 2dx.y_k + C$$

- The sign of the decision parameter P_k is the same as that of $d_{lower} - d_{upper}$.
- If p_k is negative, then choose the lower pixel, otherwise choose the upper pixel.
- Remember, the coordinate changes occur along the x axis in unit steps, so you can do everything with integer calculations. At step k+1, the decision parameter is given as:

$$p_{k+1} = 2dy.x_{k+1} - 2dx.y_{k+1} + C$$

Subtracting pk from this we get:

$$p_{k+1} - p_k = 2dy(x_k + 1 - x_k) - 2dx(y_{k+1} - y_k)$$

But, xk+1 is the same as x_{k+1}. So:

$$p_{k+1} = p_k + 2dy - 2dx(y_{k+1} - y_k)$$

- Where, $Y_{k+1} - Y_k$ is either 0 or 1 depending on the sign of P_k.
- The first decision parameter p_0 is evaluated at (x_0, y_0) is given as:

$$p_0 = 2dy-dx$$

Now, keeping in mind all the above points and calculations, here is the Bresenham algorithm for slope m < 1:

Step 1 : Input the two end-points of line, storing the left end-point in (x_0, y_0).

Step 2 : Plot the point (x_0, y_0).

Step 3 : Calculate the constants dx, dy, 2dy, and (2dy – 2dx) and get the first value for the decision parameter as:

$$p_0 = 2dy - dx$$

Step 4 : At each Xk along the line, starting at k = 0, perform the following test:

If $p_k < 0$, the next point to plot is $(x_k + 1, y_k)$ and $p_k + 1 = p_k + 2dy$

Otherwise,

$$p_{k+1} = p_k + 2dy - 2dx$$

Step 5: Repeat step 4 (dx – 1) times.

For m > 1, find out whether you need to increment x while incrementing y each time.

- After solving, the equation for decision parameter P_k will be very similar, just the x and y in the equation gets interchanged.

4.2.3 Mid-Point Algorithm

- Mid-point algorithm is due to Bresenham which was modified by Pitteway and Van Aken.
- Assume that you have already put the point P at (x, y) coordinate and the slope of the line is $0 \leq k \leq 1$ as shown in the following illustration, (See Fig. 4.6).
- Now you need to decide whether to put the next point at E or N. This can be chosen by identifying the intersection point Q closest to the point N or E. If the intersection point Q is closest to the point N then N is considered as the next point; otherwise E.

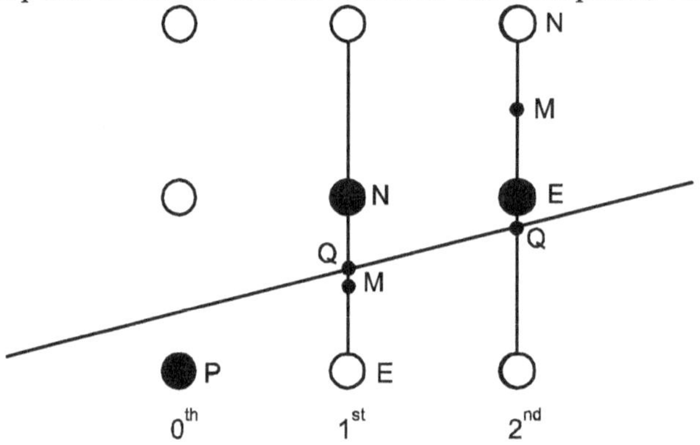

Fig. 4.6

- To determine that, first calculate the mid-point M(x + 1, y + ½). If the intersection point Q of the line with the vertical line connecting E and N is below M, then take E as the next point; otherwise take N as the next point.
- In order to check this, we need to consider the implicit equation:

$$F(x,y) = mx + b - y$$

- For positive m at any given X,
  - If y is on the line, then F(x, y) = 0.
  - If y is above the line, then F(x, y) < 0.
  - If y is below the line, then F(x, y) > 0.

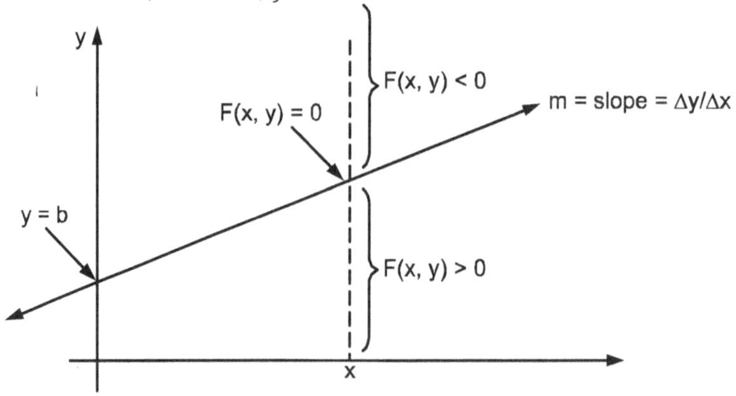

Fig. 4.7

4.2.4 Circle Generation Algorithm

- Before knowing circle generating algorithms let's see the symmetry of circle. Very first of all circle is a symmetrical figure.
- The shape of circle is similar in each quadrant. After that circle is also symmetrical between octants. Thus, circle has eight way symmetry i.e. symmetrical in all octants.
- Once, one point in one octant is calculated, it can be mapped into other seven circle points in other octants.
- A circle is defined as "the set of points that are all at a given distance r from a center position ($x_{c,}$, y_c)".
- Fig. 4.8 shows symmetry of a circle where point (x, y) in first octant gives circle points in other seven octants.

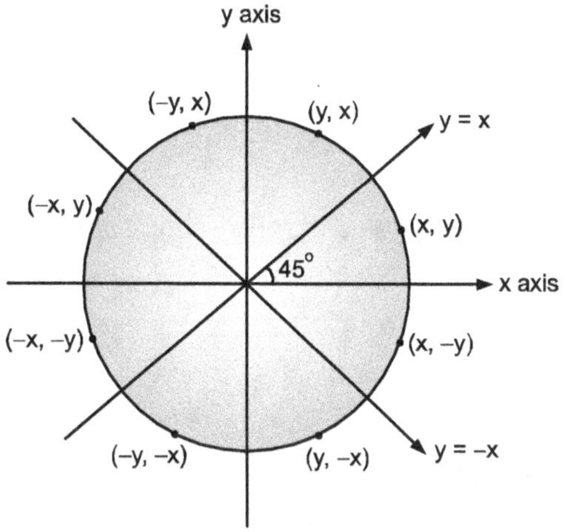

Fig 4.8: Symmetry of Circle

- Drawing a circle on the screen is a little complex than drawing a line. There are two popular algorithms for generating a circle – Bresenham's Algorithm and Midpoint Circle Algorithm. These algorithms are based on the idea of determining the subsequent points required to draw the circle.
- The equation of circle is $X^2 + Y^2 = r^2$, where r is radius.

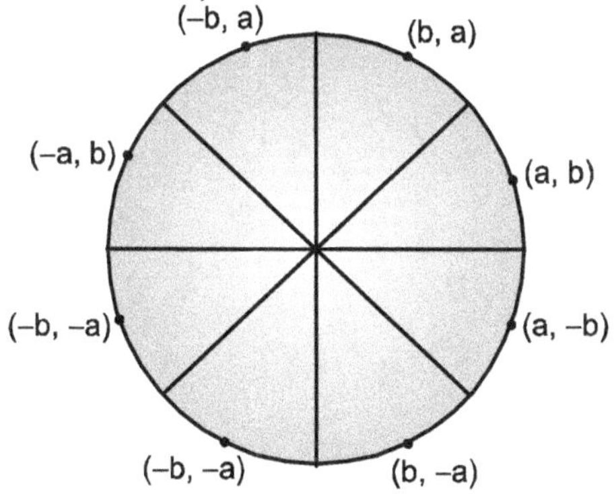

Fig. 4.9

1. **DDA Circle Generating Algorithms:**

The differential equation of a circle with center as origin is

$$\frac{dy}{dx} = \frac{-x}{y}$$

From above equation we can construct a circle by using x and y incremental values Δx and Δy as,

$$\Delta x = \varepsilon y \text{ and}$$
$$\Delta y = -\varepsilon x$$

Where,

$$\varepsilon = 2^{-n}$$

$2n - 1 \leq r \leq 2^n$ and r is radius of circle.

Thus, we can get next pixel by using following equation

$$x_{n+1} = x_n + \varepsilon y_n$$
$$y_{n+1} = y_n - \varepsilon x_n$$

Unfortunately above equations gives a spiral shape instead of a circle. To make it a circle we need to do correction in above equation as,

$$x_{n+1} = x_n + \varepsilon y_n$$
$$y_{n+1} = y_n - \varepsilon x_{n+1}$$

Merits of DDA Algorithm:

(i) It is well suited to hardware implementation.

- This algorithm is summarized as below:

Algorithm: DDA Circle Drawing Algorithm:

Step 1: Read radius of Circle (r) and calculate value of ε (epsilon).

Step 2: $x = 0$
$y = r$

Step 3: $x_1 = x$
$y_1 = y$

Step 4: While $((y_1 - y) < \varepsilon \ || \ (x - x_1) > \varepsilon)$

{

$x_1 = x_1 + \varepsilon y_1$

$y_1 = y_1 + \varepsilon x_1$

plot (int (x_1), int (y_1))

}

Step 5: Stop.

2. **Bresenham's Algorithm:**

- We cannot display a continuous arc on the raster display. Instead, we have to choose the nearest pixel position to complete the arc.
- From the following illustration (See Fig. 4.10), you can see that we have put the pixel at (X, Y) location and now need to decide where to put the next pixel – at N (X + 1, Y) or at S (X + 1, Y – 1).

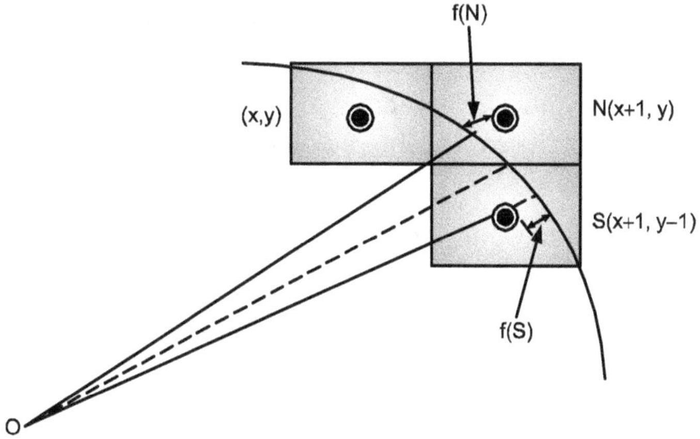

Fig. 4.10

This can be decided by the decision parameter d.

- If d <= 0, then N(X + 1, Y) is to be chosen as next pixel.
- If d > 0, then S(X + 1, Y – 1) is to be chosen as the next pixel.

Algorithm:

Step 1: Get the coordinates of the center of the circle and radius, and store them in x, y, and R respectively. Set P=0 and Q=R.

Step 2: Set decision parameter D = 3 – 2R.

Step 3: Repeat through step-8 while X < Y.

Step 4: Call Draw Circle (X, Y, P, Q).

Step 5: Increment the value of P.

Step 6: If D < 0 then D = D + 4x + 6.

Step 7: Else Set Y = Y + 1, D = D + 4(X-Y) + 10.

Step 8: Call Draw Circle (X, Y, P, Q).

- Draw Circle Method (X, Y, P, Q).

```
Call Putpixel (X + P, Y + Q).
Call Putpixel (X - P, Y + Q).
Call Putpixel (X + P, Y - Q).
Call Putpixel (X - P, Y - Q).
Call Putpixel (X + Q, Y + X).
Call Putpixel (X - Q, Y + X).
Call Putpixel (X + Q, Y - X).
Call Putpixel (X - Q, Y - X).
```

3. **Mid Point Algorithm:**

- Although Bresenham's algorithm is based upon integral operations only and is much faster than other algorithms, yet there is one drawback of this algorithm. This method is not uniformly applicable to all sorts of conics.
- For example, for the ellipse drawing procedure, we need to treat two different regions in the first quadrant differently. This complication can be avoided by the mid-point method.

Step 1: Input radius r and circle center (x_c, y_c) and obtain the first point on the circumference of the circle centered on the origin as,

$(x_0, y_0) = (0, r)$

Step 2: Calculate the initial value of decision parameter as,

$$P_0 = 5/4 - r$$

(See the following description for simplification of this equation.)

$$f(x, y) = x^2 + y^2 - r^2 = 0$$

$$\begin{aligned} f(x_i - 1/2 + e, y_i + 1) &= (x_i - 1/2 + e)^2 + (y_i + 1)^2 - r^2 \\ &= (x_i - 1/2)^2 + (y_i + 1)^2 - r^2 + 2(x_i - 1/2)e + e^2 \\ &= f(x_i - 1/2, y_i + 1) + 2(x_i - 1/2)e + e^2 = 0 \end{aligned}$$

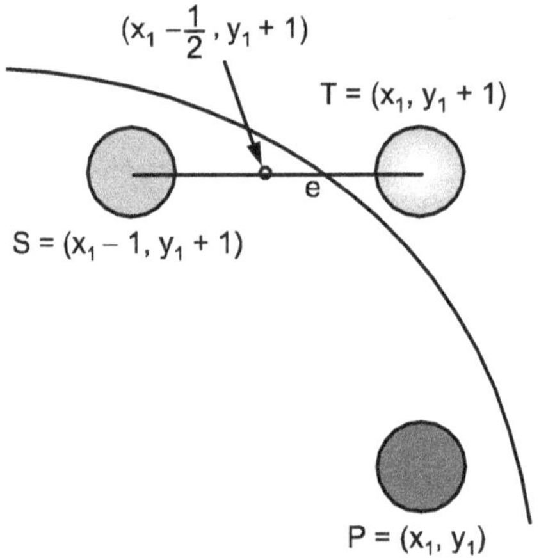

Fig. 4.11

Let $d_i = f(x_i - 1/2, y_i + 1) = -2(x_i - 1/2)e - e^2$

Thus,

If $e < 0$ then $d_i > 0$ so choose point $S = (x_i - 1, y_i + 1)$.

$$\begin{aligned} d_i + 1 &= f(x_i - 1 - 1/2, y_i + 1 + 1) \\ &= ((x_i - 1/2) - 1)^2 + ((y_i + 1) + 1)^2 - r^2 \\ &= d_i - 2(x_i - 1) + 2(y_i + 1) + 1 \\ &= d_i + 2(y_i + 1 - x_i + 1) + 1 \end{aligned}$$

If e >= 0 then d_i <= 0 so choose point T = $(x_i, y_i + 1)$

$$d_i + 1 = f(x_i - 1/2, y_{i+1} + 1)$$
$$= d_i + 2y_{i+1} + 1$$

The initial value of d_i is

$$d_0 = f(r - 1/2, 0 + 1) = (r - 1/2)2 + 1^2 - r^2$$
$$= 5/4 - r \{1 - r \text{ can be used if r is an integer}\}$$

When point S = $(x_i - 1, y_i + 1)$ is chosen then

$$d_i + 1 = d_i + -2x_{i+1} + 2y_{i+1} + 1$$

When point T = $(x_i, y_i + 1)$ is chosen then

$$d_i + 1 = d_i + 2y_{i+1} + 1$$

Step 3: At each X_K position starting at K = 0, perform the following test:

If PK < 0 then next point on circle (0, 0) is (X_{K+1}, Y_K) and

$$P_{K+1} = P_K + 2X_{K+1} + 1$$

Else

$$P_{K+1} = P_K + 2X_{K+1} + 1 - 2Y_{K+1}$$

Where, $2X_{K+1} = 2X_{K+2}$ and $2Y_{K+1} = 2Y_{K-2}$

Step 4: Determine the symmetry points in other seven octants.

Step 5: Move each calculate pixel position (X, Y) onto the circular path centered on (X_C, Y_C) and plot the coordinate values.

$$X = X + X_C, \quad Y = Y + Y_C$$

Step 6: Repeat step 3 through 5 until X >= Y.

4.3 SCAN CONVERSIONS [Oct. 16]

- The process of representing continuously graphic objects as a collection of discrete pixels is called scan conversion.
- In other words, we can say that scan conversion is continuous-to-discrete transformation.
- Fig. 4.12 show continuous-to-discrete transformation.

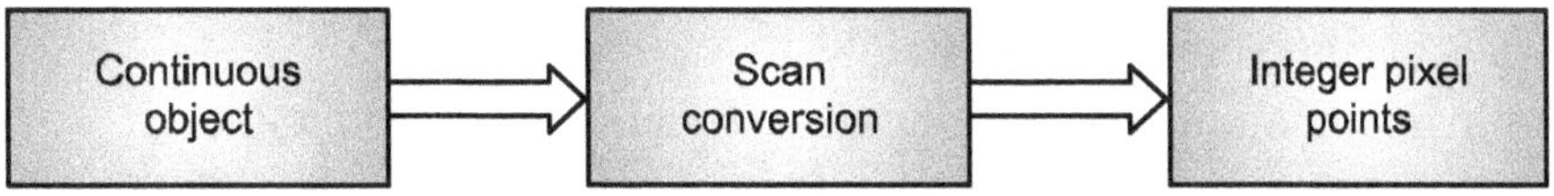

Fig. 4.12: Continuous-to-discrete transformation

- The most used graphic objects are the lines, the sectors, the arcs, the ellipses, the rectangles and the polygons.
- The process of representing continuous graphical objects as a collection of discrete pixels by identifying their locations and setting them ON is called scan conversion.

- Two ways to create an image:
    1. Scan existing photograph, and
    2. Procedurally compute values, (rendering).

4.3.1 Generation of the Display

- Following are the various way to display object:

1. **Sharper Text:**

- The text appears much sharper on a high-density display.
- The font size is the same relative to the rest of the page, but the text is drawn at the hardware pixel level. So, a font size of 14px will take up 14 CSS pixels but render at 28 hardware pixels.

2. **Sharper Icons:**

- Technically this could fall under "text", but lately there's been a movement to use icon fonts such as FontAwesome to render icons instead of traditional images.
- The advantages include the ability to specify the color, size and hover effects via CSS so you don't need separate images for each color variant.
- Essentially this is a creative and easy way to use vectors in web design that are sharp at any size, and the same high-DPI benefits apply here too. An icon-font icon will be sized with CSS pixels but rendered with hardware pixels.

3. **High-resolution Images:**

- These are also called Retina images because the techniques were first pioneered by Apple.
- It involves delivering a different set of images to higher-density displays so that they render using hardware pixels instead of software pixels. This results in a much sharper image while still being fully backwards-compatible with 1:1 density screens.

4.3.2 Image Compression

- The number of bytes needed to represent an uncompressed image is very large. In order to reduce the amount of storage space required for a document, the image must be convened into a smaller form by removing surplus information. There are three ways of convening image data:
    - Text in document images may be converted from raster to ASCII.
    - Line art can be vectorised, using mathematical formulae.
    - Bitonal and continuous tone still images can be digitized and encoded using a variety of established algorithms.
- Compression techniques may be of two types – Lossy (data is not exactly recoverable) and Lossless (data can be recovered without loss).

- Image compression is minimizing the size in bytes of a graphics file without degrading the quality of the image to an unacceptable level.
- Image compression is the method of data compression on digital images.
- The main objective in the image compression is:
  1. Store data in an efficient form, and
  2. Transmit data in an efficient form.
- Compression is achieved by the removal of one or more of the three basic data redundancies:
  1. Coding Redundancy,
  2. Interpixel Redundancy, and
  3. Psychovisual Redundancy.
- Coding redundancy is present when less than optimal code words are used. Interpixel redundancy results from correlations between the pixels of an image. Psychovisual redundancy is due to data that is ignored by the human visual system (i.e. visually non essential information).
- Image compression techniques reduce the number of bits required to represent an image by taking advantage of these redundancies.
- An inverse process called decompression (decoding) is applied to the compressed data to get the reconstructed image.
- The objective of compression is to reduce the number of bits as much as possible, while keeping the resolution and the visual quality of the reconstructed image as close to the original image as possible.
- Image compression systems are composed of two distinct structural blocks: an encoder and a decoder.
- Methods for Lossless Image Compression:
  1. Run-length encoding – used as default method in PCX and as one of possible in BMP, TGA, TIFF.
  2. Area image compression.
  3. DPCM and Predictive Coding.
  4. Entropy encoding.
  5. Adaptive dictionary algorithms such as LZW – used in GIF and TIFF.
  6. Deflation – used in PNG, MNG, and TIFF.
  7. Chain codes.

- Methods for Lossy Image Compression:
  1. **Reducing the color space** to the most common colors in the image. The selected colors are specified in the color palette in the header of the compressed image. Each pixel just references the index of a color in the color palette, this method can be combined with dithering to avoid posterization.
  2. **Chroma subsampling:** This takes advantage of the fact that the human eye perceives spatial changes of brightness more sharply than those of color, by averaging or dropping some of the chrominance information in the image.
  3. **Transform coding:** A Fourier-related transform such as the Discrete Cosine Transform (DCT) is widely used. The DCT is sometimes referred to as "DCT-II" in the context of a family of discrete cosine transforms; e.g., discrete cosine transform.

4.4 POLYGON FILLING [Oct. 16]

4.4.1 Introduction

- A polygon is a closed plane Fig. made up of several line segments that are joined together. The sides do not cross each other. Exactly two sides meet at every vertex.
- Basically, there are two types of polygons as explained below:

1. **Convex Polygon:**

- **Definition:** "A polygon in which the line segment joining any two points within polygon lies completely inside the polygon is called as convex polygon. "
- Fig. 4.13 demonstrates few examples of convex polygon.

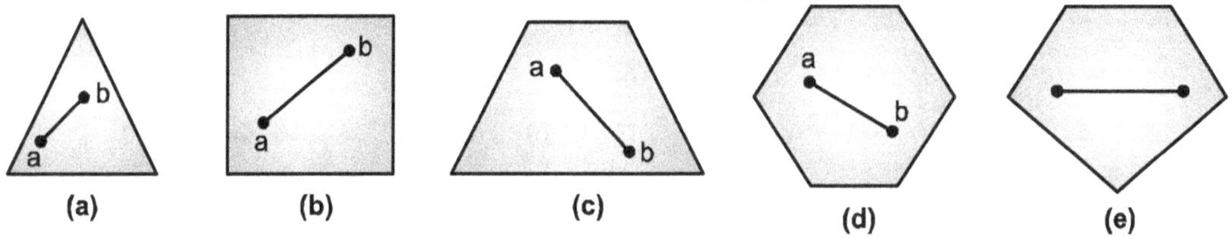

Fig. 4.13: Convex Polygons

2. **Concave Polygon:**

- **Definition:** "A polygon in which the line segment joining any two points within polygon may or may not lie completely inside polygon is called as concave polygon."
- Fig. 4.13 demonstrates few examples of concave polygon.

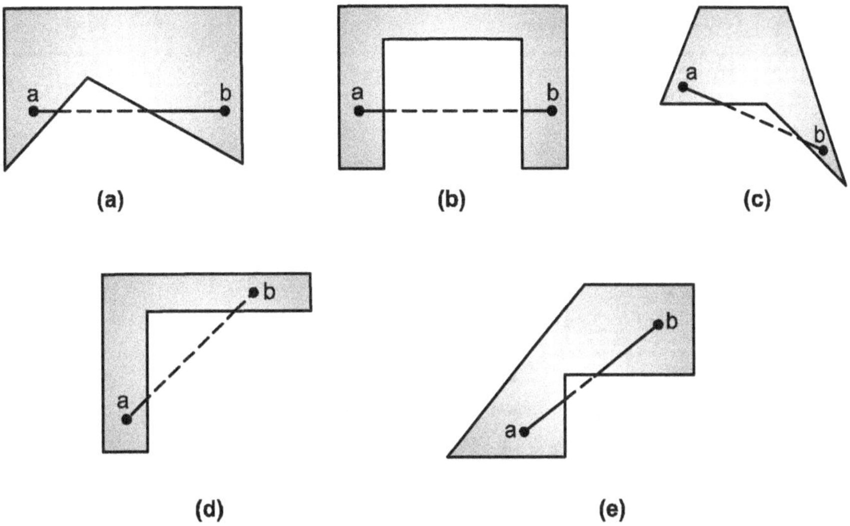

Fig. 4.14: Concave Polygons

4.4.2 Polygon Filling [Oct. 16]

- For filling polygons with particular colors, you need to determine the pixels falling on the border of the polygon and those which fall inside the polygon.
- Filling any polygon means highlighting all the pixels which lie inside the polygon with any colour other than background colour.

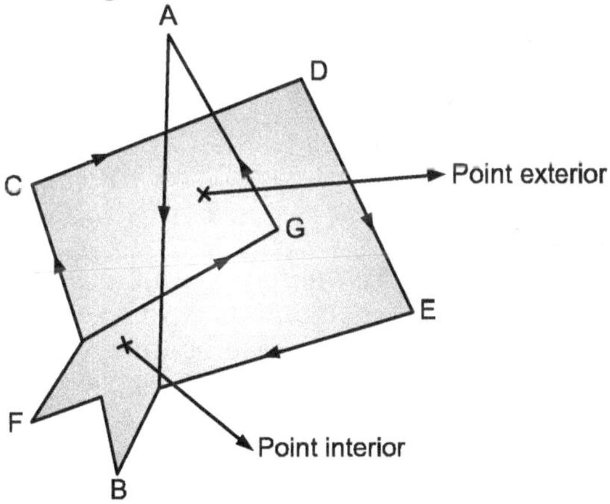

Fig. 4.15: Non-zero winding number test

- We try to fill the interior of a (polygon) area with a solid fill colour or pattern.
- There are two known approaches used to fill a polygon:
  1. Determine the overlap intervals of scan lines that cross the (polygon) area. This approach is known as scan-line algorithm.
  2. Start from a known interior point and flood the interior until you reach the boundary. This approach is known as Boundary fill algorithm.
- In this section, we will see how we can fill polygons using different techniques.

4.4.2.1 Scan Line Algorithm

- For each scan line crossing a polygon, the area-fill algorithm locates the intersection points of the scan line with the polygon edges.
- These intersection points are then sorted from left to right, and the corresponding frame-buffer positions between each intersection pair are set to the specified fill color.
- Scan line algorithm works by intersecting scan line with polygon edges and fills the polygon between pairs of intersections. The following steps depict how this algorithm works.

Step 1 : Find out the Y_{min} and Y_{max} from the given polygon.

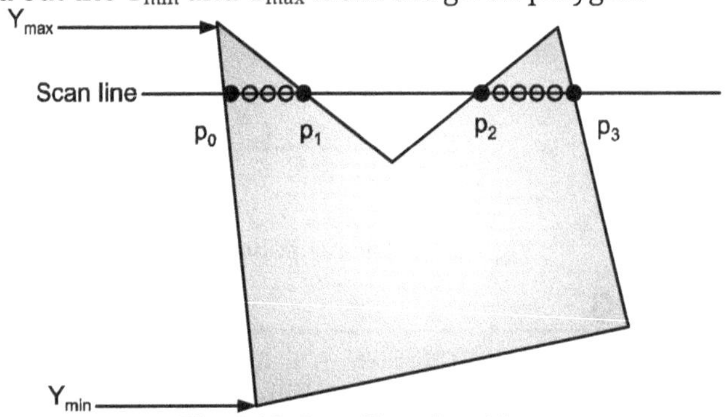

Fig. 4.16: Scan line algorithm

Step 2 : ScanLine intersects with each edge of the polygon from Y_{min} to Y_{max}. Name each intersection point of the polygon. As per the Fig. 4.16 shown, they are named as p_0, p_1, p_2, p_3.

Step 3 : Sort the intersection point in the increasing order of X coordinate i.e. (p_0, p_1), (p_1, p_2), and (p_2, p_3).

Step 4 : Fill all those pair of coordinates that are inside polygons and ignore the alternate pairs.

4.4.2.2 Flood Fill Algorithm

- Sometimes, we come across an object where we want to fill the area and its boundary with different colors. We can paint such objects with a specified interior color instead of searching for particular boundary color as in boundary filling algorithm.
- In other words, sometimes if we want to fill in (or recolor) an area that is not defined within a single color boundary.
- Fig. 4.17 shows an area bordered by several different color regions. We can paint such areas by replacing a specified interior color instead of searching for a boundary color value. This approach is called a flood-fill algorithm.

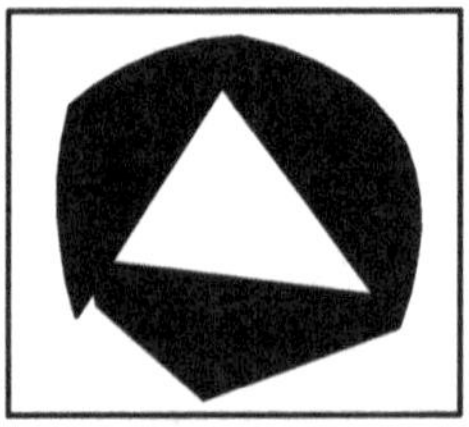

Fig. 4.17: Flood fill algorithm

- Instead of relying on the boundary of the object, it relies on the fill color. In other words, it replaces the interior color of the object with the fill color. When no more pixels of the original interior color exist, the algorithm is completed.
- Once again, this algorithm relies on the Four-connect or Eight-connect method of filling in the pixels. But instead of looking for the boundary color, it is looking for all adjacent pixels that are a part of the interior.

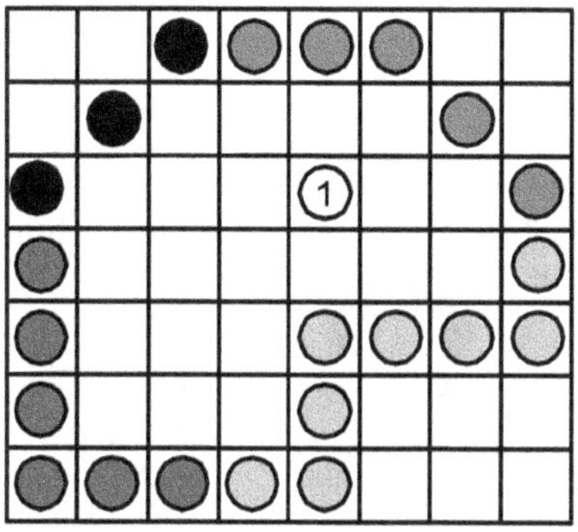

Fig. 4.18

4.4.2.3 Boundary Fill Algorithm [April 16]

- The boundary fill algorithm works as its name. This algorithm picks a point inside an object and starts to fill until it hits the boundary of the object. The color of the boundary and the color that we fill should be different for this algorithm to work.
- In this algorithm, we assume that color of the boundary is same for the entire object. The boundary fill algorithm can be implemented by 4-connected pixels or 8-connected pixels.

1. **4-Connected Polygon:**

- In this technique 4-connected pixels are used as shown in the Fig. 4.19.
- We are putting the pixels above, below, to the right, and to the left side of the current pixels and this process will continue until we find a boundary with different color.

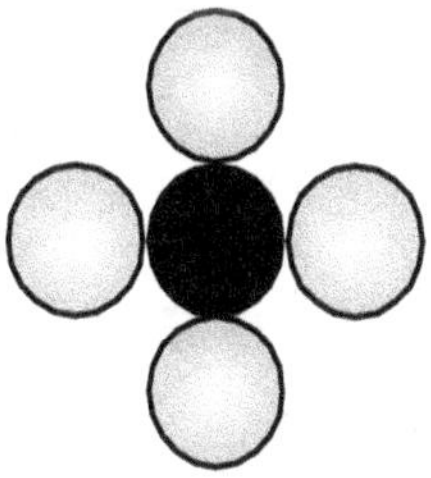

Fig. 4.19: Boundary fill algorithm

Algorithm:

Step 1: Initialize the value of seed point (seedx, seedy), fcolor and dcol.

Step 2: Define the boundary values of the polygon.

Step 3: Check if the current seed point is of default color, then repeat the steps 4 and 5 till the boundary pixels reached.

```
If getpixel(x, y) = dcol then repeat step 4 and 5
```

Step 4: Change the default color with the fill color at the seed point.

```
setPixel(seedx, seedy, fcol)
```

Step 5: Recursively follow the procedure with four neighborhood points.

```
FloodFill (seedx - 1, seedy, fcol, dcol)
FloodFill (seedx + 1, seedy, fcol, dcol)
FloodFill (seedx, seedy - 1, fcol, dcol)
FloodFill (seedx - 1, seedy + 1, fcol, dcol)
```

Step 6: Exit

- There is a problem with this technique. Consider the case as shown in Fig. 4.20, where we tried to fill the entire region. Here, the image is filled only partially. In such cases, 4-connected pixels technique cannot be used.

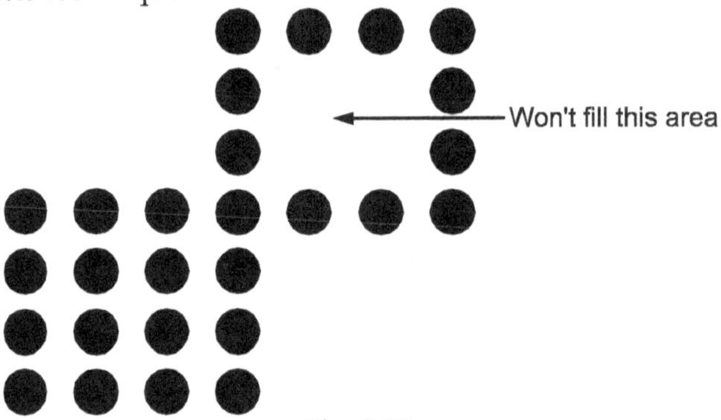

Fig. 4.20

2. **8-Connected Polygon:**

- In this technique 8-connected pixels are used as shown in the Fig. 4.21.
- We are putting pixels above, below, right and left side of the current pixels as we were doing in 4-connected technique.
- In addition to this, we are also putting pixels in diagonals so that entire area of the current pixel is covered. This process will continue until we find a boundary with different color.

Fig. 4.21: 8-connected pixels

Algorithm:

Step 1: Initialize the value of seed point (seedx, seedy), fcolor and dcol.

Step 2: Define the boundary values of the polygon.

Step 3: Check if the current seed point is of default color then repeat the steps 4 and 5 till the boundary pixels reached

```
If getpixel(x,y) = dcol then repeat step 4 and 5
```

Step 4: Change the default color with the fill color at the seed point.

```
setPixel(seedx, seedy, fcol)
```

Step 5: Recursively follow the procedure with four neighbourhood points

```
FloodFill (seedx - 1, seedy, fcol, dcol)
FloodFill (seedx + 1, seedy, fcol, dcol)
FloodFill (seedx, seedy - 1, fcol, dcol)
FloodFill (seedx, seedy + 1, fcol, dcol)
FloodFill (seedx - 1, seedy + 1, fcol, dcol)
FloodFill (seedx + 1, seedy + 1, fcol, dcol)
FloodFill (seedx + 1, seedy - 1, fcol, dcol)
FloodFill (seedx - 1, seedy - 1, fcol, dcol)
```

Step 6: Exit

- The 4-connected pixel technique failed to fill the area as marked in the Fig. 4.22 which won't happen with the 8-connected technique.

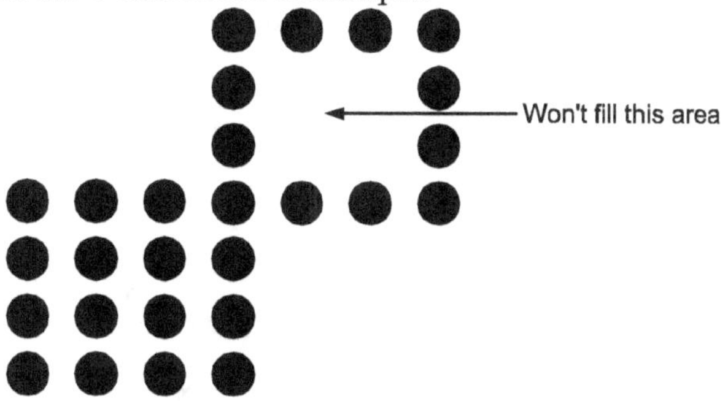

Fig. 4.22: 4-connected pixel technique

Inside-outside Test:

- This method is also known as counting number method. While filling an object, we often need to identify whether particular point is inside the object or outside it.
- There are two methods by which we can identify whether particular point is inside an object or outside:

  1. Odd-Even Rule, and 2. Non-zero winding number rule.

1. Odd-Even Rule:

- In this technique, we count the edge crossing along the line from any point (x, y) to infinity. If the number of interactions is odd then the point (x, y) is an interior point. If the number of interactions is even then point (x, y) is an exterior point.
- Here is the example to give you the clear idea, (See Fig. 4.23).

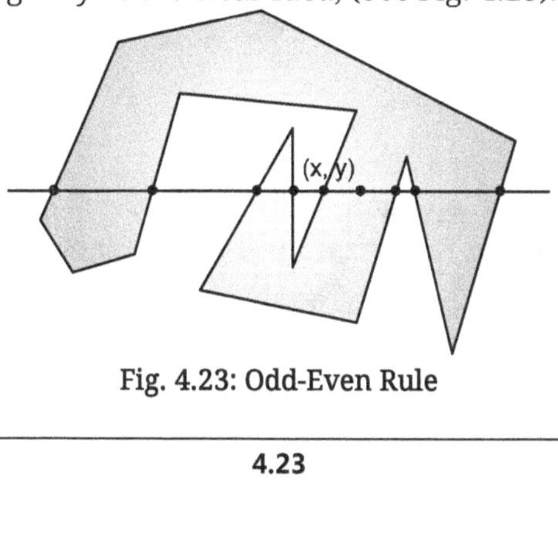

Fig. 4.23: Odd-Even Rule

- From the Fig. 4.23, we can see that from the point (x, y), the number of interactions point on the left side is 5 and on the right side is 3. So the total number of interaction point is 8, which is odd. Hence, the point is considered within the object.

2. **Non-zero Winding Number Rule:**

- This method is also used with the simple polygons to test the given point is interior or not. It can be simply understood with the help of a pin and a rubber band.
- Fix up the pin on one of the edge of the polygon and tie-up the rubber band in it and then stretch the rubber band along the edges of the polygon.
- When all the edges of the polygon are covered by the rubber band, check out the pin which has been fixed up at the point to be test. If we find at least one wind at the point consider it within the polygon, else we can say that the point is not inside the polygon.

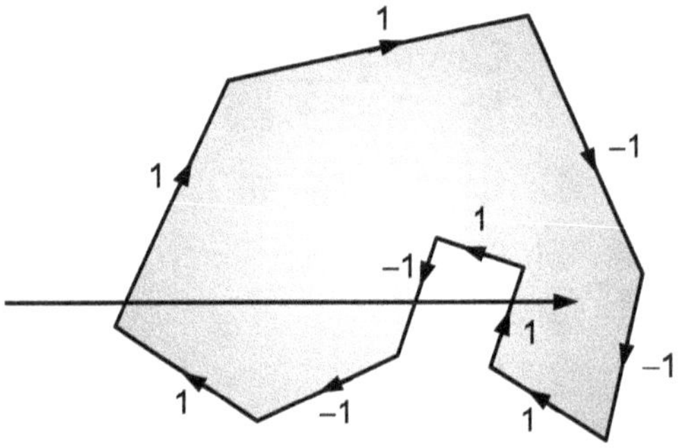

Fig. 4.24: Non-zero Winding Number Rule

- In another alternative method, give directions to all the edges of the polygon. Draw a scan line from the point to be test towards the left most of X direction.
  - Give the value 1 to all the edges which are going to upward direction and all other – 1 as direction values.
  - Check the edge direction values from which the scan line is passing and sum up them.
  - If the total sum of this direction value is non-zero, then this point to be tested is an interior point, otherwise it is an exterior point.
  - In the above figure, we sum up the direction values from which the scan line is passing then the total is 1 – 1 + 1 = 1; which is non-zero. So the point is said to be an interior point.

SUMMARY

- DDA is used for linear interpolation of variables over an interval between start and end point. DDAs are used for rasterization of lines, triangles and polygons.
- Symmetrical DDA (digital differential analyzer) generates lines from their differential equations. It is important to note that DDAs can also be used to generate arcs and other curves.

- Simple DDA - choose a line length estimate that is equal to the max(Δx, Δy) in such a way that e(Δx) or e(Δy) is of unit magnitude. This implies that one of the counters is simply an increment by 1. That is, if e=1/(max(Δx, Δy)) then either e(Δx) = 1 or e(Δy) = 1.
- The Bresenham line algorithm is an algorithm which determines which points in an n-dimensional raster should be plotted in order to form a close approximation to a straight line between two given points. It is commonly used to draw lines on a computer screen, as it uses only integer addition, subtraction and bit shifting, all of which are very cheap operations in standard computer architectures. It is one of the earliest algorithms developed in the field of computer graphics. A minor extension to the original algorithm also deals with drawing circles.
- Scan conversion or scan rate converting is a technique for changing the vertical / horizontal scan frequency of video signal for different purposes and applications. The device which performs this conversion is called scan converter. The application of scan conversion is wide and covers video projectors, cinema equipment , TV and video capture cards, standard and HDTV televisions, LCD monitors and many different aspects of picture and video processing.
- A Circle is a symmetric figure. It has 8-way symmetry. Thus a circle generating algorithm can take advantage of circle symmetry to plot 8 points by calculating the co-ordinate of any one point.
- The midpoint circle algorithm is an algorithm used to determine the points needed for drawing a circle. The algorithm is a variant of Bresenham's line algorithm, and is thus sometimes known as Bresenham's circle algorithm, although not actually invented by Bresenham.
- In the mid-point circle algorithm we use eight-way symmetry so only ever calculate the points for the top right eighth of a circle, and then use symmetry to get the rest of the points.
- When starting point & the terminal point of any polyline is same i.e. when polyline is
- closed then it is called as a polygon.
- There are two types of polygons i.e., convex and concave polygons. A convex polygon is a polygon in which the line segment joining any 2 points within the polygon lies completely inside the polygon. A Concave Polygon is a polygon in which the line segment joining any 2 points within the polygon lies partially outside the polygon.
- To show that a polygon is a solid object we need to set pixel inside the polygon as well as on the boundary. One simple method to determine whether a point is inside a polygon or not is to determine an inside outside test.
- Filling in the polygon means highlighting all the pixels while lie inside the polygon with any colour other than the background colour.

- In flood fill method approach we start from a given seed point known to be inside the polygon and highlight outwards from this point until we encounter the boundary pixels.
- This approach is called the flood fill because colour flows from the seed pixel until
- reaching the polygon boundary like water flooding on the surface of a container.
- There are 2 methods for proceeding to the neighboring pixels i.e., 4 Connected (In this case, the pixel-position that are to the right, left, above and below. The current pixel are tested) and 8 Connected (In this case, along with the 4 pixel positions used in the 4-connected method, 4-diagonal pixels are also tested).
- The DDA is an algorithm for calculating the pixel positions along a line.

PRACTICE QUESTIONS

1. What is raster graphics?
2. List out the key features of raster graphics.
3. What is rasterization?
4. List out advantages of DDA
5. What is non-zero winding number rule.
6. What is scan conversion.
7. What is interior and exterior point.
8. Differentiate concave and convex polygon.
9. Explain the concept of polygon filling.
10. Explain the working of Bresenham's line drawing algorithm.
11. Write a note on circle generation algorithm.
12. Highlight Generation of Display.
13. Compare various techniques of polygon feeling.
14. Write down steps for flood fill algorithm.
15. List out and compare different line drawing algorithm.

CHAPTER 5

Transformations

Contents ...

Objectives...

- To Study Transformation Concepts
- To Learn Transformation of various Shapes
- To Study Viewing Pipeline

5.1 INTRODUCTION

- The term 'transform' means to 'change'.
- Transformation means changing some graphics into something else by applying rules.
- Transformations play an important role in computer graphics to reposition the graphics on the screen and change their size or orientation.

Need of Transformations:

- In many applications of computer graphics, we need to alter and manipulate displayed graphical objects either interactively or non-interactively. One such an application is animation.
- In animation, one need to move object along some specified path. Such changes in orientation, size and shape of an object alter co-ordinates of object and this is done with geometric transformation.
- Also in CAD/CAM, where we need to design a wire-frame structure of some object, the facility layout diagrams and their components such as lines, curves and surfaces undergo frequent changes interactively. Such kinds of alternation and manipulation of displayed graphical objects are classified under the generic name geometrical transformations.
- In other words, geometrical transformations are the tools using which we can change shape, size, position and orientation of displayed objects on active output devices.
- Basic geometric transformations are:
    1. Translation,
    2. Scaling, and
    3. Rotation.
- Other transformations are:
    1. Reflection, and
    2. Shear.
- Following Fig. 5.1 demonstrates the visual effect of different transformations.

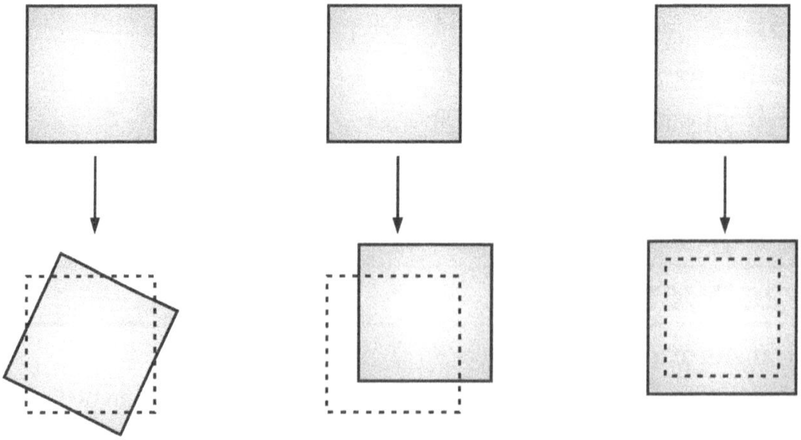

(a) Rotation (b) Translation (c) Uniform Scaling

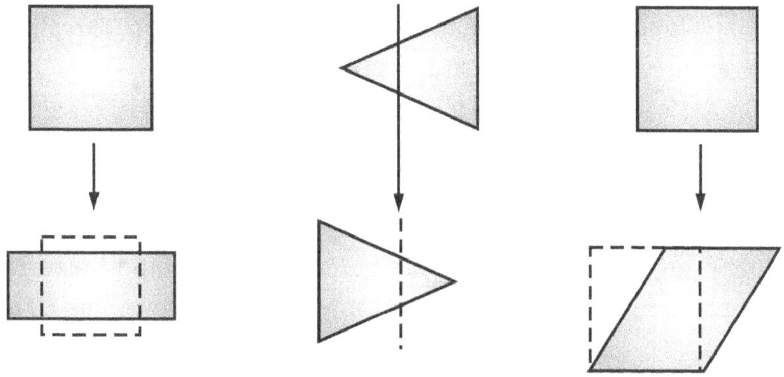

(d) Non-uniform Scaling (e) Reflection (f) Shearing

Fig. 5.1

5.2 BASIC TRANSFORMATIONS

5.2.1 Translation

- A translation is applied to an object by repositioning it along a straight-line path from one coordinate location to another.
- Translation refers to the shifting (moving) of a point to some other place, whose distance with regard to the present point is known.
- Translation can be defined as "the process of repositioning an object along a straight line path from one co-ordinate location to new co-ordinate location."
- A translation moves an object to a different position on the screen. You can translate a point in 2D by adding translation coordinate (t_x, t_y) to the original coordinate (X, Y) to get the new coordinate (X', Y').

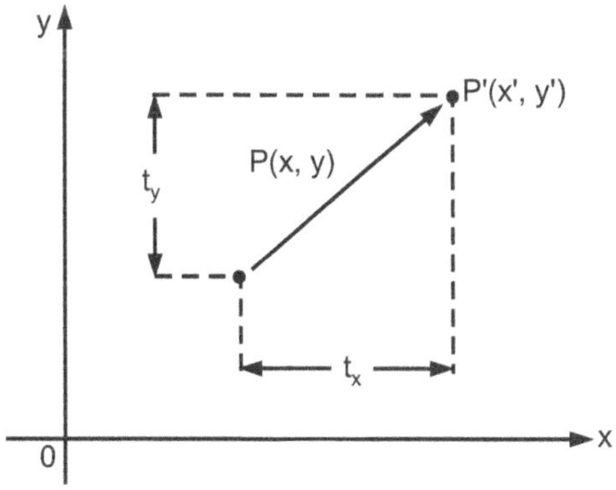

Fig. 5.2

- From the Fig. 5.2, you can write that:

$$X' = X + t_x$$

$$Y' = Y + t_y$$

- The pair (t_x, t_y) is called the translation vector or shift vector. The above equations can also be represented using the column vectors.

$$P = [X] [Y] \quad p' = [X'] [Y'] \quad T = [t_x] [t_y]$$

- We can write it as,

$$P' = P + T$$

Example:

- To translate (move) a two dimensional point one need to add translation distance tx and ty along x and y axis respectively (or any one of it) to original co-ordinate position as,

$$x' = x + t_x$$
$$y' = y + t_y$$

Where,

(x, y) = Original co-ordinates of a point.

(x', y') = New co-ordinates of a point.

t_x, t_y = Translation distance (factor) in x and y direction. Translation is rigid motion of points to new locations and moves object without deformation.

- Matrix form defined with column vectors:

$$\begin{bmatrix} x' \\ y' \end{bmatrix} = \begin{bmatrix} x \\ y \end{bmatrix} \begin{bmatrix} t_x \\ t_y \end{bmatrix}$$

i.e.

$$P' = P + T$$

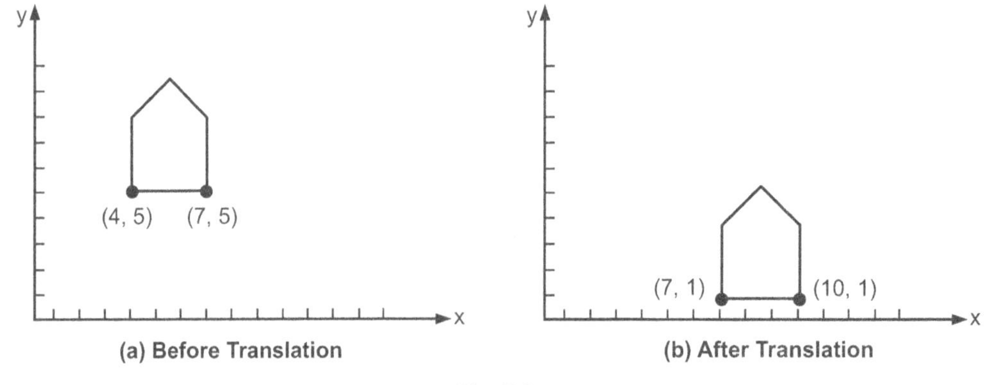

Fig. 5.3

5.2.2 Rotation [April 16]

- Rotation as the name suggests is to rotate a point about an axis. The axis can be any of the co-ordinates or simply any other specified line also.
- In rotation, we rotate the object at particular angle θ (theta) from its origin. From the following figure, we can see that the point P(X, Y) is located at angle ϕ from the horizontal X coordinate with distance r from the origin.

- Let us, suppose you want to rotate it at the angle θ. After rotating it to a new location, you will get a new point P' (X', Y').

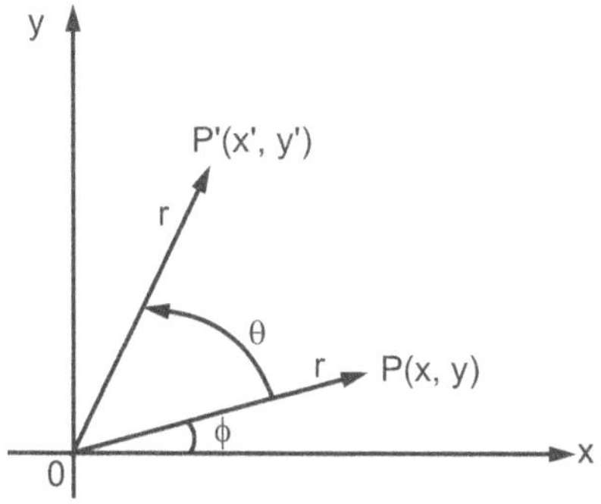

Fig. 5.4

- Using standard trigonometric the original coordinate of point P(X, Y) can be represented as:

$$X = r\cos\phi \quad \ldots (1)$$
$$Y = r\sin\phi \quad \ldots (2)$$

- Same way we can represent the point P' (X', Y') as:

$$x' = r\cos(\phi + \theta) = r\cos\theta\cos\theta - r\sin\phi\sin\theta \quad \ldots (3)$$
$$y' = r\sin(\phi + \theta) = r\cos\theta\sin\theta + r\sin\phi\cos\theta \quad \ldots (4)$$

- Substituting equation (1) and (2) in (3) and (4) respectively, we will get

$$x' = x\cos\theta - y\sin\theta$$
$$y' = x\sin\theta + y\cos\theta$$

- Representing the above equation in matrix form,

$$[X'\ Y'] = [X'\ Y']\begin{bmatrix} \cos\theta & \sin\theta \\ -\sin\theta & \cos\theta \end{bmatrix}$$

OR

$$P' = P \cdot R$$

- Where, R is the rotation matrix

$$R = \begin{bmatrix} \cos\theta & \sin\theta \\ -\sin\theta & \cos\theta \end{bmatrix}$$

- The rotation angle can be positive and negative.
- For positive rotation angle, we can use the above rotation matrix. However, for negative angle rotation the matrix will change as shown below:

$$R = \begin{bmatrix} \cos(-\theta) & \sin(-\theta) \\ -\sin(-\theta) & \cos(-\theta) \end{bmatrix}$$
$$= \begin{bmatrix} \cos\theta & -\sin\theta \\ \sin\theta & \cos\theta \end{bmatrix}$$

($\because \cos(-\theta) = \cos\theta$ and $\sin(-\theta) = -\sin\theta$)

- Rotation may be the X-axis, the Y-axis or any arbitrary line on the X-Y plane. Rotations are performed about some fixed point called the pivot point or centre of rotation.

Example: Fig. 5.5 shows example of rotation.

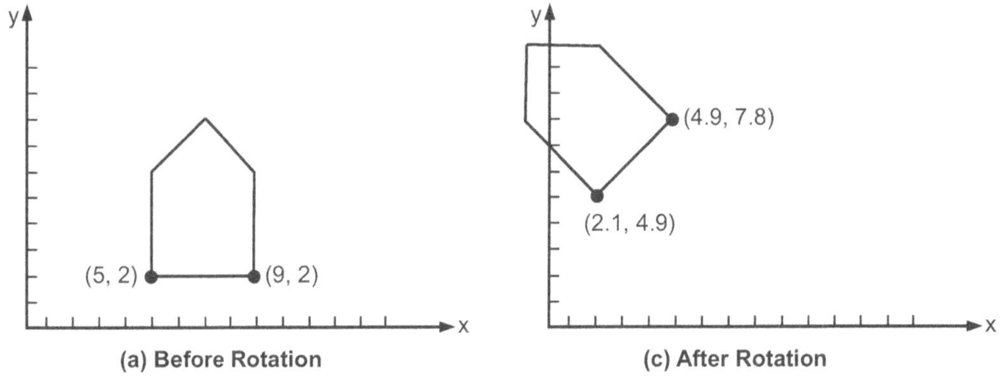

Fig. 5.5

5.2.3 Scaling [April 16]

- Scaling means to change the size of object. This change can either be positive or negative.
- To change the size of an object, scaling transformation is used. In the scaling process, you either expand or compress the dimensions of the object.
- Scaling can be achieved by multiplying the original co-ordinates of the object with the scaling factor to get the desired result.
- Let us assume that the original co-ordinates are (X, Y), the scaling factors are (S_X, S_Y), and the produced co-ordinates are (X', Y'). This can be mathematically represented as shown below:

$$X' = X \cdot S_X \text{ and } Y' = Y \cdot S_Y$$

- The scaling factor S_X, S_Y scales the object in X and Y direction respectively. The above equations can also be represented in matrix form as below:

$$\begin{bmatrix} X' \\ Y' \end{bmatrix} = \begin{bmatrix} X \\ Y \end{bmatrix} \begin{bmatrix} S_x & 0 \\ 0 & S_y \end{bmatrix}$$

OR

$$P' = P \cdot S$$

Where, S is the scaling matrix.

- The scaling process is shown in the Fig. 5.6.

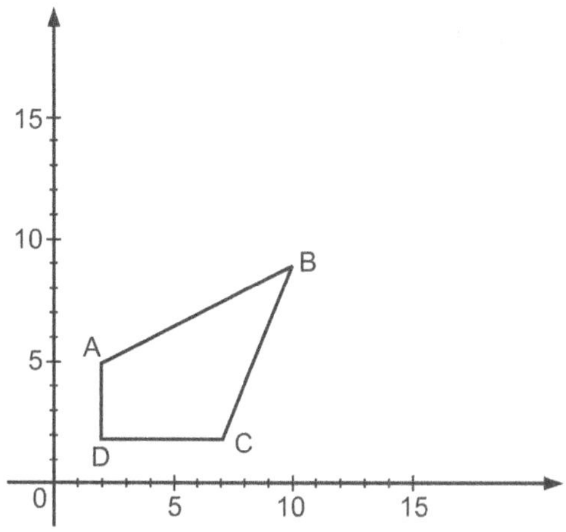

(a) Before Scaling

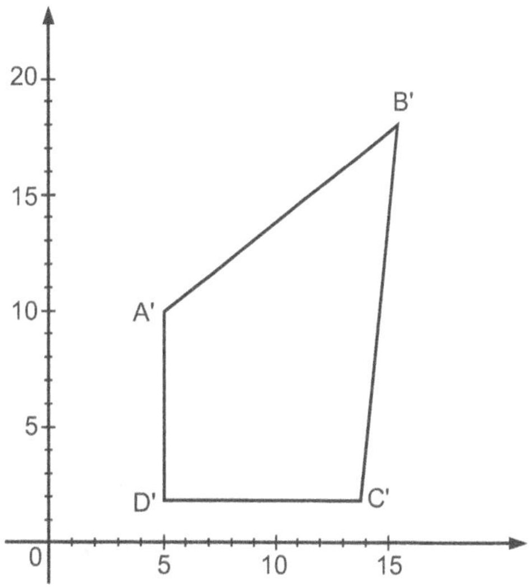

(b) After Scaling

Fig. 5.6

- If we provide values less than 1 to the scaling factor S, then we can reduce the size of the object. If we provide values greater than 1, then we can increase the size of the object.

5.2.4 Matrix Representation

- We can now write down a general formula for the transformation of points,

$$x' = a \cdot x + b \cdot y + c$$
$$y' = d \cdot x + e \cdot y + f$$

where a, b, c, d, e and f are all constants. The expressions for x' and y' are linear functions for x and y. This can be re-expressed using matrices as:

$$\begin{bmatrix} x' \\ y' \end{bmatrix} = \begin{bmatrix} a & b \\ d & e \end{bmatrix} \cdot \begin{bmatrix} x \\ y \end{bmatrix} + \begin{bmatrix} c \\ f \end{bmatrix}$$

- Now include all of the constants in one matrix,

$$\begin{bmatrix} x' \\ y' \end{bmatrix} = \begin{bmatrix} a & b & c \\ d & e & f \end{bmatrix} \cdot \begin{bmatrix} x \\ y \\ 1 \end{bmatrix}$$

- A square matrix is much easier to deal with, so the matrix is extended to as 3×3 matrix, as given below:

$$\begin{bmatrix} x' \\ y' \\ \omega' \end{bmatrix} = \begin{bmatrix} a & b & c \\ d & e & f \\ g & h & i \end{bmatrix} \cdot \begin{bmatrix} x \\ y \\ 1 \end{bmatrix}$$

- A column vectors representing points now have an extra entry. If the bottom row of the matrix is [0 0 1] then ω' will be 1 and we can ignore it. The effect of setting the bottom row of the matrix to values other than [0 0 1].
- The formulae for each of the different types of transformation can now be rewritten using this matrix notation:
  - **Translate:** $\begin{bmatrix} 1 & 0 & t_x \\ 0 & 1 & t_y \\ 0 & 0 & 1 \end{bmatrix}$
  - **Scale:** $\begin{bmatrix} s_x & 0 & 0 \\ 0 & s_y & 0 \\ 0 & 0 & 1 \end{bmatrix}$
  - **Rotate:** $\begin{bmatrix} \cos\alpha & -\sin\alpha & 0 \\ \sin\alpha & \cos\alpha & 0 \\ 0 & 0 & 1 \end{bmatrix}$
  - **Shear:** $\begin{bmatrix} 1 & a & 0 \\ b & 1 & 0 \\ 0 & 0 & 1 \end{bmatrix}$
- There is a special matrix which leaves the co-ordinates x' and y' equal to x and y. This is known as the unit or identity matrix:

$$\begin{bmatrix} x' \\ y' \\ \omega' \end{bmatrix} = \begin{bmatrix} 1 & 0 & 0 \\ 0 & 1 & 0 \\ 0 & 0 & 1 \end{bmatrix} \cdot \begin{bmatrix} x \\ y \\ 1 \end{bmatrix}$$

$$x' = x$$

$$y' = y$$

$$\omega' = 1$$

5.2.5 Homogenous Co-ordinates

- To perform a sequence of transformation such as translation followed by rotation and scaling, we need to follow a sequential process:
  1. Translate the co-ordinates,
  2. Rotate the translated co-ordinates, and then
  3. Scale the rotated co-ordinates to complete the composite transformation.
- To shorten this process, we have to use 3 × 3 transformation matrix instead of 2 × 2 transformation matrix. To convert a 2 × 2 matrix to 3 × 3 matrix, we have to add an extra dummy coordinate W.

- In this way, we can represent the point by 3 numbers instead of 2 numbers, which is called Homogenous co-ordinate system.
- In homogeneous co-ordinate system, we can represent all the transformation equations in matrix multiplication. Any Cartesian point P(X, Y) can be converted to homogenous co-ordinates by P' (X_h, Y_h, h).
- Very important advantage of co-ordinate system is it allows us to express all transformation equations as matrix multiplications, which is very much useful in composite transformations.

Homogeneous Matrix Representation of 2D Transformations :

- **Translation:** $$\begin{bmatrix} x' \\ y' \\ 1 \end{bmatrix} = \begin{bmatrix} 1 & 0 & t_x \\ 0 & 1 & t_y \\ 0 & 0 & 1 \end{bmatrix} \cdot \begin{bmatrix} x \\ y \\ 1 \end{bmatrix}$$
- **Scale:** $$\begin{bmatrix} x' \\ y' \\ 1 \end{bmatrix} = \begin{bmatrix} S_x & 0 & 0 \\ 0 & S_y & 0 \\ 0 & 0 & 1 \end{bmatrix} \cdot \begin{bmatrix} x \\ y \\ 1 \end{bmatrix}$$
- **Rotation:** $$\begin{bmatrix} x' \\ y' \\ 1 \end{bmatrix} = \begin{bmatrix} \cos\theta & -\sin\theta & 0 \\ \sin\theta & \cos\theta & 0 \\ 0 & 0 & 1 \end{bmatrix} \times \begin{bmatrix} x \\ y \\ 1 \end{bmatrix}$$
- **Shear:** $$Sh_x = \begin{bmatrix} 1 & 0 & 0 \\ Sh_x & 1 & 0 \\ 0 & 0 & 1 \end{bmatrix}$$
- **Reflection:** $$F_y = \begin{bmatrix} 1 & 0 & 0 \\ 0 & -1 & 0 \\ 0 & 0 & 1 \end{bmatrix}$$

5.2.6 Reflection

- The term 'reflection' means to simply reflect an object in the plane mirror. The image is made on the opposite side.
- In short, reflection is the mirror image of original object. In other words, we can say that it is a rotation operation with 180°.
- In reflection transformation, the size of the object does not change.
- Fig. 5.7 show reflections with respect to X and Y axes, and about the origin respectively.

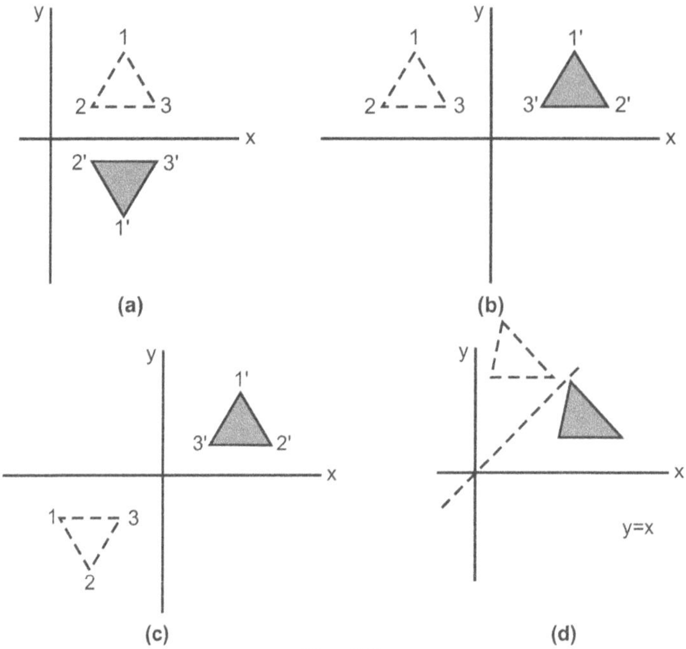

Fig. 5.7

5.2.7 Shear

- A transformation that distorts (deform or alter) the shape of an object such that the transformed shape appears as if the object were composed of internal layers that had been caused to slide over each other is called a shear.
- A transformation that slants the shape of an object is called the shear transformation.
- There are two shear transformations X-Shear and Y-Shear. One shifts X co-ordinates values and other shifts Y coordinate values. However; in both the cases only one coordinate changes its co-ordinates and other preserves its values.
- Shearing is also termed as Skewing.

1. **X-Shear:**

- The X-Shear preserves the Y coordinate and changes are made to X co-ordinates, which causes the vertical lines to tilt right or left as shown in Fig. 5.8 (i).

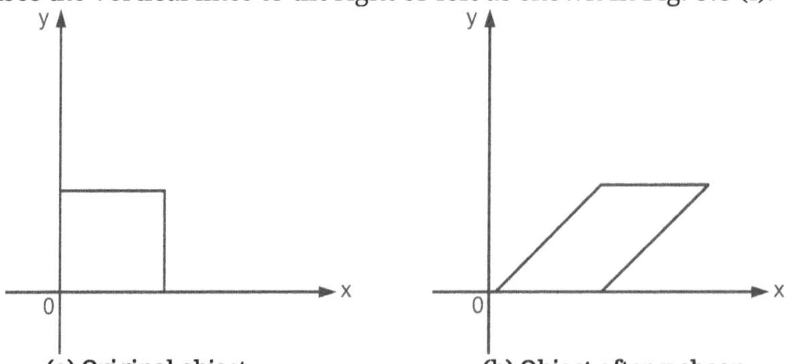

(a) Original object (b) Object after x shear

(i)

Fig. 5.8

- The transformation matrix for X-Shear can be represented as:

$$X_{sh} = \begin{bmatrix} 1 & 0 & 0 \\ Sh_x & 1 & 0 \\ 0 & 0 & 1 \end{bmatrix}$$

$$X' = X + Sh_x \cdot Y$$

$$Y' = Y$$

2. **Y-Shear:**

- The Y-Shear preserves the X co-ordinates and changes the Y co-ordinates which causes the horizontal lines to transform into lines which slopes up or down as shown in Fig. 5.8 (ii).

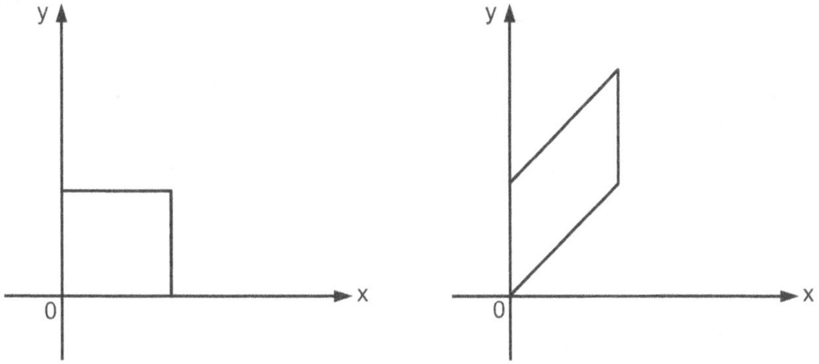

(a) Original object **(b) Object after y shear**

(ii)

Fig. 5.8

- The Y-Shear can be represented in matrix from as:

$$Y_{sh} = \begin{bmatrix} 1 & Sh_y & 0 \\ 0 & 1 & 0 \\ 0 & 0 & 1 \end{bmatrix}$$

$$Y' = Y + Sh_y \cdot X$$

$$X' = X$$

Example:

- Fig. 5.9 illustrates several different kinds of shear transformation applied to a rectangular object.

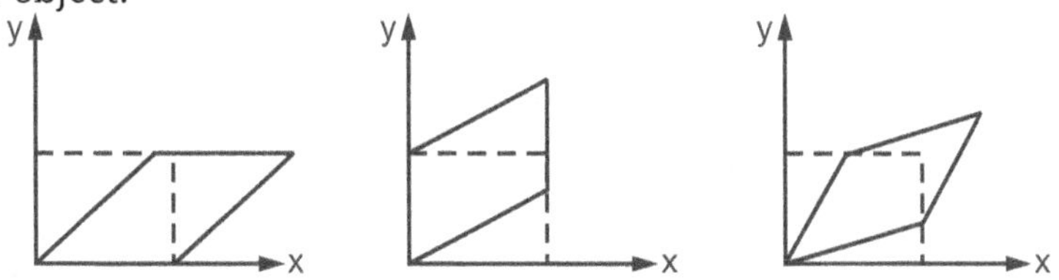

(a) Shear in x **(b) Shear in y** **(c) Shear in x and y**

Fig. 5.9: Shear transformations

- Fig. 5.9 (a) shows a shear in x in which the x-coordinates of points are displaced as a function of their height.
- Fig. 5.9 (b) shows a shear in y, where the y-coordinates are displaced according to their x-coordinate.
- Finally, a shear in both x and y is shown in Fig. 5.9 (c). The new x- and y-coordinates of a point after shearing are given by,

$$x' = x + y \cdot a$$
$$y' = y + x \cdot b$$

If $a \neq 0$ then a shear in x is obtained. Similarly, if $b \neq 0$ then a shear in y is obtained.

5.3 TRANSFORMATION OF VARIOUS SHAPES (Points, Lines, Parallel Lines, Intersecting Lines)

- We already knew that the term 'transform' means 'to change'. This change can either be of shape, size or position of the object. To perform transformation on any object, object matrix 'X' is multiplied by the transformation matrix 'T'.

$$[X^*] = [X]\ [T]$$

where,

[X*] is matrix of transformed object.

[X] is man ii of original object.

[T] is transformation matrix.

- The various transformations possible on an object are as follows:
  - Rotation
  - Shearing
  - Reflection
  - Translation
  - Scaling.

  Each or the above transformations is carried out by using a different transformation matrix.

1. **Points:**

- A transformation is any operation on a point in space (x, y) that maps the point's co-ordinates into a new set of co-ordinates (x_1, y_1).Where x represents the horizontal distance and y represents the vertical distance, while negative values are intended to represent moment in reverse direction.
- However, in context of graphics we tend to represent point as 3 value entity [x y 1] where, x, y are co-ordinates and 1 is added for representation Use of this additional value become significant.

- The mathematics of computer graphics is closely related to matrix multiplication. If you are not very familiar with the idea, this is the time to try to understand how to describe the basic transformations with matrices.
- Look carefully at the form of each standard 2×2 matrix A that describes the given transformation. For the transformation that rotates each point about the origin through an angle θ, the entries are cosines and sines of the angle θ. The standard matrix for the counterclockwise rotation with positive θ has the form $A = \begin{pmatrix} \cos\theta & -\sin\theta \\ \sin\theta & \cos\theta \end{pmatrix}$.

Note: For detail information Refer Section 1.2.3.

2. **Lines and Parallel lines, Intersecting Lines:**

- Line is given by two points , P_1 (starting point) and P_2 (ending point) where P_1 (x_1, y_1) and P_2 (x_2, y_2).
- Line transformation deals with its rotation. The rotation may be clockwise or anticlockwise.
- If anticlockwise angle of rotation is θ then rotate all points to around P_1 and P_2 by θ.
- The term affine transformation is used for transformation of lines. An affine transformation or an affinity is a function between affine spaces which preserves points, straight lines and planes. Sets of parallel lines remain parallel after an affine transformation.
- An affine transformation does not necessarily preserve angles between lines or distances between points, though it does preserve ratios of distances between points lying on a straight line.
- If X and Y are affine spaces, then every affine transformation $f : X \to Y$ is of the form $x \to Mx + b$, where M is a linear transformation on X and b is a vector in Y. Unlike a purely linear transformation, an affine map need not preserve the zero point in a linear space. Thus, every linear transformation is affine, but not every affine transformation is linear.
- Following are some definitions given for Geometric Line Transformations :

  Definition: Let $G_1 = (P_1, L_1)$ and $G_2 = (P_2, L_2)$ be two abstract geometries, and let $f : P_1 \to P_2$ a function that is objective. Then we say that f is a geometric transformation if f also maps L_1 onto L_2.
- In other words, a 1-1 transformation $f : P_1 \to P_2$ is geometric if takes the set P_1 of all points in L_1 onto the set P_2 of all points in L_2, and takes the set L_1 of all lines in G_1 onto the set L_2 of all lines in G_2.

- More generally line transformation can be given as, Any fixed line m, let f be the mapping defined by reflection in the line m. In other words, f maps any point in the plane to its 'mirror image' with respect to the mirror line m. For instance, when m is the x-axis, then f takes the point P = (x, y) in the plane to its mirror image P'(x, –y) with respect to the x-axis. Given a point P, let m' be the straight line through P that is perpendicular to m. Then P' is the point on m' on the opposite side of m to P that is equidistant from m.

Example: Consider a line A(2, 3) and B(8, 10). Obtain the coordinates of transformed line, using $[T] = \begin{bmatrix} 4 & 0 \\ 0 & 1 \end{bmatrix}$

Solution:

$$[X^*] = [X]\ [T]$$

$$= \begin{bmatrix} 2 & 3 \\ 8 & 10 \end{bmatrix} \begin{bmatrix} 4 & 0 \\ 0 & 1 \end{bmatrix}$$

$$[X^*] = \begin{bmatrix} 8 & 3 \\ 32 & 10 \end{bmatrix} \begin{matrix} A^* \\ B^* \end{matrix}$$

Hence, point A (2, 3) has been transformed into A* (8, 3) and point B(8, 10) has been transformed into B* (32, 10), as shown in Fig. 5.10 (a).

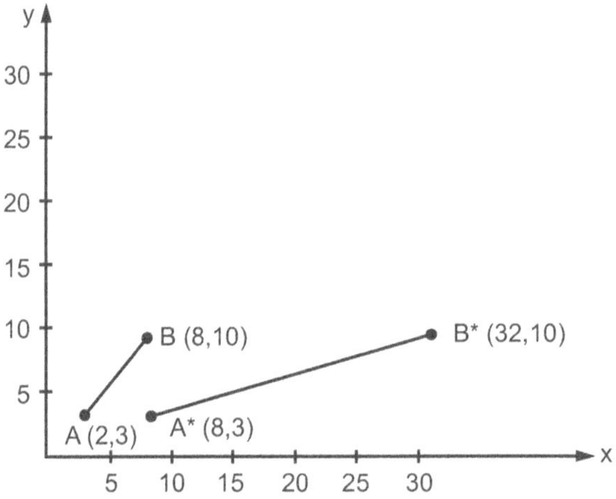

Fig. 5.10 (a): Transformation of a line

3. Transformation of Intersecting Lines:

When two intersecting lines are transformed using general 2 × 2 transformation matrix the resulting lines are also intersecting.

Consider two intersection lines,

$$y = m_1x + b_1$$

$$y = m_2x + b_2$$

The point of intersection:

$$[X_i] = [x_i \ y_i] = \begin{bmatrix} \dfrac{b_1 - b_2}{m_2 - m_1} & \dfrac{b_1m_2 - b_2m_1}{m_2 - m_1} \end{bmatrix}$$

$$\Rightarrow \qquad [X_i] = \begin{bmatrix} a & b \\ c & d \end{bmatrix}$$

Transformed point of intersection:

$$\begin{bmatrix} x_i' & y_i' \end{bmatrix} = \begin{bmatrix} \dfrac{a(b_1 - b_2) + c(b_1m_2 - b_2m_1)}{m_2 - m_1} & \dfrac{b(b_1 - b_2) + d(b_1m_2 - b_2m_1)}{m_2 - m_1} \end{bmatrix}$$

- A pair of non-perpendicular lines get transformed to perpendicular lines.
- By inverse T^{-1} a pair of perpendicular lines can get transformed to non-perpendicular lines.
- Such a result can have disastrous effect on the resulting geometry.

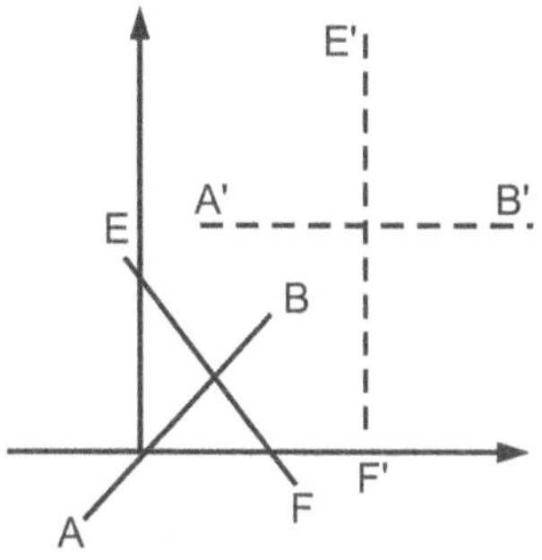

Fig. 5.10 (b)

4. **Intersecting Lines and Rigid Body Transformations:**

When two perpendicular lines transform as perpendicular lines?

Consider the scalar(dot) and vector products of two vectors as follows:

$$V_1 \cdot V_2 = V_{1x} V_{2x} + V_{1y} V_{2y} = |V_1| \ |V_2| \cos\theta$$

$$V_1 \times V_2 = (V_{1x} V_{2x} V_{1y} V_{2y}) \bar{k} = |V_1| \ |V_2| \bar{k} \sin\theta$$

Let us, now transform these vectors by general 2 × 2 T and find dot and cross products again

$$\begin{bmatrix} a & c \\ b & d \end{bmatrix} \begin{bmatrix} V_{1x} & V_{2x} \\ V_{1y} & V_{2y} \end{bmatrix} = \begin{bmatrix} aV_{1x} + cV_{1y} & aV_{2x} + cV_{2y} \\ bV_{1x} + dV_{1y} & bV_{2x} + dV_{2y} \end{bmatrix}$$

$$(a^2 + b^2) V_{1x} V_{2x} + (c^2 + d^2) V_{1y} V_{2y} + (ac + bd) (V_{1x} V_{2y} + V_{1y} V_{2x}) = |V_1'| \, |V_2'| \cos\theta$$

$$(ad - bc) \ (V_{1x} V_{2y} - V_{2x} V_{1y}) \bar{k} \, |V_1'| \, |V_2'| \, \bar{k} \sin\theta$$

We require for magnitude and angle to remain unchanged,

$a^2 + b^2 = c^2 + d^2 = 1$; $ac + bd = 0$; $ad - bc = +1$ OR $[T] [T]^{-1} = [T] [T]^T = [I]$

5. **Transformation of Two Parallel Lines:**

When two parallel lines are transformed using general 2 × 2 transformation matrix the resulting lines remain parallel.

Consider two lines parallel to each other between the end points $A(x_1, y_1)$, $B(x_2, y_2)$ and CD. Since they are parallel the slope is the same given by,

$$m = \frac{y_2 - y_1}{x_2 - x_1}$$

$$[T]\,[X] = \begin{bmatrix} a & c \\ b & d \end{bmatrix} \begin{bmatrix} x_1 & x_2 \\ y_1 & y_2 \end{bmatrix} = \begin{bmatrix} ax_1 + cy_1 & ax_2 + cy_2 \\ bx_1 + dy_1 & bx_2 + dy_2 \end{bmatrix}$$

$$m' = \frac{(bx_2 + dy_2) - (bx_1 + dy_1)}{(ax_2 + cy_2) - (ax_1 + cy_1)} = \frac{b(x_2 - x_1) + d(y_2 - y_1)}{a(x_2 - x_1) + c(y_2 - y_1)}$$

$$m' = \frac{b + d\dfrac{(y_2 - y)}{(x_2 - x_1)_1}}{a + c\dfrac{(y_2 - y_1)}{(x_2 - x_1)}} = \frac{b + dm}{a + cm}$$

5.4 VIEWING PIPELINE

- A world-coordinate area selected for display is called a window. An area on a display device to which a window is mapped is called a viewport.
  1. The window defines what is to be viewed.
  2. The viewport defines where it is to be displayed.
- Often, windows and viewports are rectangles in standard position, with the rectangle edges parallel to the coordinate axes.
- In general, the mapping of a part of a world-coordinate scene to device co-ordinates is referred to as a viewing transformation.
- Sometimes, the two-dimensional viewing transformation is simply referred to as the window-to-viewport transformation or the windowing transformation.
- The term window to refer to an area of a world-coordinate scene that has been selected for display.

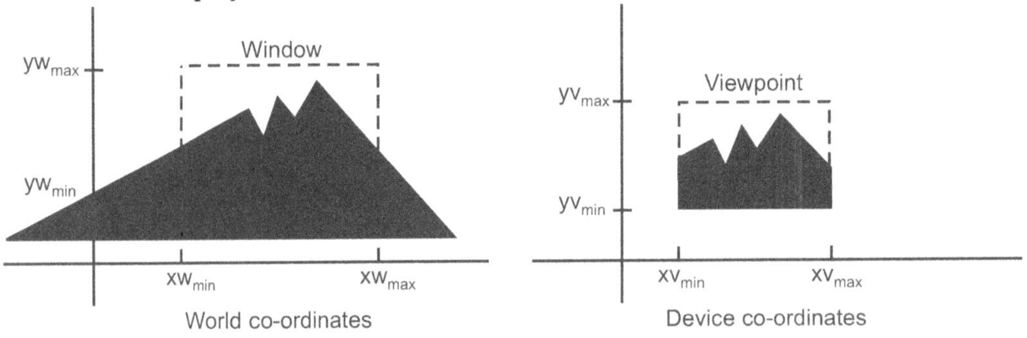

Fig. 5.11: Viewing Transformation

- We carry out the viewing transformation in several steps as indicated below:

  Step 1 : First, we construct the scene in world co-ordinates using the output primitives and attributes.

  Step 2 : Next, to obtain a particular orientation for the window, we can set up a two-dimensional viewing coordinate system in the world-coordinate plane and define a window in the viewing coordinate system.

  Step 3 : The viewing coordinate reference frame is used to provide a method for setting up arbitrary orientations for rectangular windows. Once the viewing reference frame is established, we can transform descriptions in world co-ordinates to viewing co-ordinates.

  Step 4 : We then define a viewport is normalized co-ordinates (in the range from 0 to 1) and map the viewing-coordinate description of the scene to normalized co-ordinates.

  Step 5 : At the final step, all parts of the picture that lie outside the viewport are clipped and the contents of the viewport are transferred to device co-ordinates.

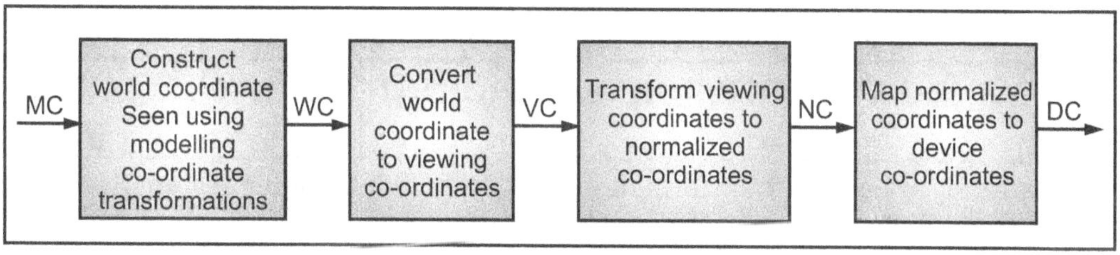

Fig. 5.12

- Fig. 5.12 shows the following points:

1. **Modeling Co-ordinates (MC):** The graphics pipeline uses the objects modeling co-ordinates to determine how to draw the object on the screen. Modeling co-ordinate may be a specification of object in the form of Global or Local co-ordinates. The co-ordinates mostly locates the geometry of items like nodes, keypoints, and results.
2. **Construction of World Co-ordinate (WC):** This step is general which converts the modeling co-ordinates to World co-ordinates.
3. **Convert World Co-ordinate to Viewing Co-ordinates (VC):** In this step world co-ordinate positions are converted to viewing co-ordinates. Viewing co-ordinate reference frame is used to provide a method for setting up arbitrary orientations for rectangular windows.Once the viewing reference frame is established , we can transform descriptions in world co-ordinates to viewing co-ordinates.

4. **Transform Viewing Co-ordinates into Normalized Co-ordinates (NC):** Here viewport is defined in normalized co-ordinates (in the range of 0 to 1)and map the viewing co-ordinate description of the scene to normalized co-ordinates.
5. **Mapping Normalized Co-ordinates to Device Co-ordinates (DC):** All parts of the picture are that lie outside the viewport are clipped and the content of viewport are transferred to device co-ordinates.

- Fig. 5.13 illustrates a rotated viewing coordinate reference frame and the mapping to normalized coordinate.

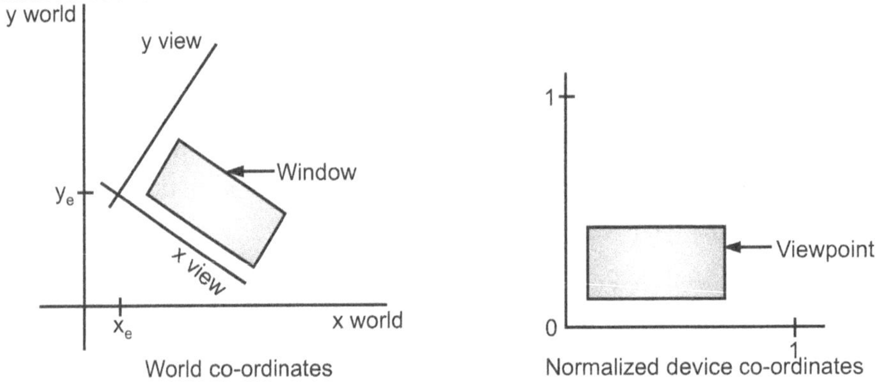

Fig. 5.13: Rotated viewing coordinate reference frame

5.5 WINDOW TO VIEWPORT CO-ORDINATE TRANSFORMATION [April 16]

- To perform a viewing transformation, we deal with a finite region in the WCS (World Co-ordinate System) called a window.
- The window can be mapped directly on to the display area of the device or on to a subregion of the display called a viewport.
- Window frame outlines and defines the portion of the object. While viewport is the zone of the monitor screen within which we wish to view the selected object.
- In short, 'Window' is what is to be viewed and 'viewport' is where it is to be viewed.
- The clipping window is mapped into a viewport.

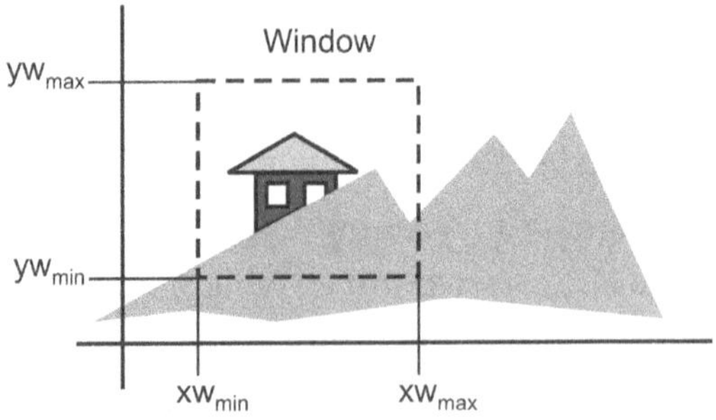

Fig. 5.14

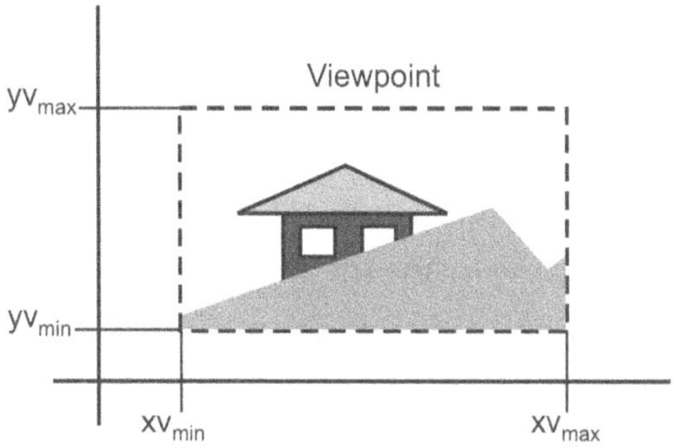

Fig. 5.15

- Viewing world has its own co-ordinates, which may be a non-uniform scaling of world co-ordinates. Generally user's prefer to work in world-coordinates.
  1 unit can be 1 micron
  1 unit can be 1 meter
  1 unit can be 1 kilometer
  1 unit can be 1 mile
- These co-ordinates must then be translated to screen co-ordinates to be displayed in a rectangular region of the screen called the viewport.
- The objects are in world co-ordinates (with n dimensions) The viewport is in screen co-ordinates (with n=2).
- Want one matrix that can be applied to all points: rectangular area of world from (Xmin,Ymin) to (Xmax,Ymax) - world-coordinate window rectangular area of screen from (Umin,Vmin) to (Umax,Vmax) - viewport need to rescale the world-coordinate rectangle to the screen rectangle.
  1. translate world-coordinate window to the origin of the world coordinate system.
  2. rescale the window to the size and aspect ratio of the viewport.
  3. translate the viewport to its position on the screen in the screen coordinate system.

$$P_{screen} = M * P_{world}$$

$$M = T(U_{min}, V_{min}) * S(\Delta U/\Delta X, \Delta V/\Delta Y) * T(-X_{min}, -Y_{min})$$

5.6 SETTING WINDOW AND VIEWPORT IN OpenGL [April 16]

- Following functions are used in OpenGL to create viewport.

1. **gluOrtho2D(left, right, bottom, top):** Function sets up a 2-D orthographic viewing region or world window.

- It defined by two vertical:
  (i) Clipping planes left and right and two horizontal clipping planes bottom and top. The world window by default is (-1,1,-1,1).
  (ii) Defines a 2-D orthographic projection matrix, sets up the window-viewport mapping, being the viewport defined by the following function:

2. **glViewport(x, y, width, height):**

- Sets up the viewport in the interface window, where x,y specify the lower left corner, and width, height its dimensions.
- By default, it uses the whole graphics area of the interface window.
- There may be various viewports inside the interface window.
- glViewport specifies the affine transformation of x and y from normalized device co-ordinates to window co-ordinates. Let x nd y nd be normalized device co-ordinates. Then the window co-ordinates x w y w are computed as follows:

  x w = x nd + 1 width 2 + x

  y w = y nd + 1 height 2 + y

- Viewport width and height are silently clamped to a range that depends on the implementation. To query this range, call glGet with argument GL_MAX_VIEWPORT_DIMS.

Errors:

- GL_INVALID_VALUE is generated if either width or height is negative.
- **Examples in OpenGL:**
  1. A single viewport by default,
  2. A single viewport, and
  3. Two viewports.

A Default Viewport:

```
default viewport           /* Using the default viewport */
#include <OpenGL/gl.h>     // Header File For The OpenGL Library
#include <OpenGL/glu.h>    // Header File For The GLu Library
#include <GLUT/glut.h>     // Header File For The GLut Library
#include <stdlib.h>
void draw()
{
   // Make background colour yellow
   glClearColor( 100, 100, 0, 0 );
   glClear ( GL_COLOR_BUFFER_BIT ); // Sets up the PROJECTION matrix
   glMatrixMode(GL_PROJECTION);
   glLoadIdentity();
   gluOrtho2D(0.0,50.0,-10.0,40.0); // also sets up world window
```

```
    // Draw BLUE rectangle
    glColor3f( 0, 0, 1 );
    glRectf(0.0,0.0,10.0,30.0); // display rectangles
    glutSwapBuffers();
}
// Keyboard method to allow ESC key to quit
void keyboard(unsigned char key,int x,int y)
{
    if(key==27)
    exit(0);
}
int main(int argc, char ** argv)
{
    glutInit(&argc, argv);  // Double Buffered RGB display
    glutInitDisplayMode( GLUT_RGB | GLUT_DOUBLE); // Set window size
    glutInitWindowSize( 500,500 );
    glutCreateWindow("Default viewport spans the whole interface window");
    // Declare the display and keyboard functions
    glutDisplayFunc(draw);
    glutKeyboardFunc(keyboard); // Start the Main Loop
    glutMainLoop();
    return 0;
}
```

A Single Viewport:

```
#include <OpenGL/gl.h>     // Header File For The OpenGL Library
#include <OpenGL/glu.h>    // Header File For The GLu Library
#include <GLUT/glut.h>     // Header File For The GLut Library
#include <stdlib.h>
void draw()
{
    // Make background colour yellow
    glClearColor( 100, 100, 0, 0 );
    glClear ( GL_COLOR_BUFFER_BIT );
```

```
    // Sets up viewport spanning the left-bottom quarter of the interface
    window
    glViewport(0,0,250,250);
    // Sets up the PROJECTION matrix
    glMatrixMode(GL_PROJECTION);
    glLoadIdentity();
    gluOrtho2D(0.0,50.0,-10.0,40.0); // also sets up world window
    // Draw BLUE rectangle
    glColor3f( 0, 0, 1 );
    glRectf(0.0,0.0,10.0,30.0); // display rectangles
    glutSwapBuffers();
}
void keyboard(unsigned char key,int x,int y)
{
    if(key==27) exit(0);
}
int main(int argc, char ** argv)
{
    glutInit(&argc, argv); // Double Buffered RGB display
    glutInitDisplayMode( GLUT_RGB | GLUT_DOUBLE); // Set window size
    glutInitWindowSize( 500,500 );
    glutCreateWindow("Single viewport spans the left-bottom interface window
    quarter");
    // Declare the display and keyboard functions
    glutDisplayFunc(draw);
    glutKeyboardFunc(keyboard); // Start the Main Loop
    glutMainLoop();
    return 0;
}
```

Two Viewport:

```
#include <OpenGL/gl.h>     // Header File For The OpenGL Library
#include <OpenGL/glu.h>    // Header File For The GLu Library
#include <GLUT/glut.h>     // Header File For The GLut Library
#include <stdlib.h>
```

```
void draw()
{
    // Make background colour yellow
    glClearColor( 100, 100, 0, 0 );
    glClear ( GL_COLOR_BUFFER_BIT );
    // Sets up viewport spanning the left-bottom quarter of the interface
    window glViewport(0,0,250,250);
    // Sets up the PROJECTION matrix
    glMatrixMode(GL_PROJECTION);
    glLoadIdentity();
    gluOrtho2D(0.0,50.0,-10.0,40.0); // also sets up world window
    // Draw BLUE rectangle
    glColor3f( 0, 0, 1 );
    glRectf(0.0,0.0,10.0,30.0); // display rectangles
    glutSwapBuffers();
    // Sets up SECOND viewport spanning the right-top quarter of the
    interface window
    glViewport(250,250,250,250); // Sets up the PROJECTION matrix
    glMatrixMode(GL_PROJECTION);
    glLoadIdentity();
    gluOrtho2D(0.0,50.0,-10.0,40.0); // also sets up world window
    // Draw RED rectangle
    glColor3f( 1, 0, 0 );
    glRectf(0.0,0.0,10.0,30.0); // display rectangles
    glutSwapBuffers();
}
void keyboard(unsigned char key,int x,int y)
{
    if(key==27) exit(0);
}
int main(int argc, char ** argv)
{
    glutInit(&argc, argv); // Double Buffered RGB display
    glutInitDisplayMode( GLUT_RGB | GLUT_DOUBLE); // Set window size
    glutInitWindowSize( 500,500 );
    glutCreateWindow("Two viewport spanning the left-bottom and right-top
    quarters");
                // Declare the display and keyboard functions
    glutDisplayFunc(draw);
    glutKeyboardFunc(keyboard); // Start the Main Loop
    glutMainLoop();
    return 0;
}
```

Program to draw Line and Points:

```
#include <stdio.h>
#include <string.h>
#include <stdlib.h>
#include <math.h>
#include <GL/glut.h>

#define VORDER 10
#define CORDER 10
#define TORDER 3

#define VMAJOR_ORDER 2
#define VMINOR_ORDER 3

#define CMAJOR_ORDER 2
#define CMINOR_ORDER 2

#define TMAJOR_ORDER 2
#define TMINOR_ORDER 2

#define VDIM 4
#define CDIM 4
#define TDIM 2

#define ONE_D 1
#define TWO_D 2

#define EVAL 3
#define MESH 4

GLenum doubleBuffer;

float rotX = 0.0, rotY = 0.0, translateZ = -1.0;

GLenum arrayType = ONE_D;
GLenum colorType = GL_FALSE;
GLenum textureType = GL_FALSE;
GLenum polygonFilled = GL_FALSE;
GLenum lighting = GL_FALSE;
GLenum mapPoint = GL_FALSE;
GLenum mapType = EVAL;
```

```
double point1[10 * 4] =
{
  -0.5, 0.0, 0.0, 1.0,
  -0.4, 0.5, 0.0, 1.0,
  -0.3, -0.5, 0.0, 1.0,
  -0.2, 0.5, 0.0, 1.0,
  -0.1, -0.5, 0.0, 1.0,
  0.0, 0.5, 0.0, 1.0,
  0.1, -0.5, 0.0, 1.0,
  0.2, 0.5, 0.0, 1.0,
  0.3, -0.5, 0.0, 1.0,
  0.4, 0.0, 0.0, 1.0,
};
double cpoint1[10 * 4] =
{
  0.0, 0.0, 1.0, 1.0,
  0.3, 0.0, 0.7, 1.0,
  0.6, 0.0, 0.3, 1.0,
  1.0, 0.0, 0.0, 1.0,
  1.0, 0.3, 0.0, 1.0,
  1.0, 0.6, 0.0, 1.0,
  1.0, 1.0, 0.0, 1.0,
  1.0, 1.0, 0.5, 1.0,
  1.0, 1.0, 1.0, 1.0,
};
double tpoint1[11 * 4] =
{
  0.0, 0.0, 0.0, 1.0,
  0.0, 0.1, 0.0, 1.0,
  0.0, 0.2, 0.0, 1.0,
  0.0, 0.3, 0.0, 1.0,
  0.0, 0.4, 0.0, 1.0,
  0.0, 0.5, 0.0, 1.0,
  0.0, 0.6, 0.0, 1.0,
  0.0, 0.7, 0.0, 1.0,
  0.0, 0.8, 0.0, 1.0,
  0.0, 0.9, 0.0, 1.0,
};
double point2[2 * 3 * 4] =
{
  -0.5, -0.5, 0.5, 1.0,
  0.0, 1.0, 0.5, 1.0,
  0.5, -0.5, 0.5, 1.0,
  -0.5, 0.5, -0.5, 1.0,
  0.0, -1.0, -0.5, 1.0,
  0.5, 0.5, -0.5, 1.0,
};
double cpoint2[2 * 2 * 4] =
{
  0.0, 0.0, 0.0, 1.0,
  0.0, 0.0, 1.0, 1.0,
  0.0, 1.0, 0.0, 1.0,
  1.0, 1.0, 1.0, 1.0,
};
```

```
double tpoint2[2 * 2 * 2] =
{
  0.0, 0.0, 0.0, 1.0,
  1.0, 0.0, 1.0, 1.0,
};
float textureImage[4 * 2 * 4] =
{
  1.0, 1.0, 1.0, 1.0,
  1.0, 0.0, 0.0, 1.0,
  1.0, 0.0, 0.0, 1.0,
  1.0, 1.0, 1.0, 1.0,
  1.0, 1.0, 1.0, 1.0,
  1.0, 0.0, 0.0, 1.0,
  1.0, 0.0, 0.0, 1.0,
  1.0, 1.0, 1.0, 1.0,
};

static void
Init(void)
{
  static float ambient[] =
  {0.1, 0.1, 0.1, 1.0};
  static float diffuse[] =
  {1.0, 1.0, 1.0, 1.0};
  static float position[] =
  {0.0, 0.0, -150.0, 0.0};
  static float front_mat_diffuse[] =
  {1.0, 0.2, 1.0, 1.0};
  static float back_mat_diffuse[] =
  {1.0, 1.0, 0.2, 1.0};
  static float lmodel_ambient[] =
  {1.0, 1.0, 1.0, 1.0};
  static float lmodel_twoside[] =
  {GL_TRUE};
  static float decal[] =
  {GL_DECAL};
  static float repeat[] =
  {GL_REPEAT};
  static float nr[] =
  {GL_NEAREST};

  glFrontFace(GL_CCW);

  glEnable(GL_DEPTH_TEST);
```

```
  glMap1d(GL_MAP1_VERTEX_4, 0.0, 1.0, VDIM, VORDER, point1);
  glMap1d(GL_MAP1_COLOR_4, 0.0, 1.0, CDIM, CORDER, cpoint1);

  glMap2d(GL_MAP2_VERTEX_4,  0.0,  1.0,  VMINOR_ORDER  *  VDIM,  VMAJOR_ORDER,
0.0,
    1.0, VDIM, VMINOR_ORDER, point2);
  glMap2d(GL_MAP2_COLOR_4, 0.0, 1.0, CMINOR_ORDER * CDIM, CMAJOR_ORDER, 0.0,
    1.0, CDIM, CMINOR_ORDER, cpoint2);
  glMap2d(GL_MAP2_TEXTURE_COORD_2, 0.0, 1.0, TMINOR_ORDER * TDIM,
    TMAJOR_ORDER, 0.0, 1.0, TDIM, TMINOR_ORDER, tpoint2);

  glLightfv(GL_LIGHT0, GL_AMBIENT, ambient);
  glLightfv(GL_LIGHT0, GL_DIFFUSE, diffuse);
  glLightfv(GL_LIGHT0, GL_POSITION, position);

  glMaterialfv(GL_FRONT, GL_DIFFUSE, front_mat_diffuse);
  glMaterialfv(GL_BACK, GL_DIFFUSE, back_mat_diffuse);

  glLightModelfv(GL_LIGHT_MODEL_AMBIENT, lmodel_ambient);
  glLightModelfv(GL_LIGHT_MODEL_TWO_SIDE, lmodel_twoside);

  glTexEnvfv(GL_TEXTURE_ENV, GL_TEXTURE_ENV_MODE, decal);
  glTexParameterfv(GL_TEXTURE_2D, GL_TEXTURE_WRAP_S, repeat);
  glTexParameterfv(GL_TEXTURE_2D, GL_TEXTURE_WRAP_T, repeat);
  glTexParameterfv(GL_TEXTURE_2D, GL_TEXTURE_MAG_FILTER, nr);
  glTexParameterfv(GL_TEXTURE_2D, GL_TEXTURE_MIN_FILTER, nr);
  glTexImage2D(GL_TEXTURE_2D, 0, 4, 2, 4, 0, GL_RGBA, GL_FLOAT,
    (GLvoid *) textureImage);
}

static void
DrawPoints1(void)
{
  GLint i;

  glColor3f(0.0, 1.0, 0.0);
  glPointSize(2);
  glBegin(GL_POINTS);
  for (i = 0; i < VORDER; i++) {
    glVertex4dv(&point1[i * 4]);
  }
  glEnd();
}
```

```
static void
DrawPoints2(void)
{
  GLint i, j;

  glColor3f(1.0, 0.0, 1.0);
  glPointSize(2);
  glBegin(GL_POINTS);
  for (i = 0; i < VMAJOR_ORDER; i++) {
    for (j = 0; j < VMINOR_ORDER; j++) {
      glVertex4dv(&point2[i * 4 * VMINOR_ORDER + j * 4]);
    }
  }
  glEnd();
}

static void
DrawMapEval1(float du)
{
  float u;

  glColor3f(1.0, 0.0, 0.0);
  glBegin(GL_LINE_STRIP);
  for (u = 0.0; u < 1.0; u += du) {
    glEvalCoord1d(u);
  }
  glEvalCoord1d(1.0);
  glEnd();
}

static void
DrawMapEval2(float du, float dv)
{
  float u, v, tmp;

  glColor3f(1.0, 0.0, 0.0);
  for (v = 0.0; v < 1.0; v += dv) {
    glBegin(GL_QUAD_STRIP);
    for (u = 0.0; u <= 1.0; u += du) {
      glEvalCoord2d(u, v);
      tmp = (v + dv < 1.0) ? (v + dv) : 1.0;
      glEvalCoord2d(u, tmp);
    }
```

```
      glEvalCoord2d(1.0, v);
      glEvalCoord2d(1.0, v + dv);
      glEnd();
    }
}

static void
RenderEval(void)
{

  if (colorType) {
    glEnable(GL_MAP1_COLOR_4);
    glEnable(GL_MAP2_COLOR_4);
  } else {
    glDisable(GL_MAP1_COLOR_4);
    glDisable(GL_MAP2_COLOR_4);
  }

  if (textureType) {
    glEnable(GL_TEXTURE_2D);
    glEnable(GL_MAP2_TEXTURE_COORD_2);
  } else {
    glDisable(GL_TEXTURE_2D);
    glDisable(GL_MAP2_TEXTURE_COORD_2);
  }

  if (polygonFilled) {
    glPolygonMode(GL_FRONT_AND_BACK, GL_FILL);
  } else {
    glPolygonMode(GL_FRONT_AND_BACK, GL_LINE);
  }

  glShadeModel(GL_SMOOTH);

  switch (mapType) {
  case EVAL:
    switch (arrayType) {
    case ONE_D:
      glDisable(GL_MAP2_VERTEX_4);
      glEnable(GL_MAP1_VERTEX_4);
      DrawPoints1();
      DrawMapEval1(0.1 / VORDER);
      break;
```

```
      case TWO_D:
        glDisable(GL_MAP1_VERTEX_4);
        glEnable(GL_MAP2_VERTEX_4);
        DrawPoints2();
        DrawMapEval2(0.1 / VMAJOR_ORDER, 0.1 / VMINOR_ORDER);
        break;
      }
      break;
    case MESH:
      switch (arrayType) {
      case ONE_D:
        DrawPoints1();
        glDisable(GL_MAP2_VERTEX_4);
        glEnable(GL_MAP1_VERTEX_4);
        glColor3f(0.0, 0.0, 1.0);
        glMapGrid1d(40, 0.0, 1.0);
        if (mapPoint) {
          glPointSize(2);
          glEvalMesh1(GL_POINT, 0, 40);
        } else {
          glEvalMesh1(GL_LINE, 0, 40);
        }
        break;
      case TWO_D:
        DrawPoints2();
        glDisable(GL_MAP1_VERTEX_4);
        glEnable(GL_MAP2_VERTEX_4);
        glColor3f(0.0, 0.0, 1.0);
        glMapGrid2d(20, 0.0, 1.0, 20, 0.0, 1.0);
        if (mapPoint) {
          glPointSize(2);
          glEvalMesh2(GL_POINT, 0, 20, 0, 20);
        } else if (polygonFilled) {
          glEvalMesh2(GL_FILL, 0, 20, 0, 20);
        } else {
          glEvalMesh2(GL_LINE, 0, 20, 0, 20);
        }
        break;
      }
      break;
    }
  }
```

```
static void
Reshape(int width, int height)
{

  glViewport(0, 0, width, height);

  glMatrixMode(GL_PROJECTION);
  glLoadIdentity();
  glOrtho(-1.0, 1.0, -1.0, 1.0, -0.5, 10.0);
  glMatrixMode(GL_MODELVIEW);
}

/* ARGSUSED1 */
static void
Key(unsigned char key, int x, int y)
{
  switch (key) {
  case '1':
    arrayType = ONE_D;
    glDisable(GL_AUTO_NORMAL);
    glutPostRedisplay();
    break;
  case '2':
    arrayType = TWO_D;
    glEnable(GL_AUTO_NORMAL);
    glutPostRedisplay();
    break;
  case '3':
    mapType = EVAL;
    glutPostRedisplay();
    break;
  case '4':
    mapType = MESH;
    glutPostRedisplay();
    break;
  case '5':
    polygonFilled = !polygonFilled;
    glutPostRedisplay();
    break;
  case '6':
    mapPoint = !mapPoint;
    glutPostRedisplay();
    break;
```

```
    case '7':
      colorType = !colorType;
      glutPostRedisplay();
      break;
    case '8':
      textureType = !textureType;
      glutPostRedisplay();
      break;
    case '9':
      lighting = !lighting;
      if (lighting) {
        glEnable(GL_LIGHTING);
        glEnable(GL_LIGHT0);
        if (arrayType == TWO_D) {
          glEnable(GL_AUTO_NORMAL);
        } else {
          glDisable(GL_AUTO_NORMAL);
        }
      } else {
        glDisable(GL_LIGHTING);
        glDisable(GL_LIGHT0);
        glDisable(GL_AUTO_NORMAL);
      }
      glutPostRedisplay();
      break;
    case 27:              /* Escape key. */
      exit(0);
    }
  }

  static void
  Menu(int value)
  {
    /* Menu items have key values assigned to them.  Just pass
       this value to the key routine. */
    Key(value, 0, 0);
  }

  /* ARGSUSED1 */
  static void
  SpecialKey(int key, int x, int y)
  {
    switch (key) {
    case GLUT_KEY_LEFT:
      rotY -= 30;
      glutPostRedisplay();
      break;
```

```
  case GLUT_KEY_RIGHT:
    rotY += 30;
    glutPostRedisplay();
    break;
  case GLUT_KEY_UP:
    rotX -= 30;
    glutPostRedisplay();
    break;
  case GLUT_KEY_DOWN:
    rotX += 30;
    glutPostRedisplay();
    break;
  }
}

static void
Draw(void)
{

  glClear(GL_COLOR_BUFFER_BIT | GL_DEPTH_BUFFER_BIT);

  glPushMatrix();

  glTranslatef(0.0, 0.0, translateZ);
  glRotatef(rotX, 1, 0, 0);
  glRotatef(rotY, 0, 1, 0);
  RenderEval();

  glPopMatrix();

  if (doubleBuffer) {
    glutSwapBuffers();
  } else {
    glFlush();
  }
}

static void
Args(int argc, char **argv)
{
  GLint i;

  doubleBuffer = GL_FALSE;
```

```
    for (i = 1; i < argc; i++) {
      if (strcmp(argv[i], "-sb") == 0) {
        doubleBuffer = GL_FALSE;
      } else if (strcmp(argv[i], "-db") == 0) {
        doubleBuffer = GL_TRUE;
      }
    }
}

int
main(int argc, char **argv)
{
  GLenum type;

  glutInit(&argc, argv);
  Args(argc, argv);

  type = GLUT_RGB | GLUT_DEPTH;
  type |= (doubleBuffer) ? GLUT_DOUBLE : GLUT_SINGLE;
  glutInitDisplayMode(type);
  glutInitWindowSize(300, 300);
  glutCreateWindow("Evaluator Test");

  glutCreateMenu(Menu);
  glutAddMenuEntry("One dimensional", '1');
  glutAddMenuEntry("Two dimensional", '2');
  glutAddMenuEntry("Eval map type", '3');
  glutAddMenuEntry("Mesh map type", '4');
  glutAddMenuEntry("Toggle filled", '5');
  glutAddMenuEntry("Toggle map point", '6');
  glutAddMenuEntry("Toggle color", '7');
  glutAddMenuEntry("Toggle texture", '8');
  glutAddMenuEntry("Toggle lighting", '9');
  glutAddMenuEntry("Quit", 27);
  glutAttachMenu(GLUT_RIGHT_BUTTON);
  glutAttachMenu(GLUT_LEFT_BUTTON);

  Init();

  glutReshapeFunc(Reshape);
  glutKeyboardFunc(Key);
  glutSpecialFunc(SpecialKey);
  glutDisplayFunc(Draw);
  glutMainLoop();
  return 0;
}
```

Output:

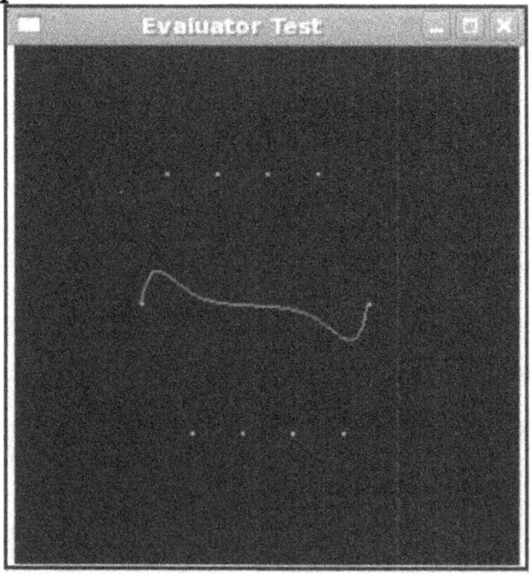

SUMMARY

- Translation refers to the shifting of a point to some other place, whose distance with regard to the present point is known.
- Rotation as the name suggests is to rotate a point about an axis. The axis can be any of the co-ordinates or simply any other specified line also.
- Scaling is the concept of increasing (or decreasing) the size of a picture. (in one or in either directions.
- Transformation matrix is a basic tool for transformation. A matrix with n x m dimensions is multiplied with the coordinate of objects. Usually 3 x 3 or 4 x 4 matrices are used for transformation.
- We can represent the point by 3 numbers instead of 2 numbers, which is called Homogenous Coordinate system.
- Mirror Reflection produces a mirror image of an object.
- A transformation that slants the shape of an object is called the shear transformation. There are two shear transformations X-Shear and Y-Shear. Shearing is also termed as Skewing.
- Composite transformation can be achieved by concatenation of transformation matrices to obtain a combined transformation matrix.

PRACTICE QUESTIONS

1. What do you mean by transformation?
2. List out different geometric transformation.
3. What is translation?
4. What is rotation?

5. What is scaling?
6. Define Homogeneous co-ordinate.
7. What is X-shear and Y-shear?
8. Explain the concept of geometric transformation. Write a note on rotation and scaling.
9. How matrix is represented in different 2-D transformation. Explain in brief.
10. Write a note on transformation of lines.
11. Explain the concept of viewing pipeline for 2D-Transformation.
12. Explain window to viewport co-ordinate system?
13. Write a openGL code to create 2 viewport in single window.
14. What is X-shear and Y-shear.

■■■

CHAPTER 6

Clipping

Contents ...

Objectives...

- To Understand Concept of Clipping and Need of Clipping Process
- To Learn various Line Clipping Algorithms
- To Study different Algorithms for Polygon Clipping

6.1 INTRODUCTION

- In this chapter, you are introduced to the concept of handling pictures that are larger than available display screen size, since any part of the picture that lies beyond the confines of screen cannot be displayed.
- We compare the screen to window which allows us to view only that portion of the scene outside as the limits of the window would permit. Any portion beyond that gets simply blocked out.

- But in graphics, this "blocking out" is to be done by algorithms that decide point beyond which the picture should not be shown. This concept is called clipping.
- Thus, we are clipping a picture that is viewable on window. The primary use of clipping in computer graphics is to remove objects, lines, or line segments that are outside the viewing pane.
- The viewing transformation is insensitive to the position of points relative to the viewing volume ; especially those points behind the viewer and it is necessary to remove these points before generating the view.

6.2 CLIPPING OPERATIONS [April 16]

- **Definition of Clipping**: Any procedure that identifies those portions of a picture that are either inside or outside of a specified region of space is referred to as a clipping.

OR

- Clipping is a procedure for spatially partitioning geometric primitives, according to their containment within some region.
- The region against which an object is to clip is called a clip window. It is usually rectangular window.

Applications of Clipping:

1. Extracting part of a defined scene for viewing,
2. Identifying visible surfaces in three-dimensiona1 clews,
3. Antialiasing line segments or object boundaries,
4. Creating objects using solid-modeling procedures, and
5. Displaying a multi-window environment.

- Drawing and painting operations that allow parts of a picture to be selected for copying, moving, erasing, or duplicating.
- The clipping window is usually a rectangular window although it could be of any shape (circular, polygonal or others).
- Rectangular windows are easy to be mapped to computer screen using a transformation called 'window to viewport mapping'.
- The parameters of the rectangular clipping window are (x_{left}, y_{bottom}) and (x_{right}, y_{top}) expressed in real-world units.
- Screen viewport parameters are given in pixels.
- Clipping window should be described relative to world coordinate system.
- For the viewing transformation, we want to display only those picture parts that are within the window area. Everything outside the window is discarded.
- Clipping algorithm can be applied in World Coordinates, so that only the contents of the window interior are mapped to Device coordinate.

- In the following sections, we consider algorithms for clipping the following primitive types:
  1. Point clipping,
  2. Line clipping, and
  3. Polygon clipping.
- We consider clipping methods using rectangular clip regions.

6.2.1 Point Clipping

- Let W denote a clip window with coordinates ($x\omega_{min}$, $y\omega_{min}$), ($x\omega_{min}$, $y\omega_{max}$), ($x\omega_{max}$, $y\omega_{min}$), ($x\omega_{max}$, $y\omega_{max}$), then a vertex (x, y) is displayed only if all four of the following "point clipping" inequalities are satisfied:

  $x\omega_{min} \leq x \leq x\omega_{max}$,

  $y\omega_{min} \leq y \leq y\omega_{max}$
- If any one of these four inequalities is not satisfied, the point is clipped (not saved for display).
- Although point clipping is applied less often than line or polygon clipping, some applications may require a point clipping procedure.
- For example, point clipping can be applied to scenes involving explosions or sea foam that is modelled with particles (points) distributed in some region of the scene.

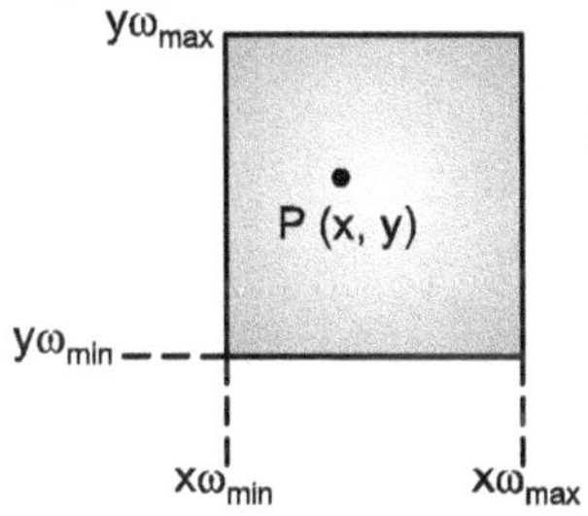

Fig. 6.1: Point Clipping

Disadvantages:

1. It requires more time.
2. It is not suitable for line drawing displays.

6.3 LINE CLIPPING

Definition:

- Line clipping is "the process of removing lines or portions of lines outside of an area of interest". Typically, any line or part thereof which is outside of the viewing area is removed.
- The expensive part of a line-clipping procedure is in calculating the intersection positions of a line.

- The intersection between the line and an edge of the window is costly since it incorporates floating point operations.
- Possible relationships between line position and standard rectangular clipping region can be:
  1. Completely inside the clipping window,
  2. Completely outside the window, and
  3. Partially inside the window.
- So we have to first perform tests to determine whether line is completely inside or completely outside test. If it is unable to identify, then perform intersection calculations.
- As shown in Fig. 6.2 inside-outside test is as follows:
  - If both endpoints are inside clipping boundaries, save the line (P_1, P_2).
  - If both endpoints are outside, discard the line (P_3, P_4).
  - If both these tests fail, the line segment intersects at least one clipping boundary.

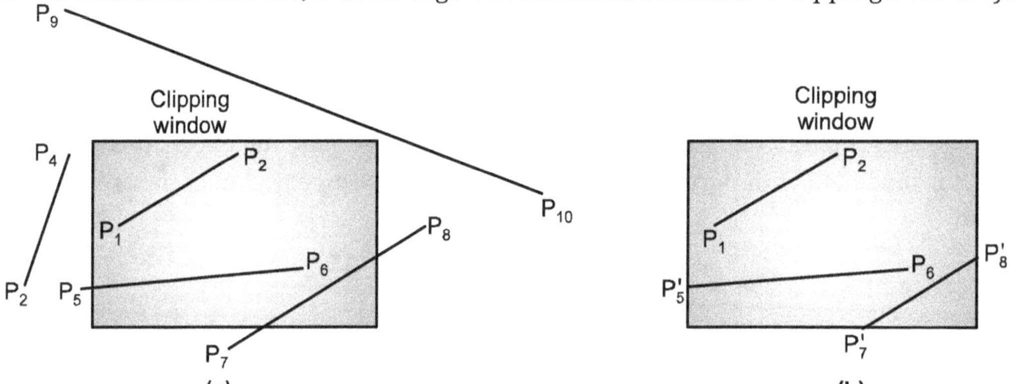

(a) Before clipping (b) After clipping

Fig. 6.2: Line clipping

- For a line segment with endpoints (x_1, y_1) and (x_2, y_2) and one or both endpoints outside the clipping rectangle, the parametric representation:

  $$x = x_1 + u(x_2 - x_1)$$

  $$y = y_1 + u(y_2 - y_1)$$

  could be used to determine values of parameter u for intersections with the clipping boundary coordinates.
- If the value of u for an intersection with a rectangle boundary edge is outside the range 0 to 1, the line does not enter the interior of the window that boundary.
- If the value of u is within the range from 0 to 1, the line segment does indeed cross into the clipping area.
- This method can be applied to each clipping boundary edge in turn to determine whether any part of the line segment is to be displayed.

- Clipping line segments with these parametric tests requires a good deal of computation, processing time and not efficient.
- Efficient algorithms try to minimize the number of intersections as much as possible. Several algorithms are introduced to clip lines against rectangular and non-rectangular windows.
- In this section, we will introduce Cohen-Sutherland algorithm, Midpoint subdivision algorithm, Cyrus beck algorithm.

6.3.1 Cohen Sutherland Line Clipping Algorithm [Oct. 16]

- This is one of the oldest and most popular line-clipping procedures. To speed up the processing of line segments, this algorithm performs initial tests that reduce the number of the intersections that must be calculated.
- It uses four-digit binary code, called a region code or outcode that identifies the location of the point relative to the boundaries of the clipping rectangle as shown in Fig. 6.3.

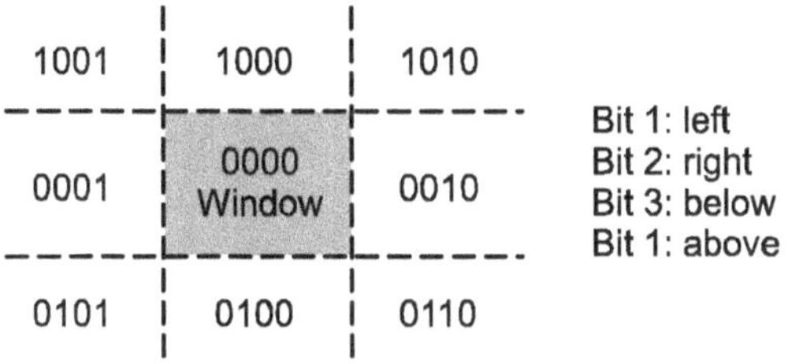

Fig. 6.3: 4-bit region codes for nine regions

How to Set region Code ?

- Each bit position is used to indicate whether the point is inside or outside one of the clipping-window boundaries.

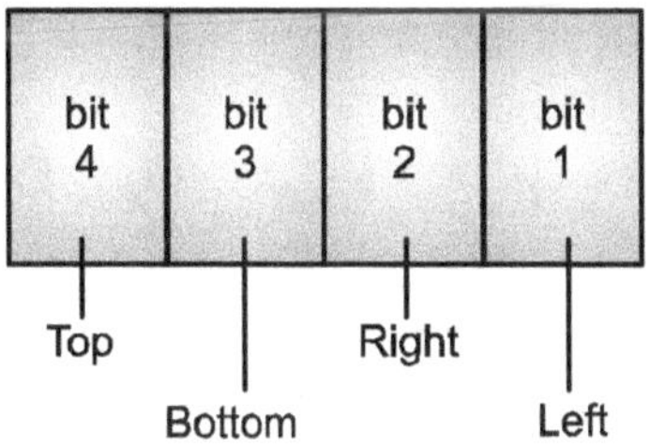

- Rightmost position (bit 1) references the left clipping-window boundary and leftmost position (bit 4) references the top window boundary.
- 1 (or true) in any bit position indicates endpoint is outside and 0(or false) indicates endpoint is inside.
- Determine the values for a region code using bit-processing operations as follows:
  1. Calculate differences between endpoint coordinates and clipping boundaries.
  2. Use the resultant sign bit of each difference calculation to set the corresponding bit value.

Bit 1 is set to 1 if $(x - x\omega_{min}) > 0$ i.e. if the endpoint is to the left of window Bit 2 is set to 1 if $(x\omega_{max} - x) > 0$ i.e. if the endpoint is to the right of window Bit 3 is set to 1 if $(y - y\omega_{min}) > 0$ i.e. if the endpoint is to the bottom of window Bit 4 is set to 1 if $(y\omega_{max} - y) > 0$ i.e. if the endpoint is to the top of window Otherwise, bits are set to 0.

- Once, we have established region codes for all line endpoints, we can quickly determine which lines are completely inside the clip window and which are clearly outside.
- Consider the following Fig. 6.4 in which we want to find region code for each line and identify whether line is completely visible or invisible.

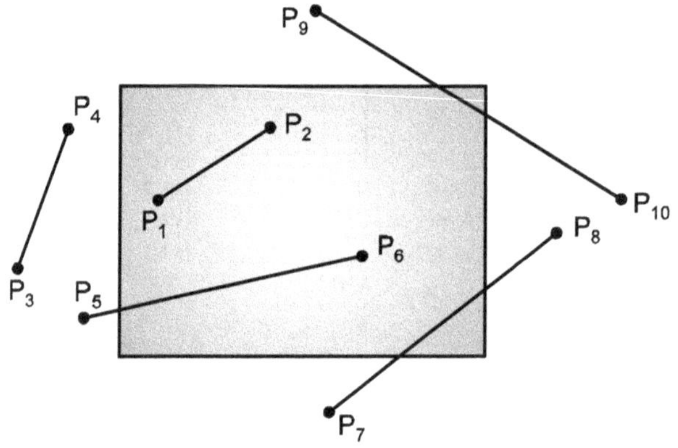

Fig. 6.4: Find region code

- The region codes for lines are shown below in Fig. 6.5.

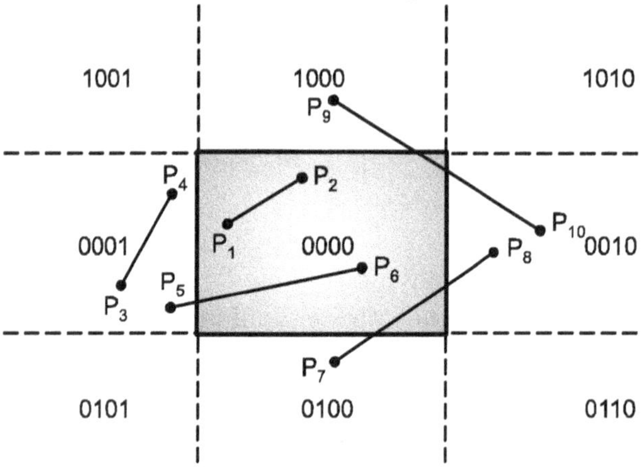

Fig. 6.5: Region codes

- The following table shows region codes and identify visibility of line.

Line	End Point Codes		Logical ANDing	Result
P_1P_2	0000	0000	0000	Completely visible
P_3P_4	0001	0001	0001	Completely invisible
P_5P_6	0001	0000	0000	Partially visible
P_7P_8	0100	0010	0000	Partially visible
P_9P_{10}	1000	0010	0000	Partially visible

- Any lines that are completely contained within the window boundaries have a region code of 0000 for both endpoints, and we trivially accept these lines.
- Any lines that have a 1 in the same bit position in the region codes for each endpoint are completely outside the clipping rectangle, and we trivially reject these lines.
- A method that can be used to test lines for total clipping is to perform the logical AND operation with both region codes. If the result is true (not 0000), the line is completely outside the clipping region. The AND operation between two endpoint region codes is false (0000), then line is inside.
- Lines that cannot be identified are next checked for intersection with the window border lines.
- To determine whether a line crosses a selected clipping boundary, Window edges are processed in the order: left right bottom top order.
- If one of these bit values is 1 and the other is 0 the line segment crosses that boundary.
- Intersection points with a clipping boundary can be calculated using the slope-intercept form of the line equation. For a line with end point coordinates (x_1, y_1) and (x_2, y_2), they coordinate of the intersection point with a vertical boundary can be obtained with the calculation,

  $$y = y_1 + m(x - x_1)$$

  where, the x value is set either to xmin, or to xmax and the slope of the line is calculated as $m = (y_2 - y_1) / (x_2 - x_1)$.
- Similarly, if we are looking for the intersection with a horizontal boundary, the x coordinate can be calculated as,

  $$x = (y - y_1) / m + x_1$$

  where, y is set either to y_{min} or to y_{max}.
- Therefore, the intersections with the clipping boundaries of the window are given as:
  - Bit1(Left) is set, then intersection point will be,

    $(x_{min}, y = m(x_{min} - x_1) + y_1)$ where $m \neq \infty$

- If Bit2(right) is set, then intersection point will be,

  $(x_{max}, y = m(x_{max} - x_1) + y_1)$ where $m \neq \infty$

- Bit3(bottom)is set, then intersection point will be,

  $(y_{max}, x = x_1 + (1/m)(y_{max} - y_1))$ where $m \neq 0$

- Bit4(top)is set, then intersection point will be,

  $(y_{min}, x = x_1 + (1/m)(y_{min} - y_1))$ where $m \neq 0$

Algorithm is as follows:

Step 1 : Accept the endpoints of line segment (x_1, y_1) (x_2, y_2) and window boundaries (x_{min}, y_{min}) (x_{max}, y_{max})

Step 2 : Assign 4-bit code to each of line segment i.e. B_4, B_3, B_2, B_1.

where,

$B_1 = \text{sign}(x_{min} - x)$

$B_2 = \text{sign}(x - x_{max})$

$B_3 = (y_{min} - y)$

$B_4 = (y - y_{max})$

Bit is set to 1 if sign(result) > 0 otherwise, Bit is set to 0.

- The code is determined according to which of the following nine legions of the plane the endpoint lies in,

1001	1000	1010
0001	0000	0010
0101	0100	0110

Step 3 : If both the endpoint codes are 0000, the line is visible. Display the line segment STOP.

If the logical AND of the endpoint codes is not 0000, the line segment is not visible. Discard the line segment and STOP.

If the logical AND of the endpoint codes is 0000, then line segment is clipping candidate.

Step 4 : Determine the intersecting boundary:

If B_1 (bit 1) is set then intersect with $x = x_{min}$

If B_2 (bit 2) is set then intersect with $x = x_{max}$

If B_3 (bit 3) is set then intersect with $y = y_{min}$

If B_4 (bit 4) is set then intersect with $y = y_{max}$

Step 5 : Determine the intersecting point co-ordinates

Bit 1 (Left) = (x_{min}, $y = m(x_{min} - x_1) + y_1$) where $m \neq \infty$

Bit 2 (right) = (x_{max}, $y = m(x_{max} - x_1) + y_1$) where $m \neq \infty$

Bit 3 (bottom) = (y_{min}, $x = x_1 + (1/m)(y_{min} - y_1)$) where $m \neq 0$

Bit 4 (top) = (y_{max}, $x = x_1 + (1/m)(y_{max} - y_1)$) where $m \neq 0$

Step 6 : Goto step 2.

Example: Find the clipping co-ordinates of line joining $A(x_1, y_1)$ and $B(x_2, y_2)$.

Solution:

Step 1 : $A(x_1 = -1, y_1 = 5)$

$B(x_2 = 3, y_2 = 8)$

$x\omega_{min} = -3$ $\quad$ $y\omega_{min} = 1$

$x\omega_{max} = -2$ $\quad$ $y\omega_{max} = 6$

Step 2 : For $A(x_1, y_1)$; $B_4\ B_3\ B_2\ B_1$

$B_1 = \text{sign}(x\omega_{min} - x)$

$= \text{sign}(-3 + 1) = \text{sign}(-2) = 0$

$B_2 = \text{sign}(x - x\omega_{max})$

$= \text{sign}(-1 - 6) = \text{sign}(-7) = 0$

$B_3 = \text{sign}(y\omega_{min} - y)$

$= \text{sign}(1 - 5) = \text{sign}(-4) = 0$

$B_4 = \text{sign}(y - x\omega_{max})$

$= \text{sign}(5 - 6) = \text{sign}(-1) = 0$

Code for $A(x_1, y_1) = 0000$. Point A (– 1, 5) is visible.

Similarly, code for $B(x_2, y_2) = 1010$.

Step 3 : $A(x_1, y_1)$ code AND $B(x_2, y_2)$ code

(0000) AND (1010) = 0000

The line segment is clipping candidate.

Step 4 : $B_2 = 1$, intersect with $x = x\omega_{max}$

$B_4 = 1$, intersect with $y = y\omega_{max}$

First select $x\omega_{max}$ as a clipping boundary.

Step 5 : $x' = x\omega_{max} = 2$

$y' = y_1 + m(x' - x_1)$

$$m = \frac{y_2 - y_1}{x_2 - x_1} = \frac{8 - 5}{+3 - (-1)} = \frac{3}{4}$$

$$y' = +5 + \frac{3}{4}[2 - (-1)]$$

$$= +5 + \frac{3}{4} \times 3 = 5 + \frac{9}{4} = \frac{29}{4}$$

$$I_1\left(2, -\frac{5}{4}\right)$$

Step 6 : Clipped line segment is $\overline{AI_1}$.

and

Step 2 : Code for $I_1\left(2, \frac{29}{4}\right)$ is $B_4\ B_3\ B_2\ B_1$, where

$$B_1 = \text{sign}(-3_0, -2) = \text{sign}(-5) = 0$$
$$B_2 = \text{sign}(2, -6) = \text{sign}(-4) = 0$$
$$B_3 = \text{sign}\left(1 - \frac{29}{4}\right) = \text{sign}\left(-\frac{25}{4}\right) = 1$$
$$B_4 = \text{sign}\left(\frac{29}{4} - 6\right) = \text{sign}\left(\frac{5}{4}\right) = 0$$

Step 3 : Point $I_1\left(2, \frac{29}{4}\right)$ is not visible, lie outside the window.

AI_1, (0000) AND (1000) = 0000

The line segment is clipping candidate.

Step 4 : $B_4 = 1$, intersect with $y = y\omega_{max} = 6$.

Step 5 : $y = 6$

$$m = \frac{3}{4}$$

$$x' = x_1 + \frac{1}{m}(y' - y_1)$$

$$= -1 + \frac{4}{3}(6 - 5)$$

$$= -1 + \frac{4}{3} = \frac{1}{3}$$

$$I_2(x', y') = I_2\left(\frac{1}{3}, 6\right)$$

Step 6 :

Step 2 : Code for $I_2\left(\frac{1}{3}, 6\right) = B_4B_3B_2B_1$

$$B_1 = \text{sign}(6 - 6) = 0$$
$$B_2 = \text{sign}(1 - 6) = 0$$
$$B_3 = \text{sign}\left(\frac{1}{3} - 2\right) = 0$$
$$B_4 = \text{sign}\left(-3 - \frac{1}{3}\right) = 0$$

Therefore, $I_2\left(\frac{1}{3}, 6\right)$ is visible

Hence, $\overline{AI_2}$ is visible.

Display the line segment $\overline{AI_2}$.

Advantages:

1. It is simple to implement.
2. Most lines can be eliminated based on region codes.
3. It can be easily extended to 3D.
4. It provides plane-line intersection instead of line-line intersection.

Disadvantages:

1. It has to be applied recursively.
2. Clipping window must be rectangular.
3. Each intersection calculation requires both a division and a multiplication operations.

6.3.2 Midpoint Subdivision Algorithm [Oct. 16]

- Cohen Sutherland line clipping algorithm requires the calculation of intersection of lines with window edge.
- These calculations can be avoided by repeatedly subdividing the line at its midpoint. It follows principle of divide and conquer strategy.
- The line is tested for visibility. If line is completely visible then it is drawn and completely invisible then rejected. If line is partially visible, then it is divided in equal subparts and visibility test is applied for each part.
- The subdivision process is repeated until we get completely visible and completely invisible line segments
- The process is explained by following Figs. 6.6 (a to g). As shown in Fig. 6.6 (a) line P_1, P_2 is partially visible. It is subdivided in two equal parts P_1, P_3 and P_3, P_2 (Fig. 6.6 (b)). Both line segments are tested for visibility and found to be partially visible. Both line segments are then subdivided in two equal parts to get midpoints P_4 and P_5 (Fig. 6.6 (c)).
- It is observed that line segments P_1P_4 and P_5P_2 are completely invisible and hence rejected. However line segments P_3P_5 are completely visible (Fig. 6.6 (d)) and hence drawn.
- The remaining line segment P_4P_3 is still partially visible. It is then subdivided to get midpoint P_6. It is observed that P_6P_3 is completely visible whereas P_4P_6 is partially visible (Fig. 6.6 (e)).
- Hence, P_4P_6 is further subdivided in equal parts to get midpoint P_7. Now it is observed that P_4P_7 is completely invisible whereas line segment P_7P_6 is completely visible (Fig. 6.6 (f)) and there is no further partially visible segment.

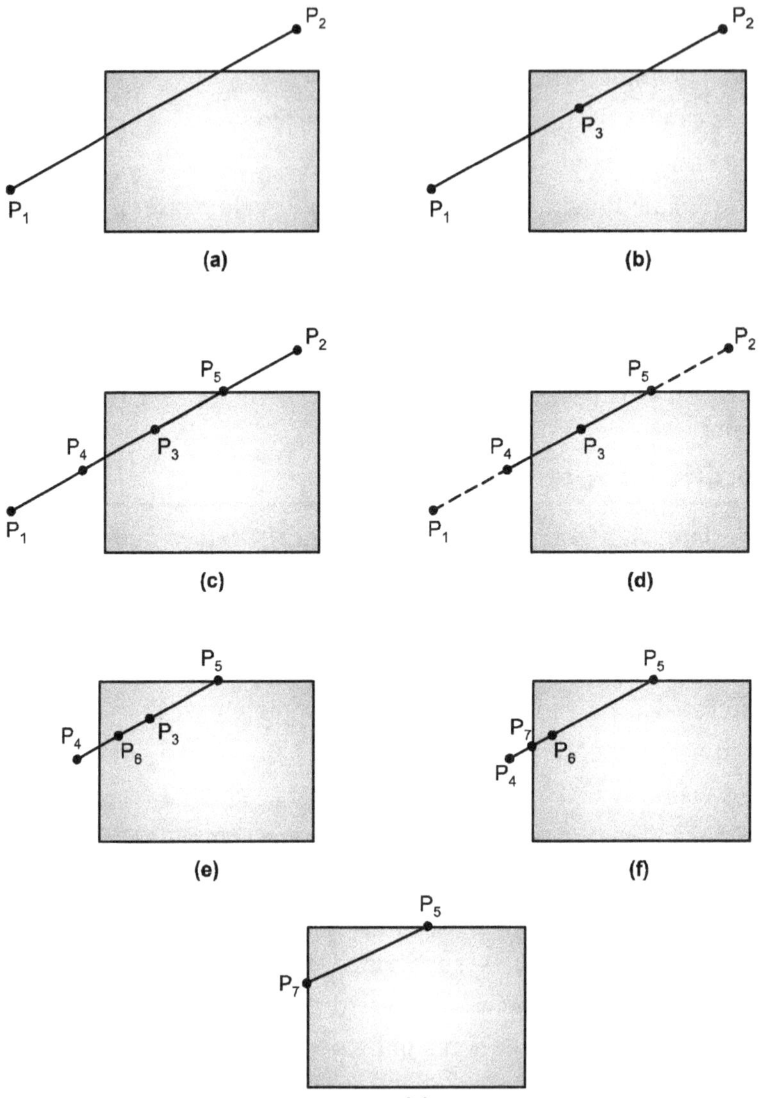

Fig. 6.6: Clipping line with Midpoint Subdivision algorithm.

Algorithm for Midpoint Subdivision:

Step 1 : Scan two end points for the line $P_1(x_1, y_1)$ and $P_2(x_2, y_2)$.

Step 2 : Scan corners for the window as $(\omega x_1, \omega y_1)$ and $(\omega x_2, \omega y_2)$.

Step 3 : Assign the region codes for endpoints P_1 and P_2 by initializing code with 0000.

Bit 1 - if $(x < \omega x_1)$

Bit 2 - if $(x > \omega x_2)$

Bit 3 - if $(y < \omega y_2)$

Bit 4 - if $(y > \omega y_1)$

Step 4 : Check for visibility of line P_1, P_2.

(i) If region codes for both end points are zero then the line is visible, draw it and jump to step 6.

(ii) If region codes for end points are not zero and the logical Anding operation of them is also not zero then the line is invisible, reject it and jump to step 6.

(iii) If region codes for end points does not satisfies the condition in 4 (i) and 4 (ii) then line is partly visible.

Step5 : Find midpoint of line and divide it into two equal line segments and repeat steps 3 through 5 for both subdivided line segments until you get completely visible and completely invisible line segments.

Step 6 : Exit.

- The midpoint subdivision algorithm requires repeated subdivision of line segments and hence many times it is slower than using directs calculation of the intersection of the line with clipping window edge.
- However, it can be implemented efficiently using parallel architecture since it involves parallel operations.

6.3.3 Cyrus Beck Line Clipping Algorithm [April 16]

- This algorithm is developed by Cyrus and Beck in 1978 and used to clip 2D/3D lines against convex polygon/polyhedron.
- Cyrus Beck Line clipping algorithm is actually, a parametric line-clipping algorithm.
- The term parametric means that we require finding the value of the parameter t in the parametric representation of the line segment for the point at that the segment intersects the clipping edge.
- Consider line segment P_1P_2. The parametric equation of line segment P_1P_2 is

  $$P(t) = P_1 + t(P_2 - P_1) \quad \ldots (1)$$

  Where, t value defines a point on the line going through P_1 and P_2.

  $0 <= t <= 1$ defines line segment between P_1 and P_2.

  If $t = 0$ then $P(0) = P_1$. If $t = 1$ then $P(1) = P_2$.

- Consider a convex clipping region R, f is a boundary point of the convex region R and n is an inner normal for one of its boundaries as shown in Fig. 6.7.

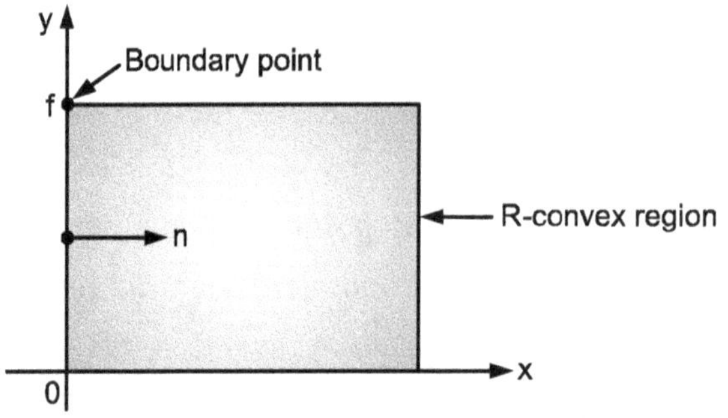

Fig. 6.7: Convex region, boundary point and inner normal.

- Then we can distinguish in which region a point lie by looking at the value of the dot product n.[P(t) – f], as shown in Fig. 6.8.
- If dot product is negative i.e.,

  $n.[P(t) - f\,] < 0$ ... (2)

  then the vector P(t) – f] is pointed away from the interior of R.
- If dot product is zero i.e.,

  $n.[P(t) - f\,] = 0$ ... (3)

  then the vector P(t) – f] is pointed parallel to the plane containing f and perpendicular to the normal.
- If dot product is positive i.e.,

  $n.[P(t) - f\,] > 0$ ... (4)

  then the vector P(t) – f] is pointed towards the interior of R.

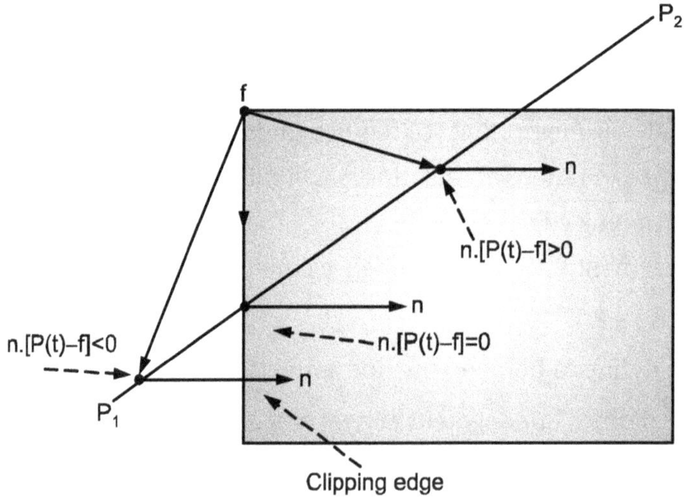

Fig. 6.8: Dot products for three points inside, outside and on the boundary of the clipping region

- As shown in Fig. 6.8 if the point f lies in the boundary plane or edge for which n is the inner normal, then that point t on the line P(t) which satisfies,

  n.[P(t) – f] = 0 condition is the intersection of the line with the boundary edge.
- To get the formal statement of the Cyrus-Beck algorithm we substitute value of P(t) in equation 3.

  $n \cdot [P(t) - f] = n \cdot [P_1 + (P_2 - P_1)t - f] = 0$ ... (5)
- The relation should be applied for each boundary plane or edge of the window to get the intersection points. Thus in general form equation (5) can be written as,

  $n_i \cdot [P_1 + (P_2 - P_1)t - f_i] = 0$ ... (6)

  where, i is edge number.
- Solving equation (6) we get,

  $n_i \cdot [P_1 - f_i] + n_i \cdot (P_2 - P_1)t = 0$ ... (7)
- Here the vector $P_2 - P_1$ defines the direction of the line. The direction of the line is important to correctly identify the visibility of the line. The vector $P_1 - f_i$ is proportional to the distance from the end point of the line to the boundary point.
- Let us define,

  $D = P_2 - P_1$ as the direction of a line and

  $W_i = P_1 - f_i$ as weighting factor.
- Substituting newly defined variable D and W_i in Equation (7) we get,

  $n_i.W_i + (n_i \cdot D)t = 0$ ... (8)

  $t = -\ (n_i \cdot W_i)/(n_i.D)$ ... (9)

  where, $D \neq 0$ and i = 1, 2, 3 .....
- The equation (9) is used to obtain the value of t for the intersection of the line with each edge of the clipping window. We must select the proper value for t using following tips :
  1. If t is outside the range $0 <= t <= 1$, then it can be ignored.
  2. We know that, the line can intersect the convex window in at most two points , i.e. at two values of t. With equation (9) , there can be several values of t in the range of $0 <= t <= 1$. We have to choose the largest lower limit and the smallest upper limit.
  3. If $(n_i \cdot Di) > 0$ then equation (9) gives lower limit value for t and if $(n_i \cdot Di) < 0$ then equation (9) gives upper limit value for t.

Algorithm Cyrus Beck Line Clipping Algorithm:

Step 1 : Read end points of line P_1 and P_2.

Step 2 : Read vertex coordinates of clipping window.

Step 3 : Calculate $D = P_2 - P_1$.

Step 4 : Assign boundary point b with particular edge.

Step 5 : Find inner normal vector for corresponding edge.

Step 6 : Calculate D.n and W = $P_1 - b$

Step 7 : If D.n > 0

$t_L = -(W.n)/(D.n)$

else

$t_U = -(W.n)/(D.n)$

end if

Step 8 : Repeat steps 4 through 7 for each edge of clipping window.

Step 9 : Find maximum lower limit and minimum upper limit.

Step 10: If maximum lower limit and minimum upper limit do not satisfy condition $0 \le t \le 1$ then ignore line.

Step 11: Calculate intersection points by substituting values of maximum lower limit and minimum upper limit in parametric equation of line P_1P_2.

Step 12: Draw line segment $P(t_L)$ to $P(t_U)$.

Step 13: Stop.

Example: Fig 6.9 shows the Hexagonal clipping window. The line $P_1(-2, 1)$ to $P_2(6, 3)$ is to be clipped to this window. Find the intersection points.

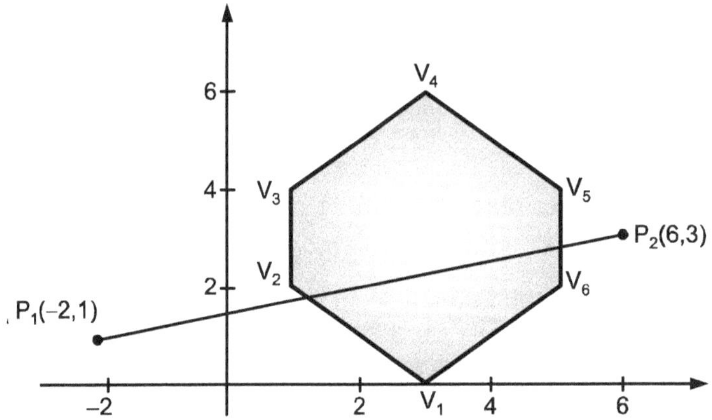

Fig. 6.9: Hexagonal clipping window

Solution: We know that,

$$D = P_2 - P_1 = [6\ 3] - [2 - 1] = [8\ 2]$$

For boundary points f(3, 0)

$$W = P_1 - f = [-2\ 1] - [3\ 0] = [-5\ 1]$$

For the edge $V_1 V_2$ the inner normal is,

$$n = [1\ 1]$$

Hence, $$D \cdot n = [8\ 2] \cdot [1\ 1] = 10 > 0$$

∴ The lower limit can be given as:

$$t_L = \frac{W \cdot n}{D \cdot n} = \frac{[-5\ \ 1]\ [1\ \ 1]}{10}$$

$$= -\frac{(-4)}{10} = \frac{4}{10}$$

Similar calculation with each edge gives the complete results of the Cyrus-Beck algorithm. These results are tabulated in following table:

Edge	n	f	W	W·n	D·n	t_L	t_U
$V_1 V_2$	[1 1]	(3, 0)	[–5 1]	– 4	10	4/10	–
$V_2 V_3$	[1 0]	(1, 4)	[–5 –3]	– 3	8	3/8	–
$V_3 V_4$	[1 –1]	(1, 4)	[–3 –3]	0	6	0	–
$V_4 V_5$	[–1 –1]	(5, 4)	[–7 –3]	10	–10	–	10/10
$V_5 V_6$	[–1 0]	(5, 4)	[–7 –3]	7	–8	–	7/8
$V_6 V_1$	[–1 1]	(3, 0)	[–5 1]	6	–6	–	6/6

Referring above table we have,

The maximum lower limit $(t_L) = \frac{4}{10}$ and

The minimum upper limit (t_U) = 7/8

Substituting these values of t in parametric equation,

We get,

$$P\left(\frac{4}{10}\right) = [-2\ \ 1] + [8\ \ 2]\left(\frac{4}{10}\right)$$

$$= [-2\ \ 1] + [3.2\ \ \ 0.8]$$

$$= [1.2\ \ \ 1.8]$$

$$P\left(\frac{7}{8}\right) = [-2\ \ 1] + [8\ \ 2]\left(\frac{7}{8}\right)$$

$$= [-2\ \ 1] + [7\ \ 1.75]$$

$$= [5\ \ 2.75]$$

Thus, the two intersection points to line P_1P_2 are [1.2 1.8] and [5 2.75] with edges V_1V_2 and V_5V_6 respectively.

Advantages:

1. It is more powerful trivial rejection algorithm that detects lines that cross several outside clip regions.
2. It avoids calculation and follows the basic principle of coordinate geometry.

3. It is non-iterative
4. It faster and efficient than Cohen-Sutherland Algorithm.
5. Clipping window can be convex.

Disadvantages:

1. The main disadvantage of the CB algorithm is a direct line intersection computation for all planes which form the boundary of the given convex polyhedron.

6.4 POLYGON CLIPPING [Oct. 16]

- Polygon clipping is removal of part of an object outside a polygon.
- A polygon is nothing but collection of lines. Therefore, we might think that line clipping algorithm can be used directly for polygon clipping.
- However, when a closed polygon is clipped as a collection of lines with line clipping algorithm, the original closed polygon becomes one or more open polygon or discrete lines as shown in the Fig. 6.10.
- Thus, we need to modify the line clipping algorithm to clip polygons.

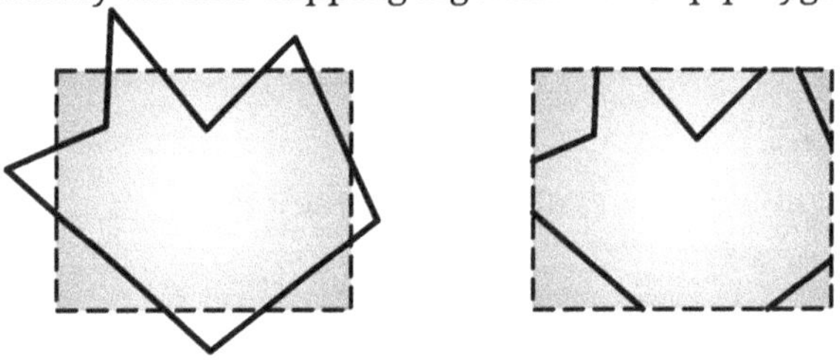

(a) Before clipping (b) After clipping

Fig. 6.10: Polygon clipping by line clipping algorithm

- As we consider a polygon as a closed area; hence after clipping it should remain closed.
- To achieve this we require an algorithm that will generate additional line segment which make the polygon as closed area.
- Polygon can be of two types i.e. Convex polygon and Concave polygon.
  1. **Convex Polygon**: It is a polygon in which if you take any two positions of polygon then all the points on the line segment joining these two points fall within the polygon itself.
  2. **Concave Polygon**: It is a polygon in which if you take any two positions of polygon then all the points on the line segment joining these two points does not fall entirely within the polygon.

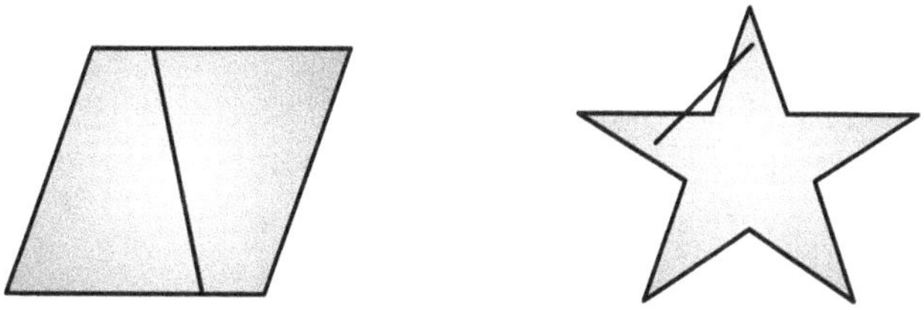

(a) Convex polygon (b) Concave polygon

Fig. 6.11

6.4.1 Sutherland-Hodgeman Polygon Clipping [April 16]

- In Sutherland-Hodgeman, a polygon is clipped by processing the polygon boundary as a whole against each window edge. Clipping window must be convex.
- This could be accomplished by processing all polygon vertices against each clip rectangle boundary in turn beginning with the original set of polygon vertices, first clip the polygon against the left rectangle boundary to produce a new sequence of vertices.
- The new set of vertices could then be successively passed to a right boundary clipper, a top boundary clipper and a bottom boundary clipper.
- At each step a new set of polygon vertices us generated and passed to the next window boundary clipper. This is the logic used in Sutherland-Hodgeman algorithm.

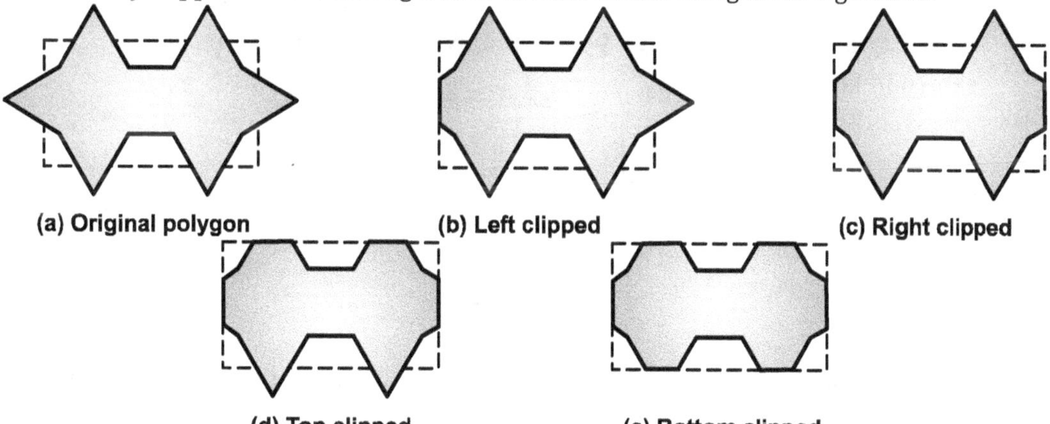

Fig. 6.12: Clipping polygon against successive window boundaries

- The output of algorithm is a list of polygon vertices all of which are on the visible side of clipping plane. Such each edge of the polygon is individually compared with the clipping plane.
- This is achieved by processing two vertices of each edge of the polygon around the clipping boundary or plane.

- This results in four possible relationships between the edge and clipping plane.
  1. If first vertex of polygon edge is outside and second is inside window boundary, then intersection point of polygon edge with window boundary and second vertex are added to output vertices set as shown in Fig. 6.13.

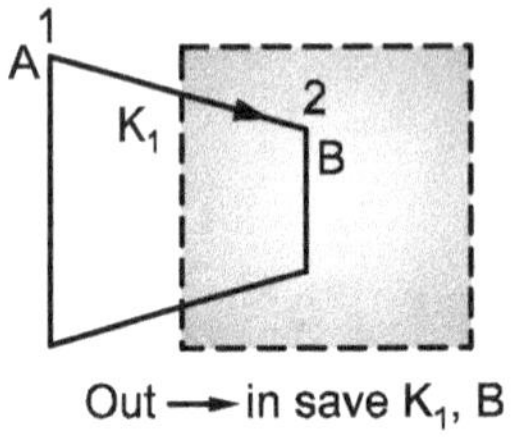

Fig. 6.13

  2. If both vertices of edge are inside window boundary, then add only second vertex to output set as shown in Fig. 6.14.

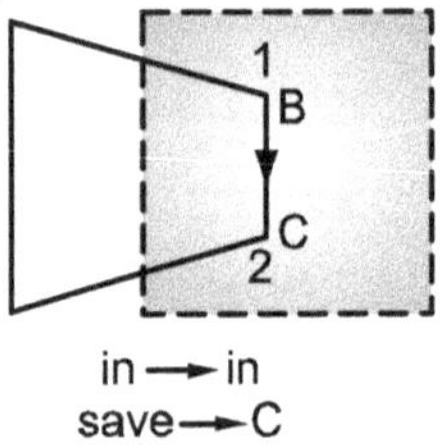

Fig. 6.14

  3. If first vertex of edge is inside and second is outside of window boundary then point of intersection of edge with window boundary is stored in output set as shown in Fig. 6.15.

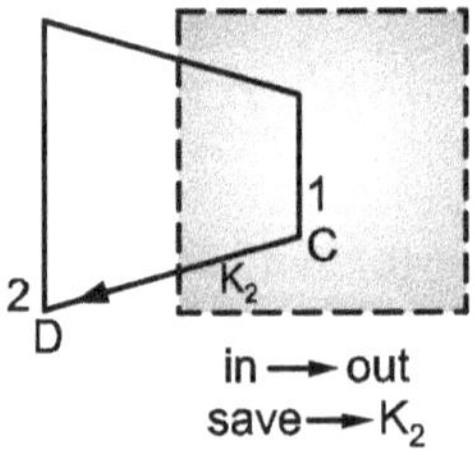

Fig. 6.15

  4. If both vertices of edges are outside of window boundary then those vertices are rejected as shown in Fig. 6.16.

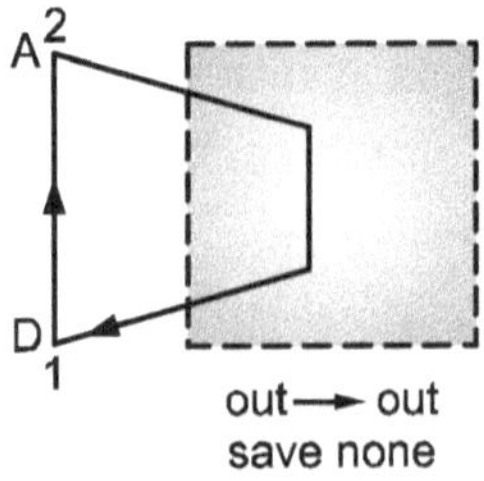

Fig. 6.16

- Going through above four cases we can realize that there are two key processes in this algorithm:
  1. Determine the visibility of point or vertex (Inside – Outside Test)
  2. Determine the intersection of the polygon edge and clipping plane.
- The second key process in Sutherland-Hodgeman polygon clipping algorithm is to determine the intersection of the polygon edge and clipping plane.
- Assume that we're clipping a polgon's edge with vertices at (x_1, y_1) and (x_2, y_2) against a clip window with vertices at (x_{min}, y_{min}) and (x_{max}, y_{max}).
  1. The location (I_X, I_Y) of the intersection of the edge with the left side of the window is:
     (i) $I_X = x_{min}$
     (ii) $I_Y = slope*(x_{min} - x_1) + y_1$, where the slope $= (y_2 - y_1)/(x_2 - x_1)$.
  2. The location of the intersection of the edge with the right side of the window is:
     (i) $I_X = x_{max}$
     (ii) $I_Y = slope*(x_{max} - x_1) + y_1$, where the slope $= (y_2 - y_1)/(x_2 - x_1)$
  3. The intersection of the polygon's edge with the top side of the window is:
     (i) $I_X = x_1 + (y_{max} - y_1) / slope$
     (ii) $I_Y = y_{max}$
  4. Finally, the intersection of the edge with the bottom side of the window is:
     (i) $I_X = x_1 + (y_{min} - y_1) / slope$
     (ii) $I_Y = y_{min}$

Algorithm for Sutherland-Hodgeman Polygon Clipping:

Step 1 : Read co-ordinates of all vertices of the polygon.

Step 2 : Read co-ordinates of the clipping window.

Step 3 : Consider the left edge of window.

Step 4 : Compare vertices of each of polygon, individually with the clipping plane.

Step 5 : Save the resulting intersections and vertices in the new list of vertices according to four possible relationships between the edge and the clipping boundary.

Step 6 : Repeat the steps 4 and 5 for remaining edges of clipping window. Each time resultant list of vertices is successively passed to process next edge of clipping window.

Step 7 : Stop.

Advantages:

1. It is simple to implement.
2. It can be extended to 3-D cubic volumes.

Disadvantages:

1. Clipping window must be rectangular or convex.
2. The Sutherland-Hodgeman Polygon Clipping algorithm clips convex polygons correctly but in case of concave polygons, clipped polygon may be displayed with extraneous lines.

Example 1: Illustrate the Sutherland - Hodgman algorithm for clipping the polygon P_1 P_2 P_3 P_4 P_5 P_6 against a rectangular window ABCD.

Solution:

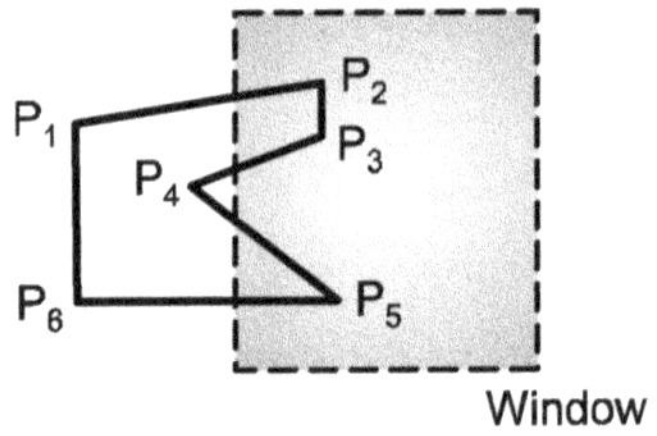

Fig. 6.17

Step 1 : Clip the polygon P_1 P_2 P_3 P_4 P_5 P_6 against the left boundary.

(a) For P_1 P_2:

Vertex P_1 is outside and vertex P_2 is inside the window boundary.

$P_1 \to P_2$ $\quad\therefore$ Save S_1 and P_2

out $\to$ in

(b) For P_2 P_3:

P_2 is inside and P_3 is inside

$P_2 \to P_3$ $\quad\therefore$ Save P_3

in $\to$ in

(c) For P_3 P_4:

P_3 is inside and P_4 is outside

$P_3 \to P_4$ $\quad\therefore$ Save S_2

in $\to$ out

(d) For P_4 P_5:

P_4 is outside and P_5 is inside

$P_4 \to P_5$ $\quad\therefore$ save S_3 and P_5

out $\to$ in

(e) For P_5 P_6:

P_5 is inside and P_6 is outside

$P_5 \to P_6$ $\quad\therefore$ save S_4

in $\to$ out

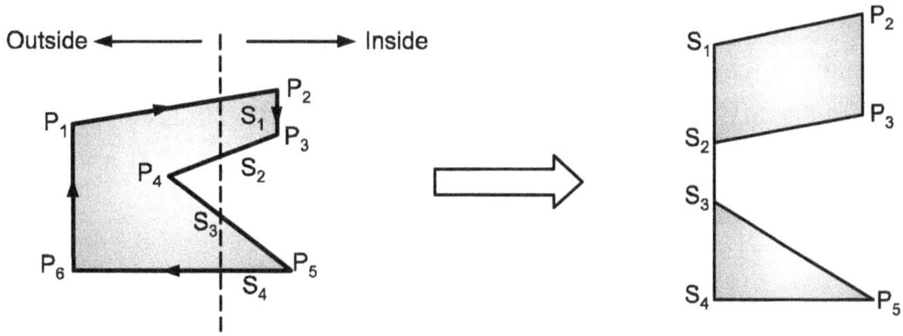

Fig. 6.18

Step 2 : Clip the polygon S_1 P_2 P_3 S_2 S_3 P_5 S_4 against the right boundary.

All the vertices are inside the right window boundary.

Therefore,

(a) For $S_1 \rightarrow P_2$, save P_2 (b) For $P_2 \rightarrow P_3$, save P_3

(c) For $P_3 \rightarrow S_2$, save S_2 (d) For $S_2 \rightarrow S_3$, save S_3

(e) For $S_3 \rightarrow P_5$, save P_5 (f) For $P_5 \rightarrow S_4$, save S_4

(g) For $S_4 \rightarrow S_1$, save S_1

P_2 P_3 S_2 S_3 P_5 S_4 S_1 as the result of right boundary clipper.

Step 3 : Clip the polygon P_2 P_3 S_2 S_3 P_5 S_4 S_1 against the bottom boundary.

All the vertices are inside the bottom window boundary.

Therefore, P_3 S_2 S_3 P_5 S_4 S_1 P_2 is the result of bottom boundary clipper.

Step 4 : Clip the polygon P_3 S_2 S_3 P_5 S_4 S_1 P_2 against the top boundary.

All the vertices are inside the top window boundary.

Therefore, S_2 S_3 P_5 S_4 S_1 S_2 P_3 is the result of top boundary clipper.

6.4.2 Weiler-Atherton Algorithm

- In previously discussed section, the clipping algorithms have used convex polygon as clipping window. But in many applications e.g. hidden surface removal, ability to clip concave polygon is required. To meet this requirement, Weiler and Atherton developed complex but powerful algorithm.
- Weiler-Atherton algorithm defines the polygon to be clipped as a subject polygon and the clipping region as the clip polygon.
- The algorithm describes both the subject and clip polygon by maintaining a circular list of vertices.
- The boundaries of subject polygon and the clip polygon may or may not intersect. If they intersect, then the intersections occur in pairs.

- One of the intersections occurs when subject polygon edge enters the inside of the clip polygon and one when it leaves.
- As shown in Fig. 6.19 there are four intersections vertices I_1, I_2, I_3 and I_4.
- In these intersections I_1 and I_3 are entering intersections, and I_2 and I_3 are leaving intersections.
- The clip polygon vertices are marked as C_1, C_2, C_3 and C_4.

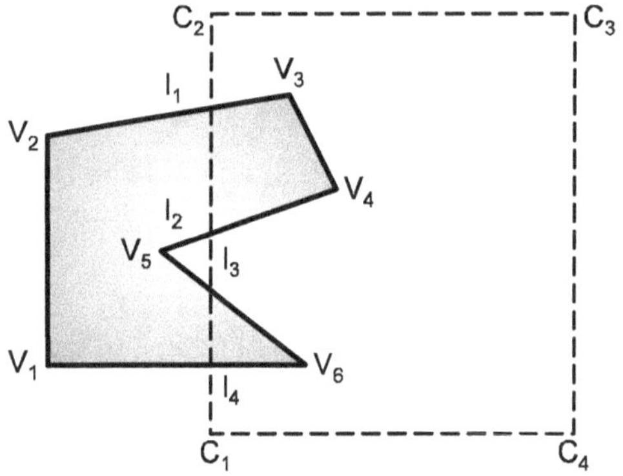

Fig. 6.19: Weiler-Atherton Algorithm

- In this algorithm two separate vertices lists are made one for clip polygon and one for subject polygon including intersections points.
- The following table shows these two lists for polygons shown in Fig. 6.19.

For subject polygon	For clip polygon
V_1	C_1
V_2	I_4
Start I_1	I_3 Finish
V_3	I_2
V_4	I_1 Finish
I_2	C_2
V_5	C_3
Start I_3	C_4
V_6	
I_4	
V_1	

- In this algorithm, we start at an entering section (I_1) and follows the subject polygon vertex list in downward direction (i.e. I_1, V_3, V_4, I_2).
- At occurrence of leaving intersection the algorithm follows the clip polygon vertex list from leaving vertex in downward direction (i.e. I_2, I_1).

- At occurrence of entering intersection the algorithm follows subject polygon vertex list from the entering intersection vertex.
- This process is repeated till we get starting vertex. This process has to be repeated for all remaining entering intersections which are not included in the previous traversing of vertex list.
- Since, I_3 was not included in first traverse, hence, we start the second traversal from I_3.
- Therefore, first traversal gives polygon as: I_1, V_3, V_4, I_2, I_1 and second traversal gives polygon as: I_3, V_6, I_4, I_3.

Programs in OpenGL

1. **Cohen-Sutherland Line Clipping Algorithm with Window to viewport Mapping using OpenGL API.**

   Objective: In this program the students will learn to implement Cohen-Sutherland Line Clipping Algorithm with Window to viewport Mapping with OpenGL API.

```
#include <stdio.h>
#include <GL/glut.h>
#define outcode int
#define true 1
#define false 0
double xmin=50,ymin=50, xmax=100,ymax=100; // Window boundaries
double xvmin=200,yvmin=200,xvmax=300,yvmax=300; // Viewport boundaries
//int x1, x2, y1, y2;
//bit codes for the right, left, top, & bottom
const int RIGHT = 8;
const int LEFT = 2;
const int TOP = 4;
const int BOTTOM = 1;
//used to compute bit codes of a point
outcode ComputeOutCode (double x, double y);
//Cohen-Sutherland clipping algorithm clips a line from
//P0 = (x0, y0) to P1 = (x1, y1) against a rectangle with
//diagonal from (xmin, ymin) to (xmax, ymax).
void CohenSutherlandLineClipAndDraw (double x0, double y0,double x1, double y1)
{
   //Outcodes for P0, P1, and whatever point lies outside the clip rectangle
   outcode outcode0, outcode1, outcodeOut;
   bool accept = false, done = false;
```

```
    //compute outcodes
    outcode0 = ComputeOutCode (x0, y0);
    outcode1 = ComputeOutCode (x1, y1);
    do{
    if (!(outcode0 | outcode1))     //logical or is 0 Trivially accept & exit
     {
        accept = true;
        done = true;
     }
     else if (outcode0 & outcode1) //logical  and  is  not  0.  Trivially  reject
and exit
     done = true;
    else
    {
        //failed both tests, so calculate the line segment to clip
        //from an outside point to an intersection with clip edge
        double x, y;
        //At least one endpoint is outside the clip rectangle; pick it.
        outcodeOut = outcode0? outcode0: outcode1;
        //Now find the intersection point;
        //use formulas y = y0 + slope * (x - x0), x = x0 + (1/slope)* (y - y0)
        if (outcodeOut & TOP)           //point is above the clip rectangle
        {
           x = x0 + (x1 - x0) * (ymax - y0)/(y1 - y0);
           y = ymax;
        }
        else if (outcodeOut & BOTTOM)  //point is below the clip rectangle
        {
           x = x0 + (x1 - x0) * (ymin - y0)/(y1 - y0);
           y = ymin;
        }
        else if (outcodeOut & RIGHT) //point is to the right of clip rectangle
        {
           y = y0 + (y1 - y0) * (xmax - x0)/(x1 - x0);
           x = xmax;
        }
```

```
    else      //point is to the left of clip rectangle
    {
       y = y0 + (y1 - y0) * (xmin - x0)/(x1 - x0);
       x = xmin;
    }
    //Now we move outside point to intersection point to clip
    //and get ready for next pass.
    if (outcodeOut == outcode0)
    {
       x0 = x;
       y0 = y;
       outcode0 = ComputeOutCode (x0, y0);
    }
    else
    {
       x1 = x;
       y1 = y;
       outcode1 = ComputeOutCode (x1, y1);
    }
}
}while (!done);
if (accept)
{   // Window to viewport mappings
    double sx=(xvmax-xvmin)/(xmax-xmin); // Scale parameters
    double sy=(yvmax-yvmin)/(ymax-ymin);
    double vx0=xvmin+(x0-xmin)*sx;
    double vy0=yvmin+(y0-ymin)*sy;
    double vx1=xvmin+(x1-xmin)*sx;
    double vy1=yvmin+(y1-ymin)*sy;  //draw a red colored viewport
          glColor3f(1.0, 0.0, 0.0);
          glBegin(GL_LINE_LOOP);
                glVertex2f(xvmin, yvmin);
                glVertex2f(xvmax, yvmin);
                glVertex2f(xvmax, yvmax);
                glVertex2f(xvmin, yvmax);
          glEnd();
```

```
            glColor3f(0.0,0.0,1.0); // draw blue colored clipped line
            glBegin(GL_LINES);
                glVertex2d (vx0, vy0);
                glVertex2d (vx1, vy1);
            glEnd();
    }
}
//Compute the bit code for a point (x, y) using the clip rectangle
//bounded diagonally by (xmin, ymin), and (xmax, ymax)
outcode ComputeOutCode (double x, double y)
{
    outcode code = 0;
    if (y > ymax)                   //above the clip window
        code |= TOP;
    else if (y < ymin)              //below the clip window
        code |= BOTTOM;
    if (x > xmax)                   //to the right of clip window
        code |= RIGHT;
    else if (x < xmin)              //to the left of clip window
        code |= LEFT;
    return code;
}
void display()
{
    double x0=120,y0=10,x1=40,y1=130;
    glClear(GL_COLOR_BUFFER_BIT);
    //draw the line with red color
    glColor3f(1.0,0.0,0.0);
    //bres(120,20,340,250);
    glBegin(GL_LINES);
            glVertex2d (x0, y0);
            glVertex2d (x1, y1);
            glVertex2d (60,20);
            glVertex2d (80,120);
            glEnd();
```

```
    //draw a blue colored window
    glColor3f(0.0, 0.0, 1.0);
    glBegin(GL_LINE_LOOP);
        glVertex2f(xmin, ymin);
        glVertex2f(xmax, ymin);
        glVertex2f(xmax, ymax);
        glVertex2f(xmin, ymax);
        glEnd();
    CohenSutherlandLineClipAndDraw(x0,y0,x1,y1);
    CohenSutherlandLineClipAndDraw(60,20,80,120);
    glFlush();
}
void myinit()
{
    glClearColor(1.0,1.0,1.0,1.0);
    glColor3f(1.0,0.0,0.0);
    glPointSize(1.0);
    glMatrixMode(GL_PROJECTION);
    glLoadIdentity();
    gluOrtho2D(0.0,499.0,0.0,499.0);
}
int main(int argc, char** argv)
{
    glutInit(&argc,argv);
    glutInitDisplayMode(GLUT_SINGLE|GLUT_RGB);
    glutInitWindowSize(500,500);
    glutInitWindowPosition(0,0);
    glutCreateWindow("Cohen Suderland Line Clipping Algorithm");
    glutDisplayFunc(display);
    myinit();
    glutMainLoop();
}
```

2. Write C/C++ program to implement the Sutherland Hodgman polygon clipping algorithm, (work on Windows platform).

```
#include <windows.h>
#include <gl/glut.h>
struct Point{
    float x,y;
} w[4],oVer[4];
int Nout;
void drawPoly(Point p[],int n){
    glBegin(GL_POLYGON);
    for(int i=0;i<n;i++)
        glVertex2f(p[i].x,p[i].y);
    glEnd();
}
bool insideVer(Point p){
        if((p.x>=w[0].x)&&(p.x<=w[2].x))
            if((p.y>=w[0].y)&&(p.y<=w[2].y))
                return true;
        return false;
}
void addVer(Point p){
    oVer[Nout]=p;
    Nout=Nout+1;
}
Point getInterSect(Point s,Point p,int edge){
    Point in;
    float m;
    if(w[edge].x==w[(edge+1)%4].x){ //Vertical Line
        m=(p.y-s.y)/(p.x-s.x);
        in.x=w[edge].x;
        in.y=in.x*m+s.y;
    }
    else{//Horizontal Line
        m=(p.y-s.y)/(p.x-s.x);
        in.y=w[edge].y;
        in.x=(in.y-s.y)/m;
    }
    return in;
}
```

```
void clipAndDraw(Point inVer[],int Nin){
    Point s,p,interSec;
    for(int i=0;i<4;i++)
    {
        Nout=0;
        s=inVer[Nin-1];
        for(int j=0;j<Nin;j++)
        {
            p=inVer[j];
            if(insideVer(p)==true){
                if(insideVer(s)==true){
                    addVer(p);
                }
                else{
                    interSec=getInterSect(s,p,i);
                    addVer(interSec);
                    addVer(p);
                }
            }
            else{
                if(insideVer(s)==true){
                    interSec=getInterSect(s,p,i);
                    addVer(interSec);
                }
            }
           s=p;
       }
       inVer=oVer;
            Nin=Nout;
        }
        drawPoly(oVer,4);
    }
```

```
void init(){
    glClearColor(0.0f,0.0f,0.0f,0.0f);
    glMatrixMode(GL_PROJECTION);
    glLoadIdentity();
    glOrtho(0.0,100.0,0.0,100.0,0.0,100.0);
    glClear(GL_COLOR_BUFFER_BIT);
    w[0].x =20,w[0].y=10;
    w[1].x =20,w[1].y=80;
    w[2].x =80,w[2].y=80;
    w[3].x =80,w[3].y=10;
}
void display(void){
    Point inVer[4];
    init();
    // As Window for Clipping
    glColor3f(1.0f,0.0f,0.0f);
    drawPoly(w,4);
    // As Rect
    glColor3f(0.0f,1.0f,0.0f);
    inVer[0].x =10,inVer[0].y=40;
    inVer[1].x =10,inVer[1].y=60;
    inVer[2].x =60,inVer[2].y=60;
    inVer[3].x =60,inVer[3].y=40;
    drawPoly(inVer,4);
    // As Rect
    glColor3f(0.0f,0.0f,1.0f);
    clipAndDraw(inVer,4);
    // Print
    glFlush();
}
int main(int argc,char *argv[]){
    glutInit(&argc,argv);
    glutInitDisplayMode(GLUT_SINGLE|GLUT_RGB);
    glutInitWindowSize(400,400);
    glutInitWindowPosition(100,100);
    glutCreateWindow("Polygon Clipping!");
    glutDisplayFunc(display);
    glutMainLoop();
    return 0;
}
```

SUMMARY

- The primary use of clipping in computer graphics is to remove objects, lines, or line segments that are outside the viewing pane.
- Any procedure that identifies those portions of a picture that are either inside or outside of a specified region of space is referred to as a clipping.
- The region against which an object is to clip is called a clip window. It is usually rectangular window.
- Rectangular windows are easy to be mapped to computer screen using a transformation called 'window to viewport mapping'.
- Clipping algorithm can be applied in World Coordinates, so that only the contents of the window interior are mapped to Device coordinate.
- Let W denote a clip window with coordinates x_{min}, y_{min}), (x_{min}, y_{max}), (x_{max}, y_{min}), (x_{max}, y_{max}), then a point (x, y) is displayed only if all four of the following "point clipping" inequalities are satisfied: $x_{min} \leq x \leq x_{max}$, and, $y_{min} \leq y \leq y_{max}$
- Line-clipping algorithms include the Cohen-Sutherland method, Midpoint sub-division algorithm and Cyrus Beck Line clipping algorithm
- Cohen Sutherland line clipping algorithm is one of the oldest and most popular line-clipping procedures. Generally, the method speeds up the processing of line segments by performing initial tests that reduce the number of the intersections that must be calculated. In this, every line endpoints are assigned a four-digit binary code, called a region code that identifies the location of the point relative to the boundaries of the clipping rectangle. Bit values in the region code are determined by comparing endpoint coordinate values (x, y) to the clip boundaries. Once we have established region codes for all line endpoints, we can quickly determine which lines are completely inside the clip window and which are clearly outside. A method that can be used to test lines for total clipping is to perform the logical AND operation with both region codes. If the result is not 0000, the line is completely outside the clipping region.
- Midpoint subdivision algorithm avoids calculation of intersecting point by repeatedly subdividing the line at its midpoint. It follows principle of divide and conquer strategy. The line is tested for visibility. If line is completely visible then it is drawn and completely invisible then rejected. If line is partially visible, then it is divided in equal subparts and visibility test is applied for each part. The subdivision process is repeated until we get completely visible and completely invisible line segments.
- Cyrus Beck line clipping algorithm is actually, a parametric line-clipping algorithm. The term parametric means that we require finding the value of the parameter t in the parametric representation of the line segment for the point at that the segment intersects the clipping edge.

- Polygon-clipping algorithms include the Sutherland-Hodgman method, Weiler and Atherton method.
- In Sutherland-Hodgeman, a polygon is clipped by processing the polygon boundary as a whole against each window edge. This could be accomplished by processing all polygon vertices against each clip rectangle boundary in turn beginning with the original set of polygon vertices, first clip the polygon against the left rectangle boundary to produce a new sequence of vertices. The new set of vertices could then be successively passed to a right boundary clipper, a top boundary clipper and a bottom boundary clipper. At each step a new set of polygon vertices us generated and passed to the next window boundary clipper. This is the logic used in Sutherland-Hodgeman algorithm.
- Weiler and Atherton developed complex but powerful algorithm for concave polygons. This algorithm defines the polygon to be clipped as a subject polygon and the clipping region is the clip polygon. The boundaries of subject polygon and the clip polygon may or may not intersect. If they intersect, then the intersections occur in pairs. One of the intersections occurs when subject polygon edge enters the inside of the clip polygon and one when it leaves.

PRACTICE QUESTIONS

1. What is clipping? Give applications of clipping.
2. Distinguish between concave and convex polygon.
3. What are the constraints for point clipping?
4. Which are inside-outside tests performed for line clipping?
5. How the 4-bit region codes are set?
6. Line clipping algorithm cannot be used for polygon clipping. Justify.
7. Explain Cohen-Sutherland Line clipping algorithm.
8. Explain Mid-point subdivision Line clipping algorithm.
9. Explain Cyrus Beck Line clipping algorithm.
10. Explain Sutherland-Hodgeman polygon clipping algorithm.
11. Explain Weiler-Atherton polygon clipping algorithm.

■■■

CHAPTER 7

3D Transformation and Viewing

Contents ...

Objectives...

- To Learn 3D Transformation on Object like Translation, Rotation, Scaling etc.
- To Understand Concept of Three Dimensional Viewing and Projection
- To Study General Projection Transformation for Parallel and Perspective Projection
- To Learn Concept of 3D Clipping

7.1 INTRODUCTION

- The field of computer graphics concerned with generating and displaying three-dimensional objects in a two-dimensional space (e.g., the display screen).
- Pixels in a two-dimensional graphic have the properties of position, colour, and brightness, whereas a 3-D pixel adds a depth property that indicates where the point lies on an imaginary Z-axis.
- When many 3-D pixels are combined, each with its own depth value, the result is a three-dimensional surface, called a texture.
- 3D graphics techniques and their application are fundamental to the entertainment, games, and computer-aided design industries. It is a continuing area of research in scientific visualization.
- Viewing procedures for three-dimensional scenes follow the general approach used in two-dimensional viewing. That is, we first create a world-coordinate scene from the definitions of objects in modelling coordinates.
- Then we set up a viewing coordinate reference frame and transfer object descriptions from world coordinates to viewing coordinates.
- Finally, viewing-coordinate descriptors are transformed to device coordinates. Unlike two-dimensional viewing, however, three-dimensional viewing requires projection routines to transform object descriptions to a viewing plane before the transformation to device coordinates.

7.2 3D TRANSFORMATION

- Manipulation viewing and construction of three dimensional graphics image requires the use of three dimensional geometric and co-ordinate transformation.
- We will consider here only geometric transformation. In geometric transformation, an object is transformed to new position or new size keeping the co-ordinate system stationary.
- Methods for geometric transformations and object modelling in 3D are extended from 2D methods by including the considerations for the z coordinate. Like two dimensional transformations, these transformations are formed by composing basic transformations of translation, scaling, and rotation.
- Each of these transformations can be represented as matrix transformations with homogeneous coordinates. Therefore, any sequence of transformations can be represented as a single matrix, formed by combining the matrices for the individual transformations in the sequence. In homogeneous coordinates, 3D transformations are represented by 4×4 matrices.
- Basic geometric transformations are Translation, Rotation, and Scaling.

7.2.1 Translation

- Translation means shifting an object to new position by given factor and direction from its original position.
- In 3D, translation matrix is,

$$T = \begin{bmatrix} 1 & 0 & 0 & 0 \\ 0 & 1 & 0 & 0 \\ 0 & 0 & 1 & 0 \\ t_x & t_y & t_z & 1 \end{bmatrix}$$

- Therefore, new homogeneous co-ordinates of the translated point are as follows :

$$\therefore \quad P' = P \cdot T$$

$$\therefore \quad [x' \ y' \ z' \ 1] = [x \ y \ z \ 1] \begin{bmatrix} 1 & 0 & 0 & 0 \\ 0 & 1 & 0 & 0 \\ 0 & 0 & 1 & 0 \\ t_x & t_y & t_z & 1 \end{bmatrix}$$

$$= [x + t_x \quad y + t_y \quad z + t_z \quad 1]$$

- Like two dimensional transformation, an object is translated in three dimensions by transforming each vertex of the object. Fig. 7.1 Shows 3D translation.

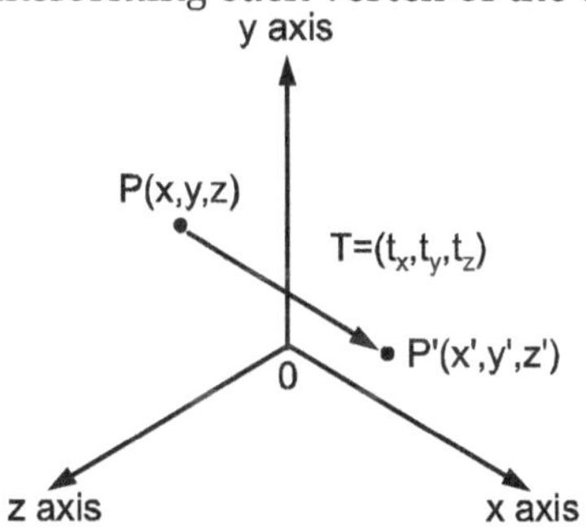

(a) Translating point

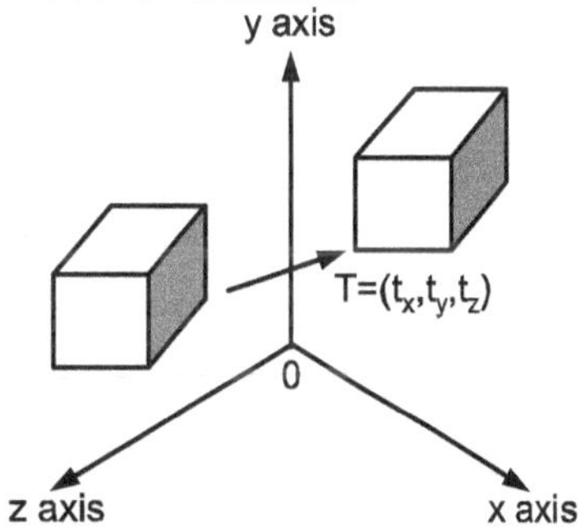

(b) Translating object

Fig. 7.1: 3D translation

7.2.2 Scaling

- Scaling is defined as the process of compressing and expanding of object or changing dimensions of object.
- 3D transformation matrix for scaling is as follows:

$$S = \begin{bmatrix} S_x & 0 & 0 & 0 \\ 0 & S_y & 0 & 0 \\ 0 & 0 & S_z & 0 \\ 0 & 0 & 0 & 1 \end{bmatrix}$$

- It specifies three co-ordinates with their own scaling factors. If scale factors,

  $S_x = S_y = S_z = S > 1$ then the scaling is called as magnification.

  $S_x = S_y = S_z = S < 1$ then the scaling is called as reduction.

  Therefore, point after scaling with respect to origin can be calculated as,

$$\therefore \quad P' = P \cdot S$$

$$\therefore \quad [x' \; y' \; z' \; 1] = [x \; y \; z \; 1] \begin{bmatrix} S_x & 0 & 0 & 0 \\ 0 & S_y & 0 & 0 \\ 0 & 0 & S_z & 0 \\ 0 & 0 & 0 & 1 \end{bmatrix}$$

$$= [x \cdot S_x \quad y \cdot S_y \quad z \cdot S_z \quad 1]$$

- The Fig. 7.2 shows 3D scaling of an object.

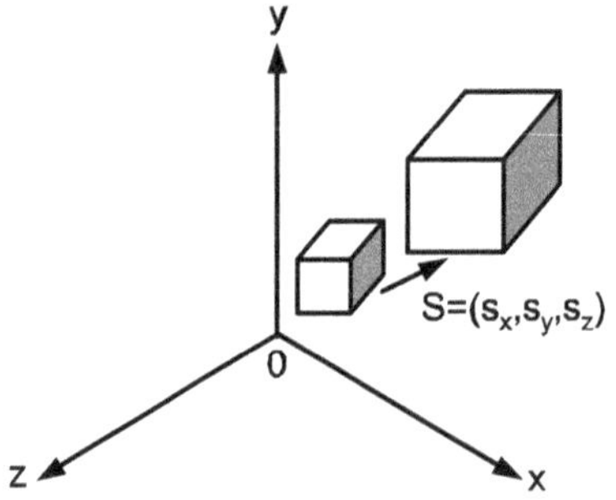

Fig. 7.2: 3D Scaling

- A scaling of an object with respect to a selected fixed position can be represented with the following transformation sequence:
  1. Translate the fixed point to the Origin.
  2. Scale the object relative to the coordinate Origin.
  3. Translate the fixed point back to its original Position.

7.2.3 Rotation

- Unlike two dimensional rotation, where all transformations are carried out in the xy plane, a three-dimensional rotation can be specified around any line in space.
- Therefore, for three dimensional rotation we have to specify an axis of rotation about which the object is to be rotated alongwith the angle of rotation.
- The easiest rotation axes to handle are those that are parallel to the coordinate axes.
- It is possible to combine the coordinate axis rotations to specify any general rotation.
- The positive value of angle θ indicates counterclockwise rotation. For clockwise rotation value of angle θ is negative.

- Rotation about X-axis is given by matrix in clockwise direction:

$$R_x(\theta) = \begin{bmatrix} 1 & 0 & 0 & 0 \\ 0 & \cos\theta & -\sin\theta & 0 \\ 0 & \sin\theta & \cos\theta & 0 \\ 0 & 0 & 0 & 1 \end{bmatrix}$$

$$P' = R_x(\theta) \cdot P$$

$$\therefore \quad [x' \ y' \ z' \ 1] = \begin{bmatrix} 1 & 0 & 0 & 0 \\ 0 & \cos\theta & -\sin\theta & 0 \\ 0 & \sin\theta & \cos\theta & 0 \\ 0 & 0 & 0 & 1 \end{bmatrix} [x \ y \ z \ 1]$$

- The following Fig. 7.3 shows rotation about X-axis.

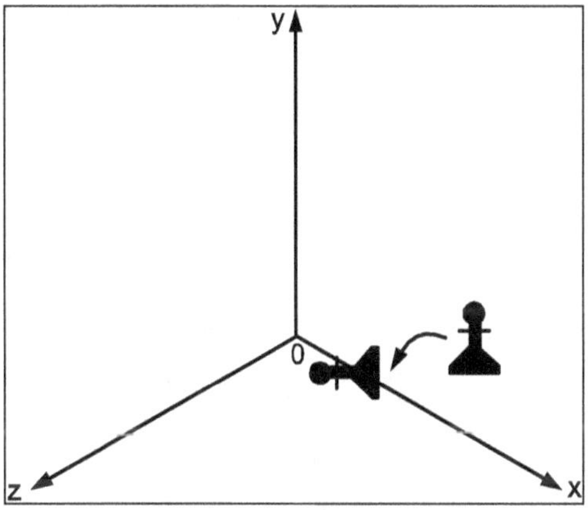

Fig. 7.3: Rotation about X-axis

- Rotation about Y-axis is given by matrix in clockwise direction:

$$R_y(\theta) = \begin{bmatrix} \cos\theta & 0 & \sin\theta & 0 \\ 0 & 1 & 0 & 0 \\ -\sin\theta & 0 & \cos\theta & 0 \\ 0 & 0 & 0 & 1 \end{bmatrix}$$

$$P' = R_y(\theta) \cdot P$$

$$\therefore \quad [x' \ y' \ z' \ 1] = \begin{bmatrix} \cos\theta & 0 & \sin\theta & 0 \\ 0 & 1 & 0 & 0 \\ -\sin\theta & 0 & \cos\theta & 0 \\ 0 & 0 & 0 & 1 \end{bmatrix} [x \ y \ z \ 1]$$

- The following Fig. 7.4 shows rotation about Y-axis.

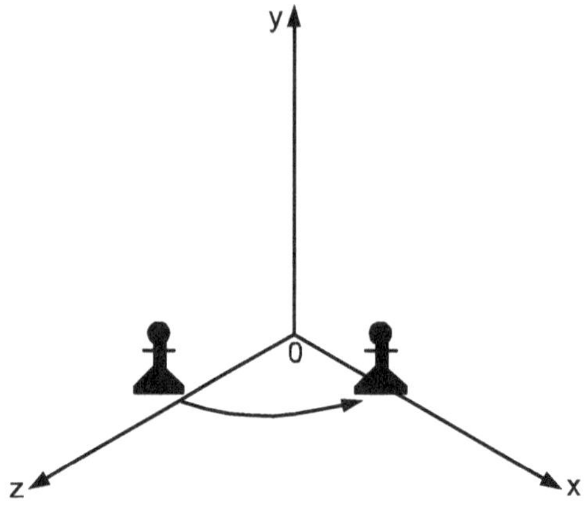

Fig. 7.4: Rotation about Y-axis

- Rotation about Z-axis is given by matrix in clockwise direction:

$$R_z(\theta) = \begin{bmatrix} \cos\theta & -\sin\theta & 0 & 0 \\ \sin\theta & \cos\theta & 0 & 0 \\ 0 & 0 & 1 & 0 \\ 0 & 0 & 0 & 1 \end{bmatrix}$$

$$P' = R_z(\theta) \cdot P$$

$$\therefore \quad [x' \; y' \; z' \; 1] = \begin{bmatrix} \cos\theta & -\sin\theta & 0 & 0 \\ \sin\theta & \cos\theta & 0 & 0 \\ 0 & 0 & 1 & 0 \\ 0 & 0 & 0 & 1 \end{bmatrix} [x \; y \; z \; 1]$$

- The following Fig. 7.5 shows rotation about Z-axis.

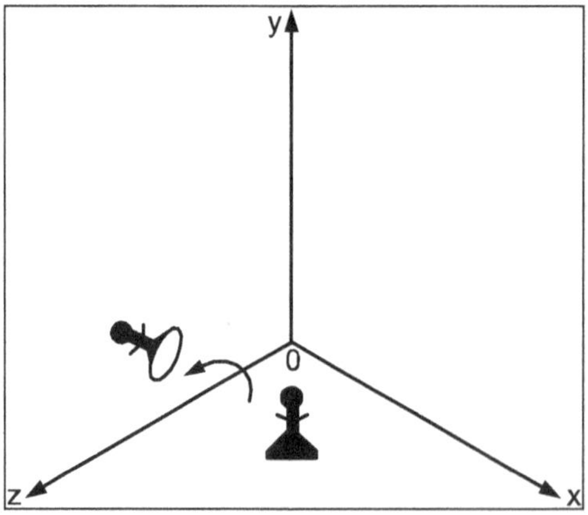

Fig. 7.5: Rotation about Z-axis

Rotation of Object about an Arbitrary Line :

- When an object is to be rotated about an axis that is not parallel to one of the coordinate axes, we have to perform some additional transformations.
- The sequence of these transformations is given below:
  1. Translate object so that the rotation axis passes through the origin.
  2. Rotate object about the x axis so that the rotation axis lies in the xz plane.
  3. Rotate object about the y axis so that the rotation axis lies along the z axis.
  4. Perform the desired rotation by θ about the z axis.
  5. Apply the inverse of step (3). i.e. Rotate object about y axis to bring rotation axis back to original orientation.
  6. Apply the inverse of step (2). i.e. Rotate object about x axis to bring rotation axis back to original orientation.
  7. Apply the inverse of step (1). i.e. Apply inverse translation to move rotation axis back to original orientation.
- The above steps are shown in following Figs. 7.6 to 7.12.
- For example, consider a point (x, y, z). We want to rotate this point by an angle θ which is in space and lying on an arbitrary axis. That is, we follow some steps now:

Step 1 : Translate the arbitrary axis so that it passes through the origin.

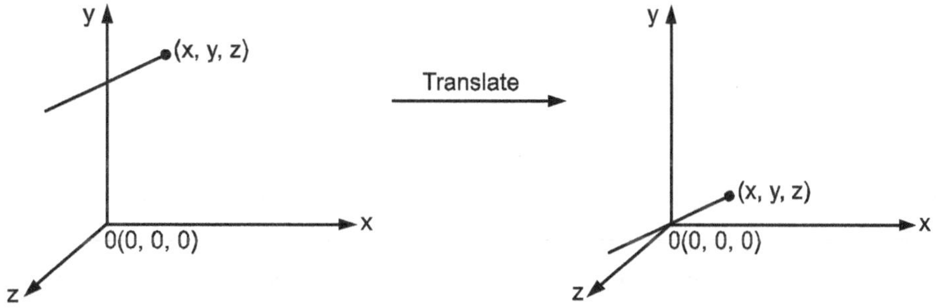

Fig. 7.6: Translation about arbitrary axis

Step 2 : Perform the rotation about x-axis until the arbitrary axis completely lies in xz plate.

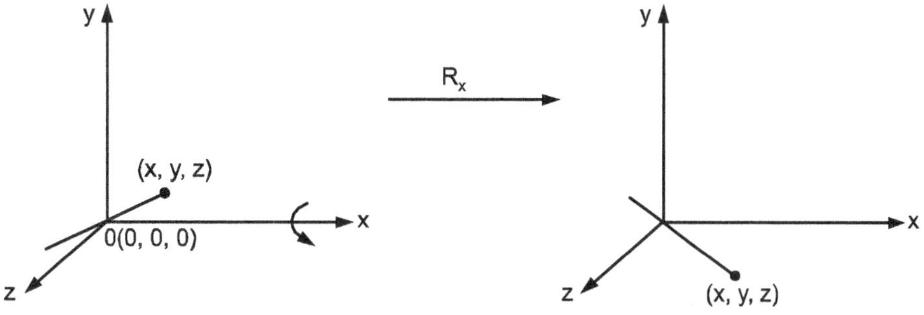

Fig. 7.7: Rotation about x axis

Step 3 : We want arbitrary axis to match one of the coordinate axis. So, we rotate arbitrary axis about y-axis in clockwise direction so that arbitrary axis matches with z-axis i.e.

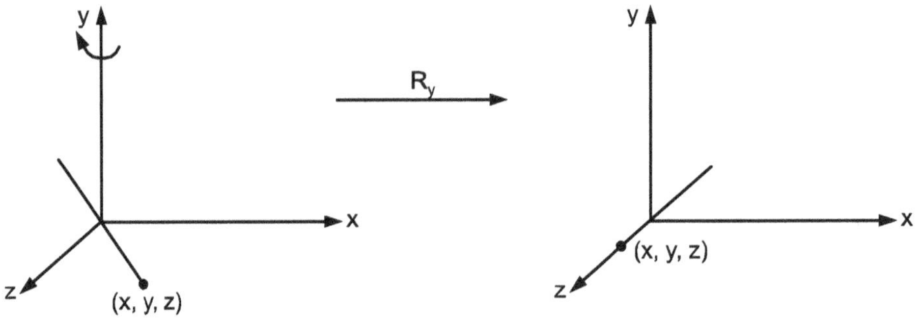

Fig. 7.8: Rotate arbitrary axis about y axis

Step 4 : Now, we rotate arbitrary axis about z-axis i.e.,

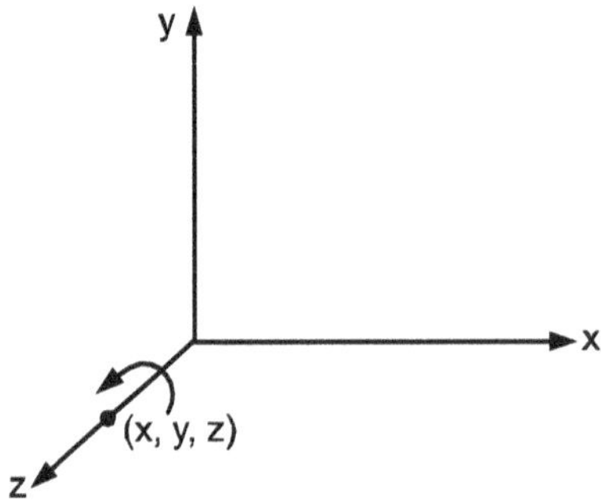

Fig. 7.9 Rotate arbitrary axis about z axis

Step 5 : Now, we have to perform reverse transformations. Please note that we should not perform reverse rotation about z-axis because it is rotation about arbitrary axis. Thus, we have to perform reverse rotation about y-axis. Also note that here we rotate the arbitrary axis about y-axis in anticlockwise direction i.e.,

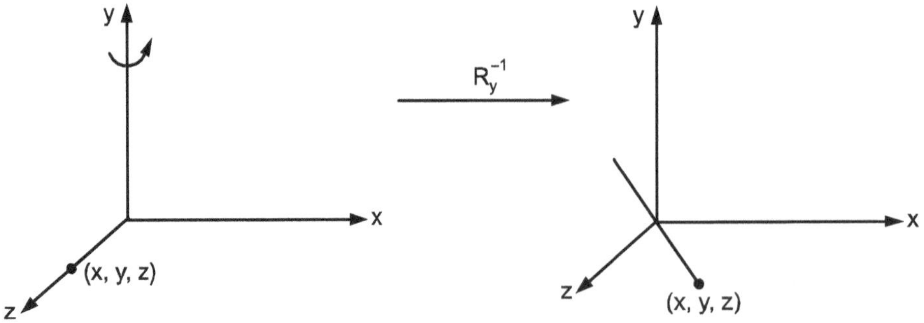

Fig. 7.10: Reverse transformation (Rotation about Y axis)

Step 6 : Now, we rotate about x-axis in clockwise direction i.e.,

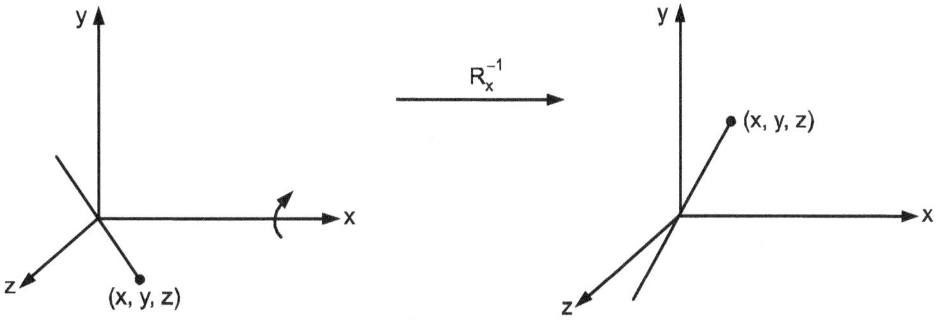

Fig. 7.11: Rotation about X axis

Step 7 : Finally, we apply inverse translation to bring the arbitrary axis back to its original position i.e.,

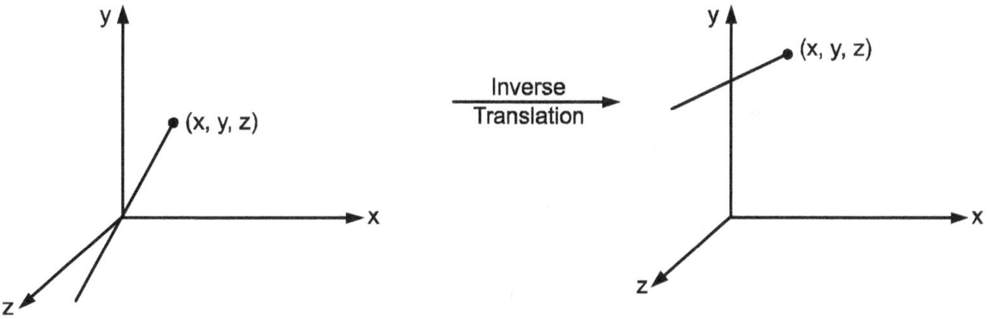

Fig 7.12: Inverse Translation

7.2.4 Shearing

- A transformation that slants the shape of an object is called the shear transformation. Like in 2Dshear, we can shear an object along the X-axis, Y-axis, or Z-axis in 3D.
- The general form of shearing along the X-axis, Y-axis, or Z-axis is as follows:

$$Sh = \begin{bmatrix} 1 & sh_x^y & sh_x^z & 0 \\ sh_y^x & 1 & sh_y^z & 0 \\ sh_z^x & sh_z^y & 1 & 0 \\ 0 & 0 & 1 & 1 \end{bmatrix}$$

$$P' = P \cdot Sh$$

$$X' = X + Sh_x^y Y + Sh_x^z Z$$

$$Y' = Sh_y^x X + Y + Sh_y^z Z$$

$$Z' = Sh_z^x X + Sh_z^y Y + Z$$

- The following Fig. 7.13 shows shearing about z-axis.

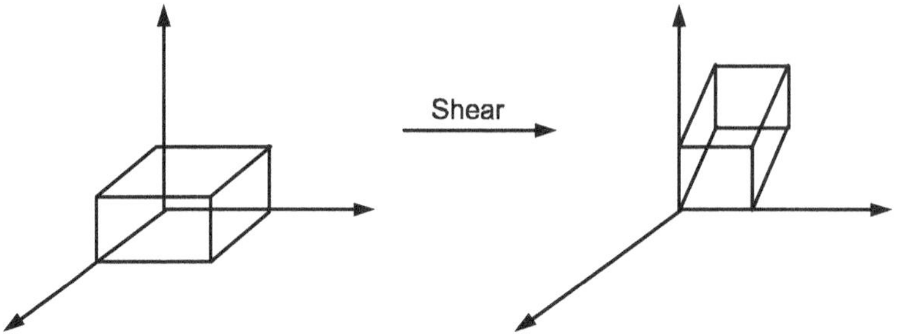

Fig 7.13: Shearing about z-axis

7.2.5 Mirror Reflection

- In 3D, reflection occurs through plane i.e. xy plane , yz plane , xz plane.

1. **Reflection through xy plane:** Transformation matrix for xy plane is as follows :

$$[T_{xy}] = \begin{bmatrix} 1 & 0 & 0 & 0 \\ 0 & 1 & 0 & 0 \\ 0 & 0 & -1 & 0 \\ 0 & 0 & 0 & 1 \end{bmatrix}$$

$$P'(x', y', z') = [T_{xy}]\,(x, y, z)$$

where, $\left.\begin{aligned} x' &= x \\ y' &= y \\ z' &= -z \end{aligned}\right\}$

The mirror reflection of point P(x,y,z) is shown in Fig. 7.14.

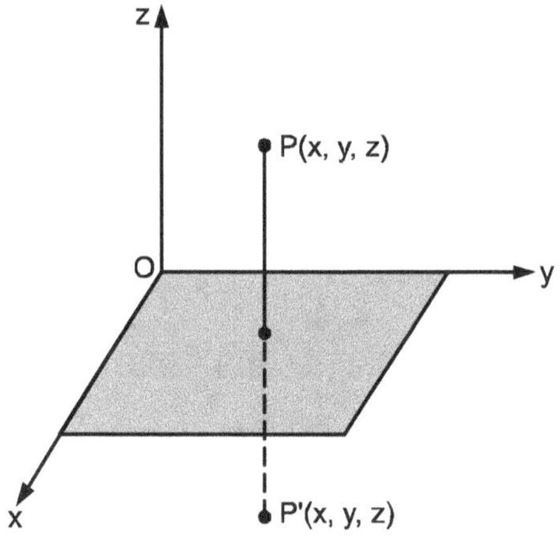

Fig. 7.14: Reflection through XY plane

2. **Reflection through YZ plane:** The transformation matrix is as follows:

$$[T_{yz}] = \begin{bmatrix} -1 & 0 & 0 & 0 \\ 0 & 1 & 0 & 0 \\ 0 & 0 & 1 & 0 \\ 0 & 0 & 0 & 1 \end{bmatrix}$$

3. **Reflection through XZ plane:** The transformation matrix is as follows:

$$[T_{xz}] = \begin{bmatrix} 1 & 0 & 0 & 0 \\ 0 & -1 & 0 & 0 \\ 0 & 0 & 1 & 0 \\ 0 & 0 & 0 & 1 \end{bmatrix}$$

7.3 THREE DIMENSIONAL VIEWING

- As mentioned earlier, the 3D viewing process is inherently more complex than the 2D viewing process. In two dimensional viewing we have 2D window and 2D viewport and objects in the world coordinates are clipped against the window and are then transformed into the viewport for display.
- The complexity in added in the three dimensional viewing is because of the added dimension and the fact that eventhough objects are three dimensional the display devices are only 2D.
- The mismatch between 3D objects and 2D displays is compensated by introducing projections. The projections transform 3D objects into a 2D projection plane.
- The following Fig. 7.15 shows the conceptual model of the 3D transformation process.
- In 3D viewing, we specify a view volume in the world coordinates using modelling transformation. The world coordinate positions of the objects are then converted into viewing coordinates by viewing transformation.
- The projection transformation is then used to convert 3D description of objects in viewing coordinates to the 2D projection coordinates.
- Finally, the workstation transformation transforms the projection coordinates into the device coordinates.

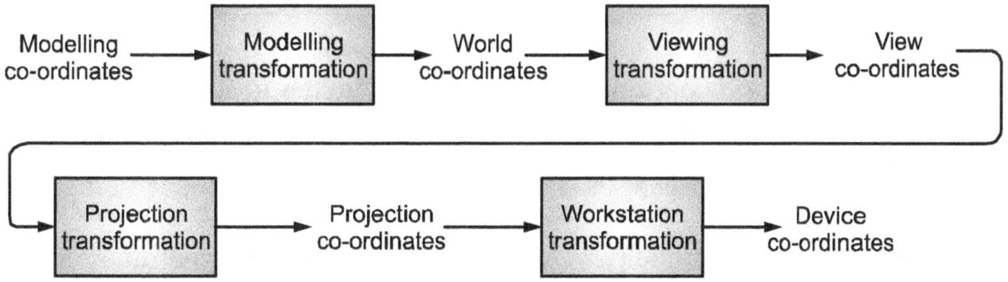

Fig. 7.15: Conceptual model of 3D transformation

Viewing Parameters:

- As mentioned earlier, we can view the object from the side, or the top, or even from behind. Therefore, it is necessary to choose a particular view for a picture by first defining a view plane.
- View plane can be defined by establishing the viewing - coordinate system or view reference coordinate system.
- The first viewing parameter we must consider is the view reference point. This point is the center of our viewing coordinate system. It is often chosen to be close to or on the surface of some object in a scene. Its coordinates are specified as X_R, Y_R and Z_R.
- The next viewing parameter is a view-plane normal vector, N. This normal vector is the direction perpendicular to the view plane and it is defined as (DXN, DYN, DZN).
- This means that the camera is pointed in the direction of the view plane normal.
- As shown in the Fig. 7.16 the view plane normal vector is a directed line segment from the view plane to the view reference point. The length of this directed line segment is referred to as view-distance. This is another viewing parameter. It tells how far the camera is positioned from the view reference point.
- At different angles, the view plane will show the same scene, but rotated so that a different part of the object is up. The rotation of a camera or a camera or view plane is specified by a view-up vector V [XUP YUP ZUP] which is another important viewing parameter.

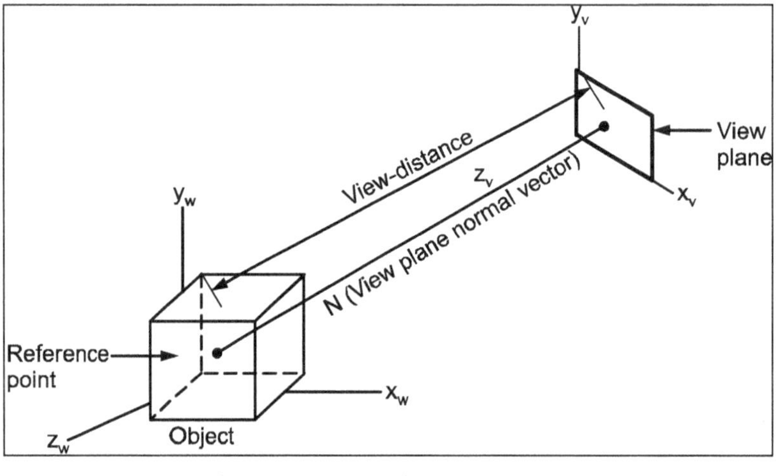

Fig. 7.16: 3-D Viewing parameters

Transformation from World Coordinate to Viewing Coordinates in 3D:

- The conversion of object description from world coordinates to viewing coordinates is achieved by following transformation sequence:
  1. Translate the view reference point to the origin of the world coordinate system.
  2. Apply rotations to align the x_v, y_v, and z_v axes with the world coordinate x_w, y_w and z_w axes, respectively.

- The view point specified at world position I (x_p, v_p, z_p) can be translated to the world coordinate origin with the matrix transformation.

$$T = \begin{bmatrix} 1 & 0 & 0 & 0 \\ 0 & 1 & 0 & 0 \\ 0 & 0 & 1 & 0 \\ -x_p & -y_p & -z_p & 1 \end{bmatrix}$$

$$P' = P \cdot T$$

- For alignment of three axes we require the three coordinate-axis rotations, depending on the direction we choose for N. In general, if N is not aligned with any world coordinate axis, we can align the viewing and world coordinate systems with the transformation sequence $R_x \cdot R_y \cdot R_z$. That is, we first rotate around the world x_w, axis to bring z_v, into the x_w, z_w, plane.
- Then, we rotate around the world y_w axis to align the z_w, and z_v axes. Finally, we rotate about the z_w axis to align the y_w and y_v axes. In case of left handed view reference system, a reflection of one of the viewing axes is also necessary.
- This is illustrated in Fig. 7.17.

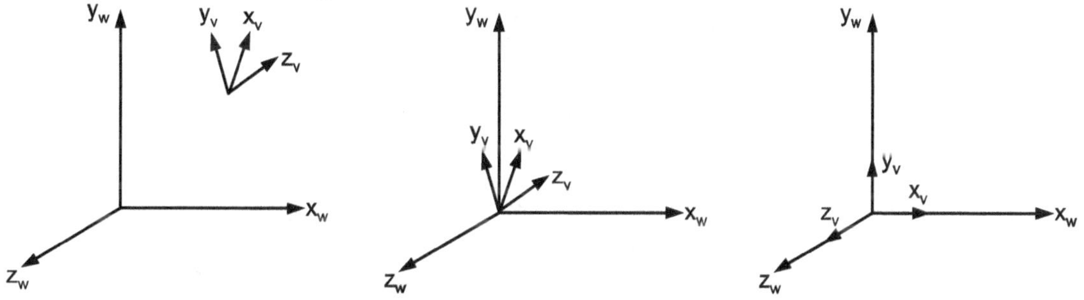

(a) Original positions (b) Translation (c) 3 axes rotation

Fig. 7.17: Aligning of viewing and world coordinate axes using a sequence of translate - rotate transformations

- Therefore, the composite transformation matrix is given as,

$$T_c = T \cdot R_x \cdot R_y \cdot R_z$$

7.3.1 Projections [April 16]

- After converting the description of objects from world coordinates to viewing coordinates, we can project the three dimensional objects onto the two dimensional view plane.
- There are two basic ways of projecting objects onto the view plane i.e., Parallel projection and Perspective projection.

- There are some basic terminologies related to projection, here:
  1. **Centre of projection:** It is a point from where projection is taken. It can either be light source or eye position.
  2. **Projection plane:** The plane on which the projection of the object is formed.
  3. **Projectors:** Lines emerging from centre of projection and hitting the projection plane after passing through a point in the object to be projected.
  4. **Projection:** It is process which transforms a point in n-dimensional co-ordinate system to point in co-ordinate system having less than n-1 dimension.
- The following Fig. 7.18 shows basic terminologies of projection.

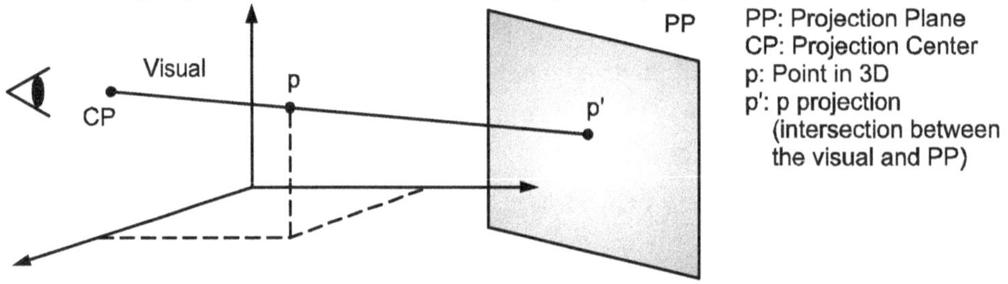

Fig. 7.18: Projection

- The following chart shows types of projection.

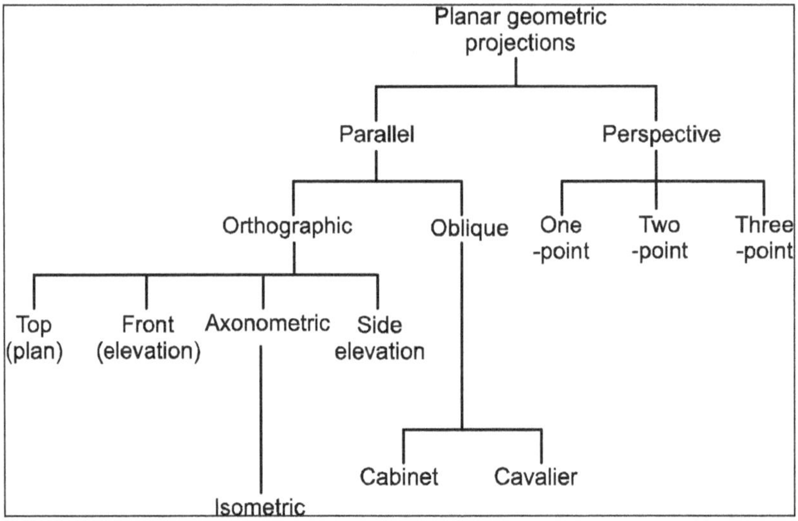

7.3.1.1 Parallel Projection [Oct. 16]

- In parallel projection, coordinate positions are transformed to view plane along parallel lines.
- In parallel projection, z - coordinate is discarded and parallel lines from each vertex on the object are extended until they intersect the view plane.

- The point of intersection is the projection of the vertex.
- We connect the projected vertices by line segments which correspond to connections on the original object.
- A parallel projection preserves relative proportions of objects. Accurate views of the various sides of an object are obtained with a parallel projection, but not a realistic representation.
- The following Fig. 7.19 shows parallel projection of object.

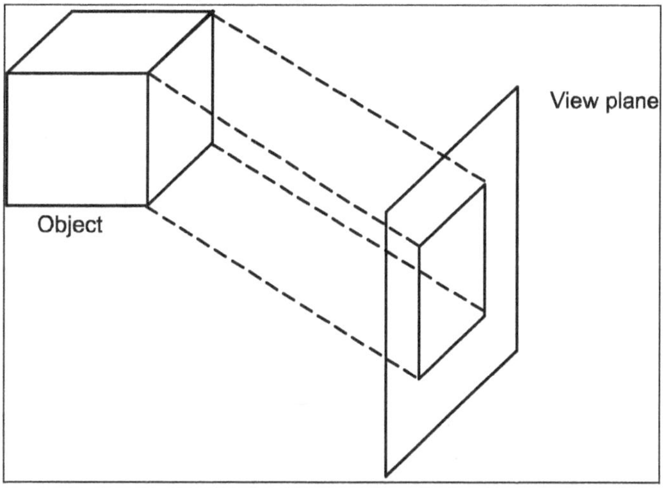

Fig. 7.19: Parallel projection of objection to view plane

Types of Parallel Projection:

- Parallel projections are basically categorized into two types, depending on the relation between the direction of projection and the normal to the view plane.
  1. Orthographic parallel projection, and
  2. Oblique parallel projection.

1. Orthographic Parallel Projection:

- Orthographic parallel projections are done by projecting points along parallel lines that are perpendicular to the projection plane.
- As shown in Fig. 7.20 most common types of orthographic projections are the front projection, top projection and side projection.
- In all these, the projection plane (view plane) perpendicular to the principle axis.
- These projections are often used in engineering drawing to depict machine parts, assemblies, buildings and so on.

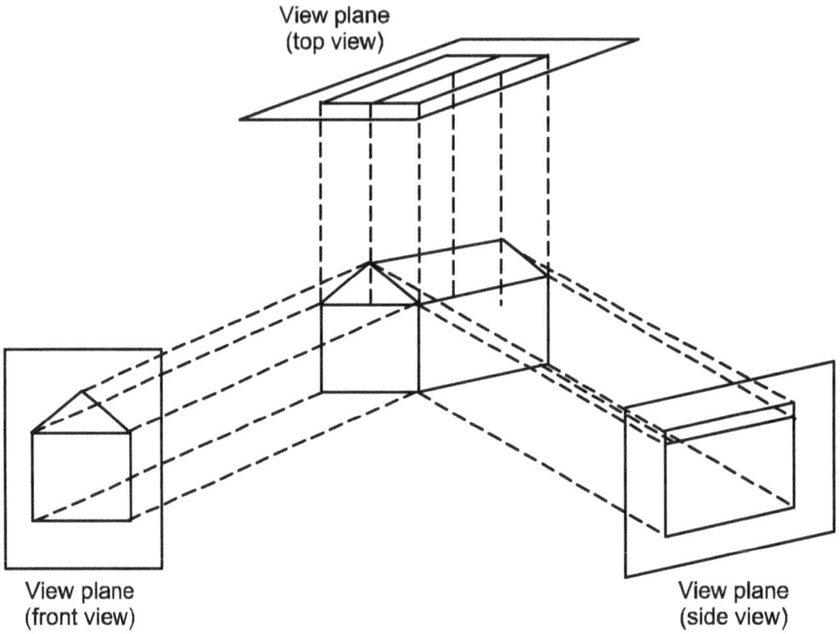

Fig. 7.20: Orthographic parallel projection

- The orthographic projection can display more than one face of an object. Such orthographic projection is called axonometric orthographic projection. It uses projection plane that are not principal axis.
- **Isometric Projection** is most commonly used axonometric orthographic projection. The projection plane is aligned such that it intersects each co-ordinate axis of object at same distance from origin.
- The following Fig. 7.21 shows Isometric Projection.

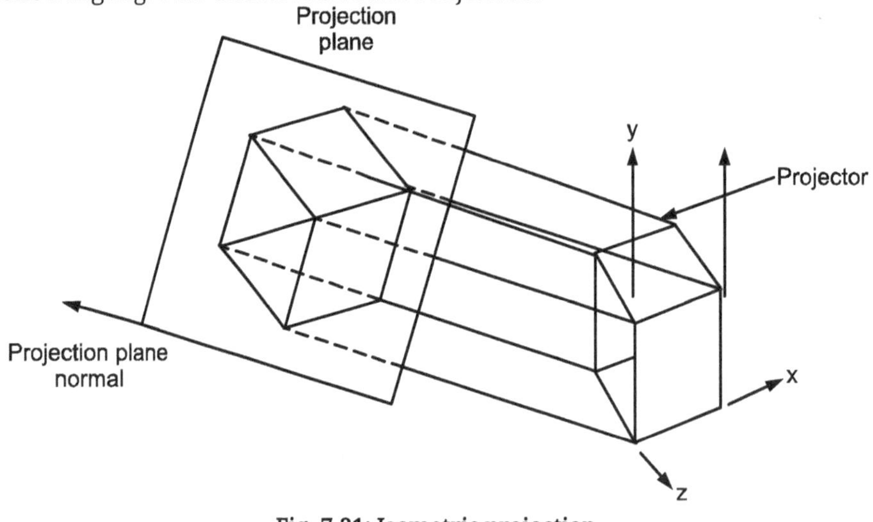

Fig. 7.21: Isometric projection

2. **Oblique parallel projection**

- Oblique projections are obtained by projecting along parallel lines that are NOT perpendicular to the projection plane.
- In oblique projection, we can view the object better than orthographic projection.
- The Fig. 7.22 shows oblique parallel projection.

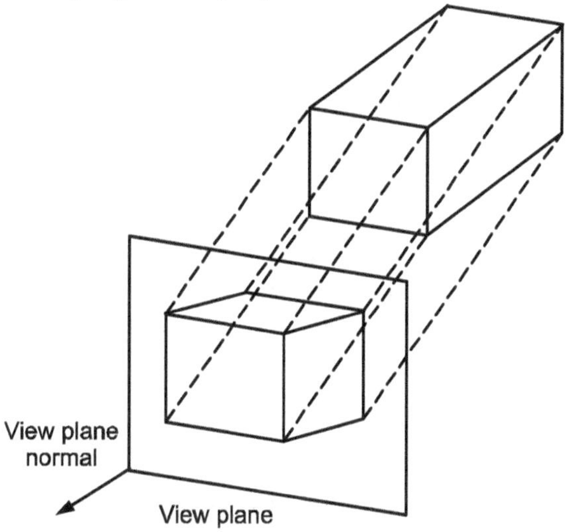

Fig. 7.22: Oblique parallel projection

- There are two types of oblique projections i.e., Cavalier and Cabinet.
- The **Cavalier Projection** makes 45° angle with the projection plane. The projection of a line perpendicular to the view plane has the same length as the line itself in Cavalier projection. In a cavalier projection, the foreshortening factors for all three principal directions are equal.
- The Fig. 7.23 shows cavalier projections of unit cube with $\alpha = 45^{\circ}$ and $\alpha = 30^{\circ}$.

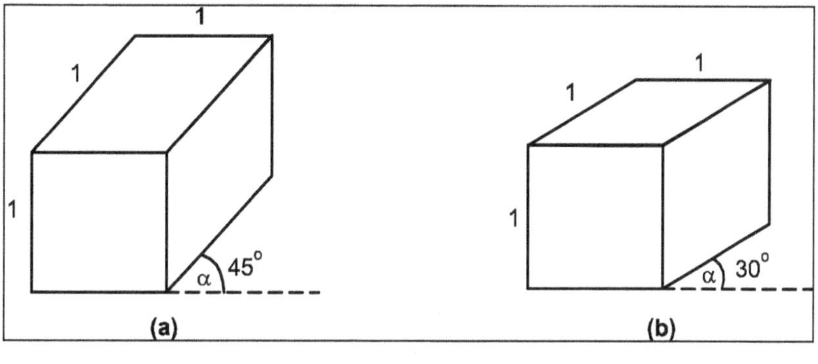

Fig. 7.23: Cavalier projection of unit cube

- The **Cabinet Projection** makes 63.4° angle with the projection plane. In Cabinet projection, lines perpendicular to the viewing surface is projected at ½ their actual length as shown in Fig. 7.24.

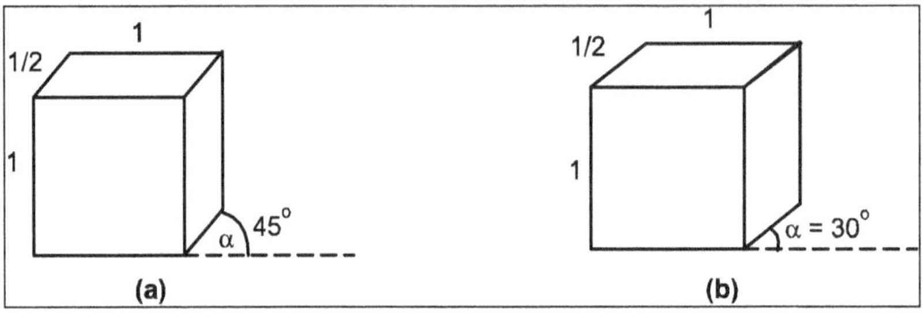

Fig. 7.24: Cabinet projection of unit cube

7.3.1.2 Perspective Projection

- The perspective projection, on the other hand, produces realistic views but does not preserve relative proportions.
- In perspective projection, the lines of projection are not parallel. Instead, they all converge at a single point called the center of projection or projection reference point.
- The object positions are transformed to the view plane along these converged projection lines and the projected view of an object is determined by calculating the intersection of the converged projection lines with the view plane, as shown in the Fig. 7.25.

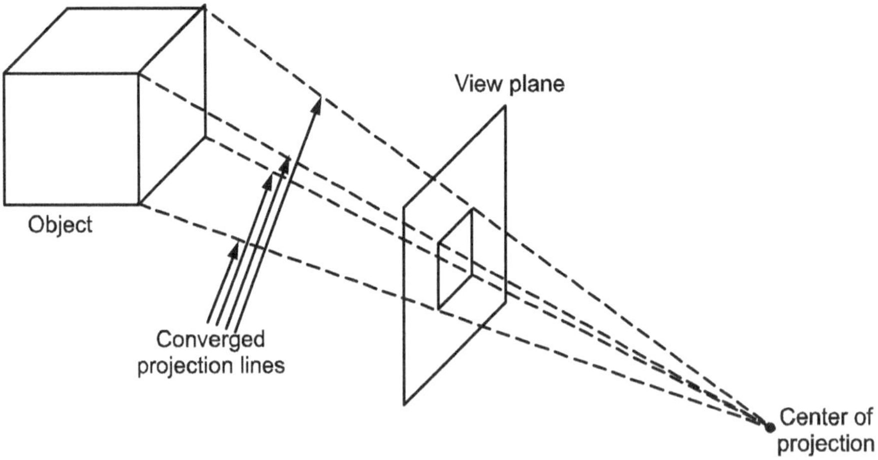

Fig. 7.25: Perspective projection of an object

- The perspective projection of any set of parallel lines that are not parallel to the projection plane converge to a vanishing point.
- The vanishing point for any set of lines that are parallel to one of the three principle axes of an object is referred to as a principle vanishing point or axis vanishing point.

- There are at most three such points, corresponding to the number of principle axes cut by the projection plane.
- The perspective projection is classified according to number of principle vanishing points in a projection i.e., one-point, two points or three-point projections.

1. **One-point Perspective Projection:** It occurs when projection plane is parallel to two principal axes or when only one of the principal axes intersects the view plane as shown in Fig. 7.26.

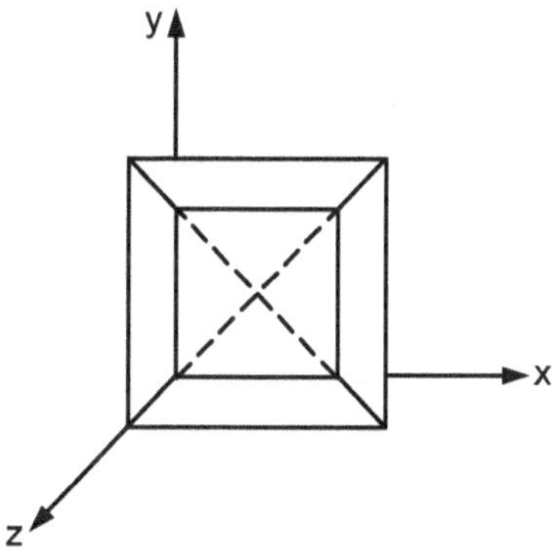

Fig. 7.26: One-point perspective projection

2. **Two-point Perspective Projection:** It occurs when projection plane is parallel to one of principal axis or when plane of projection intersects exactly two of the principal axis as shown in Fig. 7.27.

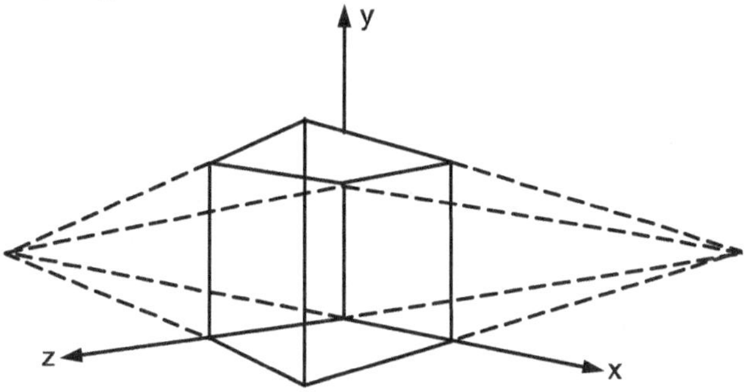

Fig. 7.27: Two-point Perspective Projection

3. **Three-point Perspective Projection:** It occurs when projection plane is not parallel to any principal axis or when plane of projection intersects all of the three principal axes as shown in Fig. 7.28.

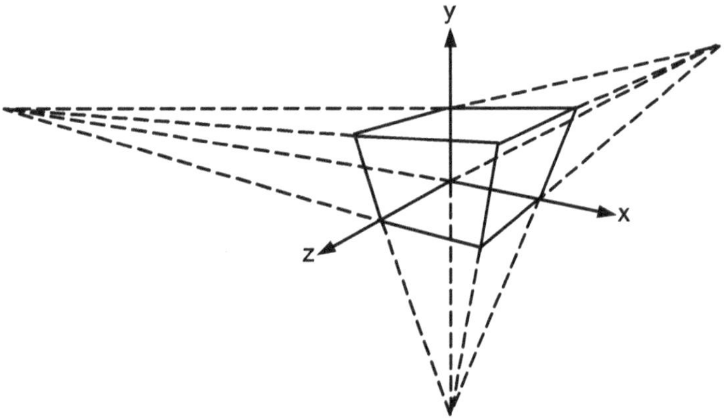

Fig. 7.28: Three-point perspective projection

- Let us see the difference between parallel and perspective projections:

Sr. No.	Parallel Projection	Perspective Projection
1.	In parallel projection, the centre of projection is at infinity.	In perspective projection, the centre of projection, is at a finite distance.
2.	Here, all projectors are parallel to each other.	Here, projectors are not parallel.
3.	It is a less realistic view.	It is more realistic.
4.	It can be used for the applications where exact measurement is required.	It resembles to that of our photographic systems (camera) and human eye.
5.	These are linear transforms implemented with a matrix.	These are non-linear transforms.
6.	Examples: Use of drawing schematic diagrams.	Examples: Use in architectural rendering realistic views.

7.4 VIEW VOLUMES

- In the camera analogy, the type of lens used on the camera is one factor that determines how much of the scene is caught on film. In three-dimensional viewing, a rectangular view window, or projection window, in the area in the view plane which controls how much of the scene is viewed.
- Edges of the view window are parallel to the xv, yv axes, and the window boundary positions are specified in viewing coordinates, as shown in Fig. 7.29.

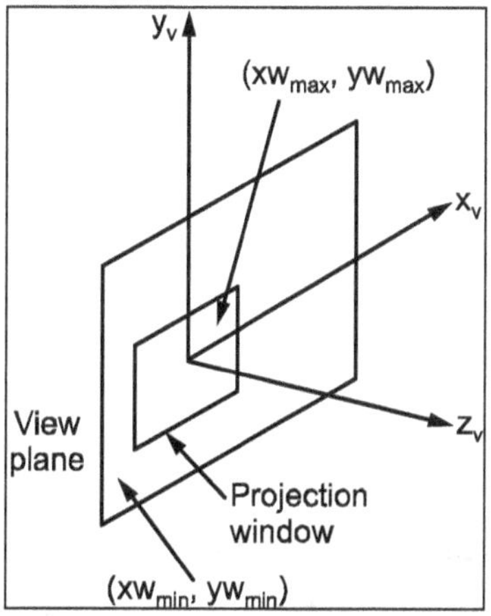

Fig. 7.29: Window Specification on the View Plane

- View volume is formed by giving the specification of the view window or the window boundaries. Only those objects within the view volume will appear in the generated display on an output device; all others are clipped from the display.
- The size of the view volume depends on the size of the window, while the shape of the view volume depends on the type of projection to be used to generate the display.
- In any case, four sides of the volume are planes that pass through the edges of the window.
- For a parallel projection, these four sides of the view volume form an infinite parallelepiped, as shown in Fig. 7.30.
- For a perspective projection, the view volume is a pyramid with apex at the projection reference point as shown in Fig. 7.30.

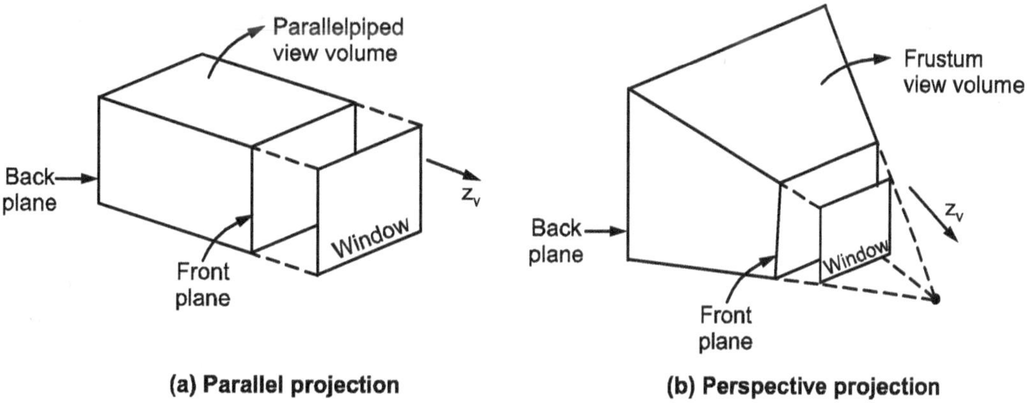

Fig. 7.30: View volume for parallel and perspective projection

- A **finite view volume** is obtained by limiting the extent of the volume in the z_v direction. This is done by specifying positions for one or two additional boundary planes. These z_v boundary planes are referred to as the front plane and back plane, or the near plane and the far plane, of the viewing volume.

- The front and back planes are parallel to the view plane at specified-positions z_{front} and z_{back}. Both planes must be on the same side of the projection reference point, and the back plane must be farther from the projection point than the front plane. Including the front and back planes produces a view volume bounded by six planes.
- With an orthographic parallel projection, the six planes form a rectangular parallelepiped, while an oblique parallel projection produces an oblique parallelepiped view volume.
- With a perspective projection, the front and back clipping planes truncate the infinite pyramidal view volume to form a frustum.
- Relative placement of the view plane and the front and hack clipping planes depends on the type of view we want to generate and the limitations of a particular graphics package.
- The view plane can be positioned anywhere along the z, axis except that it cannot contain the projection reference point.
- Orthographic parallel projections are not affected by view-plane positioning, because the projection lines are perpendicular to the view plane regardless of its location.
- Oblique projections may be affected by view-plane positioning, depending on how the projection direction is to be specified.
- Perspective effects depend on the positioning of the projection reference point relative to the view plane. If it is close to the view plane, perspective effects are emphasized, i.e. closer objects will appear larger than more distant objects of the same size.
- In Perspective projection, the projected size of an object is also affected by the relative position of the object and the view plane. If the view plane is in front of the object (nearer the projection reference point), the projected size is smaller. Conversely, object size is increased when we project onto a view plane in back of the object.
- View-plane positioning for a perspective projection also depends on whether we want to generate a static view or an animation sequence.
- For a static view of a scene, the view plane is usually placed at the viewing-coordinate origin, which is at some convenient point in the scene. Then it is easy to adjust the size of the window to include all parts of the scene that we want to view. The projection reference point is positioned to obtain the amount of perspective desired.
- In an animation sequence, we can place the projection reference point at the viewing-coordinate origin and put the view plane in front of the scene. The size of the view window is adjusted to obtain the amount of scene desired. We move through the scene by moving the viewing reference frame (i.e. the viewing coordinate system).

7.4.1 General Parallel Projection Transformation

- The direction of a parallel projection is specified with a projection vector from the projection reference point to the center of the view window as shown in following Fig. 7.31.

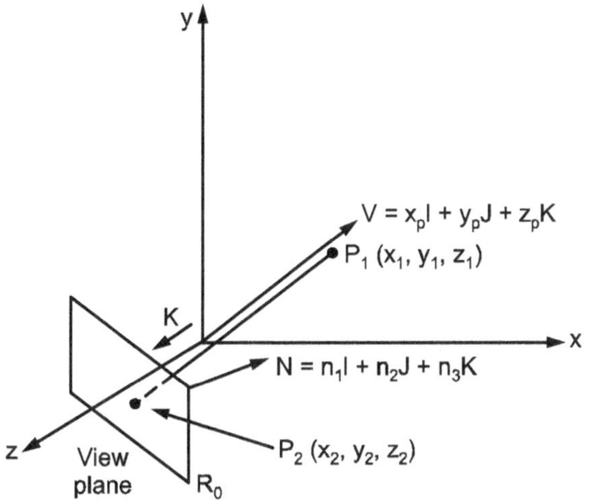

Fig. 7.31: General Parallel Projection Transformation

- Let us, consider that R_0 is the view reference point, P_1 is the object point and P_2 is the projected point. Now perform the following steps:

Step 1 : Translate the view reference point R_0 of the view plane to the origin using the translation matrix T.

Step 2 : Perform an alignment transformation R_{xy} so that the view normal vector N of the view plane points in the direction K, the normal to the xy plane.

Step 3 : Project point P_1 on to the xy plane.

Step 4 : Perform the inverse of steps 2 and 1.

$$\therefore Par_{V,N,R_0} = T \cdot R_{xy} \cdot Par_V \cdot R_{xy}^{-1} \cdot T^{-1}$$

$$= \begin{bmatrix} 1 & 0 & 0 & 0 \\ 0 & 1 & 0 & 0 \\ 0 & 0 & 1 & 0 \\ -x_0 & -y_0 & -z_0 & 1 \end{bmatrix} \begin{bmatrix} \frac{\lambda}{|N|} & 0 & \frac{n_1}{|N|} & 0 \\ \frac{-n_1 n_2}{\lambda|N|} & \frac{n_3}{\lambda} & \frac{n_2}{|N|} & 0 \\ \frac{-n_1 n_3}{\lambda|N|} & \frac{-n_2}{\lambda} & \frac{n_3}{|N|} & 0 \\ 0 & 0 & 0 & 1 \end{bmatrix} \begin{bmatrix} 1 & 0 & 0 & 0 \\ 0 & 1 & 0 & 0 \\ \frac{-x_p}{z_p} & \frac{-y_p}{z_p} & 0 & 0 \\ 0 & 0 & 0 & 1 \end{bmatrix}$$

$$\begin{bmatrix} \frac{\lambda}{|N|} & \frac{-n_1n_2}{\lambda|N|} & \frac{-n_1n_3}{\lambda|N|} & 0 \\ 0 & \frac{n_3}{\lambda} & \frac{-n_2}{\lambda} & 0 \\ \frac{n_1}{|N|} & \frac{n_2}{|N|} & \frac{n_3}{|N|} & 0 \\ 0 & 0 & 0 & 1 \end{bmatrix} \begin{bmatrix} 1 & 0 & 0 & 0 \\ 0 & 1 & 0 & 0 \\ 0 & 0 & 1 & 0 \\ x_o & y_o & z_o & 1 \end{bmatrix}$$

- This is the general equation of parallel projection on the given view plane in matrix form.

7.4.2 General Perspective Projection

- In perspective projection, the projection reference point can be located at any position in the viewing system, except on the view plane or between the front and back clipping planes.
- Let us consider the center of projection is at $P_c(x_c, y_c, z_c)$ and the point on object is $P_1(x_1, y_1, z_1)$, then the parametric equation for line containing these points can be given as:

$$x_2 = x_c + (x_1 - x_c)\,u$$
$$y_2 = y_c + (y_1 - y_c)\,u$$
$$z_2 = z_c + (z_1 - z_c)\,u$$

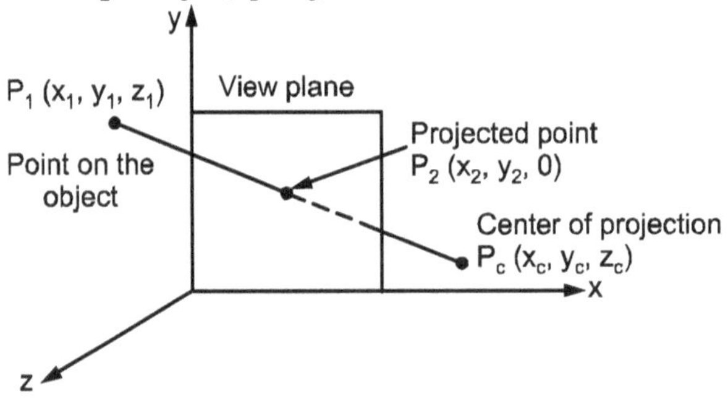

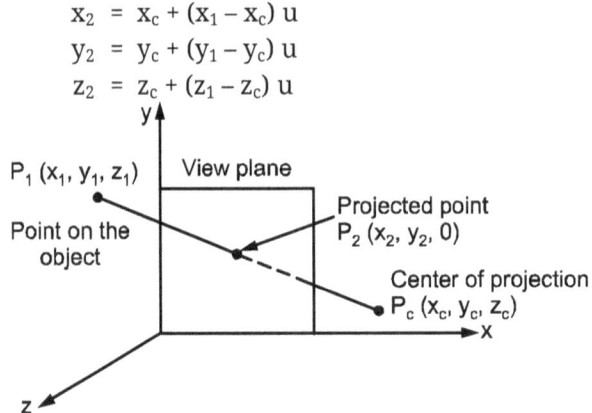

Fig. 7.32: General Perspective Projection

- For projected point z_2 is 0, therefore, the third equation can be written as:

$$0 = z_c + (z_1 - z_c)\,u$$

$$\therefore \quad u = -\frac{z_c}{z_1 - z_c}$$

- Substituting the value of u in first two equations we get,

$$x_2 = x_c - z_c\frac{x_1 - x_c}{z_1 - z_c}$$
$$= \frac{x_cz_1 - x_cz_c - x_1z_c + x_cz_c}{z_1 - z_c}$$
$$= \frac{x_cz_1 - x_1z_c}{z_1 - z_c}$$

and $$y_2 = y_c - z_c \frac{y_1 - y_c}{z_1 - z_c}$$

$$= \frac{y_c z_1 - y_c z_c - y_1 z_c + y_c z_c}{z_1 - z_c} = \frac{y_c z_1 - y_1 z_c}{z_1 - z_c}$$

- The above equations can be represented in the homogeneous matrix from as given below:

$$[\, x_2 \;\; y_2 \;\; z_2 \;\; 1 \,] = [\, x_1 \;\; y_1 \;\; z_1 \;\; 1 \,] \begin{bmatrix} -z_c & 0 & 0 & 0 \\ 0 & -z_c & 0 & 0 \\ x_c & y_c & 0 & 1 \\ 0 & 0 & 0 & -z_c \end{bmatrix}$$

- Here, we have taken the centre of projection as $P_c(x_c, y_c, z_c)$. If we take the center of projection on the negative z-axis such that,

$$x = 0$$
$$y = 0$$
$$z = -z_c$$

i.e. $P_c(0, 0, -z_c)$ then we have

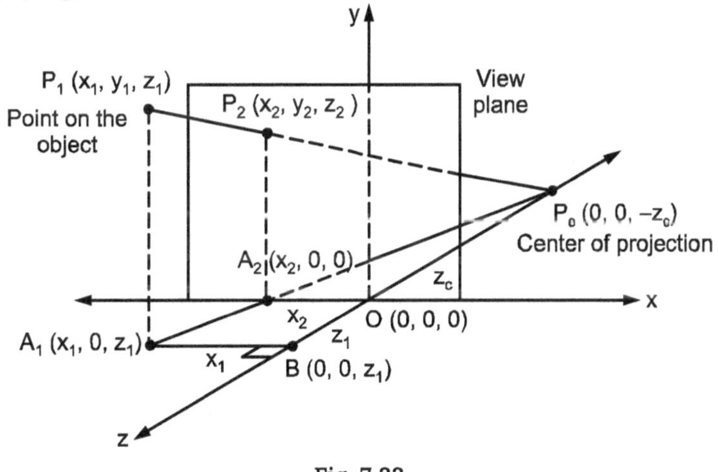

Fig. 7.33

$$\Delta P_c \, O \, A_2 \sim \Delta \, P_c \, B \, A_1$$

$\therefore$ $$x_2 = \frac{x_1 \, z_c}{z_1 + z_c}$$

Similarly, $$y_2 = \frac{y_1 \, z_c}{z_1 + z_c}$$

$$x_2 = \frac{z_c x_1}{z_c + z_1}$$

$$y_2 = \frac{z_c y_1}{z_c + z_1}$$

$$z_2 = 0$$

- Thus, we get the homogeneous perspective transformation matrix as,

$$[\, x_2 \;\; y_2 \;\; z_2 \;\; 1 \,] = [\, x_1 \;\; y_1 \;\; z_1 \;\; 1 \,] \begin{bmatrix} z_c & 0 & 0 & 0 \\ 0 & z_c & 0 & 0 \\ 0 & 0 & 0 & 1 \\ 0 & 0 & 0 & z_c \end{bmatrix}$$

7.5 3D CLIPPING

- The purpose of 3D clipping is to identify and save all surface segments within the view volume for display on the output device. All parts of objects that are outside the view volume are discarded, thus the computing time is saved.
- In Chapter 6, we have seen the concept of window, which served as clipping boundary in two-dimensional space. In three dimensional space the concept can be extended to a clipping volume or view volume.
- The two common three dimensional clipping volumes are a rectangular parallelepiped, i.e. a box, used for parallel or axonometric projections, and a truncated pyramidal volume, used for perspective projections.
- Fig. 7.34 shows these volumes. These volumes are six sided with sides i.e. left, right, top, bottom, hither (near), and yon (far).

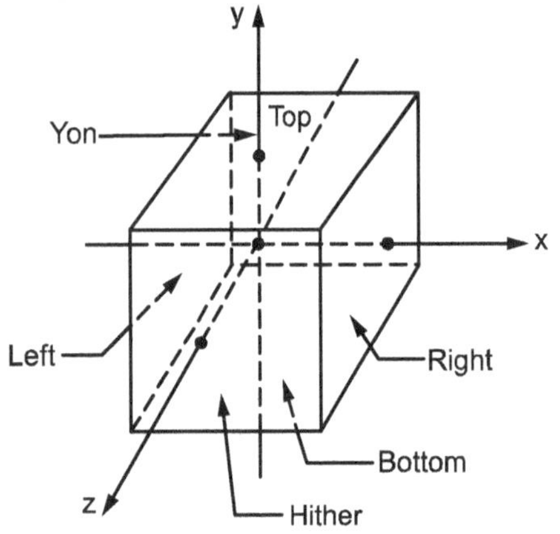

(a) Parallel

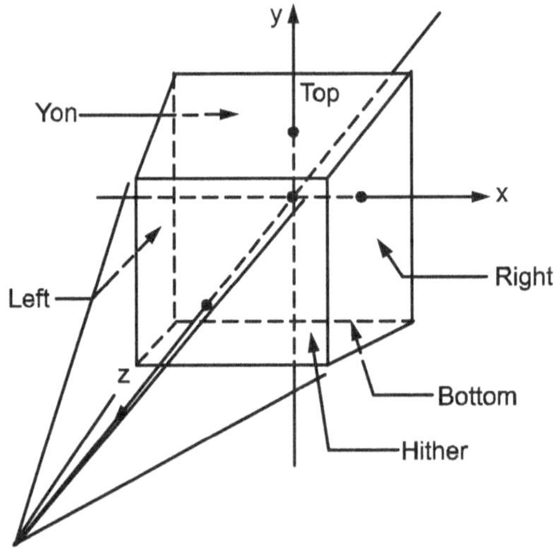

(b) Perspective

Fig. 7.34

1. **Clipping Point (3D):**

- We now need to compare the point against a plane, whereas in 2D we clip a point against a line i.e., the planes in 3D clipping are similar to lines in 2D clippings.
- We need to find out whether this point lies on the plane, lies on one side of the plane or lies on other side of the plane.

Mathematical Analysis: As we know that the equation of any plane is:

$$Ax + By + Cz + D = 0 \quad \text{... (1)}$$

This will be same for our clipping planes also. A point (x_1, y_1, z_1)

(i) Lies on the plane if,

$$Ax_1 + By_1 + Cz_1 + D = 0 \quad \text{... (2)}$$

(ii) Or lies on one side of the plane if,

$$Ax_1 + By_1 + Cz_1 + D > 0 \text{ (i.e. + ve)} \quad \text{... (3)}$$

(iii) Or lies on other side of the plane if,

$$Ax_1 + By_1 + Cz_1 + D < 0 \text{ (i.e. – ve)} \quad \text{... (4)}$$

But we have two, 3D clipping volume i.e.,

(i) At point P(x, y, z) is inside the parallel view volume if,

$$\left.\begin{array}{l} x_{u\,min} \le x \le x_{u\,max} \\ y_{u\,min} \le y \le y_{u\,max} \\ x_{u\,min} \le z \le z_{u\,max} \end{array}\right\}$$

where, $(x_{u\,min} + y_{u\,min}, z_{u\,min})$ and $(x_{u\,max}, y_{u\,max}, z_{u\,max})$ are the two end points of the view volume.

(ii) A point P(x, y, z) is inside the canonical view volume if,

$$\left.\begin{array}{l} -z \le x \le z \\ -z \le y \le z \\ -z \le z \le 1 \end{array}\right\}$$

$\because x_{u\,min} - y_{u\,min} - z_{u\,min} = 0$ and

$\because x_{u\,max} - y_{u\,max} - z_{u\,max} = 1$

- Therefore, from equation (2), (3) and (4) we can find out whether a line segment is visible or non-visible or a candidate for clipping by checking the signs of these three equations.
- If the line segment intersects with any one of the boundary plane then the point of intersections can be computed by solving equations (2), (3) and (4) above. Let us now see how we can clip a line in 3D.

2. **Clipping line in 3D:**

- Cohen-Sutherland algorithm for line clipping can be used with some modifications.
- The two-dimensional concept of region codes can be extended to three dimensions by considering six sides and 6-bit code instead of four sides and 4-bit code.
- Like two-dimension, we assign the bit positions in the region code from right to left as,

  Bit 1 = 1, if the end point is to the left of the volume.

  Bit 2 = 1, if the end point is to the right of the volume.

  Bit 3 = 1, if the end point is the below the volume.

  Bit 4 = 1, it the end point is above the volume.

  Bit 5 = 1, if the end point is in front of the volume.

  Bit 6 = 1, if the end point is behind the volume.

- Otherwise, the bit is set to zero. As an example, a region code of 101000 identifies a point as above and behind the view volume, and the region code 000000 indicates a point within the view volume.
- A line segment can be immediately identified as completely within the view volume if both endpoints have a region code of 000000. If either endpoint of a line segment does not have a region code of 000000, we perform the logical AND operation on the two endpoint codes.
- If the result of this AND operation is non-zero then both endpoints are outside the view volume and line segment is completely invisible. On the other hand, if the result of AND operation is zero then line segment may be partially visible. In this case, it is necessary to determine the intersection of the line and the clipping volume.
- We have seen that determining the end point codes for a rectangular parallelepiped clipping volume is a straight forward extension of the two dimensional algorithm.
- However, the perspective clipping volume shown in Fig. 7.35 (b) requires some additional processing.
- As shown in the Fig. 7.35 (b) the line connecting the center of projection and the center of the perspective clipping volume coincides with the z axis in a right handed coordinate system.

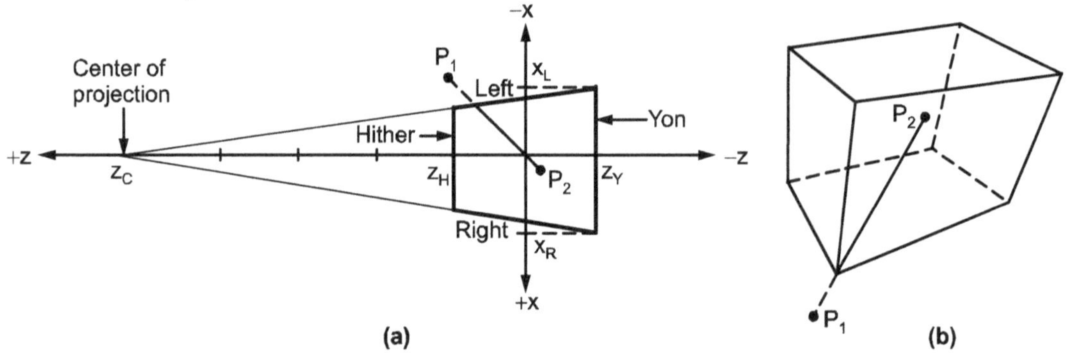

Fig. 7.35: Perspective clipping volume

- Fig. 7.35 shows a top view of the perspective clipping volume. The equation of the line which represents the right hand plane in this view can be given as,

$$x = \frac{z - z_C}{z_Y - z_C} x_R = z\,\alpha_1 + \alpha_2$$

where, $$\alpha_1 = \frac{x_R}{z_Y - z_C} \text{ and } \alpha_2 = -\alpha_1 z_C$$

- This equation of right hand plane can be used to determine whether a point is to the right, on or to the left of the plane i.e., outside the volume, on the right hand plane, or inside the volume. Substituting the x and y coordinates of a point P into $x - z\,\alpha_1 - \alpha_2$ gives the following results,

$f_R = x - z\,\alpha_1 - \alpha_2 > 0$ If P is to the right of the right plane.

$= 0$ If P is on the right plane.

< 0 If P is to the left of the right plane.

- Similarly, we can derive the test functions for the left, top bottom, hither and yon planes. Following table shows the test functions.

Sr. No.	Plane	Test Functions with Results
1.	Right	$f_R = x - z\,\alpha_1 - \alpha_2 > 0$ If P is to the right of the right plane. $= 0$ If P is to the right plane. < 0 If P is to the left of the right plane. where, $\alpha_1 = \frac{x_R}{z_Y - z_C}$ and $\alpha_2 = -\alpha_1 z_C$
2.	Left	$f_L = x - z\,\beta_1 - \beta_2 < 0$ If P is to the left of the left plane. $= 0$ If P is to the left plane. > 0 If P is to the right of the left plane. where, $\beta_1 = \frac{x_L}{z_Y - z_C}$ and $\beta_2 = -\beta_1 z_C$
3.	Top	$f_T = y - z\,\gamma_1 - \gamma_2 > 0$ If P is above the top plane. $= 0$ If P is on the top plane. < 0 If P is below the top plane. where, $\gamma_1 = \frac{y_T}{z_Y - z_C}$ and $\gamma_2 = -\gamma_1 z_C$
4.	Bottom	$f_B = y - z\,\delta_1 - \delta_2 < 0$ If P is below the bottom plane. $= 0$ If P is on the bottom plane. > 0 If P is above the bottom plane. where, $\delta_1 = z_C$ and $\delta_2 = -\delta_1 z_C$
5.	Hither	$f_H = z - z_H > 0$ If P is in front of the hither plane. $= 0$ If P is on the hither plane. < 0 If P is behind the hither plane.
6.	Yon	$f_y = z - z_y < 0$ If P is behind the yon plane. $= 0$ If P is on the yon plane. > 0 If P is in front of the yon plane.

3D Midpoint Subdivision Algorithm:

- In the previous section, we have seen how to identify location of the end points of line segments with respect to clipping volume. Once, this process is over we can determine which line segments are completely visible, which are completely invisible and which are partially visible.
- For partially visible segment we have to determine the intersection with clipping volume. This can be achieved with the help of three - dimensional midpoint subdivision algorithm.
- It is an extension of 2D midpoint subdivision algorithm discussed in Chapter 6.

Algorithm:

Step 1 : Find the locations of endpoints (endpoint codes) of line segments with respect to clipping volume, (using test functions in case of perspective clipping volume).

Step 2 : Check visibility of each line segment:

(a) If codes for both endpoints are zero then the line is completely visible. Hence, draw the line and go to Step 4.

(b) If codes for endpoints are not zero and the logical ANDing of them is also non-zero the line is completely invisible, so reject the line and go to Step 4.

(c) If codes for two endpoints do not satisfy the conditions in 2 (a) and 2 (b) the line is partially visible.

Step 3 : Divide the partially visible line segments in equal parts and repeat steps 1 and 2 for subdivided line segments until you get completely visible and completely invisible line segments. Draw the visible line segment and discard the invisible one.

Step 4 : Stop.

Programs in OpenGL:

1. Program to implement basic 3D transformation.

```
#include <math.h>
#include <GL/glut.h>
#include <stdio.h>
#include <stdlib.h>
typedef float Matrix4x4 [4][4];
Matrix4x4 theMatrix;
float ptsIni[8][3]={{80,80,-100},{180,80,-100},{180,180,-100},{80,180,-100},
                    {60,60,0},{160,60,0},{160,160,0},{60,160,0}};
```

```
//Realign above line while execution
// Initial Co-ordinates ofthe Cube to be Transformed
float ptsFin[8][3];
float refptX,refptY,refptZ;                 //Reference points
float TransDistX,TransDistY,TransDistZ;     //Translations along Axes
float ScaleX,ScaleY,ScaleZ;                 //Scaling Factors along Axes
float Alpha,Beta,Gamma,Theta;               //Rotation angles about Axes
float A,B,C;                                //Arbitrary Line Attributes
float aa,bb,cc;                             //Arbitrary Line Attributes
float x1,y11,z1,x2,y2,z2;
int choice, choiceRot,choiceRef;
void matrixSetIdentity(Matrix4x4 m)     // Initialises the matrix as Unit
Matrix
{
 int i, j;
 for (i=0; i<4; i++)
 for (j=0; j<4; j++)
 m[i][j] = (i == j);
}
void matrixPreMultiply(Matrix4x4 a, Matrix4x4 b)
{// Multiplies matrix a times b, putting result in b
 int i,j;
 Matrix4x4 tmp;
 for (i = 0; i < 4; i++)
 for (j = 0; j < 4; j++)
 tmp[i][j]=a[i][0]*b[0][j]+a[i][1]*b[1][j]+a[i][2]*b[2][j]+a[i][3]*b[3][j];
 for (i = 0; i < 4; i++)
 for (j = 0; j < 4; j++)
 theMatrix[i][j] = tmp[i][j];
}
void Translate(int tx, int ty, int tz)
{
 Matrix4x4 m;
 matrixSetIdentity(m);
 m[0][3] = tx;
 m[1][3] = ty;
 m[2][3] = tz;
 matrixPreMultiply(m, theMatrix);
}
```

```
void Scale(float sx , float sy ,float sz)
{
 Matrix4x4 m;
 matrixSetIdentity(m);
 m[0][0] = sx;
 m[0][3] = (1 - sx)*refptX;
 m[1][1] = sy;
 m[1][3] = (1 - sy)*refptY;
 m[2][2] = sz;
 m[2][3] = (1 - sy)*refptZ;
 matrixPreMultiply(m , theMatrix);
}
void RotateX(float angle)
{
 Matrix4x4 m;
 matrixSetIdentity(m);
 angle = angle*22/1260;
 m[1][1] = cos(angle);
 m[1][2] = -sin(angle);
 m[2][1] = sin(angle);
 m[2][2] = cos(angle);
 matrixPreMultiply(m , theMatrix);
}
void RotateY(float angle)
{
 Matrix4x4 m;
 matrixSetIdentity(m);
 angle = angle*22/1260;
 m[0][0] = cos(angle);
 m[0][2] = sin(angle);
 m[2][0] = -sin(angle);
 m[2][2] = cos(angle);
 matrixPreMultiply(m , theMatrix);
}
```

```
void RotateZ(float angle)
{
 Matrix4x4 m;
 matrixSetIdentity(m);
 angle = angle*22/1260;
 m[0][0] = cos(angle);
 m[0][1] = -sin(angle);
 m[1][0] = sin(angle);
 m[1][1] = cos(angle);
 matrixPreMultiply(m , theMatrix);
}
void Reflect(void)
{
 Matrix4x4 m;
 matrixSetIdentity(m);
 switch(choiceRef)
 {
 case 1: m[2][2] = -1;
 break;
 case 2: m[0][0] = -1;
 break;
 case 3: m[1][1] = -1;
 break;
 }
 matrixPreMultiply(m , theMatrix);
}
void DrawRotLine(void)
{
 switch(choiceRot)
 {
 case 1: glBegin(GL_LINES);
 glVertex3s(-1000 ,B,C);
 glVertex3s( 1000 ,B,C);
 glEnd();
 break;
```

```
 case 2: glBegin(GL_LINES);
 glVertex3s(A ,-1000 ,C);
 glVertex3s(A ,1000 ,C);
 glEnd();
 break;
 case 3: glBegin(GL_LINES);
 glVertex3s(A ,B ,-1000);
 glVertex3s(A ,B ,1000);
 glEnd();
 break;
 case 4: glBegin(GL_LINES);
 glVertex3s(x1-aa*500 ,y11-bb*500 , z1-cc*500);
 glVertex3s(x2+aa*500 ,y2+bb*500 , z2+cc*500);
 glEnd();
 break;
 }
}
void TransformPoints(void)
{
 int i,k;
 float tmp ;
 for(k=0 ; k<8 ; k++)
 for (i=0 ; i<3 ; i++)
 ptsFin[k][i] = theMatrix[i][0]*ptsIni[k][0] + theMatrix[i][1]*ptsIni[k][1]
                + theMatrix[i][2]*ptsIni[k][2] + theMatrix[i][3];
// Realign above line while execution
}
void Axes(void)
{
 glColor3f (0.0, 0.0, 0.0);                 // Set the color to BLACK
 glBegin(GL_LINES);                         // Plotting X-Axis
 glVertex2s(-1000 ,0);
 glVertex2s( 1000 ,0);
 glEnd();
```

```
 glBegin(GL_LINES);                        // Plotting Y-Axis
 glVertex2s(0 ,-1000);
 glVertex2s(0 , 1000);
 glEnd();
}
void Draw(float a[8][3])                  //Display the Figure
{
 int i;
 glColor3f (0.7, 0.4, 0.7);
 glBegin(GL_POLYGON);
 glVertex3f(a[0][0],a[0][1],a[0][2]);
 glVertex3f(a[1][0],a[1][1],a[1][2]);
 glVertex3f(a[2][0],a[2][1],a[2][2]);
 glVertex3f(a[3][0],a[3][1],a[3][2]);
 glEnd();
 i=0;
 glColor3f (0.8, 0.6, 0.5);
 glBegin(GL_POLYGON);
 glVertex3s(a[0+i][0],a[0+i][1],a[0+i][2]);
 glVertex3s(a[1+i][0],a[1+i][1],a[1+i][2]);
 glVertex3s(a[5+i][0],a[5+i][1],a[5+i][2]);
 glVertex3s(a[4+i][0],a[4+i][1],a[4+i][2]);
 glEnd();
 glColor3f (0.2, 0.4, 0.7);
 glBegin(GL_POLYGON);
 glVertex3f(a[0][0],a[0][1],a[0][2]);
 glVertex3f(a[3][0],a[3][1],a[3][2]);
 glVertex3f(a[7][0],a[7][1],a[7][2]);
 glVertex3f(a[4][0],a[4][1],a[4][2]);
 glEnd();
 i=1;
 glColor3f (0.5, 0.4, 0.3);
 glBegin(GL_POLYGON);
```

```
 glVertex3s(a[0+i][0],a[0+i][1],a[0+i][2]);
 glVertex3s(a[1+i][0],a[1+i][1],a[1+i][2]);
 glVertex3s(a[5+i][0],a[5+i][1],a[5+i][2]);
 glVertex3s(a[4+i][0],a[4+i][1],a[4+i][2]);
 glEnd();
 i=2;
 glColor3f (0.5, 0.6, 0.2);
 glBegin(GL_POLYGON);
 glVertex3s(a[0+i][0],a[0+i][1],a[0+i][2]);
 glVertex3s(a[1+i][0],a[1+i][1],a[1+i][2]);
 glVertex3s(a[5+i][0],a[5+i][1],a[5+i][2]);
 glVertex3s(a[4+i][0],a[4+i][1],a[4+i][2]);
 glEnd();
 i=4;
 glColor3f (0.7, 0.3, 0.4);
 glBegin(GL_POLYGON);
 glVertex3f(a[0+i][0],a[0+i][1],a[0+i][2]);
 glVertex3f(a[1+i][0],a[1+i][1],a[1+i][2]);
 glVertex3f(a[2+i][0],a[2+i][1],a[2+i][2]);
 glVertex3f(a[3+i][0],a[3+i][1],a[3+i][2]);
 glEnd();
}
void display(void)
{
 glClear (GL_COLOR_BUFFER_BIT | GL_DEPTH_BUFFER_BIT);
 Axes();
 glColor3f (1.0, 0.0, 0.0);                  // Set the color to RED
 Draw(ptsIni);
 matrixSetIdentity(theMatrix);
 switch(choice)
 {
 case 1:   Translate(TransDistX , TransDistY ,TransDistZ);
 break;
```

```
case 2:    Scale(ScaleX, ScaleY, ScaleZ);
break;
case 3:    switch(choiceRot)
{
case 1: DrawRotLine();
Translate(0,-B,-C);
RotateX(Alpha);
Translate(0,B,C);
break;
case 2: DrawRotLine();
Translate(-A,0,-C);
RotateY(Beta);
Translate(A,0,C);
break;
case 3: DrawRotLine();
Translate(-A,-B,0);
RotateZ(Gamma);
Translate(A,B,0);
break;
case 4: DrawRotLine();
float MOD =sqrt((x2-x1)*(x2-x1) + (y2-y11)*(y2-y11) + (z2-z1)*(z2-z1));
aa = (x2-x1)/MOD;
bb = (y2-y11)/MOD;
cc = (z2-z1)/MOD;
Translate(-x1,-y11,-z1);
float ThetaDash;
ThetaDash = 1260*atan(bb/cc)/22;
RotateX(ThetaDash);
RotateY(1260*asin(-aa)/22);
RotateZ(Theta);
RotateY(1260*asin(aa)/22);
RotateX(-ThetaDash);
Translate(x1,y11,z1);
break;
}
break;
```

```
 case 4:    Reflect();
 break;
 }
 TransformPoints();
 Draw(ptsFin);
 glFlush();
}
void init(void)
 {
 glClearColor (1.0, 1.0, 1.0, 1.0);
     // Set the Background color to WHITE
 glOrtho(-454.0, 454.0, -250.0, 250.0, -250.0, 250.0);
     // Set the no. of Co-ordinates along X & Y axes and their gappings
 glEnable(GL_DEPTH_TEST);
     // To Render the surfaces Properly according to their depths
 }
int main (int argc, char *argv)
{
 glutInit(&argc, &argv);
 glutInitDisplayMode (GLUT_SINGLE | GLUT_RGB | GLUT_DEPTH);
 glutInitWindowSize (1362, 750);
 glutInitWindowPosition (0, 0);
 glutCreateWindow (" Basic Transformations ");
 init ();
 printf("Enter your choice
          number:\n1.Translation\n2.Scaling\n3.Rotation\n4.Reflection\n=>");
 scanf("%d",&choice);
 switch(choice)
 {
 case 1:printf("Enter Translation along X, Y & Z\n=>");
 scanf("%f%f%f",&TransDistX , &TransDistY , &TransDistZ);
 break;
 case 2:printf("Enter Scaling ratios along X, Y & Z\n=>");
 scanf("%f%f%f",&ScaleX , &ScaleY , &ScaleZ);
 break;
```

```
case 3:printf("Enter your choice for Rotation about axis:\n1.parallel
to X-axis.(y=B & z=C)\n2.parallel to Y-axis.(x=A & z=C)\n3.parallel to
Z-axis.(x=A & y=B)\n4.Arbitrary line passing through (x1,y1,z1) &
(x2,y2,z2)\n =>");
//Realign above line while execution
scanf("%d",&choiceRot);
switch(choiceRot)
{
case 1:  printf("Enter B & C: ");
scanf("%f %f",&B,&C);
printf("Enter Rot. Angle Alpha: ");
scanf("%f",&Alpha);
break;
case 2:  printf("Enter A & C: ");
scanf("%f %f",&A,&C);
printf("Enter Rot. Angle Beta: ");
scanf("%f",&Beta);
break;
case 3:  printf("Enter A & B: ");
scanf("%f %f",&A,&B);
printf("Enter Rot. Angle Gamma: ");
scanf("%f",&Gamma);
break;
case 4:  printf("Enter values of x1 ,y1 & z1:\n");
scanf("%f %f %f",&x1,&y11,&z1);
printf("Enter values of x2 ,y2 & z2:\n");
scanf("%f %f %f",&x2,&y2,&z2);
printf("Enter Rot. Angle Theta: ");
scanf("%f",&Theta);
break;
}
break;
```

```
    case 4: printf("Enter your choice for reflection about plane:\n1.X-Y\n2.
                                                          Y-Z\n3.X-Z\n=>");
    scanf("%d",&choiceRef);
    break;
    default: printf("Please enter a valid choice!!!\n");
    return 0;
    }
    glutDisplayFunc(display);
    glutMainLoop();
    return 0;
}
```

2. Program to implement rotations on cube.

```
#include <GL\glut.h>
GLfloat xRotated, yRotated, zRotated;
void redisplayFunc(void)
{
    // clear the drawing buffer.
    glClear(GL_COLOR_BUFFER_BIT);
    // clear the identity matrix.
    glLoadIdentity();
    // traslate the draw by z = -4.0
    // Note this when you decrease z like 8.0 the drawing will looks far,
                                                                or smaller.
    glTranslatef(0.0,0.0,-5.0);
    // Red color used to draw.
    glColor3f(0.9, 0.0, 0.0);
    // changing in transformation matrix.
    // rotation about X axis
    glRotatef(xRotated,1.0,0.0,0.0);
    // rotation about Y axis
    glRotatef(yRotated,0.0,1.0,0.0);
    // rotation about Z axis
    glRotatef(zRotated,0.0,0.0,1.0);
```

```
    // scaling transfomation
    glScalef(1.0,1.0,1.0);
    // built-in (glut library) function , draw you a cube.
    glutWireCube(1.0);
    // Flush buffers to screen
    glFlush();
    // sawp buffers called because we are using double buffering
    glutSwapBuffers();
}
void reshapeFunc(int x, int y)
{
    if (y == 0 || x == 0) return;  //Nothing is visible then, so return
    //Set a new projection matrix
    glMatrixMode(GL_PROJECTION);
    glLoadIdentity();
    //Angle of view:40 degrees
    //Near clipping plane distance: 0.5
    //Far clipping plane distance: 20.0
    gluPerspective(40.0,(GLdouble)x/(GLdouble)y,0.5,20.0);
    glMatrixMode(GL_MODELVIEW);
    glViewport(0,0,x,y);  //Use the whole window for rendering
}
void idleFunc(void)
{
    // rotation around x axis
    xRotated += 0.03;
//    yRotated += 0.01;
//    zRotated += 0.01;
    redisplayFunc();
}
int main (int argc, char **argv)
{
    //Initialize GLUT
    glutInit(&argc, argv);
```

```
    //double buffering used to avoid flickering problem in animation
    glutInitDisplayMode(GLUT_DOUBLE | GLUT_RGB);
    // window size
    glutInitWindowSize(350,350);
    // create the window
    glutCreateWindow("Cube3d animation");
    glPolygonMode(GL_FRONT_AND_BACK,GL_LINE);
    xRotated = yRotated = zRotated = 0.0;
    glClearColor(0.0,0.0,0.0,0.0);
    //Assign  the function used in events
    glutDisplayFunc(redisplayFunc);
    glutReshapeFunc(reshapeFunc);
    glutIdleFunc(idleFunc);
    //Let start glut loop
    glutMainLoop();
    return 0;
}
```

3. Program to implement perspective projection of cube.

```
#include <GL/gl.h>
#include <GL/glut.h>
long v[8][3] = {
    {-1, -1, -1},
    {-1, -1,  1},
    {-1,  1,  1},
    {-1,  1, -1},
    { 1, -1, -1},
    { 1, -1,  1},
    { 1,  1,  1},
    { 1,  1, -1}
};
int path[16] = {
    0, 1, 2, 3,
    0, 4, 5, 6,
    7, 4, 5, 1,
    2, 6, 7, 3
};
```

```
void drawcube() {
    int i;
    glClear(GL_COLOR_BUFFER_BIT);
    glColor3f(0.0, 0.0, 0.0);
    glBegin(GL_LINE_STRIP);
    for (i=0; i < 16; i++)
        glVertex3i(v[path[i]][0], v[path[i]][1], v[path[i]][2]);
    glEnd();
    glFlush();
}
main(int argc, char **argv) {
    glutInit(&argc, argv);
    glutInitWindowSize(600, 400);
    glutInitDisplayMode(GLUT_RGB | GLUT_SINGLE);
    glutCreateWindow("glLookat example");
    glMatrixMode(GL_PROJECTION);
    glLoadIdentity();
    gluPerspective(30.0, 1.5, 0.1, 10.0);
    gluLookAt(5.0, 4.0, 6.0, 1.0, 1.0, 1.0, 0.0, 1.0, 0.0);
    glMatrixMode(GL_MODELVIEW);
    glClearColor(1.0, 1.0, 1.0, 0.0);  /* white *
    glutDisplayFunc(drawcube);
    glutMainLoop();
    return 0;
}
```

4. This program was requested Direct3D immediate mode.

```
#include <GL/glut.h>
GLfloat light_diffuse[] = {1.0, 0.0, 0.0, 1.0};  /* Red diffuse light. */
GLfloat  light_position[]  =  {1.0,  1.0,  1.0,  0.0};    /*  Infinite  light
location. */
GLfloat n[6][3] = {  /* Normals for the 6 faces of a cube. */
  {-1.0, 0.0, 0.0}, {0.0, 1.0, 0.0}, {1.0, 0.0, 0.0},
  {0.0, -1.0, 0.0}, {0.0, 0.0, 1.0}, {0.0, 0.0, -1.0} };
GLint faces[6][4] = {  /* Vertex indices for the 6 faces of a cube. */
  {0, 1, 2, 3}, {3, 2, 6, 7}, {7, 6, 5, 4},
  {4, 5, 1, 0}, {5, 6, 2, 1}, {7, 4, 0, 3} };
```

```
GLfloat v[8][3];  /* Will be filled in with X,Y,Z vertexes. */
void
drawBox(void)
{
  int i;
  for (i = 0; i < 6; i++) {
    glBegin(GL_QUADS);
    glNormal3fv(&n[i][0]);
    glVertex3fv(&v[faces[i][0]][0]);
    glVertex3fv(&v[faces[i][1]][0]);
    glVertex3fv(&v[faces[i][2]][0]);
    glVertex3fv(&v[faces[i][3]][0]);
    glEnd();
  }
}
void
display(void)
{
  glClear(GL_COLOR_BUFFER_BIT | GL_DEPTH_BUFFER_BIT);
  drawBox();
  glutSwapBuffers();
}
void
init(void)
{
  /* Setup cube vertex data. */
  v[0][0] = v[1][0] = v[2][0] = v[3][0] = -1;
  v[4][0] = v[5][0] = v[6][0] = v[7][0] = 1;
  v[0][1] = v[1][1] = v[4][1] = v[5][1] = -1;
  v[2][1] = v[3][1] = v[6][1] = v[7][1] = 1;
  v[0][2] = v[3][2] = v[4][2] = v[7][2] = 1;
  v[1][2] = v[2][2] = v[5][2] = v[6][2] = -1;
  /* Enable a single OpenGL light. */
  glLightfv(GL_LIGHT0, GL_DIFFUSE, light_diffuse);
  glLightfv(GL_LIGHT0, GL_POSITION, light_position);
  glEnable(GL_LIGHT0);
  glEnable(GL_LIGHTING);
```

```
    /* Use depth buffering for hidden surface elimination. */
    glEnable(GL_DEPTH_TEST);
    /* Setup the view of the cube. */
    glMatrixMode(GL_PROJECTION);
    gluPerspective( /* field of view in degree */ 40.0,
      /* aspect ratio */ 1.0,
      /* Z near */ 1.0, /* Z far */ 10.0);
    glMatrixMode(GL_MODELVIEW);
    gluLookAt(0.0, 0.0, 5.0,  /* eye is at (0,0,5) */
      0.0, 0.0, 0.0,      /* center is at (0,0,0) */
      0.0, 1.0, 0.);      /* up is in positive Y direction */
    /* Adjust cube position to be asthetic angle. */
    glTranslatef(0.0, 0.0, -1.0);
    glRotatef(60, 1.0, 0.0, 0.0);
    glRotatef(-20, 0.0, 0.0, 1.0);
  }
  int
  main(int argc, char **argv)
  {
    glutInit(&argc, argv);
    glutInitDisplayMode(GLUT_DOUBLE | GLUT_RGB | GLUT_DEPTH);
    glutCreateWindow("red 3D lighted cube");
    glutDisplayFunc(display);
    init();
    glutMainLoop();
    return 0;             /* ANSI C requires main to return int. */
  }
```

Output:

5. **This program was requested Direct3D immediate mode.**

```
#include <GL/glut.h>
GLfloat light_diffuse[] = {1.0, 0.0, 0.0, 1.0};  /* Red diffuse light. */
GLfloat light_position[] = {1.0, 1.0, 1.0, 0.0};  /* Infinite light location. */
GLfloat n[6][3] = {  /* Normals for the 6 faces of a cube. */
  {-1.0, 0.0, 0.0}, {0.0, 1.0, 0.0}, {1.0, 0.0, 0.0},
  {0.0, -1.0, 0.0}, {0.0, 0.0, 1.0}, {0.0, 0.0, -1.0} };
GLint faces[6][4] = {  /* Vertex indices for the 6 faces of a cube. */
  {0, 1, 2, 3}, {3, 2, 6, 7}, {7, 6, 5, 4},
  {4, 5, 1, 0}, {5, 6, 2, 1}, {7, 4, 0, 3} };
GLfloat v[8][3];  /* Will be filled in with X,Y,Z vertexes. */
void
drawBox(void)
{
  int i;
  for (i = 0; i < 6; i++) {
    glBegin(GL_QUADS);
    glNormal3fv(&n[i][0]);
    glVertex3fv(&v[faces[i][0]][0]);
    glVertex3fv(&v[faces[i][1]][0]);
    glVertex3fv(&v[faces[i][2]][0]);
    glVertex3fv(&v[faces[i][3]][0]);
    glEnd();
  }
}
void
display(void)
{
  glClear(GL_COLOR_BUFFER_BIT | GL_DEPTH_BUFFER_BIT);
  drawBox();
  glutSwapBuffers();
}
```

```
void
init(void)
{
  /* Setup cube vertex data. */
  v[0][0] = v[1][0] = v[2][0] = v[3][0] = -1;
  v[4][0] = v[5][0] = v[6][0] = v[7][0] = 1;
  v[0][1] = v[1][1] = v[4][1] = v[5][1] = -1;
  v[2][1] = v[3][1] = v[6][1] = v[7][1] = 1;
  v[0][2] = v[3][2] = v[4][2] = v[7][2] = 1;
  v[1][2] = v[2][2] = v[5][2] = v[6][2] = -1;

  /* Enable a single OpenGL light. */
  glLightfv(GL_LIGHT0, GL_DIFFUSE, light_diffuse);
  glLightfv(GL_LIGHT0, GL_POSITION, light_position);
  glEnable(GL_LIGHT0);
  glEnable(GL_LIGHTING);

  /* Use depth buffering for hidden surface elimination. */
  glEnable(GL_DEPTH_TEST);

  /* Setup the view of the cube. */
  glMatrixMode(GL_PROJECTION);
  gluPerspective( /* field of view in degree */ 40.0,
    /* aspect ratio */ 1.0,
    /* Z near */ 1.0, /* Z far */ 10.0);
  glMatrixMode(GL_MODELVIEW);
  gluLookAt(0.0, 0.0, 5.0,  /* eye is at (0,0,5) */
    0.0, 0.0, 0.0,      /* center is at (0,0,0) */
    0.0, 1.0, 0.);      /* up is in positive Y direction */

  /* Adjust cube position to be asthetic angle. */
  glTranslatef(0.0, 0.0, -1.0);
  glRotatef(60, 1.0, 0.0, 0.0);
  glRotatef(-20, 0.0, 0.0, 1.0);
}
```

```
int
main(int argc, char **argv)
{
  glutInit(&argc, argv);
  glutInitDisplayMode(GLUT_DOUBLE | GLUT_RGB | GLUT_DEPTH);
  glutCreateWindow("red 3D lighted cube");
  glutDisplayFunc(display);
  init();
  glutMainLoop();
  return 0;            /* ANSI C requires main to return int. */
}
```

Output:

SUMMARY

- Methods for geometric transformations and object modelling in 3D are extended from 2D methods by including the considerations for the z coordinate.
- Like two dimensional transformations, these transformations are formed by composing basic transformations of translation, scaling, and rotation.
- Each of these transformations can be represented as matrix transformations with homogeneous coordinates. Therefore, any sequence of transformations can be represented as a single matrix, formed by combining the matrices for the individual transformations in the sequence.
- In homogeneous coordinates, 3D transformations are represented by 4×4 matrices.
- Like two dimensional transformation, an object is translated in three dimensions by transforming each vertex of the object.

- Scaling is defined as the process of compressing and expanding of object or changing dimensions of object.
- For 3D rotation, we have to specify an axis of rotation about which object is to be rotated along with the angle of rotation.
- A transformation that slants the shape of an object is called the shear transformation. Like in 2D shear, we can shear an object along the X-axis, Y-axis, or Z-axis in 3D.
- In 3D, reflection occurs through plane i.e. xy plane , yz plane , xz plane.
- 3D viewing process is inherently more complex than 2D viewing process. The complexity in added in the three dimensional viewing is because of the added dimension and the fact that even though objects are three dimensional the display devices are only 2D.
- The mismatch between 3D objects and 2D displays is compensated by introducing projections. The projections transform 3D objects into 2D projection plane.
- There are two basic projection methods: Parallel Projection and Perspective Projection
- Parallel Projection transforms object positions to the view plane along parallel. A parallel projection preserves relative proportions of objects. Accurate views of the various sides of an object are obtained with a parallel projection. But not a realistic representation
- Perspective Projection transforms object positions to the view plane while converging to a centre point of projection. Perspective projection produces realistic views but does not preserve relative proportions. Projections of distant objects are smaller than the projections of objects of the same size that are closer to the projection plane.
- There are different types of Parallel Projection and Perspective Projection .
- In three-dimensional viewing, a rectangular view window, or projection window, in the area in the view plane which controls how much of the scene is viewed. Edges of the view window are parallel to the x_v, y_v axes, and the window boundary positions are specified in viewing coordinates.
- View volume is formed by giving the specification of the view window or the window boundaries. Only those objects within the view volume will appear in the generated display on an output device; all others are clipped from the display.
- The size of the view volume depends on the size of the window, while the shape of the view volume depends on the type of projection to be used to generate the display.
- Viewing parameters are view reference point , view plane normal vector, view distance and view up vector.
- For a parallel projection, these four sides of the view volume form an infinite parallelepiped.

- For a perspective projection, the view volume is a pyramid with apex at the projection reference point.
- The direction of a parallel projection is specified with a projection vector from the projection reference point to the center of the view window.
- In perspective projection, the projection reference point can be located at any position in the viewing system, except on the view plane or between the front and back clipping planes.
- The purpose of 3D clipping is to identify and save all surface segments within the view volume for display on the output device. All parts of objects that are outside the view volume are discarded Thus the computing time is saved. 3D clipping is based on 2D clipping.

PRACTICE QUESTIONS

1. Explain 3D basic transformations on object.
2. Explain 3D viewing process
3. What are various 3D viewing parameters? Explain in brief.
4. Derive the 3D transformation matrix to transform world coordinates to viewing co-ordinates.
5. What is projection? What is need of projection?
6. What are types of projection?
7. Write short note on Parallel Projection.
8. Write short note on Perspective Projection.
9. Differentiate between parallel and perspective projection.
10. Explain various types of parallel projection.
11. Explain various types of perspective projection.
12. Write note on View volume.
13. Derive the transformation matrix for general parallel projection.
14. Derive the transformation matrix for general perspective projection.
15. Explain 3D clipping in brief.
16. Explain various 3D viewing parameters.
17. Derive the 3D transformation matrix to transform world coordinates to viewing coordinates.

■■■

CHAPTER 8

Hidden Surfaces Elimination

Contents ...

Objectives...

- To Understand What is Need of Elimination of Hidden Surfaces From Scene
- To Study Classification of Visible Surface Detection Methods - Object Space and Image Space
- To Learn various Algorithm belonging to Object and Image Space Method like Back Face Detection, Z-buffer Algorithm, Painter Algorithm etc.

8.1 INTRODUCTION

- For the generation of realistic graphics displays, we have to identify those parts of a scene that are visible from a chosen viewing position. In a real life, the opaque material of solid objects obstructs the light rays from hidden parts and prevents us from seeing them.

- In computer generation image, no such automatic elimination takes place when objects are projected into screen co-ordinates. Instead all parts of every object, including many parts that should be invisible, are displayed. In order to create real image, we must use hidden surface elimination algorithm.
- A procedure that removes any surface or lines which are not to be displayed in a 3D scene is called hidden surface/line elimination or visible surface detection.
- There are many algorithms have been devised for efficient identification of visible objects for different types of applications. Some methods require more memory, some involve more processing time, and some apply only to special types of objects.
- A method for a particular application can be chosen upon depending factors such as the complexity of the scene, type of objects to be displayed, available equipment, and whether static or animated displays are to be generated.
- In this chapter, we explore some of the most commonly used methods for detecting visible surfaces in a three-dimensional scene.

8.1.1 Classification of Visible Surface Detection Algorithm

- Visible-surface detection algorithms are broadly classified according to whether they deal with object definitions directly or with their projected images.
- There are two approaches are called object-space methods and image-space methods, respectively.

1. **Object-space Method:**

- Object-space method is implemented in the physical coordinate system in which objects are described.
- It compares objects and parts of objects to each other within the scene definition to determine which surfaces, as a whole, we should label as visible.
- Object-space methods are generally used in line-display algorithms.
- The pseudo-code for object space method is as follows:

```
For each object in the scene do
Begin
Determine those part of the object whose view is unobstructed by other parts of it
or any other object with respect to the viewing specification.
Draw those parts in the object colour.
End
```

2. **Image-space Method:**

- Image space method is implemented in the screen coordinate system in which the objects are viewed.

- In an image-space algorithm, visibility is decided point by point at each pixel position on the view plane. Most hidden line/surface algorithms use image-space methods.
- The pseudo-code for image space method is as follows:

```
For each pixel in the image do
Begin
Determine the object closest to the viewer that is pierced by the projector through the pixel.
Draw the pixel in the object colour.
End
```

Difference between Object Space Method and Image Space method:

Sr. No.	Object Space method	Image Space method
1.	It is used in physical coordinate system.	It is used in screen coordinate system.
2.	It is based on comparison of objects for their 3D positions and dimensions with respect to a viewing position.	It is based on the pixels to be drawn on 2D. It tries to determine which object should contribute to that pixel.
3.	It performs geometric calculations with as much as precision possible having more accuracy.	It performs calculation with only enough precision to match resolution of display screen used to present image.
4.	The computation time of object space algorithms will tend to grow with number of objects in the scene.	The computation time of image space algorithms will tend to grow with complexity of visible parts of image.
5.	The cost of object space algorithms is more than image space method.	The cost of image space algorithms is less than object space method.
6.	Mostly used in line display algorithm.	Mostly used in hidden surface algorithms.
7.	Examples: Back face detection, Painter's algorithm etc.	Examples: Z-buffer algorithm, Scan-line algorithm etc.

8.2 DEPTH COMPARISON [Oct. 16]

- Although there are major differences in the basic approach taken by the various visible-surface detection algorithms, most algorithms use sorting and coherence methods to improve performance.

- Depth comparison or Sorting is used to facilitate depth comparisons by ordering the individual surfaces in a scene according to their distance from the view plane.
- Coherence methods are used to take advantage of regularities in a scene.
- The coherence is defined as the "degree to which parts of an environment or its projection exhibit local similarities". Such as similarities in depth, colour, texture and so on.
- To make algorithms more efficient we can exploit these similarities (coherence) when we reuse calculations made for one part of the environment or a picture for other nearby parts, either without changes or with some incremental changes.
- Let us see different kinds of coherence we can use in visible surface algorithms.
  1. **Object coherence:** If one object is entirely separate from another, comparisons may need to be done only between the two objects, and not between their components faces or edges.
  2. **Face coherence:** Usually surface properties vary smoothly across a face. This allows the computations for one part of face to be used with incremental changes to the other parts of the face.
  3. **Edge coherence:** The visibility of edge may change only when it crosses a visible edge or penetrates a visible face.
  4. **Implied edge coherence:** If one planar face penetrates another their line of intersection can be determined from two points of intersection.
  5. **Area coherence:** A group of adjacent pixel is often belongs to the same visible face.
  6. **Span coherence:** It refers to a visibility of face over a span of adjacent pixels on a scan line. It is special case of area coherence.
  7. **Scan line coherence:** The set of visible object spans determined for one scan line of an image typically changes very little from the set on the previous line.
  8. **Depth coherence:** Adjacent parts of the same surface are typically same or very close depth. Therefore, once the depth at one point of the surface is determined the depth of the points on the rest of the surface can often be determined by at the most simple incremental calculation.
  9. **Frame coherence:** Pictures of the same scene at two successive points in time are likely to be quite similar, except small changes in objects and view ports. Therefore, the calculations made for one picture can be reused for the next picture in a sequence.

8.2.1 Back Face Detection Algorithm (Back Face Culling) [April 16]

- Back face detection and removal is simpler object space algorithm. In a solid object, there are surfaces which are facing the viewer (front faces) and there are surfaces which are opposite to the viewer (back faces).
- These back faces contribute to approximately half of the total number of surfaces. Since, we cannot see these surfaces anyway, to save processing time, we can remove them before the clipping process with a simple test.
- Each surface has a normal vector. If this vector is pointing in the direction of the center of projection, it is a front face and can be seen by the viewer. If it is pointing away from the center of projection, it is a back face and cannot be seen by the viewer shown in Fig. 8.1.

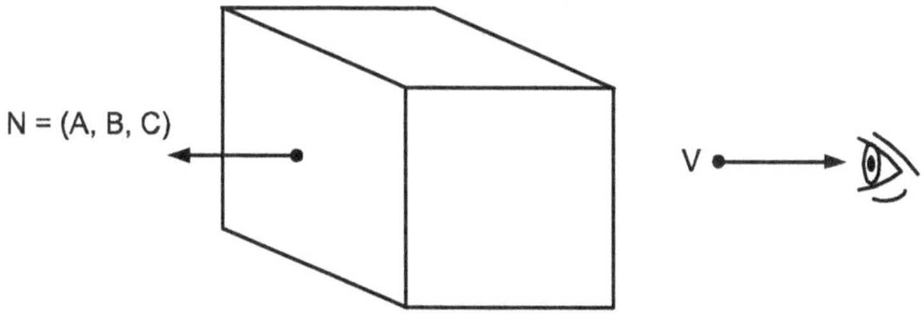

Fig. 8.1: Back Face Detection Algorithm (Back Face Culling)

- The direction of the light face can be identified by examining the result,

  $N \cdot V > 0$

  where,

  N: Normal vector to the polygon surface with cartesian components (A, B, C).

  V: A vector in the viewing direction from the eye (or "camera") position.
- We know that, the dot product of two vector gives the product of the lengths of the two vectors time the cosine of the angle between them. This cosine factor is important to us because if the vectors are in the same direction ($\theta < = 0 < \pi/2$), then the cosine is positive and the overall dot product is positive. However, if the directions are opposite ($\pi/2 < \theta < \pi$), then the cosine and the overall dot product is negative.

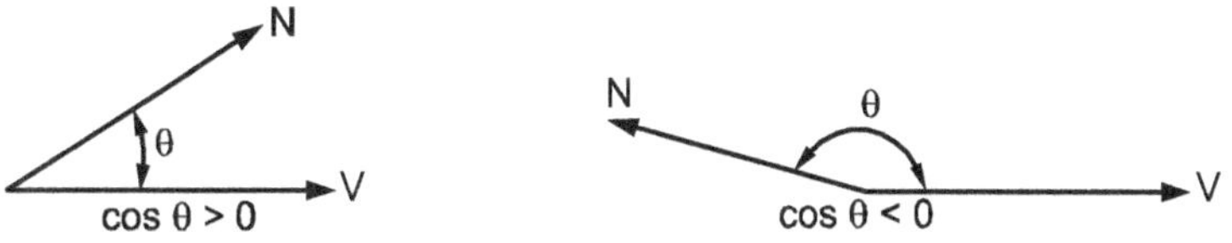

Fig. 8.2: Cosine angles between two vectors

- If the dot product is positive, we can say that the polygon faces towards the viewer; otherwise it faces away and should be removed.

- In case, if object description has been converted to projection coordinates and our viewing direction is parallel to the viewing z_v, axis, then V = (0, 0, V,) and

  $V \cdot N = V_z, C$

- So that we only have to consider the sign of C, the Z component of the normal vector N. Now, if the z component is positive, then the polygon faces towards the viewer, if negative, it faces away.
- The following Fig. 8.3 shows back face detection and removal.

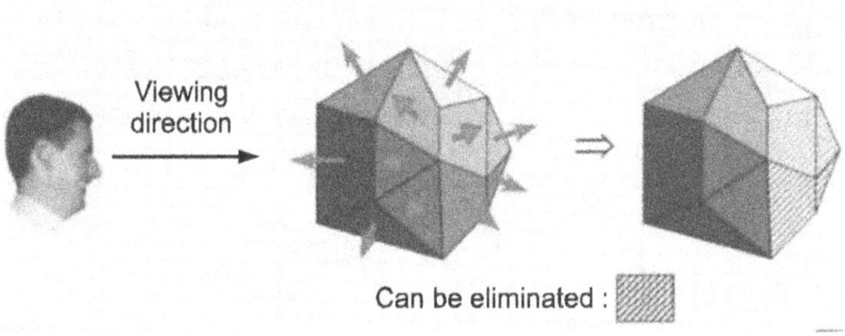

Fig. 8.3: Back face detection of polygon

Advantages:

1. It is useful for solid objects modelled as a polygon mesh.
2. It is good pre-processing step as it removes half of the polygons in the scène.

Disadvantages:

1. Partially hidden faces cannot be determined by back-face culling.
2. It only caters well for non-overlapping convex polyhedral but problematic for concave polyhedra.
3. It is not useful for ray-casting.

8.2.2 Z-buffer (Depth-buffer) Algorithm

- One of the simplest and commonly used image space approach to eliminate hidden surfaces is the Z-buffer or Depth-buffer algorithm.
- It is developed by Catmull. This algorithm compares surface depths at each pixel position on the projection plane.
- The surface depth is measured from the view plane along the z axis of a viewing system. When object description is converted to projection coordinates (x, y, z), each pixel position on the view plane is specified by x and y coordinate and z value gives the depth information. Thus, object depths can be compared by comparing the z-values.

- The Z-buffer algorithm is usually implemented in the normalized coordinates, so that z values range from 0 at the back clipping plane to 1 at the front clipping plane.
- As implied by the name of this method, two buffer areas are required. A depth buffer or Z-buffer is used to store depth values for each (x, y) position as surfaces are processed, and the refresh buffer or frame buffer stores the intensity values for each position.
- Initially, all positions in the depth buffer are set to 0 (minimum depth), and the refresh buffer is initialized to the background intensity. Each surface listed in the polygon on tables is then processed, one scan line at a time, calculating the depth (z value) at each (x, y) pixel position.
- The calculated depth is compared to the value previously stored in the depth buffer at that position. If the calculated depth is greater than the value stored in the depth buffer, the new depth value is stored, and the surface intensity at that position is determined and in the same (x, y) location in the refresh buffer.
- For example, in Fig. 8.4 among three surfaces, surface S_1 has the smallest depth at view position (x, y) and hence highest z value. So it is visible at that position.

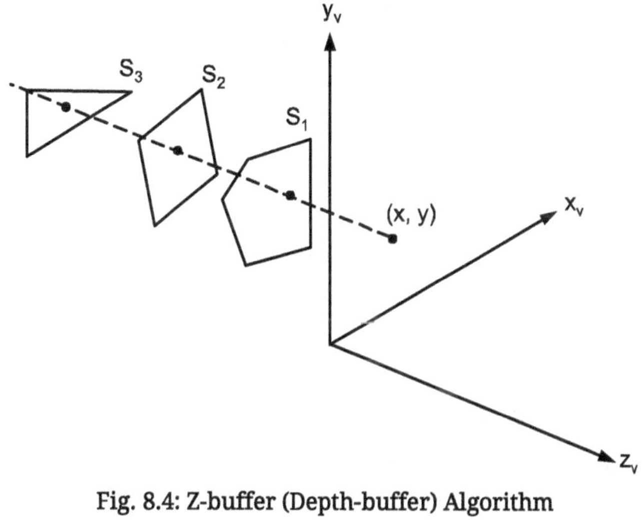

Fig. 8.4: Z-buffer (Depth-buffer) Algorithm

Z-buffer Algorithm:

1. Initialize the Z-buffer and frame buffer so that for all buffer positions, Z-buffer (x, y) = 0 and frame-buffer (x, y) = $I_{background}$.
2. During scan conversion process, for each position on each polygon surface, compare depth values to previously stored values in the depth buffer to determine visibility.

   Calculate z-value for each (x, y) position on the polygon,

   If z > Z-buffer (x, y), then set

   Z-buffer (x, y) = z, frame-buffer (x, y) = $I_{surface}$ (x, y)
3. Stop.

- Note that, $I_{background}$ is the value for the background intensity, and $I_{surface}$ is the projected intensity value for the surface at pixel position (x, y). After processing of all surfaces, the Z-buffer contains depth values for the visible surfaces and the frame buffer contains the corresponding intensity values for those surfaces.
- To calculate z-values, the plane equation,

  $$Ax + By + Cz + D = 0$$

  is used where (x, y, z) is any point on the plane, and the coefficient A, B, C and D are constants describing the spatial properties of the plane.
- Therefore, we can write

  $$z = \frac{-Ax - By - D}{C}$$

- Note, if at (x, y) the above equation evaluates to z_1, then at (x + Ax, y) the value of z, is

  $$z_1 = \frac{A}{C}(\Delta x)$$

- Only one subtraction is needed to calculate z(x + 1, y), given z(x, y), since the quotient A/C is constant and Ax = 1. A similar incremental calculation can be performed to determine the first value of z on the next scan line, decrementing by B/C for each Ay.

  depth at (x, y): $$z = \frac{-Ax - By - D}{C}$$

  depth at (x + 1, y): $$z' = \frac{-A(x+1) - By - D}{C} = z - \frac{A}{C}$$

  depth at (x, y –1): $$z'' = \frac{-Ax - B(y-1) - D}{C} = z + \frac{B}{C}$$

Advantages:

1. It is easy to implement.
2. It can be implemented in hardware to overcome the speed problem.
3. Since, the algorithm processes objects one at a time, the total number of polygons in a picture can be arbitrarily large.

Disadvantages:

1. It requires an additional buffer and hence the large memory.
2. It is a time consuming process as it requires comparison for each pixel instead of for the entire polygon.

8.2.3 A-buffer Algorithm

- The A-buffer method is an extension of the depth-buffer method for dealing with anti-aliasing, area-averaging, transparency, and translucency.
- A drawback of the depth buffer method is that it can only find one visible surface at each pixel position. This means it deals only with opaque surfaces and cannot

accumulate intensity values for more than one surface, as it necessary if transparent surfaces are to be displayed. The A-buffer method expands depth buffer so that more than one surface can be taken into consideration at each pixel position.

- This method is visibility detection method developed at Lucas film Studios for the rendering system REYES (Renders Everything You Ever Saw).
  1. The key data structure in the A-buffer is the accumulation buffer.
  2. Each position in the A-buffer has two fields:
     (i) **Depth field:** Stores a positive or negative real number, and
     (ii) **Intensity field:** Stores surface-intensity information or a pointer value.
- Two possible organizations for surface information in an A-buffer representation for a pixel position. When a single surface overlaps the pixel, the surface depth, color, and other information are stored as in (a). When more than one surface overlaps the pixel, a linked list of surface data is stored as in (b).

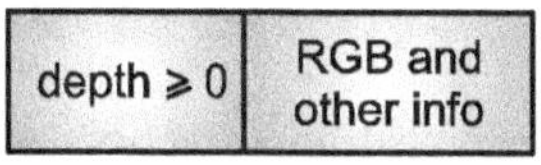

(a)

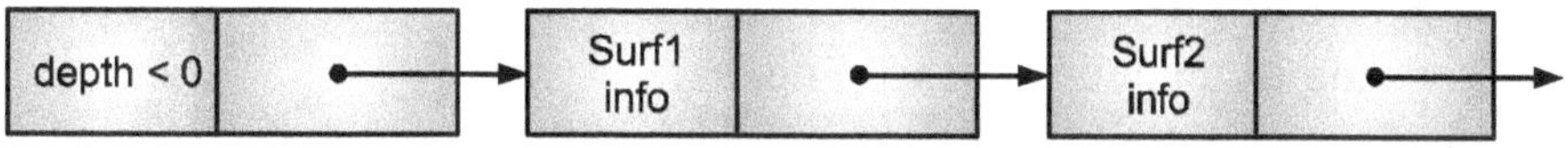

(b)

Fig. 8.5 Surface information in A-buffer representation

- If depth is >= 0, the number stored at that position is the depth of a single surface overlapping the corresponding pixel area.
- The intensity field then stores the RGB components of the surface colour at that point and the percent of pixel coverage.
- If depth < 0 this indicates multiple-surface contributions to the pixel intensity.
- The intensity field then stores a pointer to a linked List of surface data.
- Surface information in the A-buffer includes:
  (a) RGB intensity components
  (b) Opacity parameter
  (c) Depth
  (d) Percept of area coverage
  (e) Surface identifier
  (f) Other surface rendering parameters

- The algorithm proceeds just like the depth buffer algorithm. We have to process scan lines to determine surface overlaps of pixels. Surfaces are subdivided into a polygon mesh and clipped against the pixel boundaries. The depth and opacity values are used to determine the final colour of a pixel.

8.3 SCAN LINE METHOD

- A scan line method of hidden surface removal is an another approach of image space method.
- It is an extension of the scan line algorithm for filling polygon interiors. Here, the algorithm deals with more than one surfaces.
- As each scan line is processed, it examines all polygon surfaces intersecting that line to determine which are visible.
- It then does the depth calculation and finds which polygon is nearest to the view plane.
- Finally, it enters the intensity value of the nearest polygon at that position into the frame buffer.
- To implement this, two important tables are maintained the edge table and the polygon table.
  1. **The Edge Table contains:**
     - Coordinate end points of each line in the scene.
     - The inverse slope of each line.
     - Pointers into the polygon table to connect edges to surfaces.
  2. **The Polygon Table contains:**
     - The plane coefficients.
     - Surface material properties.
     - Other surface data.
     - Maybe pointers into the edge table.
     - To facilitate the search for surfaces crossing a given scan-line, an active list of edges is formed for each scan-line as it is processed.
     - The active list stores only those edges that cross the scan-line in order of increasing x.
     - Also a flag is set for each surface to indicate whether a position along a scan-line is either inside or outside the surface.
     - Pixel positions across each scan-line are processed from left to right.
     - At the left intersection with a surface, the surface flag is turned on.
     - At the right intersection point, the flag is turned off.
     - We only need to perform depth calculations when more than one surface has its flag turned on at a certain scan-line position.

- For example, Refer Fig. 8.6.

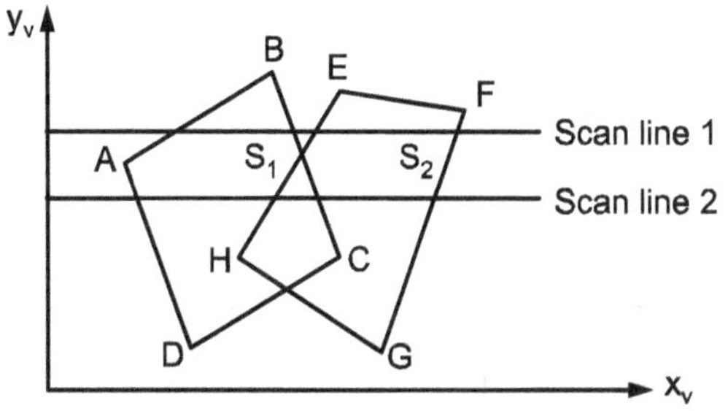

Fig. 8.6: Scan line method

The active list for scan line 1 contains,

Active Edge List (AEL) = | AB | BC | EH | FG | for scan line – 1

AB
BC
EH
FG

Span (horizontal)	FLAG → S_1	FLAG → S_2	Refresh Buffer
1. AB → BC	ON	OFF	Intensity - S_1
2. BC → EH	OFF	OFF	Background intensity
3. FH → FG	OFF	ON	Intensity - S_2

Similarly,

Active Edge List (AEL) = for scan line – 2

AD
EH
BC
FG

Span (horizontal)	FLAG → S_1	FLAG → S_2	Refresh Buffer
1. AD → EH	ON	OFF	Intensity - S_1
2. EH → BC	ON	ON	Depth calculations are made intensity of closet surface
3. BC → FG	OFF	ON	Intensity - S_2

Advantages:

1. The algorithm is applicable to non-polygonal surfaces.
2. Memory requirement is less than that for depth-buffer method.

Disadvantages:

1. Lot of sorting are done on x-y coordinates and on depths.

8.3.1 Depth Sorting Algorithm (Painter's Algorithm)

- The depth-sorting method uses both image space and object-space operations. It performs the following basic functions:
  1. Surfaces are sorted in order of decreasing depth.
  2. Resolving any ambiguities this may cause when the polygon's z extents overlap, i.e., splitting polygons if necessary.
- Surfaces are scan converted in order, starting with the surface of greatest depth.
- Sorting operations are carried out in both image and object space. The scan conversion of the polygon surfaces is performed in image space. This method for solving the hidden-surface problem is often referred to as the painter's algorithm.
- The basic idea of the Painter's algorithm developed by Newell and Sancha, is to paint the polygons into the frame buffer in order of decreasing distance from the viewpoint.
- The algorithm gets its name from the manner in which an oil painting is created. The artist begins with the background. He then adds the most distant object and then the nearer object and so forth.
- There is no need to erase portions of background; the artist simply paints on top of them. The new paint covers the old so that only the newest layer of paint is visible. This is illustrated in Fig. 8.7.

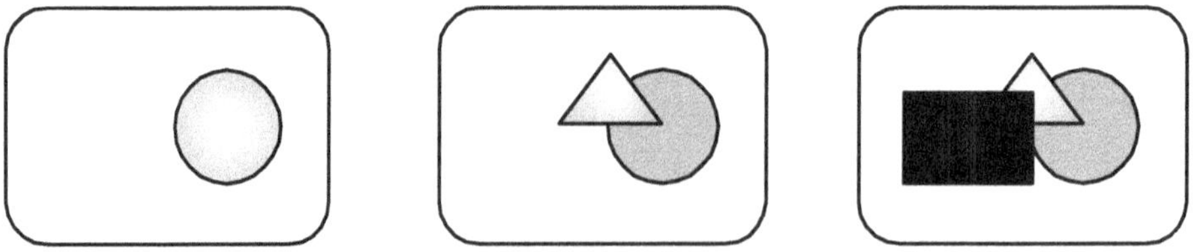

Fig. 8.7: Painter's algorithm

- Using the similar technique, we first sort the polygons according to their distance from the view point. The intensity values for the farthest polygon are then entered into the frame buffer.
- Taking each polygon is succeeding polygon in turn (in decreasing depth order), polygon intensities are painted on the frame buffer over the intensities of the previously processed polygons.

- This process is continued as long as no overlaps occur. If depth overlap is detected by any point in the sorted list, we have to make some additional comparisons to determine whether any of the polygon should be reordered.
- Surface S with the greatest depth is then compared to the other surfaces in the list to determine whether there are any overlaps in depth. We can perform the following tests for each surface that overlaps with S:
    1. The bounding rectangle in the xy plane for the two surfaces does not overlap (Fig. 8.8 (a)).
    2. Surface S is completely behind the overlapping surface relative to the viewing position. (Fig. 8.8 (b)).
    3. The overlapping surface is completely in front of S relative to the viewing position (Fig. 8.8 (c)).
    4. The projections of the two surfaces onto the view plane do not overlap (Fig. 8.8 (d)).

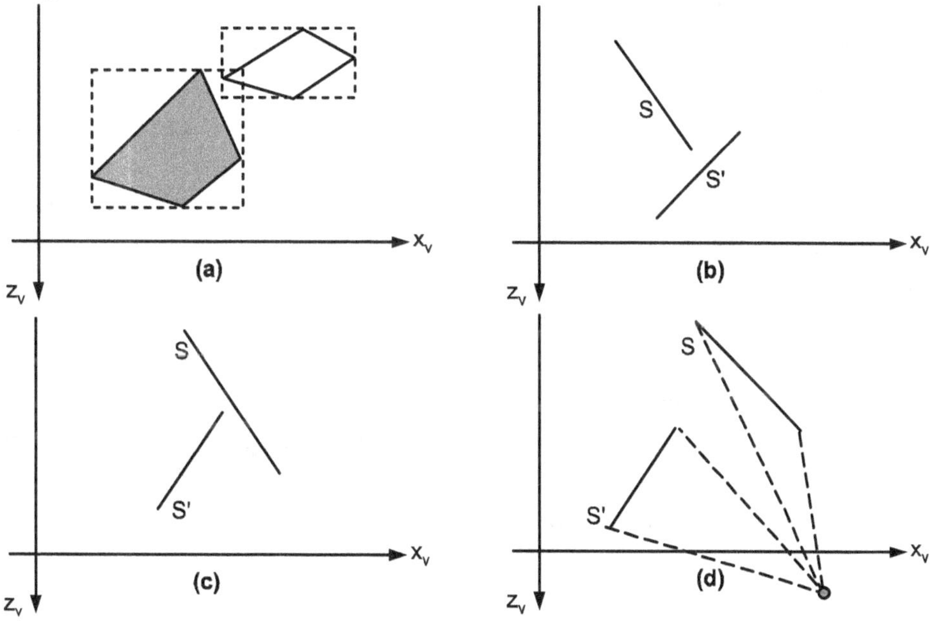

Fig. 8.8: Projections of the two surfaces onto the view plane

- If all the surfaces pass at least one of the tests, none of them is behind S and no reordering is then necessary and S is scan converted.
- If all four tests fail with S' then,
    - Interchange surfaces S and S' in the sorted list.
    - Repeat the tests for each surface that is reordered in the list as shown in Fig. 8.9.

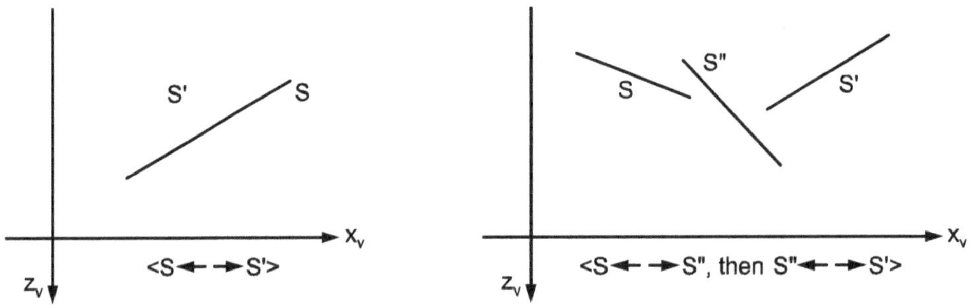

Fig. 8.9

Advantages:

1. Simple algorithm for ordering polygons.

Disadvantages:

1. Sorting criteria difficult to produce and sorting can also be expensive.
2. Redraws same pixel many times.

8.3.2 BSP-tree Method

- Binary Space Partition Trees (or BSP-trees) where introduced by Fuchs, Kedem, and Naylor around 1980.
- It is an efficient method for determining object visibility by painting surfaces onto the screen from back to front, as in the painter's algorithm.
- The BSP tree is particularly useful when the view reference point changes, but the objects in a scene are at fixed positions.
- A BSP tree is a hierarchical subdivision of n dimensional space into convex subspaces. Each node has a front and back leaf.
- Starting off with the root node, all subsequent insertions are partitioned by the hyper-plane of the current node.
- In 2 dimensional space, a hyper-plane is a line whereas in 3- dimensional space, a hyper-plane is a plane.
- It is two step process which is as follows:

  Step 1 : Construction of BSP tree, and

  Step 2 : Display of tree.

1. Construction of BSP Tree:

- Following is the procedure to build a BSP tree in the object space.

  Step 1 : Select a polygon (arbitrary) as the root of the tree i.e., the 1st partition plane.

  Step 2 : Partition the object space into two half-spaces (inside and outside of the partition plane determined by the normal to the plane), some object polygons lie in the rear half while the others in the front half w.r.t. the partition plane.

Step 3 : If a polygon is intersected by the partition plane, split it into two polygons so that they belong to different half-spaces.

Step 4 : Select one polygon in the root's front as the left node or child and another in the root's back as the right node or child.

Step 5 : Recursively subdivide spaces considering the plane of the children's as partition planes until a subspace contains a single polygon.

- Thus, we see that BSP tree's internal nodes are the partitioning planes (polygon objects) with left nodes representing front objects and right nodes the back objects. The leaves represent regions in space.

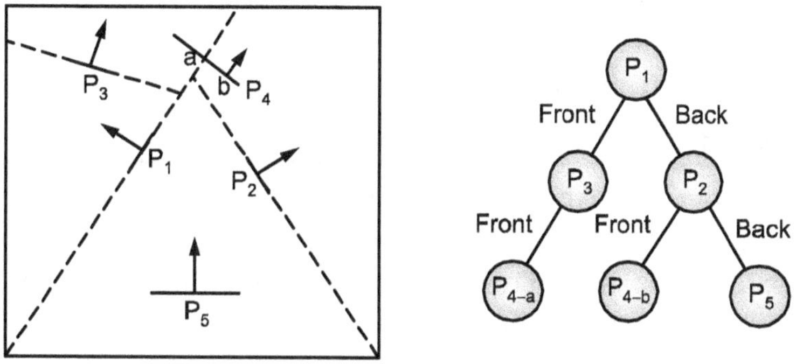

Fig. 8.10: Formation of BSP tree

- In above Fig. 8.10 p_1 dividing plane is selected as root. In front part of p_1 will be p_3 and p_4 a polygons. In back part, p_2 is selected as again dividing plane. So p_4 b will be in front part of p_2 and p_5 will be back surface p_2.

2. **Displaying BSP-tree:**

- When the BSP-tree is complete, following the principle or Painter's algorithm the tree is processed by selecting surfaces for display in back-to-front order.
- If the viewer is in the root polygons front half space, then the algorithm first displays all polygons in the roots rear half space (that too in back-to-front order recursively at each node) then the root itself and finally all polygons in its front half space (in back-to-front order recursively for each node).

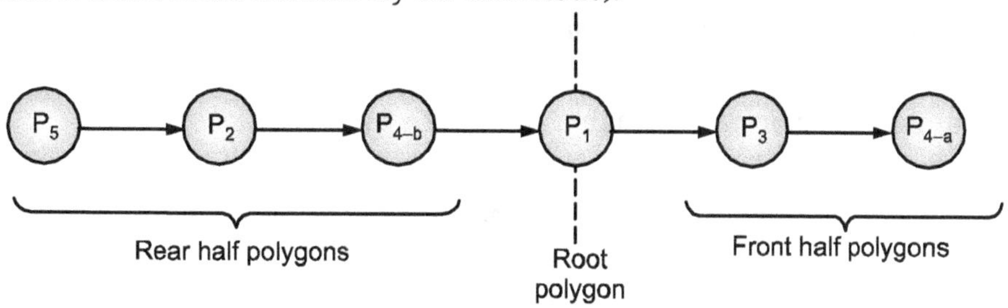

Fig. 8.11: Order of processing of polygons in BSP-tree

Advantages:

1. The main advantage of the bsp-tree algorithm for hidden surfaces is that we can use the same bsp-tree for different positions of the eye. Thus when we want to move around in a scene the bsp-tree is preferred approach to hidden surface.
2. We are not dealing with z-co-ordinates at all to decide the priority of polygons for display.

Disadvantages:

1. The main disadvantage is work involved in splitting polygons.
2. Waste of computation time as we are performing calculations for those objects which are also hidden.
3. Appropriate partitioning hyper-plane selection is quite complicated and difficult.

8.3.3 Area Sub-division Algorithm (Warnock's Algorithm)

- An interesting approach to the hidden surface problem was developed by Warnock.
- Area sub-division method is an image space method that successively divides the total viewing area into smaller and smaller rectangles until each small area is the projection of part of a single visible surface or no surface at all.
- Sub-division procedure is based on a two step strategy that, first decides which projected polygons overlap a given area A, on the screen and are therefore visible in that area. Second, in each area these polygons are further tested to determine which one will be visible within this area and should therefore be displayed.
- If a visibility decision can not be made, the screen area is further divided either until a visibility decision can be made or until the screen area is a single pixel.
- Starting with the full screen as the initial area, the algorithm divides an area at each stage into four smaller areas, thereby generating a quad tree,

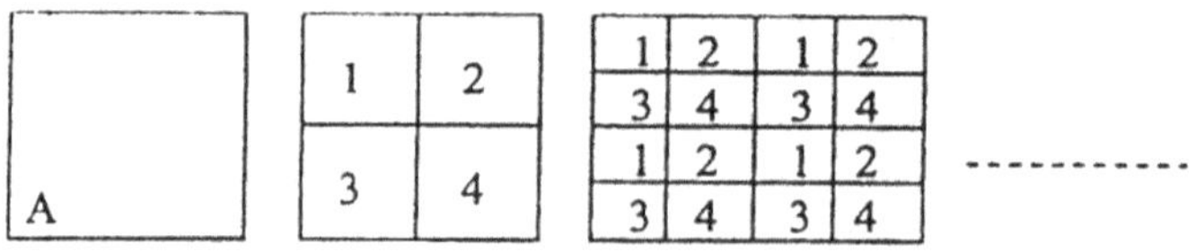

- The tests for determining surface visibility within an area can be stated in terms of the following classifications:

1. **Surrounding surface:** Polygon that completely encloses the area.

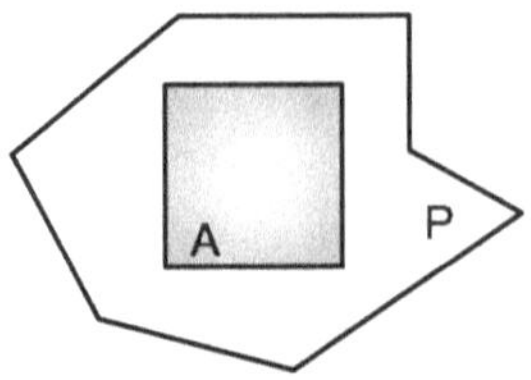

2. **Overlapping surface:** Polygon that is partly inside and partly outside the area.

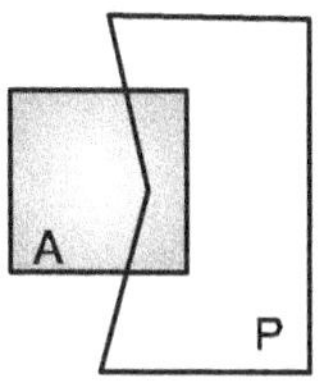

3. **Inside surface:** Polygon that is completely inside the area.

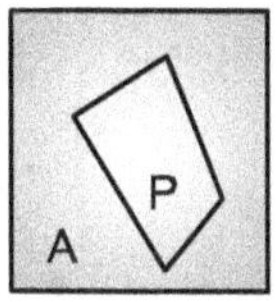

4. **Outside surface: (disjoint):** Polygon that is completely outside the area.

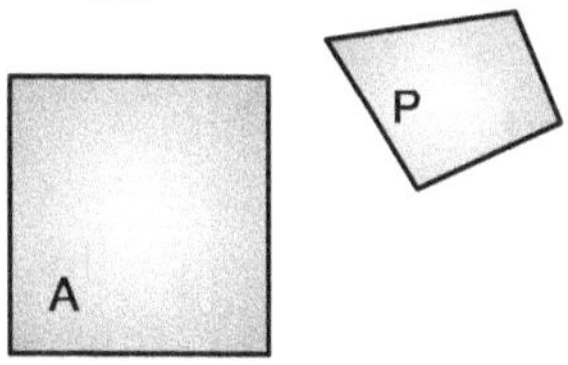

- No further subdivisions of a specified area are needed if one of the following conditions is true:
  1. All surfaces are outside surfaces with respect to the area.
  2. Only one inside, overlapping, or surrounding surface is in the area.
  3. A surrounding surface obscures all other surfaces within the area boundaries.
- Once, the visible surface is detected its pixel intensities are transferred to the appropriate area within the frame buffer.

Subdivision Algorithm:

1. Initialize the area to be the whole screen.
2. Create a visible polygon list with respect to an area sorted on Z_{min}. Remove the outside polygons. Remove the polygons that are hidden by a surrounding polygon.
3. Perform the visibility test.
   (a) If all the polygons are outside set all pixels to the background colour.
   (b) If there is exactly one polygon on the list and it is inside or overlapping scan - convert the inside polygon and colour the remaining area to the background colour.

(c) If there is exactly one polygon on the list and it is a surrounding one colour the area with the colour of the surrounding polygon.

(d) If a surrounding polygon is closer to the viewpoint than all other polygons, so that all other polygons are hidden by it, colour the area with the colour of the surrounding polygon.

(e) If the area is the pixel (x, y) calculate z-coordinate z (x, y), at pixel (x, y) of all polygons in the visible polygon list. The pixel is set to the colour of the polygon with the smallest z-coordinate.

4. If the visibility of a surface is not determined, subdivide the screen area into forths. For each area goto Step 2.

Advantages:

1. Extra memory buffer is not required.
2. Since it follows divide and conquer strategy, so parallel computers can be used to speed up the process.

Disadvantages:

1. Time complexity is at worst case $\log_2$ max(screen width, height) recursive steps will be required. At that point, the area being looked at each only single pixel which cannot be divided further. At that point, distance to each polygon intersecting, contained or surrounding the area is computed at the center of polygon to determine the closest polygon and its colour.

SUMMARY

- For the generation of realistic graphics displays, we have to identify those parts of a scene that are visible from a chosen viewing position.
- A procedure that removes any surface or lines which are not to be displayed in a 3D scene is called hidden surface /line elimination or visible surface detection.
- Visible-surface detection algorithms are broadly classified according to whether they deal with object definitions directly or with their projected images. There are two approaches are called object-space methods and image-space methods, respectively.
- Object-space Methods compare objects and parts of objects to each other within the scene definition to determine which surfaces, as a whole, we should label as visible.
- In image-space Methods visibility is determined point by point at each pixel position on the projection plane.
- Most visible-surface detection algorithms use sorting and coherence methods to improve performance.

- Depth comparison or Sorting is used to facilitate depth comparisons by ordering the individual surfaces in a scene according to their distance from the view plane.
- Coherence is the result of local similarity. As objects have continuous spatial extent, object properties vary smoothly within a small local region in the scene. Calculations can then be made incremental.
- Back face detection and removal is simpler object space algorithm. In a solid object, there are surfaces which are facing the viewer (front faces) and there are surfaces which are opposite to the viewer (back faces).These back faces contribute to approximately half of the total number of surfaces. Since we cannot see these surfaces anyway, to save processing time, we can remove them before the clipping process with a simple test.
- Z-buffer is an image-space approach. The basic idea is to test the Z-depth of each surface to determine the closest (visible) surface.In this method each surface is processed separately one pixel position at a time across the surface. The depth values for a pixel are compared and the closest (smallest z) surface determines the color to be displayed in the frame buffer.
- The A-buffer method is an extension of the depth-buffer method for dealing with anti-aliasing, area-averaging, transparency, and translucency.
- Scan line is an image-space method to identify visible surface. This method has depth information for only single scan-line. In order to require one scan-line of depth values, we must group and process all polygons intersecting a given scan-line at the same time before processing the next scan-line.
- Depth sorting method uses both image space and object-space operations. The depth-sorting method performs two basic functions –First, the surfaces are sorted in order of decreasing depth. Second, the surfaces are scan-converted in order, starting with the surface of greatest depth
- A BSP tree is a hierarchical subdivision of n dimensional space into convex subspaces. It is an efficient method for determining object visibility by painting surfaces onto the screen from back to front, as in the painter's algorithm. The BSP tree is particularly useful when the view reference point changes, but the objects in a scene are at fixed positions.
- The area-subdivision method takes advantage by locating those view areas that represent part of a single surface. Divide the total viewing area into smaller and smaller rectangles until each small area is the projection of part of a single visible surface or no surface at all.

PRACTICE QUESTIONS

1. What is need of hidden surface elimination?
2. Explain two approaches used to determine hidden surfaces.
3. What is coherence? Discuss various types of coherence that can be used to make more efficient visible algorithms.
4. Differentiate between object space and image space methods.
5. Explain back face detection algorithm.
6. Explain Z-buffer algorithm along with advantages and disadvantages.
7. Explain A-buffer algorithm for hidden surface removal and state its advantage over z-buffer algorithm.
8. Explain Scan line algorithm for hidden surface removal.
9. Explain depth sorting or painter's algorithm for hidden surface removal.
10. Explain BSP tree algorithm for hidden surface removal.

■■■

Programs for Practice

Program 1:

```
/*---------------------------------------------------------------------------
 *
 * olight.c : openGL (motif) example showing how to do hardware lighting
 * including two_sided lighting.
 * press  left   button for animation
 * middle button for two sided lighting (default)
 * right  button for single sided lighting
 *
 *
 *-------------------------------------------------------------------------*/
#include <stdio.h>
#include <stdlib.h>
#include <string.h>

#include <GL/glut.h>

/* function declarations */

void
  drawScene(void), setMatrix(void), initLightAndMaterial(void),
  animation(void), resize(int w, int h), menu(int choice), keyboard(unsigned
                                                        char c, int x, int y);

/* global variables */

float ax, ay, az;       /* angles for animation */
GLUquadricObj *quadObj; /* used in drawscene */
static float lmodel_twoside[] =
{GL_TRUE};
static float lmodel_oneside[] =
{GL_FALSE};
```

```
int
main(int argc, char **argv)
{
  glutInit(&argc, argv);

  quadObj = gluNewQuadric();  /* this will be used in drawScene
                                */
  glutInitDisplayMode(GLUT_RGB | GLUT_DOUBLE | GLUT_DEPTH);
  glutCreateWindow("Two-sided lighting");

  ax = 10.0;
  ay = -10.0;
  az = 0.0;
  initLightAndMaterial();

  glutDisplayFunc(drawScene);
  glutReshapeFunc(resize);
  glutCreateMenu(menu);
  glutAddMenuEntry("Motion", 3);
  glutAddMenuEntry("Two-sided lighting", 1);
  glutAddMenuEntry("One-sided lighting", 2);
  glutAttachMenu(GLUT_RIGHT_BUTTON);
  glutKeyboardFunc(keyboard);
  glutMainLoop();
  return 0;             /* ANSI C requires main to return int. */
}

void
drawScene(void)
{
  glClearColor(0.0, 0.0, 0.0, 0.0);
  glClear(GL_COLOR_BUFFER_BIT | GL_DEPTH_BUFFER_BIT);

  glPushMatrix();
  gluQuadricDrawStyle(quadObj, GLU_FILL);
  glColor3f(1.0, 1.0, 0.0);
  glRotatef(ax, 1.0, 0.0, 0.0);
  glRotatef(-ay, 0.0, 1.0, 0.0);
```

```
  gluCylinder(quadObj, 2.0, 5.0, 10.0, 20, 8);  /* draw a cone */

  glPopMatrix();

  glutSwapBuffers();
}

void
setMatrix(void)
{
  glMatrixMode(GL_PROJECTION);
  glLoadIdentity();
  glOrtho(-15.0, 15.0, -15.0, 15.0, -10.0, 10.0);
  glMatrixMode(GL_MODELVIEW);
  glLoadIdentity();
}

int count = 0;
void
animation(void)
{
  ax += 5.0;
  ay -= 2.0;
  az += 5.0;
  if (ax >= 360)
    ax = 0.0;
  if (ay <= -360)
    ay = 0.0;
  if (az >= 360)
    az = 0.0;
  drawScene();
  count++;
  if (count >= 60)
    glutIdleFunc(NULL);
}
```

```
/* ARGSUSED1 */
void
keyboard(unsigned char c, int x, int y)
{
  switch (c) {
  case 27:
    exit(0);
    break;
  default:
    break;
  }
}

void
menu(int choice)
{
  switch (choice) {
  case 3:
    count = 0;
    glutIdleFunc(animation);
    break;
  case 2:
    glLightModelfv(GL_LIGHT_MODEL_TWO_SIDE, lmodel_oneside);
    glutSetWindowTitle("One-sided lighting");
    glutPostRedisplay();
    break;
  case 1:
    glLightModelfv(GL_LIGHT_MODEL_TWO_SIDE, lmodel_twoside);
    glutSetWindowTitle("Two-sided lighting");
    glutPostRedisplay();
    break;
  }
}
```

```
void
resize(int w, int h)
{
  glViewport(0, 0, w, h);
  setMatrix();
}

void
initLightAndMaterial(void)
{
  static float ambient[] =
  {0.1, 0.1, 0.1, 1.0};
  static float diffuse[] =
  {0.5, 1.0, 1.0, 1.0};
  static float position[] =
  {90.0, 90.0, 150.0, 0.0};

  static float front_mat_shininess[] =
  {60.0};
  static float front_mat_specular[] =
  {0.2, 0.2, 0.2, 1.0};
  static float front_mat_diffuse[] =
  {0.5, 0.5, 0.28, 1.0};
  static float back_mat_shininess[] =
  {60.0};
  static float back_mat_specular[] =
  {0.5, 0.5, 0.2, 1.0};
  static float back_mat_diffuse[] =
  {1.0, 0.9, 0.2, 1.0};

  static float lmodel_ambient[] =
  {1.0, 1.0, 1.0, 1.0};
```

```
    setMatrix();
    glEnable(GL_DEPTH_TEST);
    glDepthFunc(GL_LEQUAL);
    glLightfv(GL_LIGHT0, GL_AMBIENT, ambient);
    glLightfv(GL_LIGHT0, GL_DIFFUSE, diffuse);
    glLightfv(GL_LIGHT0, GL_POSITION, position);

    glMaterialfv(GL_FRONT, GL_SHININESS, front_mat_shininess);
    glMaterialfv(GL_FRONT, GL_SPECULAR, front_mat_specular);
    glMaterialfv(GL_FRONT, GL_DIFFUSE, front_mat_diffuse);
    glMaterialfv(GL_BACK, GL_SHININESS, back_mat_shininess);
    glMaterialfv(GL_BACK, GL_SPECULAR, back_mat_specular);
    glMaterialfv(GL_BACK, GL_DIFFUSE, back_mat_diffuse);

    glLightModelfv(GL_LIGHT_MODEL_AMBIENT, lmodel_ambient);
    glLightModelfv(GL_LIGHT_MODEL_TWO_SIDE, lmodel_twoside);

    glEnable(GL_LIGHTING);
    glEnable(GL_LIGHT0);
    glShadeModel(GL_SMOOTH);
}
```

Output:

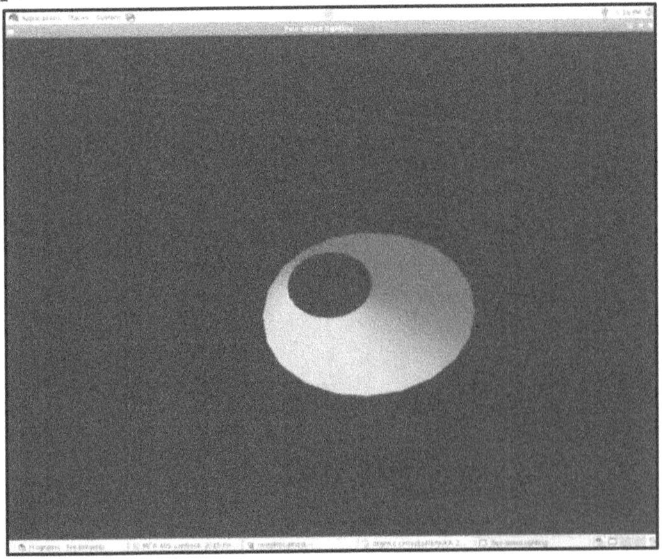

Program 2:

```
/* Program to show 3d effect

#include <stdio.h>
#include <stdlib.h>
#include <string.h>
#include <math.h>
#include <GL/glut.h>

/* Some <math.h> files do not define M_PI... */
#ifndef M_PI
#define M_PI 3.141592654
#endif

#ifdef WIN32
#define drand48() (((float) rand())/((float) RAND_MAX))
#define srand48(x) (srand((x)))
#else
extern double drand48(void);
extern void srand48(long seedval);
#endif

#define XSIZE   100
#define YSIZE   75

#define RINGS 5
#define BLUERING 0
#define BLACKRING 1
#define REDRING 2
#define YELLOWRING 3
#define GREENRING 4

#define BACKGROUND 8

enum {
  BLACK = 0,
  RED,
  GREEN,
```

```
    YELLOW,
    BLUE,
    MAGENTA,
    CYAN,
    WHITE
  };
  typedef short Point[2];

  GLenum rgb, doubleBuffer, directRender;

  unsigned char rgb_colors[RINGS][3];
  int mapped_colors[RINGS];
  float dests[RINGS][3];
  float offsets[RINGS][3];
  float angs[RINGS];
  float rotAxis[RINGS][3];
  int iters[RINGS];
  GLuint theTorus;

  void
  FillTorus(float rc, int numc, float rt, int numt)
  {
    int i, j, k;
    double s, t;
    double x, y, z;
    double pi, twopi;

    pi = M_PI;
    twopi = 2 * pi;

    for (i = 0; i < numc; i++) {
      glBegin(GL_QUAD_STRIP);
      for (j = 0; j <= numt; j++) {
        for (k = 1; k >= 0; k--) {
          s = (i + k) % numc + 0.5;
          t = j % numt;
```

```
        x = cos(t * twopi / numt) * cos(s * twopi / numc);
        y = sin(t * twopi / numt) * cos(s * twopi / numc);
        z = sin(s * twopi / numc);
        glNormal3f(x, y, z);

        x = (rt + rc * cos(s * twopi / numc)) * cos(t * twopi / numt);
        y = (rt + rc * cos(s * twopi / numc)) * sin(t * twopi / numt);
        z = rc * sin(s * twopi / numc);
        glVertex3f(x, y, z);
      }
    }
    glEnd();
  }
}
float
Clamp(int iters_left, float t)
{

  if (iters_left < 3) {
    return 0.0;
  }
  return (iters_left - 2) * t / iters_left;
}

void
Idle(void)
{
  int i, j;
  int more = GL_FALSE;

  for (i = 0; i < RINGS; i++) {
    if (iters[i]) {
      for (j = 0; j < 3; j++) {
        offsets[i][j] = Clamp(iters[i], offsets[i][j]);
      }
      angs[i] = Clamp(iters[i], angs[i]);
```

```
        iters[i]--;
        more = GL_TRUE;
      }
    }
    if (more) {
      glutPostRedisplay();
    } else {
      glutIdleFunc(NULL);
    }
}

void
DrawScene(void)
{
    int i;

    glPushMatrix();

    glClear(GL_COLOR_BUFFER_BIT | GL_DEPTH_BUFFER_BIT);
    gluLookAt(0, 0, 10, 0, 0, 0, 0, 1, 0);

    for (i = 0; i < RINGS; i++) {
      if (rgb) {
        glColor3ubv(rgb_colors[i]);
      } else {
        glIndexi(mapped_colors[i]);
      }
      glPushMatrix();
      glTranslatef(dests[i][0] + offsets[i][0], dests[i][1] + offsets[i][1],
                                                  dests[i][2] + offsets[i][2]);
      glRotatef(angs[i], rotAxis[i][0], rotAxis[i][1], rotAxis[i][2]);
                                                        glCallList(theTorus);
      glPopMatrix();
    }

    glPopMatrix();
```

```
  if (doubleBuffer) {
    glutSwapBuffers();
  } else {
    glFlush();
  }
}

float
MyRand(void)
{
  return 10.0 * (drand48() - 0.5);
}

void
ReInit(void)
{
  int i;
  float deviation;

  deviation = MyRand() / 2;
  deviation = deviation * deviation;
  for (i = 0; i < RINGS; i++) {
    offsets[i][0] = MyRand();
    offsets[i][1] = MyRand();
    offsets[i][2] = MyRand();
    angs[i] = 260.0 * MyRand();
    rotAxis[i][0] = MyRand();
    rotAxis[i][1] = MyRand();
    rotAxis[i][2] = MyRand();
    iters[i] = (deviation * MyRand() + 60.0);
  }
}
void
Init(void)
{
  int i;
```

```
float top_y = 1.0;
float bottom_y = 0.0;
float top_z = 0.15;
float bottom_z = 0.69;
float spacing = 2.5;
static float lmodel_ambient[] =
{0.0, 0.0, 0.0, 0.0};
static float lmodel_twoside[] =
{GL_FALSE};
static float lmodel_local[] =
{GL_FALSE};
static float light0_ambient[] =
{0.1, 0.1, 0.1, 1.0};
static float light0_diffuse[] =
{1.0, 1.0, 1.0, 0.0};
static float light0_position[] =
{0.8660254, 0.5, 1, 0};
static float light0_specular[] =
{1.0, 1.0, 1.0, 0.0};
static float bevel_mat_ambient[] =
{0.0, 0.0, 0.0, 1.0};
static float bevel_mat_shininess[] =
{40.0};
static float bevel_mat_specular[] =
{1.0, 1.0, 1.0, 0.0};
static float bevel_mat_diffuse[] =
{1.0, 0.0, 0.0, 0.0};

srand48(0x102342);
ReInit();
for (i = 0; i < RINGS; i++) {
  rgb_colors[i][0] = rgb_colors[i][1] = rgb_colors[i][2] = 0;
}
rgb_colors[BLUERING][2] = 255;
rgb_colors[REDRING][0] = 255;
rgb_colors[GREENRING][1] = 255;
```

```
rgb_colors[YELLOWRING][0] = 255;
rgb_colors[YELLOWRING][1] = 255;
mapped_colors[BLUERING] = BLUE;
mapped_colors[REDRING] = RED;
mapped_colors[GREENRING] = GREEN;
mapped_colors[YELLOWRING] = YELLOW;
mapped_colors[BLACKRING] = BLACK;

dests[BLUERING][0] = -spacing;
dests[BLUERING][1] = top_y;
dests[BLUERING][2] = top_z;

dests[BLACKRING][0] = 0.0;
dests[BLACKRING][1] = top_y;
dests[BLACKRING][2] = top_z;

dests[REDRING][0] = spacing;
dests[REDRING][1] = top_y;
dests[REDRING][2] = top_z;

dests[YELLOWRING][0] = -spacing / 2.0;
dests[YELLOWRING][1] = bottom_y;
dests[YELLOWRING][2] = bottom z;

dests[GREENRING][0] = spacing / 2.0;
dests[GREENRING][1] = bottom_y;
dests[GREENRING][2] = bottom_z;

theTorus = glGenLists(1);
glNewList(theTorus, GL_COMPILE);
FillTorus(0.1, 8, 1.0, 25);
glEndList();

glEnable(GL_CULL_FACE);
glCullFace(GL_BACK);
glEnable(GL_DEPTH_TEST);
glClearDepth(1.0);
```

```
  if (rgb) {
    glClearColor(0.5, 0.5, 0.5, 0.0);
    glLightfv(GL_LIGHT0, GL_AMBIENT, light0_ambient);
    glLightfv(GL_LIGHT0, GL_DIFFUSE, light0_diffuse);
    glLightfv(GL_LIGHT0, GL_SPECULAR, light0_specular);
    glLightfv(GL_LIGHT0, GL_POSITION, light0_position);
    glEnable(GL_LIGHT0);

    glLightModelfv(GL_LIGHT_MODEL_LOCAL_VIEWER, lmodel_local);
    glLightModelfv(GL_LIGHT_MODEL_TWO_SIDE, lmodel_twoside);
    glLightModelfv(GL_LIGHT_MODEL_AMBIENT, lmodel_ambient);
    glEnable(GL_LIGHTING);
    glMaterialfv(GL_FRONT, GL_AMBIENT, bevel_mat_ambient);
    glMaterialfv(GL_FRONT, GL_SHININESS, bevel_mat_shininess);
    glMaterialfv(GL_FRONT, GL_SPECULAR, bevel_mat_specular);
    glMaterialfv(GL_FRONT, GL_DIFFUSE, bevel_mat_diffuse);

    glColorMaterial(GL_FRONT_AND_BACK, GL_DIFFUSE);
    glEnable(GL_COLOR_MATERIAL);
    glShadeModel(GL_SMOOTH);
  } else {
    glClearIndex(BACKGROUND);
    glShadeModel(GL_FLAT);
  }

  glMatrixMode(GL_PROJECTION);
  gluPerspective(45, 1.33, 0.1, 100.0);
  glMatrixMode(GL_MODELVIEW);
}

void
Reshape(int width, int height)
{
  glViewport(0, 0, width, height);
}
```

```
/* ARGSUSED1 */
void
Key(unsigned char key, int x, int y)
{

  switch (key) {
  case 27:
    exit(0);
    break;
  case ' ':
    ReInit();
    glutIdleFunc(Idle);
    break;
  }
}

GLenum
Args(int argc, char **argv)
{
  GLint i;

  rgb = GL_TRUE;
  doubleBuffer = GL_TRUE;
  for (i = 1; i < argc; i++) {
    if (strcmp(argv[i], "-ci") == 0) {
      rgb = GL_FALSE;
    } else if (strcmp(argv[i], "-rgb") == 0) {
      rgb = GL_TRUE;
    } else if (strcmp(argv[i], "-sb") == 0) {
      doubleBuffer = GL_FALSE;
    } else if (strcmp(argv[i], "-db") == 0) {
      doubleBuffer = GL_TRUE;
    } else {
      printf("%s (Bad option).\n", argv[i]);
      return GL_FALSE;
    }
  }
  return GL_TRUE;
}
```

```
void
visible(int vis)
{
  if (vis == GLUT_VISIBLE) {
    glutIdleFunc(Idle);
  } else {
    glutIdleFunc(NULL);
  }
}

int
main(int argc, char **argv)
{
  GLenum type;

  glutInitWindowSize(400, 300);
  glutInit(&argc, argv);
  if (Args(argc, argv) == GL_FALSE) {
    exit(1);
  }
  type = (rgb) ? GLUT_RGB : GLUT_INDEX;
  type |= (doubleBuffer) ? GLUT_DOUBLE : GLUT_SINGLE;
  glutInitDisplayMode(type);

  glutCreateWindow("Olympic");

  Init();
  glutReshapeFunc(Reshape);
  glutKeyboardFunc(Key);
  glutDisplayFunc(DrawScene);

  glutVisibilityFunc(visible);

  glutMainLoop();
  return 0;             /* ANSI C requires main to return int. */
}
```

Output:

Program 3:

```
/* screendoor demonstrates "screen door" transparency using
   OpenGL's polygon stipple feature. */

#include <GL/glut.h>
#include <stdlib.h>
#include <stdio.h>

#define TORUS           1
#define TETRAHEDRON     2
#define ICOSAHEDRON     3

/* Screen door transparency stipple patterns, originally generated by
   Tim Hall (tjh@world.std.com) based on the 4x4 dither matrix
   described in "Computer Graphics Principles and Practice, 2nd ed." in
   the "Halftone Approximation" section (13.1.2).  Each 4x4 pattern is
   replicated over OpenGL's 32x32 pixel stipple pattern.  mjk converted
   Tim's patterns to be expressed as GLubytes instead of unsigned ints
   to avoid byte ordering problems. */

#if 0  /* Comment containing C comments. */
```

```
   Example usage:

   /* Assumes default unpack pixel store settings; see glPixelStore */

   glEnable(GL_POLYGON_STIPPLE);
   glPolygonStipple(stippleMask[0]);  /* 0% opaqueness */
   glPolygonStipple(stippleMask[8]);  /* 50% opaqueness */
   glPolygonStipple(stippleMask[16]); /* 100% opaqueness */

#endif

const GLubyte stippleMask[17][128] =
{
  /* NOTE: 0% opaqueness is faster to set and probably faster to render
with:
    glDisable(GL_POLYGON_STIPPLE);
    glColorMask(GL_FALSE, GL_FALSE, GL_FALSE, GL_FALSE); */
  {0x00, 0x00, 0x00, 0x00, 0x00, 0x00, 0x00, 0x00, 0x00, 0x00, 0x00, 0x00,
0x00, 0x00, 0x00, 0x00,
    0x00, 0x00, 0x00, 0x00, 0x00, 0x00, 0x00, 0x00, 0x00, 0x00, 0x00, 0x00,
0x00, 0x00, 0x00, 0x00,
    0x00, 0x00, 0x00, 0x00, 0x00, 0x00, 0x00, 0x00, 0x00, 0x00, 0x00, 0x00,
0x00, 0x00, 0x00, 0x00,
    0x00, 0x00, 0x00, 0x00, 0x00, 0x00, 0x00, 0x00, 0x00, 0x00, 0x00, 0x00,
0x00, 0x00, 0x00, 0x00,
    0x00, 0x00, 0x00, 0x00, 0x00, 0x00, 0x00, 0x00, 0x00, 0x00, 0x00, 0x00,
0x00, 0x00, 0x00, 0x00,
    0x00, 0x00, 0x00, 0x00, 0x00, 0x00, 0x00, 0x00, 0x00, 0x00, 0x00, 0x00,
0x00, 0x00, 0x00, 0x00,
    0x00, 0x00, 0x00, 0x00, 0x00, 0x00, 0x00, 0x00, 0x00, 0x00, 0x00, 0x00,
0x00, 0x00, 0x00, 0x00,
    0x00, 0x00, 0x00, 0x00, 0x00, 0x00, 0x00, 0x00, 0x00, 0x00, 0x00, 0x00,
0x00, 0x00, 0x00, 0x00},

  {0x88, 0x88, 0x88, 0x88, 0x00, 0x00, 0x00, 0x00, 0x00, 0x00, 0x00, 0x00,
0x00, 0x00, 0x00, 0x00,
```

```
    0x88, 0x88, 0x88, 0x88, 0x00, 0x00, 0x00, 0x00, 0x00, 0x00, 0x00, 0x00,
0x00, 0x00, 0x00, 0x00,
    0x88, 0x88, 0x88, 0x88, 0x00, 0x00, 0x00, 0x00, 0x00, 0x00, 0x00, 0x00,
0x00, 0x00, 0x00, 0x00,
    0x88, 0x88, 0x88, 0x88, 0x00, 0x00, 0x00, 0x00, 0x00, 0x00, 0x00, 0x00,
0x00, 0x00, 0x00, 0x00,
    0x88, 0x88, 0x88, 0x88, 0x00, 0x00, 0x00, 0x00, 0x00, 0x00, 0x00, 0x00,
0x00, 0x00, 0x00, 0x00,
    0x88, 0x88, 0x88, 0x88, 0x00, 0x00, 0x00, 0x00, 0x00, 0x00, 0x00, 0x00,
0x00, 0x00, 0x00, 0x00,
    0x88, 0x88, 0x88, 0x88, 0x00, 0x00, 0x00, 0x00, 0x00, 0x00, 0x00, 0x00,
0x00, 0x00, 0x00, 0x00,
    0x88, 0x88, 0x88, 0x88, 0x00, 0x00, 0x00, 0x00, 0x00, 0x00, 0x00, 0x00,
0x00, 0x00, 0x00, 0x00},

  {0x88, 0x88, 0x88, 0x88, 0x00, 0x00, 0x00, 0x00, 0x22, 0x22, 0x22, 0x22,
0x00, 0x00, 0x00, 0x00,
    0x88, 0x88, 0x88, 0x88, 0x00, 0x00, 0x00, 0x00, 0x22, 0x22, 0x22, 0x22,
0x00, 0x00, 0x00, 0x00,
    0x88, 0x88, 0x88, 0x88, 0x00, 0x00, 0x00, 0x00, 0x22, 0x22, 0x22, 0x22,
0x00, 0x00, 0x00, 0x00,
    0x88, 0x88, 0x88, 0x88, 0x00, 0x00, 0x00, 0x00, 0x22, 0x22, 0x22, 0x22,
0x00, 0x00, 0x00, 0x00,
    0x88, 0x88, 0x88, 0x88, 0x00, 0x00, 0x00, 0x00, 0x22, 0x22, 0x22, 0x22,
0x00, 0x00, 0x00, 0x00,
    0x88, 0x88, 0x88, 0x88, 0x00, 0x00, 0x00, 0x00, 0x22, 0x22, 0x22, 0x22,
0x00, 0x00, 0x00, 0x00,
    0x88, 0x88, 0x88, 0x88, 0x00, 0x00, 0x00, 0x00, 0x22, 0x22, 0x22, 0x22,
0x00, 0x00, 0x00, 0x00,
    0x88, 0x88, 0x88, 0x88, 0x00, 0x00, 0x00, 0x00, 0x22, 0x22, 0x22, 0x22,
0x00, 0x00, 0x00, 0x00},

  {0xaa, 0xaa, 0xaa, 0xaa, 0x00, 0x00, 0x00, 0x00, 0x22, 0x22, 0x22, 0x22,
0x00, 0x00, 0x00, 0x00,
    0xaa, 0xaa, 0xaa, 0xaa, 0x00, 0x00, 0x00, 0x00, 0x22, 0x22, 0x22, 0x22,
0x00, 0x00, 0x00, 0x00,
    0xaa, 0xaa, 0xaa, 0xaa, 0x00, 0x00, 0x00, 0x00, 0x22, 0x22, 0x22, 0x22,
0x00, 0x00, 0x00, 0x00,
```

```
    0xaa, 0xaa, 0xaa, 0xaa, 0x00, 0x00, 0x00, 0x00, 0x22, 0x22, 0x22, 0x22,
0x00, 0x00, 0x00, 0x00,
    0xaa, 0xaa, 0xaa, 0xaa, 0x00, 0x00, 0x00, 0x00, 0x22, 0x22, 0x22, 0x22,
0x00, 0x00, 0x00, 0x00,
    0xaa, 0xaa, 0xaa, 0xaa, 0x00, 0x00, 0x00, 0x00, 0x22, 0x22, 0x22, 0x22,
0x00, 0x00, 0x00, 0x00,
    0xaa, 0xaa, 0xaa, 0xaa, 0x00, 0x00, 0x00, 0x00, 0x22, 0x22, 0x22, 0x22,
0x00, 0x00, 0x00, 0x00,
    0xaa, 0xaa, 0xaa, 0xaa, 0x00, 0x00, 0x00, 0x00, 0x22, 0x22, 0x22, 0x22,
0x00, 0x00, 0x00, 0x00},

  {0xaa, 0xaa, 0xaa, 0xaa, 0x00, 0x00, 0x00, 0x00, 0xaa, 0xaa, 0xaa, 0xaa,
0x00, 0x00, 0x00, 0x00,
    0xaa, 0xaa, 0xaa, 0xaa, 0x00, 0x00, 0x00, 0x00, 0xaa, 0xaa, 0xaa, 0xaa,
0x00, 0x00, 0x00, 0x00,
    0xaa, 0xaa, 0xaa, 0xaa, 0x00, 0x00, 0x00, 0x00, 0xaa, 0xaa, 0xaa, 0xaa,
0x00, 0x00, 0x00, 0x00,
    0xaa, 0xaa, 0xaa, 0xaa, 0x00, 0x00, 0x00, 0x00, 0xaa, 0xaa, 0xaa, 0xaa,
0x00, 0x00, 0x00, 0x00,
    0xaa, 0xaa, 0xaa, 0xaa, 0x00, 0x00, 0x00, 0x00, 0xaa, 0xaa, 0xaa, 0xaa,
0x00, 0x00, 0x00, 0x00,
    0xaa, 0xaa, 0xaa, 0xaa, 0x00, 0x00, 0x00, 0x00, 0xaa, 0xaa, 0xaa, 0xaa,
0x00, 0x00, 0x00, 0x00,
    0xaa, 0xaa, 0xaa, 0xaa, 0x00, 0x00, 0x00, 0x00, 0xaa, 0xaa, 0xaa, 0xaa,
0x00, 0x00, 0x00, 0x00,
    0xaa, 0xaa, 0xaa, 0xaa, 0x00, 0x00, 0x00, 0x00, 0xaa, 0xaa, 0xaa, 0xaa,
0x00, 0x00, 0x00, 0x00},

  {0xaa, 0xaa, 0xaa, 0xaa, 0x44, 0x44, 0x44, 0x44, 0xaa, 0xaa, 0xaa, 0xaa,
0x00, 0x00, 0x00, 0x00,
    0xaa, 0xaa, 0xaa, 0xaa, 0x44, 0x44, 0x44, 0x44, 0xaa, 0xaa, 0xaa, 0xaa,
0x00, 0x00, 0x00, 0x00,
    0xaa, 0xaa, 0xaa, 0xaa, 0x44, 0x44, 0x44, 0x44, 0xaa, 0xaa, 0xaa, 0xaa,
0x00, 0x00, 0x00, 0x00,
    0xaa, 0xaa, 0xaa, 0xaa, 0x44, 0x44, 0x44, 0x44, 0xaa, 0xaa, 0xaa, 0xaa,
0x00, 0x00, 0x00, 0x00,
    0xaa, 0xaa, 0xaa, 0xaa, 0x44, 0x44, 0x44, 0x44, 0xaa, 0xaa, 0xaa, 0xaa,
0x00, 0x00, 0x00, 0x00,
```

```
    0xaa, 0xaa, 0xaa, 0xaa, 0x44, 0x44, 0x44, 0x44, 0xaa, 0xaa, 0xaa, 0xaa,
0x00, 0x00, 0x00, 0x00,
    0xaa, 0xaa, 0xaa, 0xaa, 0x44, 0x44, 0x44, 0x44, 0xaa, 0xaa, 0xaa, 0xaa,
0x00, 0x00, 0x00, 0x00,
    0xaa, 0xaa, 0xaa, 0xaa, 0x44, 0x44, 0x44, 0x44, 0xaa, 0xaa, 0xaa, 0xaa,
0x00, 0x00, 0x00, 0x00},

  {0xaa, 0xaa, 0xaa, 0xaa, 0x44, 0x44, 0x44, 0x44, 0xaa, 0xaa, 0xaa, 0xaa,
0x11, 0x11, 0x11, 0x11,
    0xaa, 0xaa, 0xaa, 0xaa, 0x44, 0x44, 0x44, 0x44, 0xaa, 0xaa, 0xaa, 0xaa,
0x11, 0x11, 0x11, 0x11,
    0xaa, 0xaa, 0xaa, 0xaa, 0x44, 0x44, 0x44, 0x44, 0xaa, 0xaa, 0xaa, 0xaa,
0x11, 0x11, 0x11, 0x11,
    0xaa, 0xaa, 0xaa, 0xaa, 0x44, 0x44, 0x44, 0x44, 0xaa, 0xaa, 0xaa, 0xaa,
0x11, 0x11, 0x11, 0x11,
    0xaa, 0xaa, 0xaa, 0xaa, 0x44, 0x44, 0x44, 0x44, 0xaa, 0xaa, 0xaa, 0xaa,
0x11, 0x11, 0x11, 0x11,
    0xaa, 0xaa, 0xaa, 0xaa, 0x44, 0x44, 0x44, 0x44, 0xaa, 0xaa, 0xaa, 0xaa,
0x11, 0x11, 0x11, 0x11,
    0xaa, 0xaa, 0xaa, 0xaa, 0x44, 0x44, 0x44, 0x44, 0xaa, 0xaa, 0xaa, 0xaa,
0x11, 0x11, 0x11, 0x11,
    0xaa, 0xaa, 0xaa, 0xaa, 0x44, 0x44, 0x44, 0x44, 0xaa, 0xaa, 0xaa, 0xaa,
0x11, 0x11, 0x11, 0x11},

  {0xaa, 0xaa, 0xaa, 0xaa, 0x55, 0x55, 0x55, 0x55, 0xaa, 0xaa, 0xaa, 0xaa,
0x11, 0x11, 0x11, 0x11,
    0xaa, 0xaa, 0xaa, 0xaa, 0x55, 0x55, 0x55, 0x55, 0xaa, 0xaa, 0xaa, 0xaa,
0x11, 0x11, 0x11, 0x11,
    0xaa, 0xaa, 0xaa, 0xaa, 0x55, 0x55, 0x55, 0x55, 0xaa, 0xaa, 0xaa, 0xaa,
0x11, 0x11, 0x11, 0x11,
    0xaa, 0xaa, 0xaa, 0xaa, 0x55, 0x55, 0x55, 0x55, 0xaa, 0xaa, 0xaa, 0xaa,
0x11, 0x11, 0x11, 0x11,
    0xaa, 0xaa, 0xaa, 0xaa, 0x55, 0x55, 0x55, 0x55, 0xaa, 0xaa, 0xaa, 0xaa,
0x11, 0x11, 0x11, 0x11,
    0xaa, 0xaa, 0xaa, 0xaa, 0x55, 0x55, 0x55, 0x55, 0xaa, 0xaa, 0xaa, 0xaa,
0x11, 0x11, 0x11, 0x11,
    0xaa, 0xaa, 0xaa, 0xaa, 0x55, 0x55, 0x55, 0x55, 0xaa, 0xaa, 0xaa, 0xaa,
0x11, 0x11, 0x11, 0x11,
    0xaa, 0xaa, 0xaa, 0xaa, 0x55, 0x55, 0x55, 0x55, 0xaa, 0xaa, 0xaa, 0xaa,
0x11, 0x11, 0x11, 0x11},
```

```
{0xaa, 0xaa, 0xaa, 0xaa, 0x55, 0x55, 0x55, 0x55, 0xaa, 0xaa, 0xaa, 0xaa,
0x55, 0x55, 0x55, 0x55,
    0xaa, 0xaa, 0xaa, 0xaa, 0x55, 0x55, 0x55, 0x55, 0xaa, 0xaa, 0xaa, 0xaa,
0x55, 0x55, 0x55, 0x55,
    0xaa, 0xaa, 0xaa, 0xaa, 0x55, 0x55, 0x55, 0x55, 0xaa, 0xaa, 0xaa, 0xaa,
0x55, 0x55, 0x55, 0x55,
    0xaa, 0xaa, 0xaa, 0xaa, 0x55, 0x55, 0x55, 0x55, 0xaa, 0xaa, 0xaa, 0xaa,
0x55, 0x55, 0x55, 0x55,
    0xaa, 0xaa, 0xaa, 0xaa, 0x55, 0x55, 0x55, 0x55, 0xaa, 0xaa, 0xaa, 0xaa,
0x55, 0x55, 0x55, 0x55,
    0xaa, 0xaa, 0xaa, 0xaa, 0x55, 0x55, 0x55, 0x55, 0xaa, 0xaa, 0xaa, 0xaa,
0x55, 0x55, 0x55, 0x55,
    0xaa, 0xaa, 0xaa, 0xaa, 0x55, 0x55, 0x55, 0x55, 0xaa, 0xaa, 0xaa, 0xaa,
0x55, 0x55, 0x55, 0x55,
    0xaa, 0xaa, 0xaa, 0xaa, 0x55, 0x55, 0x55, 0x55, 0xaa, 0xaa, 0xaa, 0xaa,
0x55, 0x55, 0x55, 0x55},

{0xee, 0xee, 0xee, 0xee, 0x55, 0x55, 0x55, 0x55, 0xaa, 0xaa, 0xaa, 0xaa,
0x55, 0x55, 0x55, 0x55,
    0xee, 0xee, 0xee, 0xee, 0x55, 0x55, 0x55, 0x55, 0xaa, 0xaa, 0xaa, 0xaa,
0x55, 0x55, 0x55, 0x55,
    0xee, 0xee, 0xee, 0xee, 0x55, 0x55, 0x55, 0x55, 0xaa, 0xaa, 0xaa, 0xaa,
0x55, 0x55, 0x55, 0x55,
    0xee, 0xee, 0xee, 0xee, 0x55, 0x55, 0x55, 0x55, 0xaa, 0xaa, 0xaa, 0xaa,
0x55, 0x55, 0x55, 0x55,
    0xee, 0xee, 0xee, 0xee, 0x55, 0x55, 0x55, 0x55, 0xaa, 0xaa, 0xaa, 0xaa,
0x55, 0x55, 0x55, 0x55,
    0xee, 0xee, 0xee, 0xee, 0x55, 0x55, 0x55, 0x55, 0xaa, 0xaa, 0xaa, 0xaa,
0x55, 0x55, 0x55, 0x55,
    0xee, 0xee, 0xee, 0xee, 0x55, 0x55, 0x55, 0x55, 0xaa, 0xaa, 0xaa, 0xaa,
0x55, 0x55, 0x55, 0x55,
    0xee, 0xee, 0xee, 0xee, 0x55, 0x55, 0x55, 0x55, 0xaa, 0xaa, 0xaa, 0xaa,
0x55, 0x55, 0x55, 0x55},

{0xee, 0xee, 0xee, 0xee, 0x55, 0x55, 0x55, 0x55, 0xbb, 0xbb, 0xbb, 0xbb,
0x55, 0x55, 0x55, 0x55,
    0xee, 0xee, 0xee, 0xee, 0x55, 0x55, 0x55, 0x55, 0xbb, 0xbb, 0xbb, 0xbb,
0x55, 0x55, 0x55, 0x55,
```

```
    0xee, 0xee, 0xee, 0xee, 0x55, 0x55, 0x55, 0x55, 0xbb, 0xbb, 0xbb, 0xbb,
0x55, 0x55, 0x55, 0x55,
    0xee, 0xee, 0xee, 0xee, 0x55, 0x55, 0x55, 0x55, 0xbb, 0xbb, 0xbb, 0xbb,
0x55, 0x55, 0x55, 0x55,
    0xee, 0xee, 0xee, 0xee, 0x55, 0x55, 0x55, 0x55, 0xbb, 0xbb, 0xbb, 0xbb,
0x55, 0x55, 0x55, 0x55,
    0xee, 0xee, 0xee, 0xee, 0x55, 0x55, 0x55, 0x55, 0xbb, 0xbb, 0xbb, 0xbb,
0x55, 0x55, 0x55, 0x55,
    0xee, 0xee, 0xee, 0xee, 0x55, 0x55, 0x55, 0x55, 0xbb, 0xbb, 0xbb, 0xbb,
0x55, 0x55, 0x55, 0x55,
    0xee, 0xee, 0xee, 0xee, 0x55, 0x55, 0x55, 0x55, 0xbb, 0xbb, 0xbb, 0xbb,
0x55, 0x55, 0x55, 0x55},

   {0xff, 0xff, 0xff, 0xff, 0x55, 0x55, 0x55, 0x55, 0xbb, 0xbb, 0xbb, 0xbb,
0x55, 0x55, 0x55, 0x55,
    0xff, 0xff, 0xff, 0xff, 0x55, 0x55, 0x55, 0x55, 0xbb, 0xbb, 0xbb, 0xbb,
0x55, 0x55, 0x55, 0x55,
    0xff, 0xff, 0xff, 0xff, 0x55, 0x55, 0x55, 0x55, 0xbb, 0xbb, 0xbb, 0xbb,
0x55, 0x55, 0x55, 0x55,
    0xff, 0xff, 0xff, 0xff, 0x55, 0x55, 0x55, 0x55, 0xbb, 0xbb, 0xbb, 0xbb,
0x55, 0x55, 0x55, 0x55,
    0xff, 0xff, 0xff, 0xff, 0x55, 0x55, 0x55, 0x55, 0xbb, 0xbb, 0xbb, 0xbb,
0x55, 0x55, 0x55, 0x55,
    0xff, 0xff, 0xff, 0xff, 0x55, 0x55, 0x55, 0x55, 0xbb, 0xbb, 0xbb, 0xbb,
0x55, 0x55, 0x55, 0x55,
    0xff, 0xff, 0xff, 0xff, 0x55, 0x55, 0x55, 0x55, 0xbb, 0xbb, 0xbb, 0xbb,
0x55, 0x55, 0x55, 0x55,
    0xff, 0xff, 0xff, 0xff, 0x55, 0x55, 0x55, 0x55, 0xbb, 0xbb, 0xbb, 0xbb,
0x55, 0x55, 0x55, 0x55},

   {0xff, 0xff, 0xff, 0xff, 0x55, 0x55, 0x55, 0x55, 0xff, 0xff, 0xff, 0xff,
0x55, 0x55, 0x55, 0x55,
    0xff, 0xff, 0xff, 0xff, 0x55, 0x55, 0x55, 0x55, 0xff, 0xff, 0xff, 0xff,
0x55, 0x55, 0x55, 0x55,
    0xff, 0xff, 0xff, 0xff, 0x55, 0x55, 0x55, 0x55, 0xff, 0xff, 0xff, 0xff,
0x55, 0x55, 0x55, 0x55,
    0xff, 0xff, 0xff, 0xff, 0x55, 0x55, 0x55, 0x55, 0xff, 0xff, 0xff, 0xff,
0x55, 0x55, 0x55, 0x55,
```

```
    0xff, 0xff, 0xff, 0xff, 0x55, 0x55, 0x55, 0x55, 0xff, 0xff, 0xff, 0xff,
0x55, 0x55, 0x55, 0x55,
    0xff, 0xff, 0xff, 0xff, 0x55, 0x55, 0x55, 0x55, 0xff, 0xff, 0xff, 0xff,
0x55, 0x55, 0x55, 0x55,
    0xff, 0xff, 0xff, 0xff, 0x55, 0x55, 0x55, 0x55, 0xff, 0xff, 0xff, 0xff,
0x55, 0x55, 0x55, 0x55,
    0xff, 0xff, 0xff, 0xff, 0x55, 0x55, 0x55, 0x55, 0xff, 0xff, 0xff, 0xff,
0x55, 0x55, 0x55, 0x55},

   {0xff, 0xff, 0xff, 0xff, 0xdd, 0xdd, 0xdd, 0xdd, 0xff, 0xff, 0xff, 0xff,
0x55, 0x55, 0x55, 0x55,
    0xff, 0xff, 0xff, 0xff, 0xdd, 0xdd, 0xdd, 0xdd, 0xff, 0xff, 0xff, 0xff,
0x55, 0x55, 0x55, 0x55,
    0xff, 0xff, 0xff, 0xff, 0xdd, 0xdd, 0xdd, 0xdd, 0xff, 0xff, 0xff, 0xff,
0x55, 0x55, 0x55, 0x55,
    0xff, 0xff, 0xff, 0xff, 0xdd, 0xdd, 0xdd, 0xdd, 0xff, 0xff, 0xff, 0xff,
0x55, 0x55, 0x55, 0x55,
    0xff, 0xff, 0xff, 0xff, 0xdd, 0xdd, 0xdd, 0xdd, 0xff, 0xff, 0xff, 0xff,
0x55, 0x55, 0x55, 0x55,
    0xff, 0xff, 0xff, 0xff, 0xdd, 0xdd, 0xdd, 0xdd, 0xff, 0xff, 0xff, 0xff,
0x55, 0x55, 0x55, 0x55,
    0xff, 0xff, 0xff, 0xff, 0xdd, 0xdd, 0xdd, 0xdd, 0xff, 0xff, 0xff, 0xff,
0x55, 0x55, 0x55, 0x55,
    0xff, 0xff, 0xff, 0xff, 0xdd, 0xdd, 0xdd, 0xdd, 0xff, 0xff, 0xff, 0xff,
0x55, 0x55, 0x55, 0x55},

   {0xff, 0xff, 0xff, 0xff, 0xdd, 0xdd, 0xdd, 0xdd, 0xff, 0xff, 0xff, 0xff,
0x77, 0x77, 0x77, 0x77,
    0xff, 0xff, 0xff, 0xff, 0xdd, 0xdd, 0xdd, 0xdd, 0xff, 0xff, 0xff, 0xff,
0x77, 0x77, 0x77, 0x77,
    0xff, 0xff, 0xff, 0xff, 0xdd, 0xdd, 0xdd, 0xdd, 0xff, 0xff, 0xff, 0xff,
0x77, 0x77, 0x77, 0x77,
    0xff, 0xff, 0xff, 0xff, 0xdd, 0xdd, 0xdd, 0xdd, 0xff, 0xff, 0xff, 0xff,
0x77, 0x77, 0x77, 0x77,
    0xff, 0xff, 0xff, 0xff, 0xdd, 0xdd, 0xdd, 0xdd, 0xff, 0xff, 0xff, 0xff,
0x77, 0x77, 0x77, 0x77,
    0xff, 0xff, 0xff, 0xff, 0xdd, 0xdd, 0xdd, 0xdd, 0xff, 0xff, 0xff, 0xff,
0x77, 0x77, 0x77, 0x77,
```

```
    0xff, 0xff, 0xff, 0xff, 0xdd, 0xdd, 0xdd, 0xdd, 0xff, 0xff, 0xff, 0xff,
0x77, 0x77, 0x77, 0x77,
    0xff, 0xff, 0xff, 0xff, 0xdd, 0xdd, 0xdd, 0xdd, 0xff, 0xff, 0xff, 0xff,
0x77, 0x77, 0x77, 0x77},
  {0xff, 0xff, 0xff, 0xff, 0xff, 0xff, 0xff, 0xff, 0xff, 0xff, 0xff, 0xff,
0x77, 0x77, 0x77, 0x77,
    0xff, 0xff, 0xff, 0xff, 0xff, 0xff, 0xff, 0xff, 0xff, 0xff, 0xff, 0xff,
0x77, 0x77, 0x77, 0x77,
    0xff, 0xff, 0xff, 0xff, 0xff, 0xff, 0xff, 0xff, 0xff, 0xff, 0xff, 0xff,
0x77, 0x77, 0x77, 0x77,
    0xff, 0xff, 0xff, 0xff, 0xff, 0xff, 0xff, 0xff, 0xff, 0xff, 0xff, 0xff,
0x77, 0x77, 0x77, 0x77,
    0xff, 0xff, 0xff, 0xff, 0xff, 0xff, 0xff, 0xff, 0xff, 0xff, 0xff, 0xff,
0x77, 0x77, 0x77, 0x77,
    0xff, 0xff, 0xff, 0xff, 0xff, 0xff, 0xff, 0xff, 0xff, 0xff, 0xff, 0xff,
0x77, 0x77, 0x77, 0x77,
    0xff, 0xff, 0xff, 0xff, 0xff, 0xff, 0xff, 0xff, 0xff, 0xff, 0xff, 0xff,
0x77, 0x77, 0x77, 0x77,
    0xff, 0xff, 0xff, 0xff, 0xff, 0xff, 0xff, 0xff, 0xff, 0xff, 0xff, 0xff,
0x77, 0x77, 0x77, 0x77},

  /* NOTE: 100% opaqueness is faster to set and probably faster to render
with:
        glDisable(GL_POLYGON_STIPPLE); */
  {0xff, 0xff, 0xff, 0xff, 0xff, 0xff, 0xff, 0xff, 0xff, 0xff, 0xff, 0xff,
0xff, 0xff, 0xff, 0xff,
    0xff, 0xff, 0xff, 0xff, 0xff, 0xff, 0xff, 0xff, 0xff, 0xff, 0xff, 0xff,
0xff, 0xff, 0xff, 0xff,
    0xff, 0xff, 0xff, 0xff, 0xff, 0xff, 0xff, 0xff, 0xff, 0xff, 0xff, 0xff,
0xff, 0xff, 0xff, 0xff,
    0xff, 0xff, 0xff, 0xff, 0xff, 0xff, 0xff, 0xff, 0xff, 0xff, 0xff, 0xff,
0xff, 0xff, 0xff, 0xff,
    0xff, 0xff, 0xff, 0xff, 0xff, 0xff, 0xff, 0xff, 0xff, 0xff, 0xff, 0xff,
0xff, 0xff, 0xff, 0xff,
    0xff, 0xff, 0xff, 0xff, 0xff, 0xff, 0xff, 0xff, 0xff, 0xff, 0xff, 0xff,
0xff, 0xff, 0xff, 0xff,
    0xff, 0xff, 0xff, 0xff, 0xff, 0xff, 0xff, 0xff, 0xff, 0xff, 0xff, 0xff,
0xff, 0xff, 0xff, 0xff,
    0xff, 0xff, 0xff, 0xff, 0xff, 0xff, 0xff, 0xff, 0xff, 0xff, 0xff, 0xff,
0xff, 0xff, 0xff, 0xff},
  };
```

```
GLfloat angle = 20.0;

int torusStipple = 4, icoStipple = 8, tetraStipple = 16;

/* Initialize material property and light source. */
void
myinit(void)
{
  GLfloat light_ambient[] =
  {0.2, 0.2, 0.2, 1.0};
  GLfloat light_diffuse[] =
  {1.0, 1.0, 1.0, 1.0};
  GLfloat light_specular[] =
  {1.0, 1.0, 1.0, 1.0};
  GLfloat light_position[] =
  {1.0, 1.0, 1.0, 0.0};

  glClearColor(0.49, 0.62, 0.75, 0.0);

  glLightfv(GL_LIGHT0, GL_AMBIENT, light_ambient);
  glLightfv(GL_LIGHT0, GL_DIFFUSE, light_diffuse);
  glLightfv(GL_LIGHT0, GL_SPECULAR, light_specular);
  glLightfv(GL_LIGHT0, GL_POSITION, light_position);

  glEnable(GL_LIGHT0);
  glDepthFunc(GL_LESS);
  glEnable(GL_DEPTH_TEST);
  glEnable(GL_LIGHTING);
  glEnable(GL_CULL_FACE);
  glEnable(GL_POLYGON_STIPPLE);

  glNewList(TORUS, GL_COMPILE);
  glutSolidTorus(0.275, 0.85, 10, 15);
  glEndList();
  glNewList(TETRAHEDRON, GL_COMPILE);
  glutSolidTetrahedron();
  glEndList();
  glNewList(ICOSAHEDRON, GL_COMPILE);
  glutSolidIcosahedron();
  glEndList();
}
```

```
void
display(void)
{
  glClear(GL_COLOR_BUFFER_BIT | GL_DEPTH_BUFFER_BIT);

  glPushMatrix();
  glScalef(1.3, 1.3, 1.3);
  glRotatef(angle, 1.0, 0.0, 0.0);

  glPushMatrix();
  glTranslatef(-0.75, -0.5, 0.0);
  glRotatef(270.0, 1.0, 0.0, 0.0);
  glPolygonStipple(stippleMask[tetraStipple]);
  glCallList(TETRAHEDRON);
  glPopMatrix();
  glPushMatrix();
  glTranslatef(-0.75, 0.5, 0.0);
  glRotatef(90.0, 1.0, 0.0, 0.0);
  glPolygonStipple(stippleMask[torusStipple]);
  glCallList(TORUS);
  glPopMatrix();

  glPushMatrix();
  glTranslatef(0.75, 0.0, -1.0);
  glPolygonStipple(stippleMask[icoStipple]);
  glCallList(ICOSAHEDRON);
  glPopMatrix();

  glPopMatrix();

  glutSwapBuffers();
}

void
reshape(int w, int h)
{
  glViewport(0, 0, w, h);
  glMatrixMode(GL_PROJECTION);
  glLoadIdentity();
```

```
  if (w <= h)
    glOrtho(-2.5, 2.5, -2.5 * (GLfloat) h / (GLfloat) w,
      2.5 * (GLfloat) h / (GLfloat) w, -10.0, 10.0);
  else
    glOrtho(-2.5 * (GLfloat) w / (GLfloat) h,
      2.5 * (GLfloat) w / (GLfloat) h, -2.5, 2.5, -10.0, 10.0);
  glMatrixMode(GL_MODELVIEW);
}

void
torusTransparency(int value)
{
  torusStipple = value;
  glutPostRedisplay();
}

void
icoTransparency(int value)
{
  icoStipple = value;
  glutPostRedisplay();
}

void
tetraTransparency(int value)
{
  tetraStipple = value;
  glutPostRedisplay();
}

void
noop(int value)
{
  switch(value) {
  case 1:
    angle -= 45;
    break;
```

```
  case 2:
    angle += 45;
    break;
  case 666:
    exit(0);
  }
  glutPostRedisplay();
}

void
createTransparencyMenu(void)
{
  char label[20];
  int i;

  for (i = 0; i < 17; i++) {
    sprintf(label, "%d%% opaque", i * 100 / 16);
    glutAddMenuEntry(label, i);
  }
}

int
main(int argc, char **argv)
{
  int torusMenu, icoMenu, tetraMenu;

  glutInit(&argc, argv);
  glutInitDisplayMode(GLUT_DOUBLE | GLUT_RGB | GLUT_DEPTH);
  glutCreateWindow("screen door transparency");
  glutDisplayFunc(display);
  glutReshapeFunc(reshape);
  myinit();
  torusMenu = glutCreateMenu(torusTransparency);
  createTransparencyMenu();
  icoMenu = glutCreateMenu(icoTransparency);
  createTransparencyMenu();
  tetraMenu = glutCreateMenu(tetraTransparency);
  createTransparencyMenu();
```

```
    glutCreateMenu(noop);
    glutAddSubMenu("Torus", torusMenu);
    glutAddSubMenu("Icosahedron", icoMenu);
    glutAddSubMenu("Tetrahedron", tetraMenu);
    glutAddMenuEntry("Rotate up", 1);
    glutAddMenuEntry("Rotate down", 2);
    glutAddMenuEntry("Quit", 666);
    glutAttachMenu(GLUT_RIGHT_BUTTON);

    glutMainLoop();
    return 0;            /* ANSI C requires main to return int. */
}
```

Output:

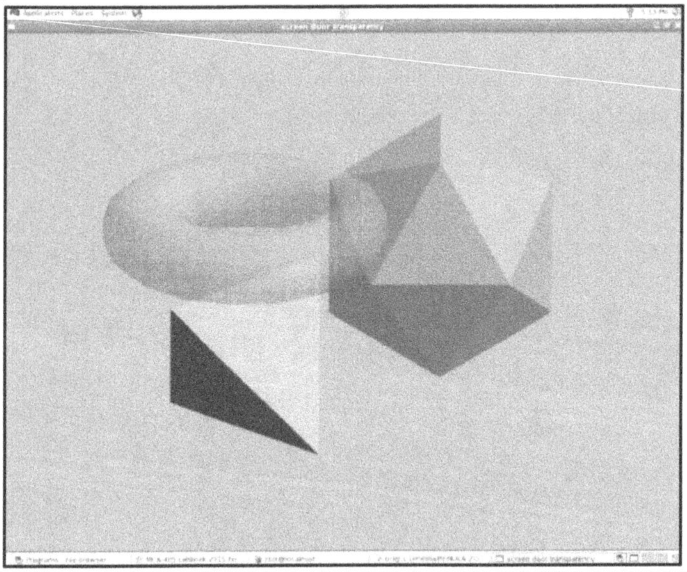

Mini Project

Mini Project to display population bar graph of different states in India.

```
#include<string.h>
#include <math.h>
#include <stdio.h>
#include <GL/gl.h>
#include <GL/glu.h>
#include <GL/glut.h>
GLint x,y;
void myinit(void)
{
    glClearColor(1.0,1.0,1.0,0.0);       //set the background color to bright
                                          white no transparency
    glColor3f(0.0, 0.0f, 0.0f);          //set the drawing color to black;
    glPointSize(4.0);                     //set the point size to 4 by 4 pixels
    glMatrixMode(GL_PROJECTION);          //set up the co-ordinate system
    glLoadIdentity();
    gluOrtho2D(0.0, 640.0, 0.0, 480.0);
}
void myDisplay(void)
{
    char *string1="MAHA";
    char *string2="GUJ";
    char *string3="UP";
    char *string4="KAR";
    char *string5="J&K";
    char *string6="GOA";
    char *string7="MP";
    char *name="BAR GRAPH OF POPULATION";

    int i,a,b,c,d,e,f,g;
    int len;
    printf("\n\tEnter the Population In Cr.\n");
    printf("\tEnter the Population for Maharashtra  : ");
    scanf("%d",&a);
    printf("\tEnter the Population for Gujrat  : ");
    scanf("%d",&b);
    printf("\tEnter the Population for UP  : ");
    scanf("%d",&c);
    printf("\tEnter the Population for Karnataka  : ");
    scanf("%d",&d);
    printf("\tEnter the Population for Jammu & Kashmir  : ");
```

```
scanf("%d",&e);
printf("\tEnter the Population for Goa  : ");
scanf("%d",&f);
printf("\tEnter the Population for MP  : ");
scanf("%d",&g);

glClear(GL_COLOR_BUFFER_BIT); //clear the entire window to background
                              color
glColor3f(0.7,0.7,0.7);
//glBegin(GL_LINE_STRIP);
//specifies a set of lines
// output(250,250,10,10,10,)
//glColor3d (255, 0, 0);

glColor3f(0.60,0.40,0.50);
//rectangle

//main rect
glClear(GL_COLOR_BUFFER_BIT); //clear the entire window to background
                              color
// X axis

glBegin(GL_LINES);                //specifies a set of lines
glVertex2i(10,10);                // starting point of the line
glVertex2i(600,10);               // end point of the line
glEnd();

 // Y axis
glBegin(GL_LINES);                //specifies a set of lines
glVertex2i(10,10);                // starting point of the line
glVertex2i(10,470);               // end point of the line
 glEnd();

// Dash o Y-axis

glBegin(GL_LINES);
glVertex2i(15,110);
glVertex2i(5,110);

glBegin(GL_LINES);
glVertex2i(15,210);
glVertex2i(5,210);

glBegin(GL_LINES);
glVertex2i(15,310);
glVertex2i(5,310);

glBegin(GL_LINES);
glVertex2i(15,410);
glVertex2i(5,410);
```

```
glBegin(GL_LINES);
glVertex2i(15,160);
glVertex2i(5,160);

glBegin(GL_LINES);
glVertex2i(15,260);
glVertex2i(5,260);

glBegin(GL_LINES);
glVertex2i(15,360);
glVertex2i(5,360);

glBegin(GL_LINES);
glVertex2i(15,60);
glVertex2i(5,60);

 //Arrow Y axis
 glBegin(GL_LINES);                //specifies a set of lines
 glVertex2i(15,450);               // starting point of the line
 glVertex2i(10,470);               // end point of the line


 glEnd();
 glBegin(GL_LINES);                //specifies a set of lines
 glVertex2i(10,470);               // starting point of the line
 glVertex2i(5,450);                // end point of the line
 glEnd();

//arrow x axis
glBegin(GL_LINES);                 //specifies a set of lines
glVertex2i(580,15);                // starting point of the line
glVertex2i(600,10);                // end point of the line
 glEnd();
glBegin(GL_LINES);                 //specifies a set of lines
glVertex2i(600,10);                // starting point of the line
glVertex2i(580,5);                 // end point of the line
 glEnd();

 glEnd();

  glColor3f(1.5,0.5,0.0);
  glRecti(50,a,100,10);

  glColor3f(0.10,0,0.50);
  glRecti(120,b,170,10);

  glColor3f(0.5,0.19,0.0);
  glRecti(190,c,240,10);

  glColor3f(0,0.5,1.5);
   glRecti(260,d,310,10);
```

```
    glColor3f(0.5,1.5,1.1);
    glRecti(330,e,380,10);

    glColor3f(0,1.1,0.0);
    glRecti(400,f,450,10);

    glColor3f(1,1,0);
    glRecti(470,g,520,10);

  glColor3f( 255,0,0 );
  glRasterPos2f(55,1);

len = (int)strlen(string1);
for (i = 0; i < len; i++)
{
glutBitmapCharacter(GLUT_BITMAP_HELVETICA_10, string1[i]);
}

  glColor3f( 255,0,0 );
  glRasterPos2f(125,1);

len = (int)strlen(string2);
for (i = 0; i < len; i++)
{
glutBitmapCharacter(GLUT_BITMAP_HELVETICA_10, string2[i]);
}

  glColor3f( 255,0,0 );
  glRasterPos2f(200,1);

len = (int)strlen(string3);
for (i = 0; i < len; i++)
{
glutBitmapCharacter(GLUT_BITMAP_HELVETICA_10, string3[i]);
}

  glColor3f( 255,0,0 );
  glRasterPos2f(270,1);

len = (int)strlen(string4);
for (i = 0; i < len; i++)
{
glutBitmapCharacter(GLUT_BITMAP_HELVETICA_10, string4[i]);
}

  glColor3f( 255,0,0 );
  glRasterPos2f(340,1);

len = (int)strlen(string5);
```

```
    for (i = 0; i < len; i++)
    {
    glutBitmapCharacter(GLUT_BITMAP_HELVETICA_10, string5[i]);
    }

     glColor3f( 255,0,0 );
     glRasterPos2f(420,1);

    len = (int)strlen(string6);
    for (i = 0; i < len; i++)
    {
    glutBitmapCharacter(GLUT_BITMAP_HELVETICA_10, string6[i]);
    }

     glColor3f( 255,0,0 );
     glRasterPos2f(480,1);

    len = (int)strlen(string7);
    for (i = 0; i < len; i++)
    {
    glutBitmapCharacter(GLUT_BITMAP_HELVETICA_10, string7[i]);
    }
     glColor3f( 255,0,0 );
     glRasterPos2f(200,450);
    len = (int)strlen(name);
    for (i = 0; i < len; i++)
    {
    glutBitmapCharacter(GLUT_BITMAP_TIMES_ROMAN_24, name[i]);
    }
        glFlush();
        //The entire data is to be processed and sent for display
}
void main(int argc, char **argv)
{
    glutInit(&argc, argv);          // Initializes the grahics toolkit
    glutInitDisplayMode(GLUT_SINGLE|GLUT_RGB);   // Single display buffer and
                                                 RGB mode
    glutInitWindowSize(600,600);                 // Initial window size
    glutInitWindowPosition(350,350);         // Initial position of windows
                                             left corner
    glutCreateWindow("My First Attempt");    // Opens a window with title
    glutDisplayFunc(myDisplay);     // Registering the display function
    myinit();                       // Do the initializations
    glutMainLoop();                 // Go into a perpetual loop
}
```

Output:

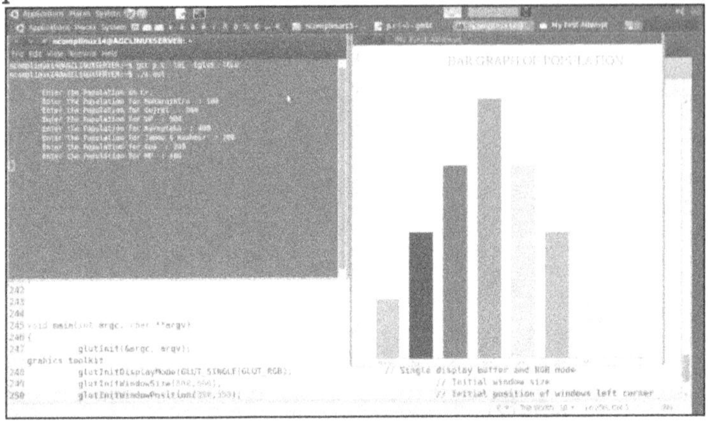
BAR GRAPH OF POPULATION
glutInitDisplayMode(GLUT_SINGLE|GLUT_RGB);
// Single display buffer and RGB mode
// Initial window size
// Initial position of windows left corner

Bibliography

Text Books:

1. Hearn, Baker – Computer Graphics (C version 2nd Ed.) – Pearson education.
2. F. S. Hill, Stephen Kelly, Computer Graphics using OpenGL, PHI Learning.
3. David F. Rogers - Procedural Elements of Computer Graphics, Tata McGRAw Hill.

Reference Books:

1. Foley, Vandam, Feiner, Hughes – Computer Graphics principles (2nd Ed.) – Pearson Education.
2. W. M. Newman, R. F. Sproull – Principles of Interactive computer Graphics – TMH.
3. D. F. Rogers, J. A. Adams – Mathematical Elements for Computer Graphics (2nd Ed.)" – TMH.
4. Z. Xiang, R. Plastock – Schaum's outlines Computer Graphics (2nd Ed.) – TMH.

■■■

Solved Question Papers

April 2016

Time : Two Hours **Maximum Marks : 40**

N.B. : (i) Figures to the right indicate full marks.

(ii) Draw neat diagram wherever necessary.

(iii) All questions are compulsory.

(iv) Use of calculator is allowed.

1. Attempt all of the following: [10 × 1 = 10]

(a) Give differences between Raster and Vector.

Ans.

Raster	Vector
• Raster graphics composed of pixels.	• Vector graphics composed of paths.
• Resolution dependent.	• Resolution independent.

(b) Touch Panel is the future of computer graphics. Comment.

Ans. Touch panel is input device layered on the top of an electronic visual display.

(c) List out any two applications of computer graphics.

Ans. CAD (Computer Aided Design)/CAM, Medical Applications, DTP (Desktop Publishing).

(d) What is scaling?

Ans. Scaling is increasing or decreasing the size of a picture.

(e) State any two applications of clipping.

Ans. Extracting part of a defined scene for viewing. Identifying visible surfaces in 3-D clews, solid modeling.

(f) List two differences between object space method and image space method.

Ans. **Object:** Used in physical coordinate system (3D).

Image: Used in screen coordinate system (2D).

(g) Differ pixel and point.

Ans. Point has no dimension in space.

Pixel: Picture element with many dots.

(h) What is projection?

Ans. The mismatch between 3D and 3D objects is compensated by projection.

(i) Name any two OpenGL libraries.

Ans. glu, gl, glut.

(j) Name the method used in OpenGL is set Window.

Ans. Gluortho 2D (0.0, 640.0, 0.0, 480.0).

2. Attempt any two: **[2 × 5 = 10]**

(a) Generate points on line with end point P_1 = (1, 2) and P_2 = (10, 5) using DDA algorithm.

Ans. $P_1 = (1, 2), P_2 = (10, 5)$

$dy = y_2 = y_1 = 5 - 2 = 3$

No. of steps k = dx = 9 (as dx > dy)

y increment $y_i = \frac{dy}{k} = \frac{3}{9} = 0.33$

x increment $x_i = \frac{dx}{k} = \frac{9}{9} = 1$

K	$x(x_{k+1} = x_k + x_i)$	$y(y_{k+1} = y_k + y_i)$
0	1	2
1	2	$2.33 \Rightarrow 2$
2	3	$2.66 \Rightarrow 3$
3	4	$2.99 \Rightarrow 3$
4	5	$3.32 \Rightarrow 3$
5	6	$3.65 \Rightarrow 4$
6	7	$3.98 \Rightarrow 4$
7	8	$4.11 \Rightarrow 4$
8	0	$4.44 \Rightarrow 4$
9	10	$4.77 \Rightarrow 5$

(b) Calculate final coordinates for points P(3, 6) after following 2D transformation:

(i) Translate with $t_x = 2$ and $t_y = 4$.

(ii) Rotate with angle 30°.

Ans. P = (3, 6) is x = 3, y = 6.

(i) For translation $t_x = 2$, $t_y = 4$.

$x = x + t_x = 3 + 2 = 5$

$y = y + t_y = 6 + 4 = 10$

∴ new values are P(5, 10).

(ii) Rotating with 30°

P(5, 10) by $\theta = 20^\circ$

P' = P.R or P' = R.P

horizontal vertical

$$[\,5 \;\; 10 \;\; 1\,]\begin{bmatrix} \cos\theta & \sin\theta & 0 \\ -\sin\theta & \cos\theta & 0 \\ 0 & 0 & 1 \end{bmatrix}$$

$$= [\,5 \;\; 10 \;\; 1\,]\begin{bmatrix} \frac{\sqrt{3}}{2} & \frac{1}{2} & 0 \\ -\frac{1}{2} & \frac{\sqrt{3}}{2} & 0 \\ 0 & 0 & 1 \end{bmatrix}$$

$$= [\,-0.67 \;\; 11.1 \;\; 1\,]$$

∴ New coordinates are (0.67, 11.1)

(c) Calculate final coordinates for point (3, 3, 3) after following 3D transformations:

(i) Rotate with angle 90° along X-axis.

(ii) Reflect along XY plane.

Ans. P(3, 3, 3)

(i) Rotate by 90° along x-axis.

$$P' = [\,3 \;\; 3 \;\; 3 \;\; 1\,]\begin{bmatrix} 1 & 0 & 0 & 0 \\ 0 & \cos\theta & \sin\theta & 0 \\ 0 & -\sin\theta & \cos\theta & 0 \\ 0 & 0 & 0 & 1 \end{bmatrix}$$

$$= [\,3 \;\; 3 \;\; 3 \;\; 1\,]\begin{bmatrix} 1 & 0 & 0 & 0 \\ 0 & 0 & 1 & 0 \\ 0 & -1 & 0 & 0 \\ 0 & 0 & 0 & 1 \end{bmatrix}$$

$$= [\,3 \;\; -3 \;\; 3 \;\; 1\,]$$

∴ New coordinates are (3, –3, 3)

(ii) Reflect along xy plane

P' = P.Ref (x, y)

$$P' = [\,3 \;\; -3 \;\; 3 \;\; 1\,]\begin{bmatrix} 1 & 0 & 0 & 0 \\ 0 & 1 & 0 & 0 \\ 0 & 0 & -1 & 0 \\ 0 & 0 & 0 & 1 \end{bmatrix}$$

$$P' = [\,3 \;\; -3 \;\; -3 \;\; 1\,]$$

∴ New coordinates are (3, –3, –3)

3. Attempt any two: [2 × 5 = 10]

(a) **Explain boundary fill algorithm for 4-connected polygon.**

Ans. Refer to Section 4.4.2.3.

(b) **Write a note on Laser Printer.**

Ans. Refer to Section 3.3.2.

(c) **Explain perspective projection in brief.**

Ans. Refer to Section 7.4.2.

4. Attempt any one (A or B): [4 + 4 + 2 = 10]

(A) (a) **Explain Cyrus-Beck line clipping algorithm.** [4]

Ans. Refer to Section 6.3.3.

(b) **Explain Bresenham's line drawing algorithm.** [4]

Ans. Refer to Section 4.2.2.

(c) **Give any two functions in OpenGL which are used for mouse interaction.** [2]

Ans. Refer to Section 2.4.

OR

(B) (a) **Explain back face detection algorithm.** [4]

Ans. Refer to Section 8.2.1.

(b) **Explain Sutherland-Hodgeman polygon clipping algorithm.** [4]

Ans. Refer to Section 6.4.1.

(c) **Discuss keyboard interaction in OpenGL.** [2]

Ans. Refer to Section 2.4.

■■■

October 2016

Time : Two Hours **Maximum Marks : 40**

N.B. : (i) Figures to the right indicate full marks.
(ii) Draw neat diagrams wherever necessary.
(iii) All questions are compulsory.
(iv) Use of calculator is allowed.

1. Attempt all of the following: [10 × 1 = 10]

(a) **Name four components of Computer Graphics.**

Ans. Representation, Presentation, Interaction, Transformation.

(b) **State four logical interactions of input devices.**

Ans. Locator, Valuator, Pick, Choices.

(c) Name the method used in OpenGL to set window.

Ans. Gluortho2D (0.0, 640.0, 0.0, 480.0)

(d) Define pixel.

Ans. Smallest addressable unit on screen.

(e) Name any two input devices.

Ans. Mouse, tablet, lightpen, joystick.

(f) List out any two polygon clipping algorithms.

Ans. **Cohen** - Sutherland algorithm.

Weiler - Atherton algorithm.

(g) State any two applications of computer graphics.

Ans. CAD / CAM, medical, DTP.

(h) What is clipping operation?

Ans. Identifying those portions of picture that are either inside or outside viewing window and removing outside part.

(i) Name any two OpenGL libraries.

Ans. glut, SDL, gl

(j) Which methods in OpenGL sets input device for interaction.

Ans. glukeyboardFunc(keyboard)

glutmouseFunc(mouse)

2. Attempt any two of the following: **[2 × 5 = 10]**

(a) Generate points on the line with end points P_1 = (0, 0) and P_2 = (– 6, – 6) using DDA algorithm.

Ans. Length $\Delta x = 6$, $\Delta y = 1$ points are:

x	y
0.5	0.5
1.167	1.5
1.833	2.5
2.5	3.5
3.167	4.5
3.833	5.5
4.5	6.5

The result should plotted by graph.

Refer to Section 4.4.1.

(b) Calculate final coordinates for point P(3, 6) after following 2D transformation (use matrix representation):

(i) Translate with $t_x = 2$ and $t_y = 4$.

(ii) Rotate with angle 30°.

Ans. P(3, 6) is x = 3, y = 6

(i) For translation $t_x = 2$, $t_y = 4$

$x = x + t_x = 3 + 2 = 5$

$y = y + t_y = 6 + 4 = 10$

∴ New values are (5, 10).

(ii) Rotating with 30°

P(5, 10) by Q = 30°

P' = P · R OR P' = R·P

Horizontal representation Vertical representation

$$= [5, 10, 1]\begin{bmatrix} \cos\theta & \sin\theta & 0 \\ -\sin\theta & \cos\theta & 0 \\ 0 & 0 & 1 \end{bmatrix}$$

$$= [5, 10, 1]\begin{bmatrix} \frac{\sqrt{3}}{2} & \frac{1}{2} & 0 \\ -\frac{1}{2} & \frac{\sqrt{3}}{2} & 0 \\ 0 & 0 & 1 \end{bmatrix}$$

$$P' = [9.3, \; 11.1, \; 1]$$

Vertical:

$$P' = \begin{bmatrix} \cos\theta & -\sin\theta & 0 \\ \sin\theta & -\cos\theta & 0 \\ 0 & 0 & 1 \end{bmatrix}\begin{bmatrix} 5 \\ 10 \\ 1 \end{bmatrix}$$

$$= \begin{bmatrix} 9.3 \\ 11.1 \\ 1 \end{bmatrix}$$

New co-ordinates of P are [9.3, 11.1, 1]

P(3, 3, 3)

(c) **Calculate final coordinates for point P(2, 3, 4) after following 3D transformation (use matrix representation):**

(i) **Rotate with angle 90° along X-axis.**

(ii) **Reflect along XY plane.**

Ans. (i) Rotate by 90° along X-axis

P' = P·R (Horizontal)

$$P' = [\,3\ \ 3\ \ 3\ \ 1\,]\begin{bmatrix} 1 & 0 & 0 & 0 \\ 0 & \cos\theta & \sin\theta & 0 \\ 0 & -\sin\theta & \cos\theta & 0 \\ 0 & 0 & 0 & 1 \end{bmatrix}$$

$$P' = [\,3\ \ 3\ \ 3\ \ 1\,]\begin{bmatrix} 1 & 0 & 0 & 0 \\ 0 & 0 & 1 & 0 \\ 0 & -1 & 0 & 0 \\ 0 & 0 & 0 & 1 \end{bmatrix}$$

$$P' = [\,3\ \ -3\ \ 3\ \ 1\,]$$

P' = R·P (Vertical)

$$P' = \begin{bmatrix} 1 & 0 & 0 & 0 \\ 0 & \cos\theta & -\sin\theta & 0 \\ 0 & \sin\theta & \cos\theta & 0 \\ 0 & 0 & 0 & 1 \end{bmatrix}\begin{bmatrix} 3 \\ 3 \\ 3 \\ 1 \end{bmatrix}$$

$$P' = \begin{bmatrix} 1 & 0 & 0 & 0 \\ 0 & 0 & -1 & 0 \\ 0 & 1 & 0 & 0 \\ 0 & 0 & 0 & 1 \end{bmatrix}\begin{bmatrix} 3 \\ 3 \\ 3 \\ 1 \end{bmatrix}$$

$$P' = \begin{bmatrix} 3 \\ -3 \\ 3 \\ 1 \end{bmatrix}$$

$\therefore$ New coordinates are (3, – 3, 3)

(ii) Reflect along XY plane

P* = Ref (x, y)

$$P' = [\,3\ \ -3\ \ 3\ \ 1\,]\begin{bmatrix} 1 & 0 & 0 & 0 \\ 0 & 1 & 0 & 0 \\ 0 & 0 & -1 & 0 \\ 0 & 0 & 0 & 1 \end{bmatrix}$$

$$P' = [\,3\ \ -3\ \ -3\ \ 1\,]$$

$$P' = \begin{bmatrix} 1 & 0 & 0 & 0 \\ 0 & 1 & 0 & 0 \\ 0 & 0 & -1 & 0 \\ 0 & 0 & 0 & 1 \end{bmatrix}\begin{bmatrix} 3 \\ -3 \\ 3 \\ 1 \end{bmatrix}$$

$$P' = \begin{bmatrix} 3 \\ -3 \\ -3 \\ 1 \end{bmatrix}$$

New P' = (3, – 3, 3)

3. **Attempt any two of the following:** [2 × 5 = 10]

(a) **What is can conversion of polygons? How is it used for polygon filling?**

Ans. Use scan lines for polygon filling

Case 1: Point on edge.

Case 2: Point on vertex with incident edges same sides.

Case 3: Point on vertex with incident edges same sides on different sides.

Ans. Refer to Sections 4.3 and 4.4.

(b) **Write a note on "working of CRT monitors"/**

Ans. **Working:** Components base and electron gun, focusing system, deflection system and screen. Refer to Section 3.2.1.1.

(c) **What is parallel projection in 3D?**

Ans. **Types:** Orthographic - Isometric

Oblique: Cavalier, cabinet.

Refer to Section 7.3.1.1.

4. **Attempt (A) or (B):** [4 + 4 + 2 = 0]

(A) (a) **What is region code and how is it used for clipping lines in Cohen-Sutherland line clipping algorithm?**

Ans. Explanation with diagram. Refer to Section 6.3.1.

(b) **How is the concept of 8-connectivity used in polygon filling? Explain any one method.**

Ans. Boundary fill / flood fill. Refer to Section 4.4.

(c) **Give any two functions in OpenGL, which are used for mouse interaction.**

Ans. Mouse call back.

Motion call back.

Refer to Section 2.4.

OR

(B) (a) **Write a note Depth comparison in hidden surface elimination.**

Ans. Refer to Section 8.2.

(b) **Explain midpoint subdivision algorithm for clipping lines.**

Ans. Refer to Section 6.3.2.

(c) **State any two GUI components in OpenGL alongwith their methods.**

Ans. glclearcolor

glcolorsf

glPointsize

Refer to Sections 1.2. and 1.8.3.

■■■

www.ingramcontent.com/pod-product-compliance
Lightning Source LLC
Chambersburg PA
CBHW081144020726
47504CB00009B/1987
* 9 7 8 9 3 5 1 6 4 9 1 3 7 *